Outstanding praise for the novels of Chris Kenry!

CONFESSIONS OF A CASANOVA

"They say that if a writer can hook his or her reader in the first few paragraphs, that reader will finish the book and ask for more. Kenry can do just that."
—*Out Front* (Denver, Colorado)

UNCLE MAX

"Zippy . . . Kenry has a knack for spinning clichéd, banal material into endearingly comical, featherweight entertainment. The great leap to more substantial literary terrain feels but a book or two away for this talented author."
—*Publishers Weekly*

"A modern-day mix of *Oliver Twist* and *Auntie Mame* set in Kenry's beloved Denver."
—*The Weekly News* (Miami, Florida)

"When it comes to gay beach reading, nobody does it better than Kensington. Its best books are escapists, humorous and upbeat."
—*Gay Today*

CAN'T BUY ME LOVE

"A rollicking debut . . . the author's talent for catchy, catty dialogue and innovative (and often quite humorous) sexual interplay buoys his story-line . . . Kenry shows promise with this first effort and his moxie shines through . . . a satisfying confection."
—*Publishers Weekly*

"With his clever comic observations and rapid-fire dialogue, Chris Kenry is a smart and funny writer."
—*The Advocate*

"A romp through every gay subculture imaginable. The lead character charges by the hour, but the book will give you a charge every minute."
—Michael Musto, *The Village Voice*

Books by Chris Kenry

CAN'T BUY ME LOVE

UNCLE MAX

CONFESSIONS OF A CASANOVA

THE SURVIVAL METHODS AND MATING RITUALS
OF MEN AND MARINE MAMMALS

SUMMER SHARE
(with William J. Mann, Andy Schell and Ben Tyler)

ALL I WANT FOR CHRISTMAS
(with Jon Jeffrey, William J. Mann and Ben Tyler)

Published by Kensington Publishing Corporation

The Survival Methods and Mating Rituals of Men and Marine Mammals

Chris Kenry

KENSINGTON BOOKS
www.kensingtonbooks.com

KENSINGTON BOOKS are published by

Kensington Publishing Corp.
119 West 40th Street
New York, NY 10018

Copyright © 2012 by G. Christopher Kenry

ISBN-13: 978-0-7582-0438-7
ISBN-10: 0-7582-0438-8

First Kensington Trade Paperback Printing: May 2012
10 9 8 7 6 5 4 3 2 1

Printed in the United States of America

For Jim Holik

ACKNOWLEDGMENTS

Thanks to Jim Holik, Lee Patton, Nancy Kenry, Michael Ensminger, John Scognamiglio, Alison Picard, and all of the blockheads at The Writer's Block.

In the time of chimpanzees I was a monkey.

—Beck

Prologue

The Reality Detection Device had come alive and was swinging pendulously, but unlike a pendulum, its swings were uneven, irregular, and their speed varied. Often the weighted end would reach one end of its path, quiver for a moment, then make a violent sweep back the other way. This might be followed by a series of low, slow sways, then another swift rise to one side of the arc, where it would hover, as if weightless or indecisive. There was never any pattern to the swings, but for the past three days it had been in constant motion. There were six marks (three on each side) along the semicircular trajectory, and above the highest of these was written, in ominous red ink, *Danger Zone*.

In reality, the Reality Detection Device was nothing more than a long piece of string with a bolt tied onto one end of it. The other end was affixed with a piece of strapping tape to the top of a small science refrigerator, itself bolted to the wall and floor next to Davis's desk. The bolt on the string gave weight to the pendulum and allowed it to swing to and fro in time with the motion of the ship. The motion was considerable and unpleasant, hence the reason the fridge, the tables, the printer, the carbon dioxide bottles, and everything else in the lab except for the RDD was fastened down, and Davis found that fixing his eyes on the swinging bolt was soothing, almost hypnotic. He sat alone in the empty room and watched the thing as it went back and forth, feeling a slight tightness in his shoulders, a tinge of suspenseful anticipation each time the little tethered bolt neared, but never quite reached, the Danger Zone. He was not pleased to notice that his belly was making similar, pendulous swoops, and he regretted how much he had eaten during his last visit to the galley. But there had been so much food, and so few people up and around to eat it. And besides, what else was there to do?

Although not seasick himself, he longed to feign the malady and take refuge in his cabin, as most of the other people on the ship had done, but his roommate, a burly, red-bearded antenna-rigger, headed down to Palmer Station, was actually very seasick, and their tiny shared space, in which the windows, for obvious reasons, did not open, reeked of vomit. But even if it hadn't, the antenna-rigger had, in their first five minutes together in the cabin, been clear about the terms of their cohabitation:

"I'll sleep from midnight to noon, you sleep from noon to midnight. My time in here is my time, your time is your time. Get it? I don't want to see you in here during my time. Don't leave your shit lying around on the floor and don't jerk off in the shower."

Even if there hadn't been that edict, Davis was not, himself, sick and was, therefore, expected to be working, although his shipboard work was not, thus far, much different from his work in the office, meaning that it involved staring at the screen of his laptop most of the day, trying to appear busy. This task of nothingness was made easier by the fact that in his sea cubicle, unlike his office cubicle, there weren't any people watching him. But there wasn't an Internet connection either, so that made wasting time much more challenging, and more often than not he found himself defaulting to yet another game of computer solitaire.

He had, of course, been given a list of documentation to update, but those manuals and procedures had long ago been farmed out to various shipboard SMEs to edit and update, and until they returned it to him he had nothing to do but wait. So he sat, and he waited.

SME, a.k.a. Subject Matter Expert. Just about everything associated with this job had an acronym, and SME was the acronym for someone who actually knew what they were doing. Someone with skills and knowledge. Someone who belonged on this boat. Someone who was not, in just about every way, shape, and form, a professional fraud.

The vessel, an icebreaker, had not been designed, as many purpose-built work vehicles are not, with the comfort of its passengers in mind. It did not have a sharp, pointed bow that could cut through the water like a knife through warm butter. Instead, its features were best described with compound adjectives that might best be used to describe an unattractive woman: bull-nosed, broad-based, flat-bottomed—features that were useful for pushing up and over the surface of the frozen sea, cracking it with its own weight, but that were terrible liabilities when it came to transiting through open water, for then the boat would bob and gyrate, tip and rock, like a fat boy on an inner tube. In all but the calmest seas there was a near-constant need for the passengers to hang onto something—a wall, a desk, a door handle—for support. At that moment, Davis was seated at his makeshift workstation. His legs were spread wide, his knees buttressed against the cabinet. His left hand clutched the edge of the counter while with his right he gallantly struggled, with the aid of his computer mouse, to move the onscreen two of clubs up onto the awaiting ace.

In the eight hours since the vessel had poked her ugly, bulbous head out of the calm, protected waters of the Straits of Magellan, the utility of the nursing-home handrails on either side of the hallway had become obvious. The ship ascended and fell, pitched and rolled, like an incessant amusement park ride, and until you learned to move with the motion, you needed to hang on.

At night back in Davis's cabin, previously inanimate objects—pens hidden in drawers, aerosol spray cans that had tipped over in the bathroom, wire coat hangers in an empty closet—all came alive. His clothes, suspended on hooks on the wall, did ghostly dances, dangling their empty legs and arms out into the room, then slapped them back against the bulkhead. In addition to that there were the creaks and moans of the vessel's joints and beams, the hum of the engines, the incessant, sparrow-like chirp of the sonar, and the occasional low thud whenever the ship crested a wave and then slammed back down onto the sea. But as loud as it all was, the back-and-forth repetitive nature of the noises blended them all into a tranquilizing blur, and Davis found that he was aware of individual sounds only if he made a concerted effort to listen and separate them from the overall din. They were all threaded together by the subtle hiss of the wind and the washing-machine swirl of seawater in the portholes—a gentle, aqueous sound that was similar to and yet altogether different from the violent splash of vomit hitting toilet water. Different, perhaps because of the sounds that preceded it: running footsteps, a slamming metal door, the sharp contraction of a human diaphragm . . . Then came the splash, followed by a series of coughs, a flush, and an anguished moan of "Oh, God! Oh, my God!" It was a sequence of aural events Davis had heard several times a day during the crossing since his workspace was in a room that shared a bulkhead with the public bathroom. This location made him a reluctant witness to the tide of human misery, and as much as he tried, as much as he was able to make white noise out of all the other sounds, he could not tune out the frequent and unmistakable sound of his shipmates eating their meals in reverse. The green-faced traffic had begun almost as soon as they exited the Straits, reached a climax, and had now slowed to a trickle, most passengers having sequestered their miserable selves in their cabins.

The night before they'd entered the Drake, Maureen had gone from lab to lab, warning everyone, in her signature bossy and condescending tone, that the barometer was falling. Davis had no idea what that implied so he nodded, waited for her to leave, and then went back to his game of solitaire. A half hour later she returned and, seeing that no precautions had been taken, barked at Davis like a border collie: "Secure *everything* for the crossing! Now, not later! Lash it down with bungee cords, put it away in drawers or down on the deck. Do not put anything up high where it could potentially fall and damage a piece of equipment. Or a person."

When they did hit rough seas a few hours later, Davis initially enjoyed the novelty of it—the rocking motion as he lay in his bunk, rolling from one side to the other, the drunken, funhouse stagger as he tried to walk down the hall. Soon, however, the novelty wore off and his only desire was that someone, somehow, please, make it stop. He was spared the worst of the seasickness because he had followed Jake's advice and taken the Coast Guard Cocktail (meclizine and Sudafed) before leaving the dock, had done his best to keep his stomach full of starchy, bland food (which is how it almost always was anyway), but in spite of those preventative measures, he still felt terrible. There was the constant—and constantly annoying—need to hang on, even while seated or lying down, the futile challenge of keeping anything on his desk, and then, too, there was the headache (blunt, persistent), and the leaden feeling in his arms, legs, and neck. It was like a hangover, but much, much worse because it went on, unabated, and was tinged with an element of injustice since it had not been caused by any moral failing or overindulgence on the part of the sufferer.

"It's what you call a poison response," the captain (a Cajun of such enormous girth that Davis always felt slim by comparison) told him one morning when he, and the few others who had not succumbed to the motion of the ocean, were seated at a table in the otherwise empty mess hall.

"Your body reacts to the sea," the captain said, between massive bites of biscuits and gravy, "the same way it does when you eats something rotten: It tries to make you barf it up and then tells your brain and your body you need sleep to fight it off. She's a tricky bitch, the sea."

Davis nodded weakly. He nibbled on a piece of dry toast and tried not to look at the gooey clots of biscuit and gravy clinging to the captain's goatee. Instead, he scanned the room for one stationary point—a wall, a tabletop, the floor—on which to focus. Anything that wasn't seesawing, but everything was in motion.

It had only been two days of rough sailing, but those two days were enough to make Davis forget what it was like not to feel miserable. And then there was the work (alleged in nature as it was) he was supposed to be doing on his laptop. Work he found nearly impossible to do since it required him to grip the edge of the desk, flex his legs to keep his chair from swiveling, and try to rivet his gaze to the small screen of his laptop, which was itself lashed to the desk with eyebolts and bungee cords to keep it from careening off onto the deck. He found he could look at the screen for about ten minutes at a time before the headache and dizziness got to be too much. Then he would have to get up and walk (or stumble) around.

"It's a disconnect," Worm said when they were again sitting in the mess, trying to eat. "Your eyes send a message to your brain that what you're looking at is stable, but the little seaweed hairs in your inner ears are screaming, 'No, it's not! No, it's not!' You can't really do much on a computer when we're in seas like this."

"What-*ever,*" Maureen countered. "Seems like an excuse for people to loll around in their rack and watch DVDs." She got up from the table and took her empty plate to the dishwasher. "I don't have a problem with it."

"Of course she don't," the captain muttered once she was out of earshot. "But for those of us what ain't got a set of concrete nuts swinging between our legs, it's good to get away from the computer every now and then." He rose like an emperor from the table and gave Davis a slap on the back. "Walk around a bit, come up to the bridge and get some air. You'll be fine. Or," he added with a laugh, "you can puke like the rest of 'em!"

"He's right about the vomiting," Worm said. "It will make you feel better—for about ten to fifteen minutes. Then you'll go back to feeling like hell. But sometimes it's worth sticking your finger down your throat just to get those ten to fifteen minutes."

Since Davis could not return to his cabin, and since he could not stay awake and keep staring at the screen playing solitaire, he did what he had done back in the Denver office and retreated to the bathroom.

There were three communal toilets (or "heads," as all the salty sailors, and ersatz salty sailors, referred to them) on the main deck, one at the aft end of the boat, and two closer to the center. The two near the center shared a common wall. Each one was roughly the size of a coffin and yet somehow managed to contain a toilet, a small sink, a wall-mounted hand dryer, and a small magazine rack. Initially, Davis attempted to nap, as he'd done at the office, sitting upright on the toilet in what he called "the Porcelain Lotus." It was a pose he'd refined and perfected in the month prior to embarking, but the heaving of the ship made that position impossible, so he resorted first to sitting, then lying on his back on the floor, a roll of toilet paper propped under his head as a pillow.

These naps were not, suffice to say, what he considered proud moments, but what else could he do? Where else could he go? In spite of the pills and the starchy food, in spite of the walks up and down the stairs, in spite of the brief sojourns outside, which had to be very brief due to the numbing winds and churning sea—in spite of all that, he still felt like he had God's own hangover. The kind you get from drinking, say, a liter of tequila on an empty stomach. The kind of hangover he had experienced many mornings with Jake but that had always attenuated (yes, that was the word: *attenuated!*) as the day progressed. This hangover seemed to be doing whatever the opposite of attenuating was. A word that, if he had studied more for the SATs, he would probably know, and would probably thus have a better job, a home, a significant other, maybe even kids. Instead, here he was, pathetically stupid, financially wrecked, terminally ill, temporarily sick, flat on his back on the bathroom floor, his belly sloshing from side to side like a giant water balloon full of liquid self-pity.

He drifted in and out of sleep, so he had no idea how long he'd been there. Occasionally, some desperate, nauseous person would try the door handle and, finding it locked, move quickly to the adjacent head, whip open the door, slam it shut, and then heave ferociously into the awaiting bowl. At first the sounds made Davis cringe, but soon they, like the poo sounds in the Denver office, became so commonplace that he hardly noticed them. Proof, he supposed, that you can get used to just about anything.

And yet, as he slouched on the floor listening to an anonymous someone moan in agony in the room next to him, he couldn't help but wonder how it had come to this. How had his life come to be punctuated by a series of bathroom naps, each more degrading, pathetic, and disgusting than the last? He lifted up his hand and gazed at the faint, faux-radium glow of his watch. Seven days ago he had left Denver, where the leaves were falling, thrilled to be heading away from the office. Twelve hours later he was on the southern tip of South America, crocus and daffodils popping up. There had been a few calm days in port, one peaceful day bobbing at sea and now this! This! How had it come to this . . . ?

Book 1

Difficulties are just things to overcome, after all.

—Ernest Shackleton

Chapter 1

Four months earlier

The worst thing about the waiting room of the STD clinic was that there weren't any magazines, as if the lack of reading material would force you to reflect, without distraction, on your sins. The waiting room was really nothing more than a hallway lined on both sides with banks of connected chairs. The design ensured that when the place was full—and it always was—you were forced to either stare at the person across from you, keep your eyes up to the heavens, or keep them closed or cast down, as if in prayer or deep remorse.

Candy-colored condoms overflowed from a Plexiglas box mounted to the wall under a sign (inviting or imperative, Davis was never sure) proclaiming *Take One!* Beneath the box was a rack of pamphlets, almost like tourist brochures in a motel lobby, with the notable difference that instead of touting the local attractions, these brochures featured gory photographs of advanced-stage syphilis, oozing gonorrhea blisters, cauliflower clusters of genital warts, and the yellow eyes of late-stage hepatitis.

For the past three years, Davis had made a habit out of going to the clinic to get checked out every six months, so he was prepared for the lack of reading material and had brought his own, but the book he had chosen was not entertaining and soon his eyes grew heavy and he dozed off. A jab in the ribs from his neighbor's elbow woke him up. Davis blinked, looked at the man, a skinny Latino in a wifebeater and a sideways baseball cap. He had a gold incisor that glinted in the fluorescent light when he spoke.

"I think you're up, bro." Davis sat up and looked down the hall where a tall woman in pink floral scrubs stood scanning the crowd. Like a shy schoolgirl, she held a clipboard and a blue notebook close against her chest. She called Davis's name again. He closed his book, lifted himself up from the chair, approached the woman, and gave her a smile. She smiled back and motioned him into one of the examination rooms. Once inside, she closed the door behind her.

"Have a seat," she said, indicating one of two chairs in the small, windowless room. Davis sat. The nurse sat. Then, without a moment of hesitation, she flipped back a page from the clipboard and said, "You've tested negative for syphilis, gonorrhea, and chlamydia, but I'm afraid you're positive for HIV."

There was a pause while her words registered. Then it was like she'd pushed a button, ejecting his chair up through the roof. Or like the wheels of his car locked up on an icy road and he watched in helpless horror as he slid through the guardrail and over the cliff. It was, he would later reflect, almost the exact feeling he'd had when, on the advice of a friend, and with more than a few beers in his system, he'd been persuaded to step off a bridge with a bungee cord attached to his ankles: a face-first downward plunge, followed by a series of harrowing recoils.

When he came back to his senses and was again aware of his clinical surroundings, he looked down and saw a freckled hand sticking out from one of the sleeves of the pink floral scrubs. The hand was resting on his forearm.

"What are you feeling right now?" the nurse asked. "Can you tell me that?" He looked up, met her eyes, and thought only about her excessive and amateurish use of eyeliner. Then she went out of focus and he repeatedly smacked his forehead with the palm of his hand, hissing, "Stupid! Stupid! You stupid, dumb-ass idiot!"

The freckled hand retreated and her chair slid back on its casters.

Had it been drugs or dick? Davis asked himself. He knew she'd ask the same thing soon enough, and he knew he really couldn't give her an accurate answer. There had been that rare and reckless night last February when he'd shot meth and shared the works with a "friend," somehow persuading himself that if he wiped the needle clean on his sock before injecting it, that would make it okay. That had been in February.

February.

February had been a rough month. Two days before Valentine's Day, Mark had left him. And in the months that followed, there had been no shortage of sexual partners with most of whom, he reflected, he had been *relatively* safe. He scrolled through the mental list but couldn't pin down one specific person or incident that could have done it.

These thoughts were then interrupted by another, heavier one. One that made his stomach muscles clench and revived the plum meting sensation. The thought was that maybe he had, in the nebulous time since he had acquired the virus, and the present moment in this small examination room, passed it on to someone else. But another quick scroll through the mental list quelled that idea. The recent expansion of his waistline, occurring inversely with the contraction of the contents of his wallet, had not helped him attract partners, and had inhibited him from affording even the cheapest of recreational drugs. The only "action" he'd had of late had been with himself, and that, he knew, didn't count.

Or did it? Another thought occurred to him and again he stepped off the bridge. The reason for this round of panic was his sudden realization that the one being that he might have infected was his dog.

This was not as unsavory as it sounds. No, the worry came from the simple fact that Davis, like most single men, often indulged in a round of beating the bishop at night before nodding off to sleep. Once finished, he would clean up with a handful of tissues, wad them up, and make a limp-wristed, three-point, shot-in-the-dark attempt to hit the trash can. The morning after, he would invariably discover that the dog, in one of the less charming aspects of canine behavior, had, at some time during the night, rooted through the trash and eaten the tissues.

The nurse was talking numbers—"about five hundred milliliter parts per million. That's not bad. In fact, that's really pretty good"— but Davis bobbed in and out of her narrative like an exhausted swimmer, catching only gurgled bits of what she said. The memory of the dog and the shredded tissues snapped him back to attention. He grabbed the nurse's forearm and with a manic intensity related the story about his nightly ritual and morning discovery, concluding the tale with the anguished, but quite genuine query, "What if I've given HIV to my dog?"

The nurse, taking a moment to stifle her initial shock and subsequent amusement, gently lifted Davis's hand from her forearm. She then gave it a few compassionate pats and explained, in the least patronizing tone she could manage, that the "H" in HIV stood for "Human," "which means it is not at all, not by any method whatsoever, transmissible to dogs."

"Oh. Well then." Davis sniffed, managing an embarrassed laugh through his tears. "I guess that's one good thing."

Chapter 2

Though not the death sentence of the 1980s and early '90s, HIV in the new millennium does still come with the realization that life will, from the point of infection on, be shaped by the mirrored labyrinth of bureaucracy through which one must wander in order to get the medication needed to keep the virus in check. If you have lots of money, or good insurance, rest assured that there's no reason you shouldn't have a long and productive life. If you have neither money nor insurance (as Davis did not), well, the prognosis is not so rosy.

And then, of course, there is the stigma; again, not as bad as it was in the '80s, when those infected were feared and avoided like lepers, but different. Different because those testing positive in the twenty-first century were less often able to claim the "innocent victim" status, bestowed on those who acquired it from a blood transfusion, an unhygienic dentist, or a cheating, duplicitous spouse. Instead, the majority of newly infected are seen as careless, reckless, and very, very stupid. Because, let's face it, the cause of the disease, and the means to prevent its transmission, have been known to just about every semiconscious man, woman, and child on every continent of the world for over twenty years: condoms, clean needles, limit your sexual partners—what could be more straightforward and easier to understand? Use the standard precautions and it won't happen to you. So ... (and here the unspoken question always hung in the air) ... what the hell happened?

As Davis saw it, what the hell happened was not all that different from what happened each and every day to any number of girls in the waiting room down the hall from the STD clinic, all hoping and praying that the little stick they'd peed on at home—the one that also showed a dreaded plus sign—had somehow been terribly wrong. Those girls, too, had known what precautions to take (condoms, the pill, be sober enough when you have sex so that you don't forget one, or both, of the first two), but somewhere along the line they, too, had come to believe that although "it" definitely, most certainly, and without a doubt *could* happen, "it" probably wouldn't, at least not to them. Which all goes to show that there are many different ways to play Russian roulette and never a shortage of willing participants.

Along with the feeling of devastation, what Davis felt as he left the clinic late that morning was something akin to buyer's remorse—like he'd just purchased an item so beyond what he could afford (and, it goes without saying, an item he didn't really want or need) that he'd have to spend the rest of his life paying for it.

Dejected, he walked along Sixth Avenue back to his apartment. He snuck quietly past the ground-floor unit housing his landlord, and tiptoed up the creaking stairs. There was a note stuck to his door. He didn't remove it, didn't even look at it. He didn't need to. He recognized the tiny print, the spacing and numbering of the penal codes. He knew that what it said, in so many long and legal words, was "Get out!" and his hope was that if the note stayed there, stuck to the door, seemingly untouched, the landlord (a retired sanitation worker with a penchant for watching television game shows at an earsplitting volume while downing shots of Manischewitz), would think Davis hadn't returned and would leave him alone for the rest of the day. Tomorrow he would deal with the rent. Tomorrow, just not today.

He dipped his hand in his pants pocket and clutched his keys, lifting them noiselessly up and out. He singled out the door key from the others on his ring and eased it into the lock with such practiced gentleness and delicacy that none of the teeth even touched the inner edges of the mechanism. When it was all the way in, Davis cupped his meaty hands around the knob to act as a silencer and then turned it to the right, stopping once he felt the pop of the lock disengaging. Then, with glacial speed, he inched the door open. This was supposed to prevent the hinges from creaking but really only succeeded at spreading the creaks apart in time. Still, he hoped that the effort, when combined with the clang and roar of *The Price Is Right* blaring up from the apartment below, would be enough to render his arrival inaudible.

When the door was open enough to allow him to cross the threshold, he squeezed inside, turned, and began the creaky glacial retreat. Before the door had traveled an inch, he heard another door open at the bottom of the stairs. The sounds of cheering and applause were louder, and Davis knew he had failed. His efforts had been for naught. He abandoned his attempt at silence, hastily closed the door, and locked the dead bolt. Turning, he scanned his apartment for a place to hide.

Davis's dog, a pug, startled out of his sunny slumber by his owner's arrival, shook the sleep out of his bulging eyes and leapt off the couch, his tail wagging. Davis held out a hand, indicating that the dog should sit. Sensing the gravity of the situation, the dog obeyed, settling on his haunches and cocking his head to the side. Davis surveyed the room for a place to hide. There was a small closet, but that would not be much help since it had no door. He looked at the couch / bed but knew he couldn't fit behind or under it. His eyes traveled to the table, with a dust-free square in the middle of it indicating the former resting place of the TV; then on to the desk, with similar dust-free squares indicating the former resting places of the computer and printer. Those four items—dog, couch, table, desk—constituted the entire contents of his apartment. There were, of course, the fixed items—the stove and refrigerator—although they were of the miniature variety and had, Davis surmised from both their size and their dated avocado green color, been salvaged from someone's wrecked Winnebago, and would be no help in concealing him.

The disappearance of his electronics hadn't bothered Davis all that much since his cable and Internet services had been shut off long before the devices that channeled them were carted off to the pawnshop. In the past week the refrigerator and stove (as well as the light switches and electrical outlets) had been rendered similarly redundant since they were no longer being fed their necessary diet of electricity. That meant, too, that the alarm clock on the floor next to the couch/bed no longer worked, but that was not so important since there really was nothing all that pressing in Davis's world that necessitated getting up for.

For Davis, mental depression had arrived first, followed shortly thereafter by economic. He had initially tried to arc up and out of them both, had read and studied self-help books, tried to stay in contact with friends and family, but the fact was he felt miserable and ashamed, like he had failed at even the most basic tenets of his life, and since he really didn't want those who loved him to see him that way, he isolated himself, told friends he was fine, didn't need a thing, and told himself he'd get back in touch when his life had stabilized.

It didn't.

He hadn't.

And when his money started to evaporate, at first he panicked. But seeing no way to recoup his losses, he embraced them and tried to put a positive spin on his economic downswing, tried to appreciate the quaint, Thoreauvian aspects of having minimal furniture, reading books and magazines by candlelight in the evening, the simplicity of eating food that did not need to be heated or refrigerated. There was, he reflected, something romantic and folksy about it—like he was guest-starring on an episode of *Little House on the Prairie,* or was hiding out from the Nazis in some abandoned French château or maybe even behind the revolving bookcase in that famous little Amsterdam walk-up that had sheltered the doomed teenage diarist and her family. Ah, the romance of adversity and persecution! It could get him through some days, but reality always came knocking.

As if on cue, these thoughts were interrupted by the all-too-familiar rap of skeletal knuckles against the hollow-core door. The dog lurched forward, growling, and snuffled the bottom edge of the door. In the corner, Davis spied the pyramid of dirty laundry and, almost without thinking, parted it and sat down. He then covered himself as best he could with shirts, pants, underwear, and socks—all so full of biological matter that they could probably have walked to the Laundromat themselves. Once concealed, he sat very still.

The knocking continued, more insistently. The dog gave a low, guttural growl that progressed into a series of pack-a-day barks.

"I know you're in there!" the landlord yelled. "I seen your car parked out front."

Beneath the laundry, Davis rolled his eyes. The car had little choice about being seen parked out front since it had been booted two weeks before. A lame bluff. Davis stayed put. He heard the muffled sound of metal jingling and imagined the man's age-spotted hands arthritically flipping through the ring of keys he kept attached to his belt on a retractable metal cord. He heard the man curse as he jabbed several erroneous keys into the lock until finally happening on the right one, which he then drove in with a force and brutality that was the polar opposite of Davis's slow, gentle technique. The lock popped, the door creaked, the dog barked, but Davis did not move, did not even breathe.

Davis had lived in this apartment for almost a year. He rented it when he and Mark broke up and he'd been forced to move out of the loft they had shared. They were on equal economic footing when they first met, Davis making money from his books and Mark having just been hired as a weekend weatherman at a local TV station. As time went on, Mark's fortunes had ascended while Davis's had gone the other way, and soon the insecurities and resentments surfaced.

Dating someone a decade younger is difficult. Dating someone a decade younger who soon makes three times the amount of money you do and never tires of reminding you of that fact requires a level of self-confidence that few possess. Nevertheless, Davis felt he should have possessed it. After all, he had very little respect for Mark's profession, which was, Mark repeatedly insisted, "a meteorologist, *not* a weatherman."

Meteorologist. What a joke. The guy had an associate degree in broadcast communications and a certificate of meteorology, meaning he had passed, with a C or better, two classes in weather forecasting. Slip up and call it *predicting* instead of *forecasting* and you got another lengthy scolding about how "predicting is what psychics do; forecasting is science."

Right.

What the guy really needed, Davis had thought after watching him in action one night, was a class in U.S. geography, since he never seemed quite certain of the location of any states other than those that were easily identifiable by their size and shape: Texas, Florida, California, and the perfectly square state in which they lived were easy, but the puzzle pieces of New England? The blobby masses of the Midwest? Forget it.

But Mark was young, clean cut, Oklahoma-accented, and, when dressed in a suit, looked as trustworthy and earnest as a Mormon missionary, which all combined to make him a favorite with the largely elderly crowd who were his audience, and allowed them to overlook his intellectual shortcomings.

And Davis's career certainly had its own shortcomings. When he'd met Mark, he'd been a successful author of children's books and had established a brand character—a naughty pug named Edgar (the same pug who now stood whining next to the pile of dirty laundry and who, unbeknownst to his cadre of juvenile fans, so relished the taste of cummy tissues). Davis's five previous books, which he had both written and illustrated, sold well, and for a very brief period of time he could not do a reading at a local preschool or toy store without being mobbed by groups of shrill, sticky-handed children. He had a following, groupies, what some might call rock-star success.

Okay, as children's book authors go, maybe it had been only very marginal success. For a while, he had made enough money to pay his bills, get himself out of debt, and woo a trophy boyfriend, but then, flush with an advance on his third book and a few royalty checks from the first two, he went back into the red by purchasing a sporty convertible (at an interest rate usually reserved for down-trodden protagonists in a Dickens novel), moved into, and then lavishly furnished, an airy loft that neither he nor the meteorologist could afford, and dined out a lot. Soon, Davis reached the limit of his credit. Even worse was the fact that by trying to maintain his relationship and lifestyle, he had become lazy and sloppy with his work, hastily cranking out two "lesser works" in order to get paid.

These effectively tarnished his earlier success and he was relegated to being what his agent, Estelle, referred to with the acronym MSCBA (Marginally Successful Children's Book Author).

In spite of his initial success, or perhaps because of it, Davis's later works were savaged by the critics, most of whom, he realized, were themselves nothing more than TUCBAs (Totally Unsuccessful Children's Book Authors). TUCBAs were notorious for exacting revenge on those who, like Davis, were ever-so-slightly more marginally successful than they. Their method for doing this was by writing reviews in which adjectives like "rambling," "weak," "unfocused," "offensively condescending," and "cloying" were flung like paint from Pollock's brush. Davis's last book, for example, had been summarized by one bitter and yet flowery TUCBA as "stale, derivative, lacking any purpose or meaning whatsoever, illustrated with all the finesse, delicacy, and color capable of a fat crayon, and enveloped in a dust jacket so horrible that its horribleness almost eclipses the horribleness of the book it envelops." And, sad to say, Davis knew there was some truth to that assessment. He had exhausted the character of Edgar, he lacked inspiration on ways to further develop him or even any idea of how to put him into an interesting plot, and should, therefore, have long ago abandoned him in favor of some other, more dynamic anthropomorphic creature. But then, along came Mark and the condo and the car, and Davis's work became secondary.

In spite of the fact that his two later works had not been profitable, Estelle had somehow managed to get him a two-book contract and an acceptable advance from a new publisher, and that had been his undoing. For with the advance came two rigid deadlines. The first descended on him with the horror of a slow-motion guillotine, effectively paralyzing his already weakened self-confidence and neutering his imagination. He didn't meet the deadline, which isn't to say that he didn't try. He did try, especially after the breakup and the change in his living situation. Motivated by a need for money and a desire for artistic redemption, he got up early, day after day, and set off, proverbial pick and shovel in hand, to mine the deepest recesses of his imagination, but the ore bucket almost always came up full of gravel. Gravel that he would dutifully unload and paw through, arranging and rearranging it, hoping that one of his arrangements might at least give the appearance of a gem.

In desperation, with the publisher and Estelle screaming at him, with bills piling up, and with Davis unable to pay back an advance he had long ago spent (on what exactly, he could not and probably did not want to remember), he dusted off the character of Edgar, placed him and a few other characters on the sandy foundation of a plot (a plot that had been largely copied—er, *inspired* by a faintly remembered episode of *Land of the Lost*), put some appropriately dumb dialogue in their canine mouths, and then, in a Ritalin-induced frenzy (Ritalin stolen from a bottle intended for his young nephew and replaced, by Davis, with identically shaped cinnamon candies, on which he painstakingly stenciled the logo of the pharmaceutical company) spent seventy-two manic hours producing the illustrations.

The end product, entitled *Reigning Cats and Dogs,* was this: Edgar and another dog, an inconsistently patterned collie (talk about cloying!), traveled back in time to the age of the dinosaurs (because really, what child doesn't love dinosaurs?) in order to catch an evil cat who had devised a plan to cut off, at the evolutionary pass, the path of dogs and thus create a feline utopia in which there would be no dogs.

It was as bad as that brief synopsis makes it sound, but somehow it was published anyway and, by just about all estimations, failed miserably. And there's nothing quite like failure, documented publicly and seemingly for all eternity, in the scathing reader reviews on Amazon.com, to pulverize a writer's already brittle confidence, to make him physically tremble at the thought of summoning the courage and audacity to ever again put pen to paper.

Some artists attempt to blunt the pain of divorce and artistic failure with bourbon; some seek the syrupy solace of Xanax or Vicodin; still others pave the road to oblivion with maxed-out credit cards, but for Davis, this last time, the drugs of choice had been food and sex.

As before, he tried to force himself up and out of his depression and humiliation. He got up each day, rolled up his sleeves, and composed pages of junk; drew sketch after sketch of cartoon animal confections, but those fickle twin sprites—Inspiration and Confidence—were habitual no-shows at the meetings he held in his brain.

So, while waiting for the muses to return, Davis ate. He went through boxes of jelly doughnuts, packages of Orco cookies, and bag after bag of tater tots. And while eating he idly cruised the M4M section of Craigslist, selecting random hook-ups from the endless parade of ads. But still the muses did not return. Oh, they made brief appearances, hovering overhead, visible but always just out of reach, watching as Davis's life and apartment became progressively vacant, but never did they come within reach.

Which brings us back to the paused plot . . . Our main character still artlessly concealed beneath the pile of dirty laundry. The two minor characters, growling pug and Manischewitz-guzzling landlord, each giving voice to his own part. The landlord entered stage right, approached the quivering pile of clothes, and pulled away, one by one, the socks, shirts, and underwear. When Davis was exposed, he was surprised to see the old man grinning, his wine-stained dentures exposed.

"Get yourself out of there," he grumbled, pulling Davis up by the sleeve of his sweater, "and let's have ourselves a talk."

Davis allowed himself to be helped out of his stinking nest and the two sat together on the sofa, staring at the blank wall.

"Son, you've been a good tenant; quiet, no complaints from the neighbors. You keep the place clean," he said, giving a grand sweep at the empty apartment, "but goddamn, you gotta pay rent!"

Davis nodded.

"I've got an order of eviction here," he said, slapping a folded bunch of yellow papers on his palm. "Give me a reason why I shouldn't file it and have the cops toss you out on your ear."

Davis shrugged.

"You gotta give me something," the man said, an empty palm held out in front of him. "Anything. Work with me."

"It's like this . . ." Davis started, but then could not follow through. He knew he needed to say something, would usually have been able to come up with an excuse, some plan of action that would sound good enough to put the man off for a while, but the shock from his morning visit to the clinic was still with him and his thoughts weren't clear. Oddly, the best excuse, the truth—that he had just that morning been diagnosed with a terminal illness—never even occurred to him, and the best he could do was shrug his shoulders and try not to cry.

Three days later when he returned from his morning walk with the dog, the couch, the table, the desk, and the pile of laundry were arranged neatly on the front lawn of the apartment building.

Chapter 3

As Jake rounded the corner, the first thing he saw was that stupid pug pissing on his hydrangeas. He could spot that dog, with its bowlegged gait and doughnut-shaped tail on its ass, from a hundred yards away, and he knew that if the dog was there, the owner must be close by. Since he didn't particularly like to drink alone, the thought that he would have a drinking companion for the evening buoyed him somewhat. And in truth, he enjoyed Davis's company in the way that most people enjoy the company of those whose life drama rises to, and often surpasses, the level of their own.

The dog lowered its leg and gazed up at Jake with bulging, cataract-covered eyes as he pulled into the driveway. It growled and approached the car, the hair rising up on the back of its neck. Then the wind shifted, providing the dog with a whiff of Jake's familiar scent, and he came bounding toward the vehicle, ears back, tongue out, ass-doughnut wobbling.

Sprawled facedown on the lawn like a bearskin rug or someone downed by an assassin's bullet was Davis, a bulging black plastic garbage bag of what could only be laundry next to him. Next to that was what looked like a table. Jake got out of the car, knelt down and patted the eager, snuffling beast at his ankles. Then he rose again, lifted his sunglasses and, addressing Davis over the roof of the car, said, "This doesn't look good."

Davis looked up, shielding his eyes from the sun, gazed at Jake for a moment, then dropped his face back onto the lawn. Jake shut the car door and walked over to Davis, the dog executing a series of hind-legged pirouettes around him as he went.

"I'm used to seeing you and the dog here, and certainly the laundry," Jake said, "but the table? That's a first."

Davis pulled himself up and sat Indian-style, his belly resting on the ground. In the three days since getting his diagnosis he'd had almost no sleep. He tried to speak, but again, the words would not come. Instead he began to cry. The kind of crying that is so severe and genuine that it initially makes no noise but is, rather, a pantomime of convulsing and tears, the mouth open but no sound or even breath coming from it.

"Whoa!" Jake exclaimed, lowering himself to the ground. "Whoa, what's this? Don't do this!" he pleaded. Jake could handle any sort of drama better than he could handle tears, especially when they came from someone usually so jovial. "What's the matter? What is it?" he said, lowering himself to the ground and trying to make eye contact, fearing that his comment about the laundry and table, as good-natured as it had been, might have been the cause of the fit. He put his hands on Davis's shoulders, but the heaving continued.

"Come on," Jake said, looking around to see if the neighbors were watching, not so much because he cared what they thought, but because he hoped that one of them might know and be able to tell him the cause of the fit. Seeing no witnesses, he decided to ameliorate the situation in the only way he knew how, first with sarcasm: "You're killing the grass," he said, rubbing the tears into the lawn. And when that failed, with the offer of his own brand of mother's milk, dispensed not from a breast but from a cocktail shaker. "Don't you need a little pick-me-up?" he inquired, lowering his head and again attempting to catch Davis's eye. "C'mon, c'mon, why don't we go inside and I'll build us a drink?"

Without looking up, Davis wiped the snot and tears from his face and tried to take a breath. Jake offered a hand to help him, knowing that the effort to pull the large man up would require both hands—and all the force he could summon from his legs and back—but that effort proved unnecessary as Davis got up by himself, collecting Edgar with one arm as he ascended. The dog licked the briny streaks from his cheeks, and the two followed Jake into the house.

In addition to his many other talents, which included an encyclopedic knowledge of geology, the ability to recite *The Love Song of J. Alfred Prufrock* in its entirety, and the know-how to fix anything, from broken hot water heaters to hopelessly frozen computers, Jake was also an expert at making all flavors and colors of martini-esque drinks. The mixing, shaking, and consuming of the first round of cocktails that evening punctuated Davis's woeful tale of his diagnosis; the second, his eviction. After the third shaker had been emptied and Davis's nerves had settled, Jake raised the inevitable question:

"So what are you going to do?"

Davis shrugged. "If I could just get some ideas together and crank out this book, then at least I could have some money. About the rest, I don't know what I'm going to do." Jake nodded and got up to mix another round. He was the type of person who was excellent in a crisis, which was why he and Davis, whose life seemed to be an endless series of crises, were such good friends. It was also why Jake had gone far in his career, which involved supplying logistical support to marine scientists: a job in which there was always some crucial piece of equipment that was supposed to have arrived yesterday in a distant port; some argument between rival scientists about the allocation of laboratory or bunk space; some sobbing young undergrad who'd gone out and gotten drunk with the locals in a rough-and-tumble seaside town and been relieved, at some point in the evening, of her wallet and passport. And for all of those dramas, and many others like them, Jake always seemed to find some satisfactory solution.

In addition to his aforementioned talents and resourceful problem-solving skills, he was also the kind of friend who was easy to like because the advice he dispensed was, more often than not, designed to improve the immediate situation rather than to remedy or eliminate the problem in the long term. He made it seem that a Band-

Aid was all that was needed when really the problem required something more like amputation. In short, he gave the type of advice that most people wanted to hear.

If life were like an old movie, Jake might be the blindly supportive wife who stands faithfully by her husband as he dumps all of the family's money into some shady Ponzi scheme; or he could be the coach who gives false courage to the stitched and dazed boxer before shoving him back in the ring for a concussion-inducing pummeling. Jake's advice, though inspirational, was, more often than not, lacking in at least one vital element of conventional wisdom. He is the kind of friend you could rely on to tell you to buy some whimsical, expensive piece of clothing that you'd probably never wear—a crushed-velvet half shirt, say, or orange ostrich-skin cowboy boots—because "you deserve it!" Or the type of friend who'll tell you—when you are well in your cups and less likely to resist—that of course it's a good idea to stop in and get that tattoo. The kind of friend who'll console you with a "morning-after" cup of coffee when you arrive on his doorstep sporting a black eye, wearing a two-sizes-too-small, vomit-encrusted shirt that clearly does not belong to you, and which you have no recollection of putting on, by saying, "You don't have a drinking problem, you just drink like a European." The kind of friend who, much to the delight of his nieces and nephews, gives live bunnies and baby chicks as Easter presents. The kind of friend who would say, "You're right, everything will fall right into place as soon as you finish this book."

"Listen," Jake said, shaking the remaining pink liquid into their glasses and getting up to mix another round, "stay here tonight—and for as long as you need to. I'm headed to sea in a few days, and I'll be gone for a month." Then, pausing in his mixing, as if just realizing the wisdom of his own words, he nodded. "Yes, you should definitely stay here while I'm gone. You'll have a roof over your head, rent free, and you'll be helping me out by watching the place. It's a no-brainer."

No-brainer. What a lovely, cautionary term, the irony of which is lost on so many.

Davis hesitated. Jake finished measuring, capped the lid, and shouted to make himself heard over the violent shaking: "It's quiet here! You can finish your book! Once that's done, everything will fall right into place." He stopped shaking, refilled their glasses, and added in a softer voice, "You'll see."

They sipped their drinks in silence, Davis considering the proposition—a proposition he had secretly hoped Jake would propose. It was, after all, the reason he'd come.

"You've got enough to worry about," Jake resumed, "without worrying about finding a place to stay, so just step down off the cross and don't try to be a martyr. And like I said, you'll be helping me out. Really. Just take it easy for a while, don't think about finding work just yet. You've got a lot to process and digest. Chill out for a week—two weeks—then maybe think about getting started on your book."

Since Davis was, at that point, drunk, and since the alternative was for him and Edgar to sleep in the bucket seats of his booted convertible in front of his old apartment, he accepted the offer without argument. That no-brainer out of the way, the discussion then turned to the more mentally challenging topic of where they should go to eat.

In the days and weeks after Jake left, time, for Davis, passed quickly, as time is wont to do when you go from a one-bedroom apartment with no electricity, electronics, or food to a well-appointed house with a full refrigerator/freezer, a flat-screen plasma TV (with premium cable), and a computer with a T1 connection. Yes, in such situations, time zips by, weight accrues around one's midsection, and not much productive work is done on artistic endeavors.

As usual, Davis had good intentions about finishing his book, and a few times he really did try to pull something together, but he never found just the right spurs to prick the sides of his intent and send it galloping off to the finish line. The same problems—dull story, uninspiring characters, complete lack of any point whatsoever—were still there, and every time he thought about sitting down at the desk to address them, he would linger for a moment in front of the TV, or computer, or refrigerator, and five minutes later his senses were numbed and all ambition lost.

In addition to those distractions, there was the ever-present distraction of the virus, silently dividing and multiplying in his body, gnawing away at his immune system. He always knew it was there—like the presence of termites in a wall, or the first Mrs. Rochester locked away in the attic—but it was so silent and abstract that it rarely gained his attention. He knew he would need to take some sort of action regarding it very soon, but taking action meant really and honestly admitting that it existed, and that was something Davis was not quite ready to do.

When Jake returned a month later, pale, exhausted, and constipated from eating nothing but airline food for the previous twenty-four hours, Davis was on the couch spooning ice cream into his mouth directly from the half-gallon container and watching a repeat of *The Biggest Loser*. He shut off the TV when he heard Jake come in, stuck the ice cream under the end table, and went downstairs to greet him.

"You look like you could use a cocktail," Davis said, but as soon as the words were out of his mouth he had cause to regret them, since all that remained in the liquor cabinet was a half pint of bourbon and a bottle of sweet vermouth. He mixed up a pathetic Manhattan and poured it into their glasses. Jake took a sip and winced.

"Sorry," Davis said, "we're a little low on product."

Five minutes later they were seated on stools at the neighborhood bar on Seventeenth Avenue drinking enormous gin martinis. After the first was gone and they'd ordered the second, Jake became buoyant again and asked the inevitable: "How's the book coming along?"

Could there be, in any known language of the world, a worse, more backhandedly accusatory and openly judgmental question to ask of a struggling writer? Davis thought not, and had to make an effort to conceal his annoyance. He'd been expecting the question, of course, but not nearly so soon. He fortified himself with another gulp of gin and spat out a well-rehearsed lie:

"Oh, it's coming along. . . . It wasn't headed in the right direction, so I ditched it all last week and started over, which was a good thing because it's going much better now. *Much* better. I just need to tweak it a bit, you know?"

And in the coming weeks, Davis was diligent in his writing efforts, rising early each morning, fortifying himself with espresso, and sitting down at the table, a notebook and sketch pad before him, ready to descend again into the artistic mine and see what he could dig up. He forced himself to keep at it until noon, digging and digging, trying to find the vein of an interesting story, but more often than not the ore bucket came up to the surface empty.

At one very low point, after a week of intellectual futility, Davis again flirted with the idea of going back to another Edgar story, but after spending a few hours on tepid drawings and sloppy plots he was forced to admit that any story lines he could devise involving that fictional animal had, like his non-fictional namesake, become gray, slow, wheezing, smelly and uninteresting.

In spite of Davis's artistic stasis, he and Jake lived compatibly for almost a month after Jake's return. Jake would come home in the evenings, he and Davis would chat, have cocktails, order dinner in or go out, and then pass out in front of the television watching sports.

Soon, however, a rip appeared in this idyll portrait of bachelor domesticity when Jake began dating a guy he'd met online. The casual dating soon progressed into nights spent at one or the other's house, and that, coupled with the fact that the battle of trying to keep white pug hairs from embedding themselves into the fabric of just about every piece of clothing or upholstery was a losing one, and thus a source of increasing annoyance for Jake's new love interest, who, as an artist, wore only black clothing, was the death knell for Davis's free ride.

"Maybe," Jake said tentatively, taking courage one evening from his second Windex-colored martini, "you should start looking for your own apartment. I could give you the deposit and first month's rent. Then," he added brightly, "you'd have a month to find a job and come up with the money for the next month."

"I don't know..." Davis said. "Sounds a little risky."

"Yes," Jake agreed. "It does. But I think it's time."

"*You* think it's time, or Nabil thinks it's time?"

"*We* think it's time. Look," Jake said, changing tack, "I'm not one to lecture, but you do remember that you've got a potentially terminal disease, right?"

Davis nodded.

"And the drugs you need aren't cheap."

Davis knew they were not cheap, but his fear of finding out just exactly how un-cheap they were had kept him from investigating the subject.

"Depending on what you need," Jake said, "they could potentially cost tens of thousands of dollars a year."

Davis was not shocked. At least not entirely. Termites, the first Mrs. Rochester, HIV—they could all be ignored, but only for so long. He'd been largely successful at keeping the disease in the margins of his life, but it was inevitable, he knew, that it would again move to the center and demand attention. Still, in that semi-subliminal, self-deluding way of his, Davis had hoped that somehow, despite the overwhelming historical evidence to the contrary, the virus might just evaporate. Might just, like a seasonal flu, run its course and be gone.

After that jarring conversation, Jake drove off to spend the night with Nabil and Davis retreated upstairs where he lay on his bed, staring at the ceiling. Much later he roused himself, ordered Chinese food, and when it came, he took it upstairs and ate it absently in bed, tasting nothing. He chewed, he swallowed, he stared at the wall. His thoughts were paralyzed, frozen by a dull sense of dread.

When Jake came home the following evening and Davis heard the familiar castanet sound of the cocktail shaker, he remained where he had been most of the day—on his back in Jake's guest room, staring up at the ceiling.

Jake stood at the bottom of the stairs and shook louder. "Don't you need a cocktail?" he called. Davis pulled himself up, put a robe over his pajamas, and walked downstairs.

Jake frowned at the attire but poured the emerald liquid into two large funnel-shaped glasses and handed one to Davis without comment.

"Cheers," Jake said. "And congratulations."

"For what?"

"Have a sip of your drink first. I know it looks like mouthwash," he said, wincing at his first swallow, "and it kind of tastes like mouthwash, but then, I guess it suits your outfit."

Davis gave a shrug and accepted the glass.

"Take a sip," Jake said. "I think I've got it all figured out for you."

"You found a cure?" Davis deadpanned.

"No."

"Maybe you've got some brochures on pre-planning a funeral?"

Jake sighed, lit two cigarettes, and gave one to Davis.

"Gallows humor. Cute. But no. I think I can get you a job. With benefits."

Davis perked up.

"Not a great job—probably boring as all fuck—but it pays well, you'll get to travel, and did I mention it has benefits? That means you can go to the doctor. You can get any meds you want—even the fun ones (for the small cost of a co-pay, of course). You'll have a regular paycheck, so you can get your car out of hock, buy some new clothes, and"—here Jake paused and clenched his hands together—"you'll be able to get your own apartment!"

Davis rolled his eyes.

"I'm not totally sure I can pull it off," Jake said, "but I've got some favors I can call in, so at the very least I can get you an interview. How's your résumé look these days?"

Davis sighed. "Not unlike my latest book."

"Huh?"

"Like a blank sheet of paper."

"Well, we can work on that, flesh it out a bit."

"What's the job?" Davis asked, closing his eyes and sipping from his drink, imagining himself alone with a clipboard in some grim warehouse, inventorying thousands of small plumbing parts; ten-keying in sheet after sheet of numerical data, maybe sorting mail. . . .

"It's writing!" Jake said.

Davis raised his eyes and looked at Jake over the rim of his glass.

"Well, technical writing anyway."

"Technical writing," Davis said, and then repeated the words again: "Technical. Writing." To his mind they were like the opposing ends of two magnets being pushed together. "You mean, like . . . manuals?"

"Yes."

"You're kidding, right?" Davis said.

"No, why? You can totally do it, I'm sure. It'll be a challenge at first, but you *can* write, and that's all you need to know. We've got all these knuckledragger technicians who somehow manage to compose sentences without using any verbs, so we need someone like you to help them out."

"...?"

"With writing manuals."

"About?"

"About equipment. And, of course, updates on all the stupid corporate policies that no one ever reads. You can totally do it. We've got one girl doing it already, but she's not going to be around much longer. If we got you in now, she'd be there to train you before she leaves."

"I don't know...."

"You don't need to know. You don't need to know anything but how to write, and you do know that."

It was true that at one time in his life Davis had been able to write. And he could still, if pressed, string a sentence together and have it make sense on a page with other sentences, apply some style and polish to it, but even he knew, even then, that Jake was not telling the truth when he said "that's all you need to know."

Since the job involved technical machinery and technicians, Davis correctly assumed that he would probably need to know something—anything—technical, but the truth was he did not. Davis was the type of person who learned to live without the functions on the computer that he couldn't immediately understand, the type who would rather burn toast forever than read the manual to figure out how to change the setting on the toaster; the type who had never learned how to set the DVD player to do anything other than "Play" and had gotten used to the *00:00* or *Err* that flashed incessantly from all of his household appliances (before the power had been shut off, of course); the type who would have preferred a simple rotary cell phone instead of the one he had, with its glittering array of "features," most of which he was too lazy and disinterested to figure out. He was, to be blunt, the embodiment of a "no-brainer," and yet here was his friend, a friend who had known him for nearly a decade and who, by now, surely knew all of Davis's intellectual limitations, proposing that he take a job writing technical manuals.

"Do you really think I could do it?" Davis asked.

"Not a doubt in my mind! Here," Jake said, collecting their glasses, "let me refresh your drink."

Chapter 4

After a sober evening spent working with Jake on Davis's résumé (the biggest work of collaborative fiction either one had ever produced), Jake took the two sheets of paper with him the next morning to be delivered to the shadowy person who would be making the decision about the job. All that remained for Davis to do was wait.

During the week it took to hear back, the majority of Davis's eating was confined to his fingernails, which he whittled down to nubs while poring over a stack of business-related books he'd checked out from the library. There was, of course, the classic tome *Sealing the Deal,* by Burkowits and Epps; Margaret Danielson's indispensable and highly praised *Navigating the Minefield: A Q&A Workbook for Interviewees,* but the one that seemed, to Davis, most relevant was the volume by a Zif Selig, entitled *Foot in the Door: How to Get the Rest of Your Body In, Too.*

When the day arrived that Jake returned home and said, "It's on for tomorrow, nine A.M.," Davis did not feel prepared. On the contrary, all the reading he had done had the opposite effect of its intended purpose and had made him a mentally jumbled mess. His outward appearance, by contrast, was well under control, although it had not been easy. At 6'6" and close to 270 pounds, finding suitable clothes had always presented a challenge for him. Miraculously he had squeezed some more credit out of one of the department stores and with it acquired a pale green dress shirt with French cuffs, a two-piece black suit, and an emerald tie with an architectural pattern. A pattern that was closely echoed on a pair of cufflinks he'd been given one Christmas by his sister-in-law. Cufflinks that had, by happy accident, missed a trip to the pawnshop because they'd been out of his possession, having been lent to Jake soon after they'd been unwrapped. Since his feet were size 14, finding shoes had been the biggest problem. He did find a pair at a department store in the mall, but the price far exceeded the amount of credit the store was willing to extend him. Proving that necessity is the mother of invention, or something like that, he resurrected a pair of lawyerly wingtips he'd inherited from a long-dead and similarly large-hoofed uncle. They were actually a pair of old brown and white golf shoes, but once he'd removed the spikes and covered the brown and white leather with two even coats of gloss black spray paint, they looked fine, almost new, not a drip in sight. And as long as he was careful not to scuff them, the color and sheen would last—at least through the interview. The only problem with this modified footwear came whenever he walked on a surface that wasn't carpeted.

On the morning of the interview he was dressed and ready by 6:00 A.M. Too nervous to eat, he busied himself reciting the mantras from his interview books, while simultaneously patting the lower half of his black pants with a sticky mitten he'd fashioned out of masking tape in a futile attempt to get rid of the pug hair. Jake walked in.

"You look nice," he said.

"I look ridiculous."

"No," Jake said, pouring them both a cup of coffee, "you look nice, very professional."

Davis waved away the coffee and rolled his eyes.

"Sarah's going to interview you," Jake said, between sips. "She's fine. A nice girl. She knows you don't have the science or computer background—"

"That's an understatement."

"So just keep telling her that you're a fast learner."

"So I should lie."

Jake set down his cup. "Would you stop? Really. Just stop."

"What?"

"Displaying your insecurities like they're some sort of stig-mata."

"But I *don't* have the computer skills. I *don't* know anything about science."

"Yes, but you're not stupid. Somehow you managed to get an agent and a publisher, and you got them to publish your books. Do you think that happened by accident?"

Davis shrugged.

"Look," Jake said, not concealing his exasperation, "you can write. You can definitely do this. And you need to. It's a great op-portunity. Just go in there, be yourself, and you'll be fine. Really."

That was what Jake said. What Davis heard was something like this:

"You are in your mid-thirties and broke. What's more, you have a terminal illness and you need benefits so you don't die. And what's more still, you need to make some money so you and your little dog can get the hell out of my house, because if you don't, my doe-eyed young boyfriend is going to prance right out of my life."

"And tell her that you don't get seasick," Jake added.

"But I don't kno—"

"No." Jake was adamant. "You do *not* get seasick. That'll be the nail in your coffin if you let on that you do, or even hint that you might. Sarah's nice, but she's also a hard-ass. Lucky for us, she's in a hurry to fill the position and she owes me some favors. Still, I've left the entire decision on whether or not to hire you up to her, so you've got to sell yourself."

Selling himself. Davis pondered the term. He'd seen it used sev-eral times in *Sealing the Deal* and all the other books, but even after reading about it he was not quite sure how to do it, not quite sure that he even wanted to do it. Giving himself away, now *that* he could do. That was, after all, what had gotten him into this predica-ment in the first place—but selling himself? That was something different. Thinking literally for a moment, his mind wandered to the idea of prostitution, and he pictured all of the oiled pectorals, peaked biceps, and bulging jockstraps he'd seen on a website for male escorts. Now, *those* were guys who had something to sell.

Davis, on the other hand, with his beer gut, flabby arms, and blood that he couldn't even donate, had a hard time considering himself a commodity. Still, he knew what Jake meant. He meant that Davis needed to sweep up the shredded confetti that once constituted his self-confidence and toss it gaily around during the interview. And Davis did think that maybe he might pull it off. After all, his last published book had been, to his mind, a real piece of crap, and yet somehow he had managed to dress it up, tout it as something it most definitely was not—a good piece of work—and get it published. He could, he supposed, do something similar with himself in this situation.

And yet that bit of self-confidence did nothing to allay his under-lying anxiety. An anxiety that lived deep back behind the often foggy foothills of his brain. It was a fear (rarely admitted and often fervently concealed) that he was just not very smart. Oh, he had a level of knowledge, education, and wit that made him occasionally able to "pass" for smart, much as the descendants of Thomas Jefferson and Sally Hemings may have been able to pass for white, or in the way that some gay men pass for straight, but like them, deep inside himself he knew what he was. And that knowledge—the knowledge of his fundamental, innate dumbness—was the bubbling source of his angst.

Once he arrived at the office building and announced to the receptionist who he was and why he was there, she sent a call out over the intercom. She motioned to a seating area behind him, saying, "She should be here in a moment."

Davis retreated to the small sofa/coffee table arrangement and took a seat. Like the STD clinic, there were no magazines, nothing with which to distract himself, so he was forced to listen to the receptionist repeat, over and over again, "Polar Support Services, this is Martha, how may I direct your call? One moment, please."

There was a mirror on the wall opposite him, and he took the opportunity it provided to examine his carefully arranged reflection. He straightened his tie, practiced a smile he hoped would not appear too saccharine. Somewhat satisfied, he turned his attention to his legs and engaged, once again, in the task of plucking pug hair from his pant legs. He heard his name, looked up, and realized in an instant that his appearance would probably not be all that important. Before him, hand extended in greeting, was an extravagantly pregnant woman dressed in a pair of faded denim overalls. Her dull brown hair, parted in the middle, was held back from a face free of makeup by two large chrome barrettes.

"I'm Sarah." Davis stood, introduced himself and shook her hand. "Let's go up into the conference room," she said, motioning to a flight of stairs to her right. Davis followed her wide denim ass as she labored down the hall and up the stairs, stopping midway to catch her breath.

"You can see," she said, turning and exposing her distended womb, "why I'm eager to fill the position."

"Looks like a big baby," Davis remarked.

"Two, actually."

"Twins?"

"Yes."

"How far along are you?"

"Oh, they could drop any day now. The due date's the twenty-seventh."

"Of September?"

"August! I know, I know, that doesn't leave much time," she said, turning and resuming her ascent. When they got to the conference room, she lowered her bulk into a chair and flipped through some paperwork, pausing to look over his résumé.

"BA in English, that's good, minor in art. Hmm. Published works of fiction . . ."

"I attached some writing samples."

"Great, okay," she said, flipping to see that they were there, "I'll look those over later. God, these shoes!" she cried, extending her stubby legs and using her swollen feet to pry off her shoes. Once freed, she rubbed them together, emitted an orgasmic sigh, and eased back into a comfortable position in the chair. She flipped back to the main page of his résumé and continued her recitation: " 'Proficient with the Microsoft Office Suite.' That's good. We use mostly Word, Excel, some drawing programs, occasionally FrameMaker and other Adobe products. I assume you're familiar with them?"

He nodded like an eager puppy. "What I don't know, I'm sure I can learn. I'm a very fast learner."

"Good, good," she said, giving her belly an affectionate series of pats, "because I'm not going to be around long to give much instruction. We do mostly SOPs, policies, O and M manuals, proposals, RFPs, some formatting of SIPs and RSPs, maybe an ORT or two, some work on the after ops report, the occasional haz waste or spill response report. That sort of stuff. Oh, and updates of existing documentation. Always lots of updates. Do you think you could handle that?"

"Of course," Davis replied, although he had no idea what on God's green earth this bloated tub of baby was talking about—or in what language. It was like listening to a skipping disc, or like talking to someone on a cell phone that kept losing reception—he could catch one word, then another, but they were punctuated by blips of incomprehensible gibberish. Then came the barrage of questions:

"What would you say are some of your strengths? Do you work better alone or in a collaborative environment? What's a word or phrase that people use to describe you? What word or phrase would you use to describe yourself? Could you give me an example of a time you had to work under extreme pressure? What are your long-term career goals? Where do you see yourself in six months? In five years? Is there any . . . thing in your life that you might need to consider when faced with the prospect of extended travel? If someone were to show up to work smelling of alcohol, what would you do?"

Davis had practiced answers to all of those questions, but the one that threw him was this:

"Do you smell paint?" Sarah asked, sitting erect in her chair and indignantly sniffing the air. Davis froze.

"God!" she exclaimed, snapping shut her leather notebook and giving Davis a look of outrage. "You try to do everything possible to not poison your unborn children—no caffeine, no cigarettes, no liquor—I even wear gloves and a respirator when I clean the house so I'm not leeching in all those chemicals!—and then I come to work and get all these paint fumes coming through the vents!"

Using her arms, she hoisted herself up from the chair and circled the room, nose up, searching for the source of the fetus-maiming odor. Hoping to distract attention away from the topic, Davis cleared his throat several times and blurted out the following non sequitur:

"Funny, my mother smoked all through her pregnancy—and beyond. And I assure you," he said, repeatedly patting his own belly, "there was no problem whatsoever with low fetal birth weight, nor has there been in all my post-fetal years, ha, ha, ha."

Sarah turned and stared at him. He went on:

"She used to joke that she loved being pregnant because it gave her a place to set the ashtray, ha, ha."

Of course Davis had intended for his comments to lighten the mood, just as Burkowits and Epps had advised and, more importantly, to distract attention away from the smell of his shoes, but Sarah wasn't laughing, or even smiling. She had that expression that is a cross between pity and horror: a scrunched-up, lemon-sucking, World Trade Center-bombing-witness look. A look that, when a woman sees it reflected in her bathroom mirror, often results in her scheduling of a series of Botox injections. Davis saw the look and instantly knew what she was thinking: She was looking at him thinking "what the fuck?!"

But he was not quite right in his assessment. Instead, his comments had pricked the bloated sack containing her hormonally charged maternal instinct and sent it coursing through her bloodstream. She looked at him and thought:

Poor, pitiful, gigantic used-to-be someone's little boy! I can only imagine the childhood he must have endured, raised by that nicotine-addicted alcoholic mother. Why, she'd probably been one of those mothers on daytime TV—the kind with five kids, all with different last names. Kids that ride in the back of open pickup trucks and have Pepsi in their baby bottles. Kids named after soap opera characters or luxury cars.

Davis sensed that he needed to appeal to her pity rather than her horror, so instead of chuckling at his little anecdote, he followed the cue of her mood swing, dropped his shoulders, and tried to project a look he'd learned from Edgar and had drawn many times in his books: the contrite puppy face. The kind of face the dog made when he'd been caught digging through the trash or chewing on one of Davis's baseball caps. And the look seemed to work, because the next question she pitched was a real maternal softball:

"Why don't you tell me about your publications. Being a published author, that must be exciting!"

Given the highly technical job for which he was applying, Davis was acutely aware of the absurdity of describing the genre—let alone the plots—of his work, but his *Interviewing for Dummies* book had cautioned him to talk more about the business aspects of his creative endeavors rather than the content, so again he cleared his throat and began to speak, thinking that he might just be able to spin this hay into gold.

Being naturally high-spirited, Davis found it easy to talk to just about anyone, and like most people, he loved to talk about himself and his work, which he then did, treating Sarah to a rollicking five-minute verbal tour of the publishing world and his part in it. He told her all about having his first book published, emphasizing the research required to find an agent and pitch his work to her. He described the contracts he'd signed (omitting the small fact that he hadn't bothered to really read any of them prior to signing) and underscored how that had helped hone his attention to detail. He mentioned his deadlines (all but one of which he had missed) and highlighted the fact that they had taught him to effectively manage his time. He told her about incorporating revisions that came back from his editor (neglecting to mention the screaming tantrums he'd thrown whenever he'd been presented with such list of revisions), and then he segued into describing the joy of having children as fans (although any time he did a book signing he invariably came down with a nasty head cold afterward, which he attributed to having to shake the sticky, filth-covered mitts of all those little walking petri dishes), and the responsibility he felt to be true in his work, since he was, after all, "molding young minds."

"And part of that responsibility," he added, his tone rising and turning more businesslike, "is to make sure that the information I convey, whether it be in a children's storybook or a technical manual, is conveyed with the utmost in clarity and conciseness."

He had hoped that she would take special note of that last bit, but she seemed far more interested in removing a pilled-up piece of wool from the cuff of her sweater. He switched gears and began narrating his recent disillusionment with the book world. Told her all about the bitter TUCBAs, and confessed to being tired of being an impoverished MSCBA, ending his narrative by expressing the wish to have "something that still involves writing but that will allow me to eat three meals a day, ha, ha!"

That elicited a brief smile, some movement of pen on paper, followed, in a tone that was the antithesis of excitement, by, "Yes, that all sounds very exciting."

Then, twirling the pen between her fingers, she directed her gaze at him and asked, "And are you currently working on anything?"

Again Davis froze.

"I only ask because I'm wondering if it would be something that might interfere with the job."

"Oh, no way!" Davis replied. "Would it interfere, I mean. In no way would it interfere." Then in an attempt to get his legs back under him, he took a deep breath, looked up and to the left, as per the suggestion of Mr. Selig in *Foot in the Door: How to Get the Rest of Your Body In, Too.* According to Selig, "looking up and to the left is a subliminal way to give the appearance of profound thought and reflection." In this situation it would, Davis figured, make him seem, well, more profound and reflective. All it actually did was cause Sarah to crane her neck around to see what it was he was looking at. Unnerved by the failure of this strategy, and feeling like he ought to say something to distract her from the gaffe, he exclaimed, almost as if it were the answer to a game show question, "Multitasker!"

Sarah raised her eyebrows.

"That's the best word I can think of to describe me. If you were going to ask me that question, which I anticipated that you might. If so, then that is the answer. The more irons I have in the air, the better."

Now, of course, completely off cue, came her laughter. "I already asked you that question," she said, "and I believe your answer was"—she paused and flipped back a few pages of notebook paper—"self-starter."

"Well, that too. As well, I mean."

She smiled, closed the notebook and set it on her lap. "I have one more question for you." Davis met her eyes. He felt tears of sweat roll down his flanks and hoped they weren't seeping through the shirt. Sarah went on: "And I want you to be completely honest with me on this, okay?"

"Okay."

"Do you get seasick?"

"No. Absolutely not."

Again, the eyebrows went up. "Then you've spent some time on the water?" she asked, reexamining the résumé for nautical experience she might have overlooked.

Time on the water, thought Davis. Maybe if she put the word "bed" after it.

"Oh, yes. I have."

"Because our boats are no picnic," she said, waving a warning finger at him. "We go through some of the roughest seas in the world."

"I'll be fine."

"You have sailed before?"

"Mmm-hmm."

"On open water?"

"Yes."

"Where, exactly?"

On the fly, Davis elaborated on the one cruise he had ever taken:

"It was during a semester break, while I was studying abroad my junior year. In England. I think that's on my résumé. Excellent year. So many opportunities. Anyway, a group of friends and I decided to go on a North Sea cruise to Sweden. You know, one of those drunken 'let's take advantage of the duty-free and the cheap gambling' junkets that are so popular with poor students eager for a weekend lark. Anyway, we'd started playing a drinking game before we'd even left the port. Funny game called Open Mike, basically involves singing the lyrics to a song with a shot glass in your mouth. Anyway, by the time we reached open water and the ship started banging around—it was the North Sea, after all—everyone, except me—who was, sad to say, as big then as I am now—were all puking in the hallways. Granted, some of that was from playing so many rounds of Open Mike, but most of it was from the sea."

He paused long enough to look over at Sarah, who was again picking at the pills on her cuff. Davis wanted to tell her to give it up, get a new sweater or use a razor on it, but then he remembered her condition and size, and realized the sweater had probably been one of those pregnancy hand-me-downs that made their way around fecund offices like this. Either that, or it had come from the same obese Iowa farmer as those horrible overalls.

"To make a long story short," Davis said, regaining his composure, "I seem immune to the effects of both the sea and the bottle."

"Okay then," Sarah said, again shifting in her chair, and using her pen as a pointer. "Great about that first one. No seasickness. And you really won't have to worry too much about the second, because our little vessel is dry."

Davis cocked his head. A dry boat? Wasn't that an oxymoron? Like jumbo shrimp, airline food, or fat-free ice cream? She sensed his confusion.

"Meaning there is no alcohol allowed on board."

"Not even before dinner?"

She shook her head.

"Or after you're done working?"

"Not ever."

How, Davis wondered, had Jake neglected to tell him something so vital? More importantly, how had Jake, whose pickled platelets flowed through his veins and arteries on a steady stream of spirits, survived—for months at a time—without the stuff?

"Would that pose a problem for you?" she asked, the pen resuming its role as a baton, twirling in and around her fingers.

"Not in the least."

"Good, because there's no wiggle room on that one. It's an insurance issue. When you're in port, fine, as long as it's off the boat. When you're at sea, no. We've got a very firm policy on that. Also, you'll be expected to work twelve-hour days, seven days a week, even when you're in port. You do get compensation for the extra hours, which they can explain to you more during the orientations."

Davis's heart leapt. "If they'll tell me about it in orientations, does that mean . . . ?"

"What?" She paused, a questioning look on her face. Then, realizing her slip, said, "No. No, no, no! I mean they *would* tell you about that, and many other details about the program and your part in it, if you *were* to get the job."

"I see."

"Yes."

The interview went on for another five or ten minutes, but Davis was much more relaxed. He even stretched out his legs and crossed them at the ankle, heedless of the exposed metal plates.

The shoe is in the door, he thought. The rest of the body will soon follow.

Chapter 5

"Am I an animal?" she asked.

"No."

"Uh-uh."

"Well," Davis said, "kind of."

She gave him an exasperated look. "How can I be kind of an animal?"

"Ah, ah, ah," Davis scolded, shaking his finger at her. "Remember the rules. Only answer yes or no questions."

"But you're the one that said 'kind of'!" Bryce cried.

"Yeah!" said Bryan. " 'Kind of' isn't a yes or no answer."

"You're both right," Davis concurred. "As usual. Such smart boys. I withdraw my answer." The boys' sister, Briana, enthroned in her car seat, resumed her line of questioning:

"Am I a person?"

"Yes," the boys replied in unison.

"Yes!" Davis exclaimed. "And you see, that's kind of an animal."

She narrowed her eyes and pursed her lips. It was remarkable to Davis that a four-year-old had so perfected the expression of stern admonishment, but then, she did have two menacing older brothers to contend with. Three if you counted her uncle, who was, in many ways, the least mature of them all.

"Uncle Davis," she said gravely, "play right, or don't play at all!" Davis apologized and she again resumed her questioning.

"Am I a man?" she asked.

"Yes."

"Do I drink a lot?" The boys, Bryan and Bryce, giggled, thus giving away the answer. Briana smiled, clearly knowing the answer but wanting to continue the game for the sake of the comedy.

"Do I like flowers?"

"Do you ever!"

"Uncle Davis!"

"Sorry," Davis said, his tone grave. "Yes. You like flowers."

"Do I walk around the yard . . . in my teeny-weeny bikini?" she asked, giggling so hard she could hardly get the question out. The van erupted in giggles.

"Am I . . . Grandpa?"

The children's mother craned around in her seat, trying to maintain parental composure.

"That's not nice," she said, shaking her head and glaring in particular at the two boys and Davis. "You three know better. Let's think about setting a better example for Briana. She has to learn from you."

Davis, playing contrite, lowered his head. He glanced up, met the eyes of his brother, Don, reflected in the rearview mirror, and tried but could not repress a nasal snort. The two boys then lost their composure, and Briana, thrilled to be the cause of such amusement, began kicking her legs in the car seat and chanting "teeny-weeny bikini! teeny-weeny bikini!"

"That's enough back there!" Don boomed from the driver's seat. They were all silent. Don was trying to contain his amusement, but his shoulders were heaving and his eyes were teary. He retrieved his sunglasses from the visor and put them on.

"Daaaaad?" Bryce queried. "You're not laughing, are you? Are you?"

"Teeny-weeny bikini!"

Don let out a laugh and then he looked over at his wife, mouthing the words "I'm sorry." She rolled her eyes and then turned back, trying to keep herself in check. From the backseat the littlest comedienne was still performing her routine, this time trying out the timing and pacing of her material.

"Teeny!

"Weeny!

"Bikini!"

"All right," their mother sighed. "Get it all out of your systems now. Laugh away. Because when we get there, I want all of you—especially you, Uncle Davis—to be on your best behavior. I want all the manners we've practiced to be put into action, okay?"

A few minutes later, the minivan arrived at its destination: the split-level house where Davis and his brother Don had grown up. This house, and all of the other houses on the block, were artless, each consisting of one rectangle lying on its side connected to another rectangle standing on end, both capped with a slightly peaked roof. The large window on the second story of the taller rectangle had shutters on either side of it, but these were for ornamental purposes only, like false eyelashes, and really fooled no one.

Although the house—and the surrounding houses in the neighborhood—was architecturally negligible, the front lawn of this particular house was remarkable in that there was no lawn. Instead it was as if some member of the seventeenth-century French aristocracy had been reincarnated in the American suburbs and had attempted, with varying degrees of success, to create a miniature replica of the gardens at Versailles. There were four triangular areas each filled with beds of blooming flowers, each bed enclosed on all sides by a foot-high box hedge. Between the beds were four gravel paths that converged on a central circular area where a slightly incongruous three-tiered Mexican fountain gurgled and spat. The manicured geometry of the space could only be fully appreciated when seen from above, but, as evidenced by the numbers of passersby who eased their foot off the accelerator and gazed in wonder, it was still quite impressive from eye level—one of those rare suburban anomalies that managed to evade scrutiny of the neighborhood covenant, which had not legislated against such a thing because they had not been able to anticipate, let alone conceive of it.

The ordered beauty of the garden in the spring and summer months was, however, often marred by the sight of the aforementioned gardener, an obese man with a hairy back, invariably clad in a skimpy swimsuit, black dress socks, and white tennis shoes. His belly and bald head slathered with Coppertone, he would wander the gravel paths admiring his handiwork, garden hose in one hand, a plastic cup full of rum and Coke in the other. The embarrassment this apparition had caused to Davis and his brother while growing up was compounded by the fact that the house was not located at the end of a remote cul-de-sac, nor on a seldom-traveled circle, but on a busy corner not far from the local high school. This kept both boys indoors, driving one toward the escape of artistic expression and the other toward the regimented normality of accounting.

When the minivan rounded the corner on that particular day—the sixty-eighth anniversary of the gardener's birth—they did not find him strutting in the garden but in the driveway, clad just as they had expected, in an orange floral Speedo, his gut hanging over the front, making it appear from certain angles that he was wearing nothing except for the socks and shoes. Judging by the wet pavement and the pile of rags on the driveway, he had just washed one of the cars, an oversized green Plymouth station wagon that had been in the family since the late 1970s. It had wood grain paneling on its doors and back end, and it was to this that Davis's father was now giving his attention, spraying it with lemon Pledge and then buffing it to a shine.

"I see Grandpa's butt! I see Grandpa's butt!" Briana said from her car seat, prompting another round of laughter from the two boys.

"Shhh!" their mother scolded, turning and giving them each a stern look. "We are all to be on our best behavior. Manners in action, okay?"

They nodded, composed themselves, and got out of the car, running to greet the old man, whose expression did not conceal the fact that he did not especially like having his ordered world intruded upon either by raucous children or his son's dog, for whom each and every finely manicured botanical feature in the yard represented nothing more than another item on which to lift his leg. The kids and their parents disappeared into the backyard in order to set up the picnic lunch they'd brought, and Edgar followed, wheezing behind them. Davis was left alone with his dad.

"Make sure you clean up after that dog this time," his father said. "I walk around here in my bare feet."

"I will."

"I'm just about finished up here," Davis's father said, spraying a cloud of milky polish onto the driver's side panel and buffing it with an old pair of underwear.

The station wagon had belonged to Davis's mother for less than a year when she died, and it had seldom been driven since. Mostly it was backed out, buffed, and then pulled back into place.

Davis picked up a rag—one that had a collar instead of a waistband—and helped polish the side panels.

"Dad, I don't think this is real wood."

"What do you mean?"

"I mean it's just a sticker."

"Oh, it's wood," his father said, pausing to wipe the sweat off his forehead and take another sip from his glass. "Very thin sheets of wood. That's why it needs so much care. Otherwise it'll warp."

Davis opened his mouth to protest, thought better of it, sprayed more Pledge on his rag, and went back to polishing.

The lunch proceeded without incident, and when it was over and the plates had been cleared away, Davis decided to tell them about his job interview.

"I think I might have a new job," he announced.

His brother looked up and stopped chewing on his toothpick.

"That's great!" Krista exclaimed, and then looked over at her husband, who quickly echoed her sentiments.

"That really is great, Davis," he said, although the tone of his voice betrayed his dubiousness. "Congratulations . . . Is it . . . another book?"

"I still have one left in my contract," Davis said, "but this is something different. I think I'm going to be a technical writer."

His father roused himself from his rummy haze and tried to focus.

"Wow!" Krista said. "When? Who will you be working for?"

Davis explained the details of working for this specific government contractor, heightened the seagoing drama and left out his professional insecurities.

"How . . . ?" Don asked, tapping the toothpick on the table. "I mean, how did you hear about the job?"

Davis knew that his brother suspected there was more to the story than Davis was relating, and saw that he was having real difficulty keeping his suspicions to himself.

"Through a friend," Davis replied. "My friend, Jake. You guys have met him."

"Oh yeah, I remember. Tall guy, little older than you."

"Yes."

"This is a real opportunity," Davis's father piped in. "When do you start?"

"I, I don't know. I just got a message yesterday with the offer. I haven't called back yet."

"What! Why not? You're going to take it."

"I . . . don't know," Davis said. "I mean, probably."

"Of course you'll take it."

It was always like this with his father. No matter what they were talking about, Davis always heard the unspoken but tacitly implied "stupid" tagged on to the end of each of his father's sentences. It had been a nightmare when the man found out he was gay; he could just imagine the reaction if he found out Davis was HIV+.

How the hell did that happen, stupid? What were you thinking, stupid?

"I just wanted to hear what you guys thought about it first," Davis said, figuring that an appeal to the paternal ego was the best route to take. "You know, before I call them back."

"Call them back!" his father said, waving his napkin in the air. "Call them right away. First thing Monday morning." Again with the implied *stupid*. "It's a good, solid company. You can't do much better."

"Okay."

"And you'll get to travel?" Krista asked, in a feeble attempt to pull the conversation back from the precipice.

"Yes."

"Davis, this is great," his father effused, downing his drink and getting up to mix himself another. "Really the sock in the arm you need. I'm proud of you. Call them Monday morning. Or call today and leave a message. Don't give them time to change their mind."

"Dad!" Don said, setting down his knife and fork and shaking his head. "It's Davis's decision."

"You know what I mean," his father said, talking to Don as if Davis wasn't in the room. "He won't get many chances like this, not at his age."

Don shook his head, gave Davis an apologetic look, and then lit into their father:

"Davis has *always* worked, Dad. It's just not the same kind of work that you did."

The children exchanged worried glances with their mother. Davis sighed and leaned back in his chair. He tuned out the conversation and stared off into space. Why had he even bothered? It had, he supposed, been an almost canine effort to gain some praise from an indifferent master. To hear, just once, that his father was proud of him. And he had got what he wanted, or so it seemed. Certainly it had been more than he'd heard from his father when any of his books had been published. He recalled with a painful vividness the day he had told his dad he wanted to write:

"Children's books?" his father had said, his tone more akin to someone spitting out the words "child molester." Then he added, "I don't suppose there's any money in *that*. And what about insurance (*stupid*)? Retirement (*stupid*)?"

Davis looked at his father, now arguing in the kitchen with his brother. He didn't especially respect his father, didn't agree with the way he led his life. Why, then, did he aspire to please him at all, let alone be like him? This was, after all, the man who had been so bored and dissatisfied with his job that he set off every morning, lunch box in hand, in a foul mood, returning in the evening in an equally foul mood that would only begin to ebb away and be replaced by something resembling happiness once he had downed a scotch, stripped out of his work clothes, and gone to work in his garden.

Davis then realized that the reason his father so wanted him to take the job was because it was the first step Davis had ever taken toward becoming more like him. Early in his life, when he'd held his father in higher esteem, Davis had actually thought he wanted to emulate the man. For most of his youth, Davis had believed his father's self-aggrandizing exaggerations about his important job with an aeronautics company, had believed his claims that he had personally built the highly publicized rocket ships and satellites, had believed that he had almost single-handedly engineered the design, construction and launch of the space shuttle. Now, of course, he knew better. For years he had known better. The reality, which Davis discovered at the age of fourteen when he and his brother had gone on a "Family Day" outing to visit the guarded compound of his father's employer, was considerably less exotic. The man worked in a ground-floor office, low-ceilinged, with some sort of large, exposed drainage pipe running over his desk. Granted, he was in his own office, with a door, but on that door was a faux-wood-grained plaque (also probably polished with lemon Pledge) with his father's name, followed by the words *Asst. Mgr., Personnel* —a position he'd held (or which had held him) for close to thirty years.

"He's loaded," Don said, when he and Davis were alone at the table, their father off in his garden and the rest of the clan inside preparing the cake and ice cream. "Don't let him get to you. You know how he is."

"I know." They were both watching their father, kneeling down on a cushion, plucking miniscule weeds and putting them in a pile on the ground.

"Hell, he'd be happiest if he could just be out there all the time."

"I know," Davis said. And he really did know the reasons for his father's bitterness. He also knew that on Monday morning he would pick up the phone, call Sarah, and accept the job, for much the same reason that his father had probably taken his job. With his father it had been because his wife had died and left him solely responsible for raising two young boys. The way that Davis saw it, his HIV was just another type of needy child.

"This isn't really what you want to do, is it, Davey," his brother asked.

"No," Davis said, "it isn't."

On the surface, his taking the job seemed an ideal solution to a number of problems: It would bring in some much-needed income, it would provide him with medical benefits, it would allow him to travel to an exotic locale—one rarely frequented by anyone in the world. . . . But underneath the excitement and relief, there was also an undeniable sadness—a feeling that by taking the job he would be putting his dreams of being a writer on ice for a while, maybe forever. Going to Antarctica was a great opportunity, he knew that, but it wasn't really what he wanted to do with his life, so there was nothing that was going to make it seem right, no matter how adventurous the job was supposed to be. It was a compromise. He had fucked himself into a corner, so to speak, and to get himself out, this was what he had to do.

He looked out at his father, tottering drunkenly in the garden, his rum and Coke sloshing out of the glass. Compromise. Then he moved his focus to his brother, whose eyes were on him, waiting for an explanation.

"Things that bad?" Don asked.

Davis nodded. He felt like he was evading his brother by not telling him about the HIV. He knew Don wouldn't judge him, would never say anything negative or mean. Instead, he would worry, and to Davis, that was even worse. He could handle the disappointment and chastising his father dished out at him, but his brother was such a good man, in spite of their chaotic upbringing, in spite of his being younger and having only Davis as a filial role model. Don was, by all accounts, a great dad; his marriage appeared solid; he was always ready to help Davis out, be it with money, or by doing his taxes, or working on his car. He had done all of those things and more so many times in the past that Davis felt guilty burdening him with anything else. And that was, Davis supposed, reason enough to take the job. It was a chance to legitimize himself in the eyes of others, yes, but more than that, it was a chance to put his family and friends at ease, to finally give them the chance to move him out of the "worry" column of their minds.

But his brother wouldn't let it drop.

"If you need money . . ."

"I do need money," Davis said, "but it's a little more complicated than that."

His brother's gaze was on the table. He was examining a napkin ring. Edgar made several futile attempts to jump into Davis's lap. Davis picked him up and the dog licked his face. The kids were talking inside, still busy with the cake and ice cream.

"Tell me what's going on," Don said, not looking up.

"It's nothing. Really. I shouldn't have said anything. What did you guys get for dad?"

"Don't change the subject. I'm your brother. You need to tell me."

Davis looked down at the dog, so content in his lap, the lids of his bulbous eyes descending as he slipped into a nap. Davis looked up.

"I'm sort of HIV positive," he said. "But I'll be all right. Really. I just need to get on some medication. I don't want you to worry. Please don't worry." He looked over at Don and saw tears sliding down his face.

The kids reemerged from the darkness of the house, their faces illuminated by the candles on the cake. They were about to burst into song when they saw their father crying. They froze in the doorway, too frightened to advance.

Book 2

The Office

The brain is a wonderful organ; it starts working the moment you get up in the morning and does not stop until you get into the office.

—Robert Frost

Chapter 6

His eyes stung, and his neck felt like it was boneless, incapable of supporting the weight of his head. He was conscious of a dull, rumbling sound, like someone blowing bubbles through a straw into a large paper cup. He tried to focus on the text projected in front of him but words, often whole sentences, slid on and off the screen with the slick precision of professional ice skaters.

VISION!
STRATEGY!
GOALS!

Sometimes the phrases would materialize slowly, appearing first as pixilated specs and then getting ominously larger as they approached.

CONTINUAL IMPROVEMENT!
TEAM MOBILIZATION!
PROCESS IMPLEMENTATION!

Once they had reached their full size, they paused, then flashed on and off, like neon Vacancy signs outside of cheap motels.

PRODUCTIVITY!
TOTAL PRECISION QC!
EFFECTIVE SUPPORT THROUGH
  NEEDS ANTICIPATION!

If the presentation were slowed down to one-quarter speed, or the slides played in reverse, Davis was sure there would be some subliminal message, something like the words spoken by Cold War hypnotists in B-movies as they swung pocket watches before the eyes of bound and gagged captives.

This particular room, and every other conference room he'd been in so far, seemed to have been designed for hypnosis—or at least for the study of sleep. It was windowless, it had carpeted walls, and the overhead lights (except for the eternally exempt Exit sign) were either dimmed or off. The ventilation system seemed to be working in reverse, slowly sucking all the air out of the room, although the lack of oxygen could certainly have been caused by the woman standing behind the podium; on and on and on she went, usually doing little more than supplying redundant commentary on the flashing text on the screen.

The voice of this particular woman, the one facilitating this particular training, was particularly anesthetizing, never moving out of the lower octaves. It came to Davis in gargled bits, as it would to one who had been floundering in the ocean for hours and was now losing the battle to keep his head above water.

"... our commitment to ..." glub, glub, glub "... internal auditing contro—" blub, blub, blub "... guidelines for proactive strategic modeling ..." glub, blub, blub.

Sometimes the tone of the one behind the podium would change from underwater gargling to, say, the purr of a large, overfed cat, but whichever tone was used, it inevitably had the same hypnotic effect and succeeded only in persuading Davis's eyelids to descend. His head simultaneously began an almost imperceptible descent toward his chest, then, reaching a critical point, it snapped back, as if yanked by some invisible string. The third time this happened he sat up in his chair and felt a strand of drool on his chin. He paused a moment before wiping it away, glancing ever so slightly to the left, and then to the right. On his left, a blond girl's moccasined foot swung in time to some tune in her head. In one hand she held a pencil at a ninety-degree angle, using the edge of its tip to precisely shade in every other line of her notebook paper. With her other hand she absently twirled her long hair around her index finger.

The bearded man on his right *appeared* to be writing, his notebook resting on his crossed legs. But when Davis took a closer look at his page he saw that instead of text, there was an elaborate drawing of a dragon-robot hybrid being ridden by a woman with flowing tresses and enormous bare breasts; breasts so out of proportion to the rest of her body that they must have been as difficult for her to support as Davis's leaden head was then for his neck.

The page of notebook paper resting on Davis's lap was considerably more prosaic. At the top he had written the training topic—which was something to do with project management—and the date on which the training began—which had surely been sometime in the last calendar year. He glanced down at his watch and saw that they had, in fact, been in the room for less than twenty minutes, provided that it was still Tuesday, and not Wednesday, or even Thursday. His mind wandered and he considered the possibility of writing a modern-day update of the Rip Van Winkle story. The hero, in a suburban office-park setting, would awaken in some dim conference room, his face covered in cobwebs and whiskers (or maybe just caked with dried-up drool), as slide #7,428,653 of a PowerPoint presentation on Workplace Ethics (or IT Security, or E-mail and Telephone Protocol, or some such thrilling topic) silently materialized on the screen and then, a few moments later, just as silently, waltzed away.

Davis grabbed his upper lip between his thumb and forefinger and pinched it. Hard. The hope was that the self-inflicted pain might shock him into alertness. It did not, so he rested the row of his upper teeth on his thumb and forced that single digit to support the entire weight of his head.

This must be what narcolepsy is like, he thought to himself, or chronic fatigue syndrome, or even slipping into death.

With his free hand, he began massaging his eyes. The luxurious, stinging relief at finally allowing them to close, coupled with the tie-dye constellations produced by the gentle pressure of his fingers, soon had him in a trance-like state of somnolence. On and on she warbled from her perch behind the podium. On and on and on, and whenever Davis's fingers inadvertently pushed one or the other eye open, it was only to have it assaulted by another bullet-pointed phrase:

PROCESS AFFINITIZATION
LESSONS LEARNED
INTRA-DEPARTMENTAL CROSS-POLLINATION

This was only his second day in the office, but it was his seventh training/orientation. So far he had endured a General Office Introduction; a nauseatingly in-depth training on e-mail regulations; the first of a six-part business ethics module, entitled What If . . . ?; an Introduction to Six Sigma: Methodology and Practice; two that he couldn't remember, and then this last one: Project Management: Things We All Must Know. He couldn't even keep track of which orientation/training was which. His notebook consisted of page after page of headings and dates, beneath which were elaborate doodles of futuristic houses, lyrics from songs that were stuck in his head, or stylized geometric renderings of one of the terms from the PowerPoint. It wasn't that he didn't try to pay attention—his intentions were always good when he walked into the room, fortified with caffeine—but then the lights would dim, he would settle into the chair, and the person speaking behind the podium would slowly unravel the topic, usually for the twenty-seventh time that week, his or her boredom for the subject matter becoming airborne and slowly infecting each and every member of the audience. Soon they were all head-bobbing and drooling, doodling and praying to God that time would somehow resume passing.

It had all started the day before. Davis, dressed far more casually than he had been in the previous week's interview, arrived at the office and went through the same drill: He announced himself to the receptionist who, in turn, summoned Sarah, via loudspeaker. Five minutes later, she had waddled into view, preceded by her unborn, the overalls and pink sweater having been replaced by a blue gingham muumuu. She greeted Davis and then stood guard at the front desk while the receptionist led him back into a room behind her chair where a camera and tripod were waiting. "Stand over there and smile," the receptionist said. "Or don't. Just don't make any goofy faces, m'kay?" Davis did as he was told and she snapped the picture. "It's for your badge," she told him. "It should be ready by the end of the day." She then handed him what looked like a credit card with a clip attached to it. "Keep this visible on your person at all times."

Davis stared at the card, unsure what to do with it. He was about to ask, but before he could do so the receptionist's eyes went blank and she began speaking into her wireless headset. "Polar Support Services, this is Martha. How may I direct your call? Mmm-hmm. Yes. Mmm-hmm. Please hold." Then, focusing on Davis and stabbing at his badge with the cardinal red nail of her index finger, she said, "You use it to get into the building," sounding a note of surprise, almost annoyance, at his naïveté. "You swipe it on one of the key pads. There's one by every door—Polar Support Services, this is Martha. Can you hold, please?—one by every door. Do *not* allow anyone to tailgate in after you. They'll tell you all about that in security training, I'm just giving you a heads-up." Then she leaned in, pinched the ant-sized microphone that was attached to her headset, and whispered conspiratorially to him: "The place has been swarming with auditors this week. You never can be too careful." Then she resumed her conversation, "Thank you for holding, how may I direct your call?" and motioned Davis back out to Sarah, who escorted him to the first of many trainings.

From the way Jake had described the job, and from the pictures on the company website, all featuring flocks of penguins and huge tabular icebergs floating in navy blue seas, Davis had somehow expected more excitement, or at least less sheer tedium. But so far it had been one meeting or lecture after another.

Some of the presentations—Information Security Breaches, Lock Out/Tag Out Procedures, Laser Safety—sounded exciting at first but soon proved as boring as all the others. He'd been particularly interested in one entitled The Importance of Branding, as it brought to Davis's mind images of cattle roundups or elaborate skin art, but when the time for that meeting arrived, he took his place in the conference room and felt a tinge of dread as the lights went down and the PowerPoint projector was fired up. In less than a minute, he was again pinching his upper lip and rubbing his eyes as the man behind the podium embarked on an hour-and-twenty-minute lecture on the importance of the company's logo, extolling, with puritanical zeal, the need to "combat nonconformance and maintain standardization at all five levels: logo, font, color, page placement, and website protocols."

The lectures and slide shows were bad enough, but when, at the end, the speaker invited questions from the audience, they invariably got worse, as there was always some eager beaver, usually seated in one of the first three rows, who, wanting to impress the facilitator with his or her intelligence (and to impress everyone else with his or her prowess at wedging his or her nose deep between the presenter's ass cheeks), would say something like, "I, for one, would just like to offer my thanks for your presentation. It really has, and I mean this sincerely, enabled me see which processes are most important to my cost center."

But even worse than that was when someone, usually someone seated in the back, and usually with a private axe to grind with the PowerPoint presenter, would try to lambaste the inadequacy of the presentation by picking the rotting meat off some tiny bone of contention: "I've been here for seven years," the complainer would begin, "which is three years longer than PSS has been at the helm of this contract, and back in the old days, we were always told that we could use an Arial twelve-point font beneath the corporate logo, as long as the document was for internal use only. Are you telling us now that that has changed? And if so, when and from where did the directive for that change come, and why was it not officially disseminated?"

These "contentious questions" were the worst, but not, as one might think, because of their absurdity. No, they were awful and hateful because they would invariably ensure that the meeting would continue for an additional ten minutes—at least—forcing the audience to sit captive as a jury while the prosecution and defense each took turns presenting their side of the esoteric case.

In the few hours left between trainings and orientations, Davis returned to the desk he would soon take over from Sarah, who was busy packing up some of her belongings and waddling them out to her car.

The building housing the Denver office of Polar Support Services was three stories high with a large, ground-level annex in the rear. Davis's cubicle was in this annex, which had once been, judging from its football-stadium size, a warehouse. The ceiling had been dropped down to office height and the floor space divided and subdivided with hundreds of "modular office systems," as they were euphemistically called. It was a massive, fluorescent-bathed metropolis, but unless you stood on a chair and looked over the tops of the walls, you never really got a sense of just how massive. Being freakishly tall, Davis could easily peer over the top edges of the cubicles, but he tried to avoid doing so since it always gave him the sensation of being in a large cave in which the water was slowly rising.

The cubicle walls were softly upholstered in cushiony taupe fabric. At first, this struck Davis as odd, almost quaint, but after less than a day confined inside one, he understood the need for the upholstery. It was to protect the inhabitants from possible skull fractures when, in ever-diminishing moments of angst-tinged clarity, they banged their heads against them and rued the quiet desperation of their eight hours of obligated time.

"The workspaces are arranged," the office manager had explained, as she clipped Davis's nameplate to the outside of his cubicle, "to foster openness, collaboration, and communication. For that reason we place two to four people in each modular system."

Within an hour, Davis realized the lie. While having four people together in a "modular system" did, in ways that were perhaps not intended, foster immense and often spirited communication, its real function was to enable the inhabitants to police one another and thus make sure that no one was frittering away company time on eBay or Craigslist, or, say, by writing a novel.

The desks of the inhabitants were arranged and angled so that each person faced into a corner, giving the impression that they were all being somehow punished. Having everyone thus positioned would, one might think, give a certain degree of privacy, but this was not so since all the chairs were rotational and could swivel a full 180 degrees in far less time than it took to minimize a computer screen, thus granting your coworkers valuable insight into how you were, to quote the orientation training manual, "engaging in unproductive time."

And then, too, there was always the threat of MBWA, an acronym for Management By Walking Around. Ostensibly, MBWA was meant to make you feel that upper management, as they strolled casually from cube to cube, was accessible, approachable, like a friend or confidant. What it really meant was that the one thing you needed in this office, above all else, was an eye in the back of your head, preferably one that worked independently of the two in front. Either that, or excellent auditory skills so that you could hear the gentle click and clack of the photo ID badge, door swipe card, five-year commemorative pin, and security key fob that swung like so many corporate testicles from the lanyards attached to all managerial belt loops.

The cubicle Davis was set to inherit was shared with four other technical writers, each with their own specialty and each with varying levels of bitterness. Bitterness that roughly corresponded to their age and to the number of years they had been with "the program."

At the time Davis was hired, the United States maintained three Antarctic stations and a research vessel. Each of the members in the cubicle was assigned to a different station. In the east corner was Janet, the pseudo-fascist neo-con. She was assigned to the station at the South Pole. In the west sat Tom, the uncompromising environmentalist, who supported an entire odorous ecosystem on his rarely washed body and clothes. Tom was assigned to the tiny outpost on the Antarctic Peninsula known as Palmer Station. Representing the largest of the three stations, McMurdo, were Gordon and Ryan.

Gordon, a frustrated scientist who had been forced to fall back on technical writing in order to pay back his student loans, felt himself superior to all the others and thus was like the personification of an interjection—never allowing anyone to finish a sentence without tacking his thoughts onto it. In addition, he suffered (and so did all those in proximity to him) from a form of conversational Tourette's syndrome, which caused him to provide unsolicited running commentary on just about each and every aspect of his day.

Gordon, Janet, and Tom deployed to their stations during the austral summer. That time of year, roughly from October to February, was referred to by those in the program as "the science season," since that was when the Antarctic continent was most sunny and accessible. Ryan, on the other hand, deployed during the austral winter, which was, Davis came to realize, about as close as one could get to being shot into outer space: It was dark, cold, inhospitable, lonely, and inaccessible. Very little science was done during that time and the populations of all the stations decreased to what was referred to as a skeleton crew, meaning there were just enough people to achieve the twin goals of 1) keeping the stations up and running, and 2) maintaining a geo-political presence on a continent that was allegedly owned and governed by no one.

Since Ryan was a "winter-over," his schedule was opposite of all the other station-based tech writers. That allowed him and Gordon to share a desk, since they were never in the same place at the same time.

Ryan was, for many months, a shadowy figure in Davis's imagination, never seen but occasionally included in teleconferences, where he was mute and invisible on the other end of the line. His presence was so infrequent that Gordon, Janet, and Tom never had much to say about him since they rarely saw or spoke to him. Davis did, later that year, cross paths with Ryan, and as soon as he did he immediately understood why he chose to deploy when he did. Ryan was the antithesis of the other three tech writers. Where they were loud, boisterous, opinionated, obnoxious, Ryan was quiet, serious, focused on his work, and almost entirely lacking in social skills. It was only later that Davis would discover that his emotional remove from the day-to-day office drama was helped along by a strict regimen of early-morning cannabis smoking.

Two of the workstations in Davis's cubicle had windows, but these slots were occupied by the more senior tech writers, Gordon/Ryan and Janet. Davis was initially envious of these prestigious roosts but soon realized that the window seats were, in a way, more depressing than his seat on the aisle, since "the view" was of a barren dirt slope, too steep to mow and, therefore, routinely sprayed with herbicide by the building maintenance man to keep anything from growing on it. The slope was at such a steep incline that it created something of a little canyon between itself and the building.

Unless you arrived at work very early in the morning (which, after the first few weeks, Davis did not bother to do), you were apt to miss the fifteen-minute gap in grimness during which the sun actually reached the window. Grimmer still, at the crest of the slope was a high chain-link fence, delicately crowned with loops of concertina wire. On the other side of that fence was allegedly a prison, but again, the slope was too steep to see an actual building so, for all the cubicle dwellers knew, the fence and concertina wire were just as likely there to keep them in as to keep the prisoners out.

On Davis's first day in the office, Sarah and Jake led him to the place that was to be his new home and made polite introductions to the other tech writers. Sarah had warned him about the hazing practices they might inflict, but he shrugged it off figuring she was probably just exaggerating. Once the pleasantries were over, the three writers stood and began their vivisection. Gordon was the first to speak:

"What is your science background?"

Davis's mouth opened but nothing came out. He looked to Sarah, who was also caught off guard, her shoulders tensed, causing the muumuu to inch up and reveal her swollen ankles.

Jake cleared his throat and said: "He's a published author."

"Yes, published," echoed Sarah.

"He had a contract," Jake said. "We were lucky to get him."

Eyebrows went up all around.

"What type of publications?" Janet asked, narrowing her right eye.

About Janet's eyes: The right eye was blue, lidded, normal; the left eye may or may not have been in the socket, Davis couldn't tell, as it was hidden behind a dark green lens of her black-framed glasses. There was no lens, green or otherwise, covering the good eye, and its absence was almost as distracting as the green one.

"I, uh . . . it's fiction," Davis said, trying to decide which eye to look at.

"Ahhhh," Tom said.

"What genre?" Gordon asked. "Mystery, thriller, science fiction?"

"Just fiction," Davis said. "Probably nothing you've ever heard of."

"What's your last name?" Janet demanded.

Davis gave it, and all three, Tom, Gordon, and Janet, pivoted on their heels, returned to their respective corners, and began typing.

"Nothing on Wikipedia," Janet said.

"There is a listing on Barnes and Noble," Gordon said, and Janet immediately began typing again.

"Kids' books," said Tom. "Four of them. Edgar's Weekday Adventure, Edgar Digs to China, Edgar Takes a Trip—that one must be about drugs—and Reigning Cats and Dogs: Edgar and Sheba in the Land That Time Forgot. You can get used copies of the first three for a penny on Amazon. 'Course it'll cost you six ninety-five in shipping."

Davis longed for another pile of laundry in which to bury himself.

"Listen to this," Gordon said, giggling as he read: "In this, the fourth, and, one hopes, final, chapter in the ongoing Edgar saga, the hero, a pug, steps into a time machine and goes back to the days of the dinosaurs. . . ."

He then went on to describe, to the evident amusement of all Davis's new coworkers, the entire messy plot of Davis's last book, as seen through the gimlet eye of one of the more bitter TUCBAs at *Publishers Weekly*. When Gordon finished reading, Tom chimed in: "Well, he *does* mention evolution. . . . And that's science, right, Janet?"

"It is," Janet assented, "if you're gullible. Or a narrow-minded, can't-think-for-himself lib—"

"Uh-oh, here it comes," Tom said, "here it comes . . ."

"Liberal!" Gordon cried.

"No," Janet said, shaking her head. "That's not what I was going to say. But I knew you'd think that. What I was going to say was 'lemming,' which is synonymous with 'liberal' because they've got the same stupid herd mentality. Regardless, the point I was trying to make (before I was rudely, but not surprisingly interrupted) is that the fact that you two exist at all is proof that there's no validity to the 'theory,' " she said, making little finger quotes around the word, "of evolution.

"Children's books," Janet said, focusing her eye on Davis with a look only slightly less dismissive than the one she'd just given to Gordon and Tom.

"Listen, bitches," Sarah sighed, "we've got a lot of outdated pieces of paper passing for documentation down on the boat and we need someone who can clean them up and make them useful. I, for obvious reasons, won't be able to do that anymore, so we needed to find someone who knows how to string words together, and Davis here has got a proven record of being able to do that."

Jake nodded. They all continued to stare at Davis.

"You all know how it is," Sarah went on. "The boat is just like the stations: You've got gearheads and techno-dorks who know their jobs but don't know how to put things down on paper without making them so complicated and convoluted that no one can understand what they're talking about. Davis here is just the kind of writer we need: Someone from the outside, someone who won't get bogged down in all the techno mumbo jumbo; someone who can make it more understandable."

As Sarah spoke, the three writers reacted to her words as if she'd been spitting them. They winced, frowned, shook their heads, and looked for any significant pause or gap in her speech that would allow them to interrupt. Before they got a chance, Jake spoke up: "We don't need someone who knows all the systems and policies and procedures, we need someone who doesn't. We need to have the technicians explain what they do—in everyday terms—so that it can be written down in language the average layman can understand."

"So are you saying," Tom said, "that you employ average laymen to facilitate the highly technical and skilled scientific work that is performed on your boat? Because those aren't the type of people we hire at Palmer Station, I can tell you that much."

"Or at McMurdo!" said Gordon.

Tom went on: "We need a technically-minded person to write our manuals because we employ technically-minded people—people who are sometimes actually referred to as 'technicians'—to read and use them."

Jake's jawbones clenched together, making little balls appear on the sides of his face. Davis knew his friend was not one to lose his temper—or even his sense of humor—easily but he was clearly about to do so.

"What Jake's saying," Gordon said, turning to address his colleagues, "is that he wants someone to dumb it down."

"Someone from the 1D-10T Department," Tom added.

Sarah rolled her eyes and started to speak but Janet cut her off.

"Aha!" she said, jumping up from her chair and raising her index finger in the air. It was a gesture so false and contrived that Davis felt certain he'd never seen it used outside of a bad sitcom. "What Jake wants," Janet declared, confining her remarks, as Gordon had done, to her coworkers, "is another person to illustrate that oft-overlooked mathematical theorem: the DCD."

"Stop it," Sarah said, again. "Will you guys just give it a rest?"

"The DCD?" Davis asked, before Sarah or Jake could stop him.

"It's like the lowest common denominator," Gordon said, "except instead of lowest it's dumbest."

Actual snickering followed this last remark. It was, Davis reflected, behavior on a level that he had not witnessed since the seventh grade, that being a period in his life he did not look back on with anything even resembling nostalgia. Rather, it had been like a stint in a prisoner-of-war camp—but with unsightly acne outbreaks, bad hairstyles, the wrong clothes, and humiliating methods of orthodontia. It appeared that this workplace situation was shaping up to be something comparable.

"It's nothing . . . to be . . . ashamed of," Tom said, trying to arrest his laughter and compose himself. "We've all been one at one time."

"Not me!" Janet said.

"All right, listen," Jake said, grinding his teeth, "there's good reason for this," he said, pointing at Davis. "For him, I mean. What if—"

"No, no, wait," Tom interrupted. "Wait! I know where this is going. We all know where this is going," he said, walking his chair, hermit crab–like, into the center of the cube. Once there, he stood up, spread his arms wide, and said, "Step back from the curb, folks, because here comes the bus!"

"I personally prefer the image of me basking in the sun on the terrace of my villa in the French Riviera while contemplating how I want to spend my lotto millions," Gordon said.

"I guess," Janet chimed in, "that leaves me with the plane crash or, heaven forbid, the massive head wound sustained when I slipped getting out of the tub."

Davis looked to Jake and Sarah for some decoding of what the three were talking about, or at least some outrage about what they were saying, but instead he saw traces of amusement.

"Enough!" Sarah said, trying to keep herself from laughing. "Let's not throw the knives at one of our own, okay?"

"Yes," Tom said, "save the knives for the girls in Human Resources."

"We were just asking about his credentials," Gordon said with a shrug, his grin quickly concealed behind his enormous coffee mug.

"Well, then ask him in a nicer way," Sarah scolded, lowering her bulk into one of the office chairs. "He's more qualified than the last one," she sighed, kicking off her shoes, "and he's available now, which is kind of the most important thing."

The last one? The words echoed in Davis's head. *Sarah was the last one, wasn't she?* It turned out she wasn't. Before Davis there had been Ed—a former high school English teacher who had also coached the wrestling team. A broad-chested, hairy-knuckled, stout-drinking Man's Man who was looking for the kind of Hemingway adventure he imagined a seafaring voyage to Antarctica might provide.

"He was a handsome guy," Jake confessed later that night, as he and Davis sat on Jake's back deck sipping cocktails. And coming from Jake, whose taste in men leaned toward the twiggy, effeminate, and ethnic (usually past the age of consent, at least old enough to drive, but with skin and bodies that could still be classified as that of an adolescent), the compliment was surprising.

"So what happened?" Davis asked.

"Oh, he started out fine, got along with the techs, knew what he was doing, but then the boat left the dock. He was fine while it was still in the straits. I guess he looked a little green around the gills, but he kept going, made appearances at meals, managed to do some of his work, but as soon they hit open water, he just totally lost it."

"Huh?"

"He got seasick. And not just a little bit. He disappeared in his cabin for days, and by the time one of the EMTs found him, he was so dehydrated, they had to turn the ship around and take him back to port, which cost a whole hell of a lot of money and really pissed off the scientists."

"So that's why it was so important for me to say I didn't get seasick," Davis said.

"Exactly."

"But—"

"No!"

"Come on! It's possible."

"It's possible, but unlike that other thick-necked dickwad, you're going to do what I tell you. The trouble with that guy, that Edward, is that he wouldn't listen. We all told him, *take pills before you leave the dock, use the patch,* but he thought those things would shrink the size of his dick, or make him grow tits, the stupid arrogant fuck. The thing you're going to learn about boat people is that nobody will admit to taking seasickness medication—especially not the girls—because that's somehow like admitting you're not strong enough, or don't have your sea legs—and out there, with all that testosterone in the air, nobody wants to admit that. So just get the pills before you head down to port and then take them, discreetly if you have to, but take them—at least an hour before the ship is scheduled to leave. They'll probably make you nauseous, but trust me, they work. And if they don't, get a patch from the EMT, even if he gives you shit about it. And eat, even if the idea of it makes you want to hurl. It'll probably do the opposite. Eat lots of starchy crap. There won't be any shortage of it, believe me."

Somehow, this did not make Davis feel better. In fact, it made him feel worse—like there was even more pressure on him to succeed, not only by faking the knowledge he didn't have, but by somehow controlling a bodily response that even some wrestling-coaching, non-dick-sucking He-Man had been unable to do.

Like Sarah, the tech writers in his cubicle spoke in a dizzying code of acronyms and numbers, always going on about AORs, SOPs, SOWs. And when they weren't doing that, they were discussing some grammatical minutiae (a favorite being the inexhaustible, always raucous, and deadly serious debate over whether there should be one or two spaces after a period). And when they weren't doing that they were "discussing" politics.

The latter discussions were the most lively, since the room was a microcosm of the country itself in that it was evenly divided between liberals and conservatives—with almost nothing moderate in between. The discussions started harmlessly enough, with someone pulling the pin out of a conversational grenade and lobbing it from his or her respective corner into the center of the room. Usually this was something small and simple, an offhand comment on global warming, say, or stem cell research. The definition of marriage was always popular, as was U.S. involvement in the Middle East, media bias, whether we as "one nation under God" should say Merry Christmas or Happy Holidays, illegal immigration, People for the Ethical Treatment of Animals, France, Indian call center outsourcing, the Israelis, the Palestinians, the Endangered Species Act, racial integration (or racial quotas, depending on your corner), the second amendment to the U.S. Constitution, the Homeland Security threat scale, slave reparations, school vouchers, school prayer, school bussing, and that perennial favorite, abortion.

The conversation would start something like this . . . Gordon, reading an article in an online scientific journal (an acceptable use of the Internet, provided it did not impinge upon productive time) on the subject of the Intelligent Design movement, would toss off, to no one in particular, the following:

"Intelligent design," he would sneer. "There's nothing intelligent about it. The only good thing is that these moronic people and their brainless theories will inevitably be weeded out by natural selection."

Janet would raise her head, her eye moving as slowly and deliberately as an iguana's. Then, whoosh! Her chair would spin around and the tongue would dart out!

"It's a theory! Just like evolution! There's no reason they shouldn't be able to teach it in schools, just like all the other theories."

"Except," Tom would say, still facing his computer, "that we have the separation of church and state in this country, although you'd never know it by listening to that fascist rant known as the

Pledge of Allegiance that they make our kids recite every morning before school."

That comment made Janet's face so red she looked like she was entering an early phase of anaphylactic shock. Her mouth fell open but she was so angry that nothing came out. Gordon was only too happy to fill the void:

"As a father, I agree. We don't need to be filling the heads of our children with all of this invented gobbledygook designed to advance the agenda of the far right."

At this point, Janet—who, because of her undisputed-by-anyone Post Traumatic Stress Disorder, acquired sometime during the first Iraq war, could not be fired from the company—would find her voice and shout, "Well, we can't expect people like you, who'll swallow, like some goddamned fifty-cent whores, whatever the liberal media pisses down their throats, to understand anything that contains the word 'intelligent'!"

And on it would go, until someone, making one final volley into enemy territory, would rise from his or her chair and exit the cube, allegedly to go to the bathroom or get more coffee, leaving the others fuming and sputtering.

And, sad to say, soon after his arrival, Davis became the most adept grenade lobber of the bunch, never taking a side, but using the technique to incite conflict between the warring factions and thus deflect attention away whenever the topic of conversation threatened to veer into the subject of his professional ineptitude. Usually this was not necessary. Usually he could wear his stupidity on his sleeve and appeal to their egos, asking them to demonstrate their superior knowledge and expertise at, say, sorting columns in a spreadsheet or getting the page numbering to stop acting up in a Word document. But whenever those tactics failed, he didn't hesitate to pull the pin and lob the grenade.

"Do you have any questions so far?" Sarah asked as they sat eating take-out in the break room on that first day. Davis thought for a moment, reflecting on the fact that although she had inundated him with a paralyzing amount of information, she had not really given him any defined tasks. He tried to come up with a diplomatic way of asking, "What the hell am I supposed to be doing?" Not finding that, he said nothing. Sarah, perhaps sensing his confusion, patted his thigh and said, "Don't worry, it will all fit together soon enough. Really all you need to worry about in the beginning is getting the techs to update the content in their documents. Then you reformat it and get it into the appropriate template."

Davis nodded. "I do have one question," he said.

"Shoot."

"What was all that talk about the bus?"

Sarah looked confused.

"You know," Davis said, "back in the cubicle when Tom was talking about getting run over by a bus, and Gordon mentioned something about lotto winnings."

"Oh, *that!*" Sarah laughed, but then stopped almost as soon as she started since laughing (or coughing or sneezing) in her advanced state put her at risk of peeing her muumuu. "Those are just some of the reasons that we seasoned tech writers spout out to reluctant SMEs when they whine about our documenting their jobs and procedures."

"SMEs?"

"Sorry. Subject Matter Experts—the people whose jobs you have to write about. For example, you're the SME on writing children's books, I'm the SME on swollen feet and never-ending pregnancy, Gordon's the SME on arrogant bitchiness, Tom's the coffee snob SME—you get the idea. Sometimes the technicians, or other people who have written documentation, don't want us to touch it—probably the way you feel when an editor pokes around in your little books—so the thing we tell them in situations like that is that we need to document what they do, and how they do it, in case, heaven forbid, they step off the curb one morning and get struck and killed by a bus. Or, more optimistically but just as improbably, if they win millions of dollars in the lotto or the Publishers Clearing House sweepstakes and decide not to return to work."

"Oh."

At this point, Janet, who had entered the break room to refill her coffee cup, added her own editorial comment:

"What they really mean is that if they catch you surfing porn or researching bomb-making materials online, or if they smell liquor on your breath after lunch, or if you fail a random drug test, they need to be able to slide a new person into your chair before the cushion even has a chance to cool down. We provide that new person with a document defining their job so that they can begin engaging in productive time ASAP."

"And that makes Janet," Sarah sighed, "the SME on decoding HR subtext—and eavesdropping."

Once Janet had gone, Sarah turned to Davis. "Listen, I know some people sound pretty bitter around this place sometimes, but you have to understand where that comes from." Davis waited for her to go on, but she seemed at a loss as to how to continue her thought. She looked around the break room, stood up, and led him over to one of the many oversized pictures of Antarctica that adorned the walls. This particular one was of a bright red helicopter taking off from the sea ice with the gently smoking volcano, Mount Erebus, in the background. "The people working in this office," she said, "are not really like the people you're going to find working in, say, an insurance company or a bank. Most of the people here have, at least once, gone halfway around the world and gotten a taste of the wild blue yonder. Once you've done that, it's kinda hard to step back into the bland tedium of this daily grind." She stared at the picture in silence, seemingly lost in her own memories, then added wistfully: "We're like dogs that have escaped from the yard and run with wolves for a while. Then we got caught and put back behind the fence. It's tough."

Chapter 7

Near the end of his third week in the office, Davis returned to the cubicle from one of his trainings to find his desk cordoned off with masking tape. There was a giant wet spot on his chair and beneath it on the floor was a pool of yellowish green fluid. Gordon and Tom were gone but Janet was still there, sitting at her desk, scrolling through a list of guns for sale on an online auction site.

"What's with the tape?" Davis asked.

"EH and S put it up," Janet said, her eye never moving from the screen.

"EH and S?"

"Environmental Health and Safety," and just as in conversations with his father, Davis heard the same implied "stupid" at the end of her statement.

"Oh."

"I wouldn't sit there if I were you."

Davis looked at the chair again, then at the congealing puddle of liquid on the plastic mat beneath it, and waited for Janet to elaborate. He hoped it was just something like spilled Mountain Dew, a can of which Tom was never without.

"Facilities has been apprised of the problem," Janet said, still scrolling. "They should have a new chair here within the half hour. For now, consider it a biohazard. Martha is bringing down a Caution placard and some yellow biohazard tape but they don't know if the cleanup team will be able to get here today or not. The head of EH and S is at an off-site meeting and neglected to give anyone his contact information or signature authority, so nobody really knows what to do."

Fearing this whole biohazard thing was some sort of cruel joke his cube mates might have devised about his undisclosed HIV status, Davis tentatively asked, "What happened?"

"Sarah," Janet said. "She went into labor. That's her broken water on your chair and on the floor there. Technically, it's not water but amniotic fluid. She's lucky she didn't have the kids right here in the cube. Tom and Gordon and your little pal Jake"—all three of the cube dwellers had taken to referring to Jake as Davis's "little pal" or "li'l buddy" or "patron" or "insert here any derogatory term denoting the boss-that-you-obviously-fucked-to-get-the-job"—"they all piled into Gordon's car and took off after the ambulance."

"Wow," Davis said, staring at the chair, a wave of nausea rising in him.

"Yeah," said Janet, still not looking up from her scrolling pistols. "Don't know why they all felt they needed to tag along with her, but whatever. Probably won't mark the time off on their time cards, either."

As he so often did in the first stressful weeks of his job, when he grew tired of the grenade lobbing, the implications of his idiocy, or during times of intense ennui due to his lack of work, or, in this instance, when he had no place to sit, Davis retreated to the bathroom. It was a strange place to seek refuge, but the truth was there was nowhere else in the entire stadium-sized office complex where an underling like Davis could go for a moment of privacy, unless it was to lock himself in one of the three stalls of the bathroom. But even there Davis was hardly alone. At its peak, when the office was full of people going through their week of mandatory training and orientation prior to their deployment, the office was crowded with people, the majority of whom were men. And yet for all those men there were only three toilets and three urinals. Consequently, the office men's room was as busy as an airport and, for that reason, it was not uncommon to enter and discover that there was, so to speak, no room at the inn. Although maybe the bathroom just seemed inadequate because there were other men in there, like Davis, who went to the stalls not to answer nature's call, but to alleviate the comparably unbearable pressure of trying to *look* busy, or avoid intra-cubicle warfare, and the only way to find this kind of relief was by hiding in the stall and reading the newspaper.

The newspaper. Printed versions are well on their way to becoming an anachronism, but one copy always appeared in the bathroom sometime in the morning. If you got there too early, sometimes it hadn't arrived yet, but if you got there too late in the day you'd find that it had been broken out into all of its individual sections: National, Local, Sports, Entertainment, Classifieds, Funnies, etc., and each section had been passed under the stalls from man to man, like one of Janet's fabled fifty-cent whores, its pages pawed over so many times that by the end of the day it was more like gauzy cloth than paper. Sometimes there were even bits of it missing, as if someone had torn out an interesting article or a coupon they wanted to save, maybe even a recipe. But no. One had only to look over at the brown cardboard tube hanging forlornly, almost mockingly in the dispenser to realize that the day's pitiful ration of toilet paper had already been consumed, which necessitated the wiping of asses with sections of the newspaper.

How had this happened? Davis wondered with disgust, the first time he himself was forced to discreetly tear a section from the Classifieds and usher it along the path between his cheeks, wondering as he did so, if, in addition to his marking the paper, it was also marking him, the way that it did to Silly Putty when you pressed it against a section of the comics. Disturbing thoughts, yes, but the worst part about the "newspaper days" was that they often reduced the three-holer to two, as the newspaper had a knack for clogging the commodes and rendering them unusable, thus increasing the misery of the office's male inhabitants and forcing many of them to make unplanned off-site visits to Starbucks or McDonald's.

As unsavory as it was, the frequency of Davis's bathroom breaks increased dramatically in the empty weeks after Sarah began her maternity leave. The reason for this was, chiefly, boredom. Oh, there was a slender file containing some manuals to update, but his problem was that after reading, rereading, and studying them, he could not determine what exactly needed updating, or who he should ask about it. Two weeks after she left, Sarah sent him a brief e-mail saying she would call as soon as she got settled and provide him with a written outline of what he was to do, closing her missive with the line, *Just hold on until you get down to the boat; it will all make more sense then.* Until then he sat doing, well, nothing.

The worst, and most exhausting, part of doing nothing is (as anyone who's been there can attest) trying to look like you aren't doing nothing, which is infinitely harder than being balls-to-the-wall overloaded with stacks of assignments that were due yesterday. Granted, both situations are stressful, the latter because there is not enough time to complete everything, the former because there seem to be too many hours to occupy and, at certain times of excruciating boredom, it does really seem as though time has come to an utter stop.

The other downside of being undertasked is that it carries the added threat that if the higher-ups realize there is not enough to keep you busy, then it is only a few mental steps until they realize that they don't really need you, or anyone else, in the position at all, which was sound business reasoning but was dangerous for someone like Davis, whose life depended on the pharmaceutical benefits that came with remaining employed. With that fact always in the back of his mind, he did what he needed to do, wishing, at times, that he had a basket of eggs to sit on so that he might feel somewhat productive.

After a week of anxiety and tedium, Davis returned to working on his book. Of course, with the omnipresent eyes of the other tech writers and the persistent risk of MBWA, Davis was required to develop some stealth methods for doing so without arousing suspicion.

First, he kept several programs open on the computer screen at all times and made sure there was a variety of them—spreadsheets, documents, graphs, charts, etc. The one containing his book was a Word document, which he reduced to the size of a piece of bread and kept open in the corner of his screen. To further camouflage it, he kept it in outline format so that all the text was pushed to the left and appeared in an eye-crippling 8-point font.

Second, when working on drawings, he was careful to do so only on Post-it Notes, for these were easy to casually wad up and toss into the trash can, should some nosy person sneak up behind him.

Third, when surfing the web, it was a good practice to keep a pencil or pen clenched horizontally between his teeth. For some reason this gave the impression of his doing research, although it often made him feel like an eager, tail-wagging dog with a bone in his mouth.

Fourth, whenever he got up and walked away from his desk, he was always careful to have a file folder, pen, and coffee cup with him, thus giving the impression of heading to a meeting. Important, too, was to walk with a purposeful stride, a stride that said, "I have important places to go and not a minute to waste getting there." Usually, the place he was headed to was either the toilet or to the parking lot, then to Starbucks or a bookstore to waste an hour, and when he returned, same props in hand, same brisk stride, no one seemed to have missed him.

Even with all those faux work pastimes in place, the labor and tedium involved in producing faux work was more mentally and physically exhausting than any actual work because it involved the additional element of acting. Usually he could do this quite well, but at those times when playing his part became too much to bear, Davis would retire, once again, to the only place where he could safely nod off (yes, nod off) without arousing righteous indignation, and where he could still hear the intercom should he be paged. That place was, again, in the bathroom stall with the door closed and latched behind him. There were several problems with this, not the least of which was the noise and stench of people defecating in the adjacent stalls. Surprisingly, Davis was able to tune out all but the most obnoxious sounds. The smells? Well, they were more problematic. But when you are bored, and when that boredom leads down the path to fatigue—fatigue so extreme that it puts you at significant risk of electrocution from drooling on your keyboard—you'd be surprised how trivial and insignificant a few unpleasant odors can seem.

In his first two months in the office, Davis discovered that the most important element of successful toilet napping was to make sure there was a fresh roll of toilet paper available to use as a pillow. If he was stuck in a bathroom without toilet paper, or with the toilet paper imprisoned in one of those locked dispensers mounted to the wall—the kind that dole out the paper sheet by miserly sheet— he could still nap, but it put more strain on his neck.

Assuming, for our current narrative purposes, that he did have a roll of toilet paper, here are the two positions for toilet repose:

Position #1: Downward Facing Drowsy

Sit on the toilet, as usual, and rest your forearms on your thighs with your palms facing up, as if offering up your sins to a forgiving god or as if you are cradling a dove or some other small bird. Set the roll of toilet paper on your upturned wrists, keeping them close together. Lean slightly forward and rest your forehead on the "pillow." N.B.: This is a surprisingly stable position; everything —the toilet, your legs, the roll of paper, your forearms and head—interlocks, with little to no chance of an embarrassing twitch or snap that could send the paper rolling off under the stall wall. Soon, the peace of mind provided by the knowledge of this stability, added to the fatigue you already feel, will have you snoozing soundly.

Position #2: Drooping Lotus

The second option should be considered only by those who are limber or more practiced at the art of toilet napping. To begin: Sit on the toilet, but instead of resting your forearms face-up on your thighs (see Position #1), cross them over your lap. Place your right hand, palm facing down, on your left thigh. Then place your left elbow into the concave space between your thumb and fingers of your right hand (think back to kindergarten when you used to draw a turkey by tracing around your hand with a pencil; your elbow goes between the turkey's head and its plumage). At this point, your right elbow should be resting on your right thigh. Place your left hand in the nape of your right elbow (on top of the arm), with the nape in between the left-hand turkey's neck and plumage. With your arms crossed in this way, you have again created an interlocking puzzle, and you can safely place the roll of toilet paper (and here is the best part) on *either* the right *or* the left side. For longer naps, you may want to occasionally switch sides, to reduce strain on the neck.*

Potential Problems:
Since no improvised plans like these are ever perfect, here are some problems you may encounter:

Snoring:
This is almost inevitable since your neck is bent so far forward you are constricting your air passage by at least one-third. Usually you will wake yourself up before the snoring becomes too audible, but sometimes it will be loud enough to be heard in the next stall, or even by those anxiously awaiting their turn outside. What you need to fear the most from this situation is the guy who will pound on the stall wall or door and yell, "Hey buddy, wake up!" If this happens, the first thing to do is remain calm. If at all possible, you want to keep it from escalating into an HR matter, so quick wit is important. Without getting up from your perch (you don't want to risk being identified), in a disguised voice say something like, "Dude, whoa! Was I asleep? The baby's got the croup. Me and my old lady were up all night," or "Dude, I met this chick at a bar last night. Damn, she just about wore me out." You get the picture.

Hallucinatory nightmares induced by the HIV medication Sustiva:
This will only be a problem for the tiny segment of the population taking this brand of HIV medication, one of the unfortunate side effects of which is hallucinatory nightmares, or daymares, as the case may be. These dreams are vivid and frequently involve something along the lines of a flaming free fall from some impossible height; scaly, taloned claws reaching out to grab your ankles as you tiptoe from stone to stone over a bubbling vat of hot lava. Or, worst of all, your saggy-breasted octogenarian neighbor, Gladys, dressed in a leather bustier lighting vanilla-scented candles on the nightstand while you lie strapped, naked, to her four-poster bed.

*your neck, not the "turkey's"

These dreams may cause you to wake with a violent start and scream or cry out, *"No, Gladys! No!"*

If something like that should happen, the atmosphere in and out of the stalls is apt to become very quiet. Again, remain calm. Flush repeatedly to restore a sense of normalcy and then wait, say, five or ten more minutes until all of the stalls have rotated out (this usually happens quickly after one of these incidents); then zip up, flush, and leave the bathroom as nonchalantly as possible.

Pins and needles:

The exact reasons for this are not yet known. Perhaps they are caused by the height of the toilet, perhaps by the rigidity of the seat, but for whatever reason both of the aforementioned positions, Downward Facing Drowsy and Drooping Lotus, severely restrict blood flow to your legs. The ultimate goal of toilet napping is for you to sleep, not your legs, but in naps longer than five minutes those appendages will, most assuredly, nod off, too. Thus extreme care must be taken when standing up and leaving the stall or you will find yourself emerging like a drunk from a bar at closing time or like a newborn colt just taking its first steps. Should that happen, stand for an agonizing minute or two gripping the edge of the sink until the supply of oxygenated blood in your legs is restored.

It was when Davis's legs were thus enslumbered that he had the misfortune to meet, for the first time, the woman who would, in the coming months, become his nemesis.

Chapter 8

From the moment he first saw her, Davis hated her. Hated her in the logical and yet pointless and frowned-upon way that insecure, overweight, less-than-beautiful people often hate those who have been blessed with good looks, intelligence, and the arrogance that often comes from an awareness of their possession of those two things.

Her name was Maureen, but few people referred to her that way.

"The Fourth Branch" is what Jake had called her when Davis gave him an account of their first meeting.

"I don't get it . . ."

"Of the armed forces," Jake said. "You've got Army, Navy, Air Force, and then"—he paused to crunch on a piece of ice from his drink—"there's the fourth and most brutal branch: the Maureens."

Had she been a dominatrix instead of a system administrator, she would have been the merciless type, deaf to the pleas of her clients. The type who would leave marks and not care if the wife, or girlfriend, or whoever it was that the meek little sop lived with were to notice.

If Antarctica had an indigenous race of people, Maureen could have been the female embodiment of it: a cool Hitchcock blonde with pale skin, her eyes the color of compressed ice; her personality, like the place itself, remote, inhospitable, inaccessible, unforgiving of mistakes.

In spite of that, the reason most men came to dislike her was because she had rejected their advances. The reason Davis disliked her was because she had seen through him immediately. She had known, less than a minute after he had stumbled into the IT Training Room for his indoctrination in Vessel IT Security, that he was an impostor.

On the morning she was to teach that particular class, Maureen arrived twenty minutes early, got the computers up and running, and then stood at the front of the room like a general: back erect, chest jutting out, hands clasped behind her. With her right thumb and index finger, she methodically counted off the beads on her bracelet. The outfit she had chosen that day consisted of a white pencil skirt, so tight that it restricted her stride but emphasized the round bump of her ass. Above the waist she wore a light blue angora sweater set, accented with a pearl choker. She caught sight of her distorted profile reflected in the dead screen of a monitor and was pleased with what she saw. The pearls and the sweater set she found especially charming (as deceptive props often are) in that they lent her an air of easygoing softness and approachability. Although she'd been in the building for over an hour, her tortoiseshell sunglasses were still resting on top of her head, adding to the false impression of leisure. She looked more like she was waiting for the start of a polo match or an afternoon cocktail party than to lead a computer class.

The true function of the glasses was to keep her hair corralled away from her face. Most of it she had been able to pull back and funnel through a small elastic band, but there were always those annoying strays that descended into her peripheral vision at the most inopportune moments, like when she was leaning over someone's computer to undo the mess they'd gotten themselves into, or to assist them in tapping out a simple series of keystrokes that, despite her clear recitation of the command, they had been unable to remember. When her hair fell forward at those times, she was forced to make a seemingly coy, and thus, in her mind, weak, gesture of tucking it back behind her ear.

Hair concerns took more of her attention than she would have liked. She was vigilant about using a costly conditioner, avoided blow-dryers, curling irons, and straighteners, had waited patiently for it all to grow out to one length before carefully trimming off the split ends, but in spite of all that, the wispy strays persisted. Even worse, in conditions of high humidity, or near the end of a long day, the strays became corkscrew spirals, making her look as if drunken spiders had leapt from her temples and rappelled down the side of her face. The sunglasses and a bit of greasy hair product kept that problem in check, at least until the end of the day, but the fact that she couldn't control it completely bothered her to no end.

When she was at sea, the hair was, thank God, less of an issue. Then she wore a baseball cap, which kept the wisps under wrap and made the sunglasses and the sticky product unnecessary. In fact, most of her life was easier at sea; her work was clearly defined, meals were chosen and prepared for her, the dimensions of the living space she was responsible for was reduced to seven feet by fourteen feet and contained nothing but the essentials (bed, bathroom, closet, small desk). Best of all, being at sea made most fashion, which she secretly detested, redundant, since soon after arrival in Chile or New Zealand (the two most common departure points for those heading to Antarctica), she, and all the other deploying personnel, were issued identical sets of rust-colored denim work clothes, polar fleece jackets, polypropylene long underwear, heavy socks, and steel-toed boots. It was only during port calls, and when doing time in the office, that she had to worry about choosing a costume.

As the trainees trickled in, she met eyes with each one, gave a slight nod, and then glanced at the clock on the wall to her left, which showed it to be a few minutes after the 10:00 start time. None were so late that she could make an issue out of it, but she knew there would be one or two stragglers who would disrupt her opening monologue, and she was prepared, almost eager, to scorch them. The fact that she had to teach these classes at all irked her. All these stupid, needy people. It was like having a nest full of hungry baby birds, and often just as irritating to listen to.

The classroom was narrow, low-ceilinged, and windowless. There were two rows of computer stations divided down the middle by an aisle. Her heels clicked on the concrete floor as she strode up and down between the desks, distributing the hard-copy synopsis. Her muscled calves—products of a quotidian twenty-five minutes on the StairMaster and a bimonthly wax—were in a near-constant flex due to the angle of her shoes. The click of the heels, as regular as a metronome, pierced the silence of the room and focused the students' attention just where she wanted it: on her. After two turns, she closed the door, switched off the overhead lights, and clicked back down the aisle toward the podium, tapping the one remaining synopsis, which she had rolled up like a policeman's baton, against her open palm.

Having the lights out, she believed, eliminated potential external distractions and forced the students to focus on the blue glow emanating from their monitors. It also, she knew, allowed her face to be lit from below by the projector, and that glow suffused her beauty with an appropriately sinister aspect.

"Please log in," she said, and then waited until the click and clack of fingers on keyboards had subsided and the faces were again looking at her. Unlike other teachers on the first day of class, she never went around the room and asked them to introduce themselves, tell little anecdotes, or describe what they did for the company. Such silliness was a waste of time and, she feared, had the power to undermine her authority. She always dove right into the topic, never waiting to hear what they had to say.

"We're here today," she began, "to talk about vessel information security. Can anyone tell me why that's important?"

A few hands went up and she selected one, a hand that was connected by a freckled arm to the body of the pimple-faced girl with the dreadlocks. Maureen selected her because she looked stupid and she figured her answer would be wrong.

"So that our systems don't get hacked?" the girl said, the tone of her voice lilting up at the end of her sentence.

"No," Maureen said, lowering her eyelids and shaking her head. "Since there is no Internet access on the ships, an attack from an online hacker is highly improbable."

Another hand shot up. She nodded to it.

"So that viruses don't get brought on board?"

"Partly correct. Viruses could present a problem, but we do have a screening process in place that all of you must submit to before we allow your laptops to be connected to the shipboard network. As part of that process, we run a very thorough virus scan to root out any potential threats."

What she neglected to tell them was that although she did run a virus scan on their laptops, she also took the opportunity the screening process provided to indulge her considerable fetish for voyeurism. Like a pig after truffles, she took perverse joy in rooting out their caches of pornography, poking her nose into their financial spreadsheets, and reading the e-mails and juvenile diary entries they were clumsy enough to keep in unimaginatively named files on their desktop. These actions she justified in her mind by telling herself that it was important to keep abreast of the methods that people used to conceal their private information. The content was secondary, negligible, not the point of her investigation. No, the point was to know where it was and how it was hidden. That she smiled while conducting her invasions was merely a by-product. That none of the invasive poking around was mentioned in her job description mattered not at all to her, nor did its probable illegality and definite breach of ethics. It was, she told herself, necessary, in order to identify security risks, even though in all her years of snooping she never had identified any, other than those highlighted by the virus scan. But then, rationalization for bad behavior is not usually governed by logic.

"The question I'm looking for an answer to," she continued, looking directly at them, one by one, "is why information security is important to the program?"

Blank faces all around the room. Just then, an out-of-breath Davis stumbled in, a pained, amused, almost maniacal expression on his face. His morning toilet nap had run long, and he had slept through the start time of the class. When he finally woke up and glanced at his watch he had leapt up, pulled up his pants, and sped from the bathroom without even stopping to wash his hands. The distance from the bathroom to the IT Training Room was less than fifty yards, but in that time the blood had begun flowing back into his previously constricted lower extremities so that when he arrived on the threshold of the training room he was suffering the most exquisite ticklish agony in his feet and could not walk, could not even stand, without clinging to the door frame.

Maureen shot him her signature expression of annoyance, which involved lowering both of her eyebrows and tilting her head back slightly so that her chin and the horizontal line of her mouth were thrust forward.

"Take a seat, please," she said. "So we can get started. Again."

Davis did not move. He could not move. The tingling sensation was so intense at that very moment that his face contorted into something from a Bosch painting. He held up a hand, indicating he would obey her in a moment, and then stood, panting, waiting, as the tingling slowly subsided.

She looked over at the clock and then back at Davis. "We've got a lot of material to cover today, and not a lot of time to cover it. Would you please take a seat." Then, in a voice both adamant and husky: "*Now.*"

Davis smiled and nodded his assent. He let go of the door frame and staggered, on Bambi legs, down the center aisle to the vacant seat in the front row, supporting himself on the desks as he went, the pins and needles gradually diminishing. His smile irritated Maureen, even more so because he seemed not to notice her irritation. She glanced at the clock again, and then back at Davis, sitting there grinning like an idiot. Could he possibly be drunk? The stagger suggested as much, and with the vessel crowd (most of whom had AA in their future and at least one DUI in their past) it would not have been at all surprising.

"Please *log in*," she said again, "so we can get started. You're holding up my class."

Davis nodded an apology, sat up straight in his chair, touched the space bar to bring the monitor to life, and then noticed something strange about the keyboard. It was crescent-shaped, like a smile, with the keys split down the middle. It was intended, he knew, to be ergonomic, but he had never used one before. His eyes hadn't yet adjusted to the darkness, so the keyboard was as strange to him as one of those surrealist melting clocks. He squinted and then attempted to peck in his username and twelve-digit passphrase, turning his head to the right and then to the left, trying to make out the location of the keys. His first entry didn't take, and an error message appeared on the screen. He tried again, more hastily this time: again the same error message. He kept his head down, squinting at the keyboard, but stole one quick glance up at Maureen, hoping that her attention was not on him. It was, of course, and he felt perspiration emerge from the pores on his forehead. Slowly, more deliberately this time, bringing his face very close to the keyboard, he again tapped in his username, hit the Tab button (or what looked like the Tab button), and then entered his passphrase. Tentatively, he hit Enter, but the third attempt did not prove to be the charm, producing instead a new error message, this one telling him that he had exceeded the permitted number of log-in attempts and was thus locked out of the system for twenty minutes.

He whispered an expletive and looked up with a dopey grin, aware that at any moment rivulets of sweat would begin rolling from his sideburns.

"Are you in?" she asked, one hand on her bony hip, the other tapping a pen against the podium.

Davis laughed nervously. "Not exactly."

Her face hardened. She stuck the pencil behind her ear and made a series of staccato steps around the podium until she was standing behind Davis's desk.

"You're locked out," she said. "Why is that?"

"My eyes," he said, "the keyboard. I've never used this . . . one like this . . ."

Now both hands were on her hips. She rolled her eyes and emitted a groan, largely to stifle the pleasure she was taking in having the other students witness her theatrical impatience and his subsequent humiliation.

This will teach him, she thought. This will teach all of them.

Although what it would teach them, other than that beautiful, intelligent women who were acutely aware of both their beauty and intelligence could be some of the most vicious bullies outside of junior high school playgrounds or POW torture chambers, was not entirely clear. And she was wrong to think that the other students were observing the spectacle with shock and awe. Most had seized on the delay as an opportunity to open and peruse their e-mail or read the latest news headlines on the Internet and were perfectly content to amuse themselves while she and Davis worked through their drama.

She leaned down close to Davis, inhaling as she descended, trying to detect the scent of booze. She slid the keyboard so that it was facing her and channeled her annoyance into the machine via a series of rapid keystrokes.

Davis leaned back and let her tap away, noticing that her nails, in contrast to the rest of her groomed elegance, were blunt and mannish. He looked at her in profile. Her hair was not naturally blond, although it had nearly been rendered thus by a talented colorist, and she had taut and flawless skin that made it difficult to determine her age, although, Davis reflected, if she continued expressing her disapproval by scrunching her eyebrows together, that smooth forehead would be the first thing to go.

Eventually, she got his machine unlocked and stood back while he logged in, not bothering to turn her head away as he entered his passphrase. This further embarrassed Davis since, in order to keep himself from forgetting the phrase, he had made it as raunchy and disgusting as possible. He tried to block the keyboard from her view by leaning over it and discreetly tapping out Pu**yCock469 as quickly as he could, without mangling, yet again, the entry. This time the passphrase took, and when the desktop screen came into view she clicked back behind the podium, cleared her throat, and resumed.

"The reason information security is so important to the program," she said, realizing that she had lost their focus, "is, as we were discussing, to prevent viral infections of our network, yes, but also, and most importantly, to prevent the loss or corruption of the data collected by the customers we are there to support, namely the scientists. Does that make sense to everyone?" Dull nods all around the room.

"Good. And can anyone give me some examples of things that might jeopardize their collection of data?"

No one could, so there followed a lengthy lecture on the consumption of precious bandwidth by e-mailing large attachments. They seemed bored and unsurprised by any of that information, so she changed topics and said, "You have all undoubtedly noticed the pop-up screen that appears after you first log on—the one that says the machine you are using is government property and that your keystrokes may be monitored. You've seen that, right?"

They nodded, and Davis realized yet another reason to regret the choice of his bawdy passphrase.

"Obviously, we in the IT Department do not have the manpower, or, frankly, the inclination to monitor all of your keystrokes, but if there is ever cause to think there may be a problem—that you may be doing something destructive to government assets, or engaging in illegal or illicit behavior using government or company resources—then we do have the ability, and the right, to delve into your machine and see where you've gone and what you've been doing."

That gave her what she wanted. They were all suddenly alert, their attention focused on her, all browsers and e-mail accounts having been discreetly closed. She let the gravity of her statement sink in, and while it did, she made eye contact with each and every one of them, as if looking for some twitch, some look of wide-eyed panic, that might betray guilt.

"There is rarely cause to take such extreme measures," she said, relishing their fear, "but it has happened, and usually results in immediate termination. In such cases, the employee is not allowed to return to his or her computer or desk, but will be escorted from the building by a member of the security staff. Your personal effects will be sorted and packed up for you by a representative from Human Resources.

"An extreme example of IT security, granted," she said, "but one we should all keep in the back of our minds."

She let them consider this a minute longer, then lightened her tone and treated them to a smile.

"What we're going to do next," she said, bringing her hands together in front of her, a gesture that almost implied she was going to give them a treat of some sort, "is a penetration test of your computers. And the way we're going to do that is through a simple question-and-answer game."

They shifted in their seats, not trusting her.

"I'll ask each of you a few questions, let's say no more than five, and on the basis of your answers I will then try to determine your passwords and penetrate your computers."

More uneasy shifting. She continued:

"The goal of this exercise is to show you how unsecure your

computers and personal data probably are, and then to suggest steps you can take to make them more secure.

"What I want you to do first is take the pencil and the three-by-five index card I placed on your desks and write down the answers to a few simple questions." She then pressed a button on the tiny wireless mouse concealed in her palm and a PowerPoint slide advanced into view on the screen, projecting a bulleted list of the following five items:

- What year were you born?
- What is your pet's name?
- What is your nickname?
- What number are you in the chronology of your siblings?
- What is your last name?

She read them off, one by one, and they all dutifully wrote down their answers. When they had finished, they put their pencils down on the table and waited.

"Please log out," she said.

They did so and then turned their attention to her. Again, she walked up and down the center aisle, but this time her movements were slow and deliberate, like a cat stalking its prey, the heels making almost no sound at all. Seemingly at random, she stopped next to the naughty doodler that Davis had been sitting next to in the Project Management training a few days before. She picked up his index card and read it aloud to the class:

"He was born in 1973. His dog's name is Murphy. His nickname is Camel. He is the second of three siblings, and his last name is Johnson."

She then held the card up to her forehead, closed her eyes, and was very still. Ten seconds passed. She opened her eyes, leaned down to the doodler's keyboard, and asked, "May I?"

He nodded and scooted to the side as she rapidly typed in a phrase. Then he gasped as his desktop screen came into view.

"MJohnson1973?" she asked. The man grinned and nodded. Some of the students applauded. She stood and half of her mouth went up in a wry smile.

"That one was almost too easy," she said, hands clasped, eyelids lowered. "Now granted, this is my job, it's what I do for a living, so I've had years of practice doing these types of penetration tests, but it does underscore the importance of developing a safe, strong passphrase. You've got to think, be creative, make it something that is difficult to crack. Let's try another one, shall we?"

She took a card from the dreadlocked girl and read her list out loud.

"She was born in 1978," Maureen began, and then reflected to herself that the poor thing was not aging well; way past the time to stop tanning and start using that eye cream, "the pet's name is Binky, her nickname is One Cent, she is the first and only child, her last name is Franklin. Any guesses?" she asked, pivoting on her heels and making eye contact with a select few.

"Binky78?" Someone ventured. Maureen leaned down next to Binky's owner, gazing with ill-disguised distaste at the rat's nest that was her hair, and said, "May I?"

The girl nodded and scooted her chair to the side. Maureen leaned in and tapped in the suggestion. An error message came up.

"No, that's not it," she said, rising again. "Any other suggestions?"

"How about 1CentFranklin?" a man in the back called out.

Maureen gave a condescending nod, hesitated, then leaned in reluctantly and typed in the suggestion. Another error message.

"Okay, one more try. Come on, come on, who's got it?"

"Franklin78," someone called out.

"How about 1Binky78?" said another.

Maureen said nothing and attempted nothing. Instead, she held the card up to her forehead, closed her eyes, and concentrated. She wasn't really concentrating, just pausing, like any good charlatan, for dramatic effect. The truth was, she already knew the girl's passphrase—and all of their passphrases—having programmed a script into their computers to display their keystrokes on the laptop she kept hidden behind the podium.

"Think, people. We've only got one more chance before we're locked out. Her nickname. What's another word for it?"

"Penny!" someone shouted.

"Exactly. And what year was she born?"

"1978."

"Yes. And how many brothers and sisters?"

"None."

So she's the . . ."

"Only child!"

"So . . ."

"OnePenny1978!" someone cried.

"Let's give it a try," she said, and leaned in to type, hesitating a moment, her hands held aloft as she relished the anticipatory silence. She looked over at Penny, saw the look of violation on her face, and then unmuted the computer before typing in the password. She paused before hitting Enter, turned her head, and looked around the room—all eyes still on her. Good—and then tapped the Enter key. The all-too-familiar piano bars of the Microsoft crescendo pealed out of the speaker. A tune that was then followed by gasps and smatterings of applause.

Davis sat very still, his attention rapt by her seeming wizardry, terrified that Pu^^yCunt469 might be her next target. What had he been *thinking!?*

What he had been thinking was this: The thought of any of those elements, alone or in combination, was completely foreign to him, and it was, for precisely that reason that he'd chosen them as elements of his passphrase. Each was easy to remember and had nothing whatsoever to do with him. It was like someone squeamish about blood selecting ClotsOGore4Me, or a straight man picking 10inC*ckS*cker.

He knew she would never be able to decipher his phrase, but if she could . . . Or, worse, if she made him confess it to the class! But he need not have worried. She had seen such randomness and filth before and was shocked by very little of it. She also knew better than to select someone like that for her illustrative purposes. And she knew, as soon as she'd observed him type in his naughty keystrokes (for she read keystrokes the way deaf people read lips), to eliminate him as a potential contestant.

"So you see," she said, "by creating not just a password, but instead an anti-intuitive twelve-digit passphrase, you will be protecting your own personal data, the scientists' data, the corporate data of Polar Support Services, and the government data of the National Science Foundation. All of you made attempts to do this, but as

I've illustrated, all of you have failed. Therefore, what you've got to do is come up with something random, and then memorize it. Yes, you must. There really is no way around it. Think of it as a phone number or the name of someone new. Memorize it. Do not write it down in an Excel sheet and place it in your documents folder under the heading Passwords. I can tell by the guilty grins I see around the room that there are several of you who know what I'm talking about. Don't do it. And do not write it on a Post-it Note and tape that to the underside of your desk or monitor. Really. Do you honestly think anyone would be stupid enough *not* to look there? Lame. Really lame. Do not do those things. Spend five to ten minutes memorizing your complex, anti-intuitive passphrase and be done with it."

She droned on and on about various other topics, but Davis drowsily ignored her until she called on him to give an answer to a question.

"Since the e-mail to the vessels is transmitted via satellite, there are size restrictions on incoming and outgoing e-mail. Nothing over seventy-five kilobytes. Again, can anyone tell me why that is? Davis?"

"Um . . . cost?"

"Yes, that's partly it, but not entirely. Anything else? Anyone? Nobody? Nobody? Come on, people. Why do we all go down to Antarctica in the first place?"

The stupid cows, she thought, looking out at them all staring up at her, slack-jawed. How many times did she have to force-feed them the same cud before they could spit it back up?

"Come on, you all know, say it with me: We go down there to support science, right?"

Dull nods all around. Yes, yes, support science. Yes, yes, whatever.

"So, although it is exciting to send pictures of icebergs and penguins to your friends and family, we must reserve the bulk of our bandwidth for the scientists and their data needs. Therefore, if you're going to send photos back home, you'll have to resize them so that they don't use up your daily seventy-five-kilobyte e-mail allotment."

She then gave them some exercises for the correct methods of resizing photos. Methods which Davis was all too familiar with, having learned and practiced the technique by sending and receiving semi-pornographic photos of himself to potential suitors via Craigslist. He thus gave himself permission to tune out while she was talking and began doodling on his notepad. No sooner had he finished drawing the third head on what was to be a village of African stick figures than he became conscious that the room had gone silent. He looked up. She was standing behind the podium, staring at him. He made an effort to conceal his notepad with his arm and looked back at his monitor, which had gone into "sleep" mode, the screen lifeless and black.

"Is there something more important that you're working on there?" she asked.

"No," Davis said, again trying to find the correct keys on the split keyboard so that he could again tap in Pu**yCunt469, and thus reengage with the rest of the class. While he was doing so, she clicked around the podium, stood next to his desk, reached down with one of her mannish hands, and slid the pad out from under his arm. She gazed at it for a moment, a faint smile on her face, and then held it up and turned it for the rest of the class to see. There were small titters of nervous laughter.

"I think he misunderstood," she said. "I said resize pictures, not let's draw pictures."

More nervous giggles.

"No, it's not that," Davis started. "It's just that I already know how to resize photos."

"You may already know one method," she said, "but you have no idea if that is the method I wish you to use. And even if it is, you'll please do me the courtesy to pay attention, or at least pretend to do so, to the material that I have taken the time to prepare for you. I don't like teaching these classes any more than many of you like attending them, but it is mandated that we do teach them, so please give me the courtesy of listening, won't you?"

He nodded, his face red and hot.

She handed the notebook back to him and went on.

"All of you are here because you are deploying, at some point, to the research vessel, correct?"

Nods.

"Some of you are electronics technicians, and you have your own drive on the network. Similarly, marine technicians have their own drive. Marine science technicians and computer technicians, like yours truly, we each have our own drives. And I ask that you use only the drive that is allotted to your position, okay? There is a general document repository accessible to PSS employees but not scientists. Similarly, there is a science drive, which is accessible to the science party but not to PSS employees. If you wish to communicate or pass documentation to members of the science party, or to members of the vessel crew, please use the public drive, being ever mindful of the sensitive nature of the information we deal with and the care necessary to preserve it."

She had thoroughly bored them all—their expressions those of children crashing from the heights of a sugar buzz—yet on she went:

"Be aware that any science cruise on which you are sailing is just that: a science cruise. The network we have on board is designed to allow you to do your work and the scientists to do their work. It is not there for you to bog down with your own photos or music. It is not there for you to download or install any of your own, potentially harmful, software. It is there for the acquisition and interpretation of science data.

"I understand we have a technical writer here," she said, looking around the room. Timidly, Davis raised his hand. The shock on her face was evident but quickly morphed into a grin as she saw another opportunity to humiliate him.

"Please stay a minute after class."

When the others had been excused and filed out, she came back down the aisle and took a seat opposite Davis.

"So, you're Jake's little friend."

Davis exhaled and clenched his jaw. Never in his life had so many people used the diminutive to describe him.

"I'm the marine technical writer," he corrected.

"Yes, so I've heard," she said, brushing a piece of lint from her skirt. "And also a romance author?"

"No, children's literature."

"Oh."

"Yes."

"And any technical background, or did that not really come into the interview process?"

Where, he wondered, was this bitch getting her information, or was it just that his incompetence was plainly obvious?

"I only ask because we have some IT procedures that are in need of an update and I was told to bring them to you."

"That would be correct. I think."

"But now tell me, do you know anything about computers or shipboard systems? You seemed to be having a fair amount of trouble today. . . ."

"It was dark, my eyes hadn't adjusted. I apologize for being late and disrupting the class. If you send me the documents you need updated, I'm sure I can figure them out." Of course he wasn't sure, not at all, but he knew the correct response and would then have said just about anything to get out of there.

"Will do," she said, rising from her chair and allowing him to pass, a devious glint in her eye. "Will do."

Chapter 9

Davis sat at his desk in front of his computer absently watching a racially diverse cast of actors, costumed in bland business attire, as they played "office" in order to realistically address the issue of sexual harassment in the workplace. The lower half of his face collapsed into the sagging expression of a stroke victim, his jaw drooping and his lower lip plopped out. He kept the upper half—the half that was viewable by passersby—slightly more animated, his brow tensed in the middle to convey an air of concentration. Once the mask was in place, he allowed his thoughts to abandon the ethical farce on screen and wander back behind the black curtain of his mind and into the dim and cluttered space that housed his own shattered moral compass.

Anyone with even an electron of ethical sentiment, he thought to himself, would quit this job. Anyone with the least bit of self-awareness would realize the character-corroding properties of this extended game of charades, all of the pretending to look busy, pretending to know what he was doing, pretending to be something and someone he absolutely was not. It was getting to the point where even he didn't know who he was anymore, only who he was supposed to be at a given time and a given place. But he knew he had to go on playing the game, at least for a while, so he could get the pills, those expensive little pills ($17,000 for a one-year supply) that he would most likely have to ingest for the rest of his days on earth. Pills that were almost as important to his existence as water and food.

He paused the online drama, picked up his file folder and pen, and wandered around. There were some other "marines" a few cubicles to the west, but they were a harried bunch and any time he tried to pass off documentation for them to review, they would wave him away and say, "have someone on the ship look it over." Which was similar to what Sarah had told him before she'd left:

"Just sit tight for a while until we can get you down to the ship," she'd said. "It will all make more sense then."

He was not scheduled to go down to the ship for another month and a half, and in the meantime he had nothing on the horizon other than corporate training and medical exams—things that seemed to have nothing whatsoever to do with his job. His wandering took him to Jake's office, where he stood in the doorway. Without looking up from his monitor, Jake motioned him in.

"What am I supposed to be doing?" Davis asked in a whisper.

"Didn't Sarah tell you?"

"She didn't really get the chance."

"Oh, yeah," Jake said, chuckling as he recalled her messy departure. "And she hasn't called or e-mailed you?"

Davis shook his head. "She said she'd call when she got settled. . . ."

"Then I'm sure she will. In the meantime just work on what you've got." He looked up at Davis, one eyebrow elevated into an arc. "You do have something, right?"

"Well, she told me a little, but there isn't much I can see to do here," he said, tapping the file folder full of manuals he'd printed up. Jake took the folder from him and glanced through it. "Yeah, most of this is stuff the techs will need to review. Just sit tight for a while until we can get you down to the ship," Jake said. "It will all make more sense then."

Davis remained standing in the doorway of Jake's office.

"What?" Jake said, still looking at his monitor. Davis closed the door and sat down. "I . . . appreciate this," he said, "I really do. But what . . . Well, what am I doing here?"

"What do you mean?"

"I mean what I said. I don't understand any of this," he said, slapping the folder. "And everyone is looking at me like I'm retarded, or like I'm your little butt-boy. And the sad part is, they're partly right. All of those backstabbing ball-busters in my cubicle are on to me, and they are not showing any mercy."

Jake leaned back in his chair, put his hands behind his head, and looked at the ceiling.

"Fuck 'em," he said. Davis rolled his eyes. "No, I'm serious."

"I don't doubt that you are," Davis said. "And I know you've done all this for me—gotten me in here—to try to help me get back on my feet, but I don't . . . I don't think I can do it. And I think I'm making you look bad."

"Listen," Jake said, crab-walking his chair around the desk and leaning forward, forearms resting on his knees, hands clasped in front of him. He looked intently at Davis. "You can do this. There's a learning curve for any job. Just give it some time. Hang on until we can get you to the ship."

Hang on until you get to the ship, It'll make more sense once you get to the ship, Everything will come together when you get to the ship. It was becoming an earworm, one that was firmly embedded in Davis's mind but that he couldn't quite accept as true. It seemed like the logic a drug addict might use to explain a move from one city to another, as if a change of scenery might be all he needed to get sober. The way Davis figured, if he was stupid on land he'd be just as stupid on water. He could feel his eyes about to start tearing up and he got up to leave, but he had not been quick enough.

"Hey," Jake said, his voice more like a sigh. "Sit back down for a minute." Davis stood facing the door, trying to compose himself. Once he had, he turned around and sat down again.

"Okay," Jake said, staring down at the floor, not wanting to make Davis more uncomfortable, "okay. So maybe you don't quite have all the skills and qualifications for the job."

Davis exhaled, relieved that the farce would not have to carry over into his friendship with Jake.

"But," Jake went on, "you've got the job now. And you need the job." Then, as if he'd been reading Davis's thoughts: "So just keep acting like you know what you're doing. Go through the motions for a while. Just fake it."

"Are you kidding?"

"No," Jake said. "I'm not."

"What about what they're all saying about you?" Davis asked.

"Fuck that. I know I'm qualified for this job, and I work my ass off for them. And this isn't about me, it's about you. So let me tell you this: There are people here a lot dumber than you, believe me, and most of them are up on Mahogany Row raking in a whole lot more money than both you and me combined. And in a way, you're doing them a favor."

"Who? Who am I doing a favor?"

"The guys upstairs. Look, Antarctica is this big place that allegedly belongs to no one, right? But the U.S. has three of the biggest bases there, one of which is smack dab on top of the South Pole. You think that was by chance? Hell, no. The government threw gobs and gobs of money at this program during the Cold War, all so that we could establish a presence on the continent and not give an inch to the commies. Now that we're not fighting that battle anymore, the people upstairs are scrambling to find a way to maintain the program's relevance, a way to show its vital importance to national security. They've just about figured out how to do that with all the panic about global warming, but as a threat, that's still a little bit too abstract and remote for most people to worry about just yet. But the one thing those people upstairs know *not* to do is make it seem like they don't still need money. You following?"

"Not really."

"Then I'll spell it out. Look at the situation with Sarah. She gets knocked up and leaves, maybe for good. We can't just say, 'We'll have one of the existing tech writers step in and pick up the slack,' or, God forbid, 'We don't really need a replacement tech writer after all.' No, we have to spend the money for her salary. Because if there's money left over from the previous year's budget, the inspector general is going to look at that surplus and say, 'Well, I guess since you didn't spend it, that means you don't need it,' and they'll snatch it away. Then, if we ever want it back, we'll have to fill out stacks of requests and justifications, and get all of those pieces of paper signed off by everyone from the lowly guy in the mail room to the resurrected Jesus."

Davis didn't say anything, but Jake read the expression on his face.

"You're listening and thinking 'that's crazy!' And you know what? You're right. But that's the way the game is played. Welcome to the business of federal government contracting.

"So stop worrying," Jake said, coming around his desk and giving Davis a pat on the shoulder. "Go back to your desk, look over the documents in that file again and maybe make a list of questions to ask Sarah when she calls."

Davis nodded and stood up to leave.

"Have you PQ'd yet?" Jake asked. Davis hesitated a moment, trying to remember that particular acronym. Physical Qualification, yes, that was it. And that meant going to a doctor and a dentist to get a physical and a checkup to prove he was fit enough to travel south of the Antarctic Circle.

"I go to the doctor tomorrow and the dentist next Tuesday," Davis said.

"Good. And you've got all the other things you need—the shoes? the laptop?"

Davis nodded. In the past few weeks, he had been outfitted with a pair of steel-toed boots, a heavy canvas jacket with the company's logo embroidered over a small cartoon map of Antarctica, a pair of sunglasses to protect his eyes from the ozone hole, a laptop computer, a PalmPilot (equipped with more bells and whistles than he would ever use or come close to understanding the utility of, and which he feared he had already broken because the screen had turned a sickly shade of violet), a digital camera (more complicated than the PalmPilot), a metallic coffee mug with an intricate architectural rendering of the ship stenciled on it, the handle on which had, within ten minutes of it being put into service, broken and spilled coffee on the chair that had been brought in to replace the one stained with Sarah's amniotic fluid. So yes, he was well-equipped with the externals necessary for his journey. The only things left for him to acquire (other than clear-cut tasking and intelligence) were signed statements from a doctor and a dentist that he was physically fit.

Davis went back to his desk and Googled, for possibly the hundredth time, Antarctica. It was always a safe way to surf, in that he could always pretend to be looking something up. Among the things he had learned were:

- Polar bears in the northern hemisphere; penguins in the southern
- Antarctica is a desert, getting less than ten inches of annual precipitation
- If all the ice in Antarctica melted it would raise world sea levels by two hundred feet
- Amundsen first to South Pole, Scott second; Scott died on way back
- No permanent residents, no indigenous population

Although, as Jake said, Antarctica was a neutral territory, a sort of World Park, belonging to no one, governed by a treaty, where the environment is fiercely protected, and in which the peaceful pursuit of scientific research is encouraged, there are several countries (Great Britain, Norway, France, New Zealand, Australia, and the always squabbling Argentina and Chile) that have all made claims to areas of the continent and to the ocean rights that go along with them. Those claims are not recognized by most countries of the world, but they are mapped and, one suspects, might someday carry some weight, especially since there is no centralized government for the continent and little rule of law. The Antarctic Treaty, stitched together in 1959 to form a sort of gentlemen's agreement, loosely governs all territory "south of 60"—the latitudinal line denoting entrance into the Southern Ocean.

The area south of 60 was deemed by the Medical Department of PSS as a crossing point into no-man's-land, or at least into a land where the cost of emergency medical and dental services, usually involving a logistically complicated medevac, expanded exponentially. Therefore, anyone traveling to the continent must be in relatively good health and pass a physical qualification exam. PQ-ing was a bigger caveat for getting and keeping a job with PSS than not getting seasick, but neither Jake nor Sarah had seemed particularly worried about that, so Davis hadn't either.

That all changed the next morning when Davis arrived at the doctor's office. Things started out fine; Davis got there twenty minutes early, as instructed, and began filling out the thick stack of paperwork. He signed and initialed sheet after sheet after sheet with very little thought, detailing his medical history, making checkmarks in the appropriate little boxes as he went down the page:

History of diabetes, no.

History of heart disease, no.

History of cancer or emphysema, no.

History of alcohol or substance abuse, (pause), no.

Then he turned the page and froze. This particular page was a waiver requiring his signature. The signature granted the doctor permission to conduct an HIV test. Davis stood up, stepped out of the office into the hallway, flipped open his cell phone, and called Jake.

"Why do they want to do an HIV test?"

"Shit," Jake said.

"Shit what?"

"Shit, I forgot about that."

"How could you forget about *that?!*" Davis hissed. "That's the whole reason I'm here!"

"No, no, I mean I forgot they were gonna test for it. Shit. Shit."

"Stop saying that. What should I do?"

"Let me think, here. Shit. Don't sign it."

"You're sure?"

"I'm sure. They don't need to know unless you're a winterover—like that weird guy, Bryan, from your cubicle. They make all the winter-overs get their blood tested in case something—some accident, or something—happens and they need people to donate blood. It's because the planes don't fly in during the winter. They need to have an on-site blood bank."

"Okay . . ."

"Yes."

"So I don't need to worry about not signing it?"

"No, I'm pretty sure not. Look, this isn't the test you should be worried about. They nix more people for testing positive for weed and blow. Have you done the piss test yet?"

"That's after this."

"Well, good luck with that one," Jake said with a chuckle. "Looks like today will either make or break everything."

Davis hung up, went back in the office, turned in the paperwork, and waited to be called for his physical, a part of him wishing that one test or the other would, in fact, disqualify him and thus bring this whole game to an end. When he was called, it was a male nurse who did his initial intake. Davis's blood pressure was, not surprisingly, high, and it went higher when the nurse, leafing through his paperwork, came across the blank consent form and, handing it and a pen to Davis, said, "Oopsie, looks like you forgot this one."

"No, I didn't!"

His response had been too vehement and swift. The nurse leaned back and looked down his nose at Davis.

"They did explain to you about the walking blood bank," he said, trying to make eye contact with Davis, who was looking at the floor.

"Yes, I know about that," Davis said. "I just don't want the test."

The nurse lowered the paper and stuck the pen behind his ear. "Any reason?" he asked.

Davis hesitated a moment. Then another moment. What could he say? That the test would be a profound waste of time and money? That he already knew the result?

The nurse continued to stare at him, although he could tell that the man's thoughts were elsewhere, probably off trying to remember which questions he could ask Davis without violating any privacy restrictions. He seesawed the pen over his index finger, then put it back behind his ear and held up his finger, indicating that he would be back momentarily, and he left the room. Davis fell back on the tissue paper-covered examination table and covered his eyes with his hands. "Shit," he said, staring through the cracks between his fingers at the geometry of ceiling tiles and fluorescent lights. "Shit, shit, shit."

He could hear a muffled discussion going on outside the door, then silence, then more discussion. Then a woman entered. She closed the door behind her. Davis sat up and the woman introduced herself as the doctor. She rested her lower back against the far counter, covered with glass canisters containing cotton swabs and tongue depressors, the clipboard held against her chest.

"Just so you know," she said, "you *can* say nothing. But if you have a pre-existing condition, we ought to be informed about it."

Davis nodded but did not offer any verbal information. She waited.

"How about we speak off the record for a minute?" she proposed.

Again, Davis nodded.

"If you're saying you're positive, that's not a deal-breaker, okay?"

"Okay."

She stared at him waiting for him to elaborate or confess. When he didn't, she said, "Your T-cells have to be below two hundred for you to qualify."

Davis smiled. "I think you mean above two hundred."

She cocked her head and looked down at the paper on the clipboard. "No, I'm pretty sure they have to be below two hundred."

"Below two hundred is technically an AIDS diagnosis," Davis said, proud that he was able to trot out the small amount of factual information he had acquired about his new disease. He then went on to explain to her the difference between the viral load, which should ideally be a low number, and the T-cell count, which should ideally be high. In the middle of his explanation, he abruptly stopped speaking, and looked at her, realizing he'd already said too much. It had been a trap and he'd stepped right into it.

"How about I send Roger back in to draw some blood?" she asked. "Just so we can verify the numbers."

Davis spent the next two days waiting for the axe to fall, waiting to hear that he would not be able to keep the job or, worse, could keep the job but would have to stay in the office. But on Friday afternoon the doctor called him personally to say that she had PQ'd him for a period of six months.

Chapter 10

Davis returned to his desk and picked up one of the files that Sarah had left for him. It was on the top of the stack and was labeled "BM." Having just come from a nap, it seemed the most appropriate file to choose, and he wondered if it might be the hazardous waste disposal document that she'd hinted at during his interview. He flipped it open and read the cover page: "Mitigation strategies for light-induced seabird mortalities." The rest consisted of some hand-scribbled notes and part of a previously published report. Davis attempted to read the report, but it was a mess of hyphenated four-syllable words and Latin names (tropospheric variability, anomalous meteorological incident, *Oceanites oceanus*) and was also missing several pages.

From what he could glean, the report detailed a catastrophic event that had happened on an Arctic cruise some years earlier in which hundreds of seabirds, disoriented by the whiteout conditions of a storm, were drawn, like moths to the proverbial flame, toward the brightly lit deck of a vessel, "where most of them," he read, "either died on impact, drowned in pools of standing water, or froze to death. The few unfortunates who did not die were frozen alive to the deck and were found wriggling in misery the next morn—"

Davis turned the page to follow the rest of the tragic tale, but it jumped from page 2 to page 5. On page 5, the narrative had morphed into descriptions of different methods for packaging and shipping "intact carcasses, esp. those flash-frozen immediately postmortem."

He looked back at Sarah's notes, all done in her now-familiar bubbly script, but still could not discern just what needed to be "policied." He looked up from the file and stared at her phone number, affixed to the fabric wall of his cubicle, debating whether or not he should call. He imagined her sitting in an overstuffed chair, the bib of her overalls lowered, the pilly pink sweater hiked up, an infant contentedly suckling on each of her pneumatic breasts. And then he imagined that tranquil scene of suburban contentedness being shattered by the peal of the telephone. He hesitated, his eyes triangulating from file, to phone number, to phone, and then back to the file. She had said that she would call him, but it had been a month since she'd been whisked away and still he hadn't heard anything. He rocked in his chair for a moment, weighing his options, then grabbed the Post-it from the wall, picked up the receiver, and quickly punched in the number. She had, after all, told him to call anytime. It rang. And rang. After the fourth ring it was picked up. The receiver was fumbled and clattered onto a hard surface. This was followed by a hissed curse, which was in turn followed by a sound like two chain saws starting up. Davis was lowering the receiver back to its cradle but his action was arrested by a brusque and mannish "Hello."

Still he hesitated.

"Hello!"

"Sarah?"

"Yeah."

"This is Davis."

Now it was she who hesitated, the babies howling in the background. "Mmm-hmm, yes, what can I do for you, Mr. Davis?" The "Mr." was disconcerting. Was she trying to be funny, or did she really not remember who he was? He decided he'd better clarify: "Davis from the office," he added. "The tech writer."

"Oh, yes, yes," she said, her tone softening. "*Davis,* I've been meaning to call you. How are you?"

"I'm fine. Fine, thanks," he said. The twins sounded as if they'd been lashed and were now being lowered in scalding vats of salt water. Either that or she was stabbing each of them with pins. "And how about you?" Davis asked. "It sounds like you've got your hands full."

"What?!"

He raised his voice and spoke directly into the receiver: "You sound *busy!*"

"Yes."

Davis wasn't sure how to proceed. Normal telephone protocol would dictate that he spend a few minutes making small talk, inquiring after her health and the health of the infants, etc., but the wailing of the latter, and Sarah's evident impatience, made such inquiries impossible, so he got to the point.

"Listen, I've been looking over some of the documentation you left me to work on, and—"

He paused as the screaming on the other end ascended.

"Shhh, shhh, shhh, it's all right, *it's all right.* For Jesus Christ's sake, it's all right. Shh, shh, shh."

"This is a bad time," Davis said. "I think I've caught you at a bad ti—"

"No, it's *fine,*" she barked. "Fine. I mean, unless they're asleep—which they almost *never* are—this is about as good as it gets. What can I do for you?"

The crying had subsided somewhat and now sounded more like the low moaning that often precedes a cat fight.

"Well," Davis began, again flipping through the pages in the folder, "I've been looking over some of the documentation you left for me, specifically the file labeled BM."

She gave no response. Davis flipped over to the report.

"It's something to do with birds landing on the boat, and, um, what to do with their . . . carcasses?"

"Oh, that."

"Yes, the BM file."

"That's funny!"

Davis agreed but couldn't believe that she shared his love of toilet humor.

"Is it such a shitty document?" he said, jokingly.

"Huh?"

"BM?"

"Oh," she said. "No, not that. But that's funny, too. No, the BM stands for 'bird murder.' "

"Ahh."

"Unofficially, of course. Do not use that anywhere in the document itself."

"No."

"So, what's your question?"

"Um . . . Where to . . . start? Yes, I guess that is my question."

"What do you mean?"

This was not going well. Again, he felt the sweat rolling down the sides of his torso.

"I mean, well, I mean I'm not sure what needs to be . . . policied."

"What's not to understand? You have the report!"

"Yes. And I, I read that. What there was of it. But there were a couple of pages missing . . ."

"*Missing?!* Christ!"

Once she'd calmed down and accepted the fact of the missing pages, she then proceeded to explain, with the background accompaniment of her shrieking litter, what he'd already read: How sometimes, during a storm at sea, birds will become disoriented and fly toward the ship, which "isn't at all surprising since it's lit up like fucking Christmas. They smash into it and usually die on impact. You following?"

Davis nodded, then remembered that she couldn't see him and said, "Yes."

"Most of the birds die right away," she said, "but some of them don't. They just sit there until they freeze to death."

The duet of infant moaning had changed to a background solo, and was oddly soothing in its in-and-out rhythm.

"Basically what we need is a policy for dealing with the dead birds and a way to euthanize the ones that didn't die. You'll have to do some more research online. I think there were a few methods mentioned."

"Would that be . . ." Davis stalled, trying to find the page of the report. "Would that be . . . thoracic compression?"

"Yes. And there's one more they listed, I think."

"Cervical dislocation?"

"That's it."

A demonic gurgle came through the receiver, followed by Sarah shouting "Fuck!" Then her tone softened: "Jesus, Jesus, Jesus!" The gurgling baby let out a gurgly, stuffy-nosed scream, which, in turn, roused the gentle moaner who, not wanting to be outdone by his sibling, ramped up several octaves. Davis held the phone away from his head and looked at it. He waited a moment, trying to discern whether or not the scene on the other end would quiet down. It didn't.

"I'll call you back," he said. "I should call you back later."

"No, no, it's fine!" she sniped. "He just spit up on me is all. Now, where were we?"

"Thoracic compression."

"What about it?"

"Well," Davis ventured, "I don't really know what that means."

"Okay, it's okay, little one. It's okaaaaay. It's when you hold the bird in both hands—shh, shh, shh, Mommy's here—and apply pressure to its chest with your thumbs until the heart stops. That only works with the smaller birds, of course—snow petrels and terns. You can't do it with an albatross or a skua."

"No, I guess not," Davis agreed, although if a petrel, tern, and skua were then to have descended simultaneously from the ceiling and alighted on the floor before him, he would have had no idea which one was which.

"For the larger birds you'll want to advocate cervical dislocation."

Davis opened his mouth to ask but was afraid of her answer.

Sarah sensed his reticence and said: "Wringing their necks." Then, to clarify she added: "But it's really more of a twisting motion, like opening a bottle. You have to squeeze and turn."

"I . . . see."

"You think I'm kidding."

"I was kind of hoping so."

"Well, I'm not. This is a directive from the customer"—customer being a euphemism for the NSF—"Ideally, we'd like to have the captain just turn down the exterior lights so that the birds wouldn't be so drawn to the ship, but there are navigation concerns, especially when they're sailing in the ice, and then there's the fact that we run science pretty much twenty-four seven on the vessels, meaning there's no downtime. So, since the boat can't really function and enable science in the dark this policy will be the next best thing. It's really kind of a CYA thing to appease the bird biologists."

"CYA?"

"Cover Your Ass."

"I see."

"Yes. If we have a policy in place, they're less likely to squawk about what we usually do with the birds, which is scrape them off the deck with snow shovels and pitch them overboard.

"Also, by retrieving them like this we can, so to speak, kill two birds with one stone, because the dead birds get collected, frozen, and shipped north to those same whining biologists, so they can pluck, dissect, taxidermy, or whatever it is they do with them. It's a win/win thing."

"I see."

"You say that a lot."

"I'm sorry."

"You say that a lot, too. Look, I know it sounds gross but you're talking to someone who's spent most of the morning having her own breast milk puked back up on her, so wringing little necks somehow doesn't sound so terrible to me." She paused, then emitted a nervous giggle. "Of course, I'm kidding. You know that, right?"

"Yes."

"Good."

Davis was afraid to ask his next question but figured he'd better not leave it unasked: "So . . . will I . . . have to do it?"

"The procedures?"

"Yes."

"Oh, no, sweetie, no. Is that what you're worried about? No, no, no. You're just the tech writer. You write the policy, maybe do a PowerPoint presentation showing them the correct methods, give them a form to document it, but you assign the task to someone else—in this case, probably the marine techs—and then wipe your hands of it. There probably won't even be an incident while you're on board, so don't worry."

"Okay."

"Just go on the Internet and find some information on how to do it," she continued. "Christ, Microsoft probably has some clip art of the procedure, and some sicko is sure to have it on YouTube by now. Throw something together and then e-mail it to me by Friday. I'll look it over and tell you if it's a go or not. When do you deploy?"

"I'm supposed to leave next Tuesday."

"Great. Get it to me on Friday and I'll try to get it back to you before you leave. Okay?"

"Okay."

"Listen, I gotta run," she said and hung up. Davis held the phone away from his face and stared at the receiver.

While Davis had been on the phone, Gordon had been behind him, eavesdropping. Davis saw his bald head reflected in the sleeping screen of his monitor and hoped that if he ignored him he might go away. He did not.

"Are they still going ahead with that stupid WOT?" Gordon sneered. When, after a suitable pause, Gordon failed to elaborate on the term, Davis sighed and asked, "Okay, I give in, what's a WOT?"

Janet's head ascended, puppet-like, from behind the low cubicle wall separating their workspaces and supplied the answer:

"It's an acronym. Stands for Waste of Time. Not to be confused with C-WOT (Complete Waste of Time) or O-WOT (Online Waste of Time), or with the noun version referring to the one engaging in those practices, the TW."

Davis thought for a moment, but couldn't get it.

Again, Janet supplied the answer: "Time Waster."

"All you can say when you get one of those projects dropped in your lap," Gordon said, "is OBNA."

Again, Davis waited.

"Oh, Brother. Not Again!"

The next day, Davis arrived at his desk and got to work on his grim task. He sat facing the computer screen unsure, as always, of how to begin. "Bird Murder." He typed the words into Google and hit enter. The first result was for the website of a heavy metal band; the second, a psychiatrist's paper about abused children who then go on to abuse small animals; the third, the predictable PETA site decrying the avian "holocaust" carried out daily by a fried chicken franchise; the fourth, an exterminator in Alabama. Davis clicked on that one and was taken to a headache-inducing bright blue web page with obnoxious red lettering. There was a header bar featuring the company name flanked by two Confederate flags. A soundtrack of dueling banjos started up. Davis hit the Mute button and scrolled down.

> We specialize in the human [sic] capture and disposal of sparrows in the chimney, problem pigeons, bats, squirrels, mice, snakes and other assorted vermin.

He scrolled down some more. The site had what he needed, both text and pictures, and Davis lifted from it with reckless abandon. The text needed work, to say the least, and often it was like deciphering the clues in a crossword to figure out what the guy was trying to say, but the pictures were perfect; graphic but tasteful demonstrations of the techniques of thoracic compression and cervical dislocation. No bulging eyes or gaping beaks. The guy was selling compassionate extermination and thus provided only still pictures demonstrating the techniques, step by step, on a bird that looked to be an already dead pigeon. There were so many pictures, and in such rapid sequence, that Davis was tempted to print them up, staple the corners together, and flip through the stack to see if it would play like a movie. He wondered, too, about who had been the photographer. Was it the euthanasian's assistant? His wife? Davis indulged in speculation for a few minutes more but then set to work downloading the pictures from the site and uploading them into his PowerPoint template. Once that was done, he minimized both screens and gnawed on his fingernails, looking around to see if anyone of the cube dwellers had been watching him, but they were all lost in their own little screens. What he had just done, Davis knew, was unethical and probably illegal. There had been two back-to-back episodes of "What if . . . ?" that specifically addressed the concept and consequences of copyright infringement, so there was no question, at least from a business standpoint, that what he had done was wrong, but what else was he supposed to do? He knew that despite what Sarah had said there wouldn't be any free clip art on this topic, knew that YouTube wouldn't allow such violent postings, and he certainly was not going to go out into the parking lot, trap sparrows and chickadees, and then request the assistance of one of his coworkers in photographing his bloody duty, although he felt certain that, if asked, Janet would have eagerly participated.

Stealing from the website would have to do. And after all, it wasn't like he was doing it for profit. Sure, Bubba Bird Killer should have been compensated for his photos, but what were the chances of an exterminator from Alabama finding out that his photos were being used for demonstration purposes in Antarctica? Slim to none. Worth the gamble. He clicked the PowerPoint screen back to life and began adding headings, numbered lists, short instructional paragraphs, and lots and lots of dramatic text effects.

When it was done, he sent it to Sarah. She replied the following Monday:

"Made a few minor changes but overall it looks good. Proceed with training the techs once you're on board."

Book 3

Deployment #1:
Western Antarctic Peninsula

And all the science, I don't understand
It's just my job five days a week.

—Elton John and Bernie Taupin, "Rocket Man"

Chapter 11

The green rubber luggage tags were sent to all deploying personnel with their travel packets. The tags were designed to hold a business card, a box of which Davis had, to his surprise, been given the week before. But, as is often the case with cheap trinkets, the tags were not all that useful for their intended purpose. They were too dark and opaque, and were embossed on both sides with a wide-eyed, maniacally grinning cartoon penguin, which made reading the card impossible and made having the tags attached to your luggage seem more like you were headed off to some Disney resort or a fancy summer camp instead of a place that was routinely touted (usually by the same department responsible for the creation and distribution of the cutesy tags) as the harshest environment in the world.

As Davis snaked his way through the security line at the Denver airport, he spied three other bags with green tags. The first belonged to Maureen, and Davis's bowels clenched when he saw her. He'd known she was going to be on this trip but had hoped they'd be on different flights. As he watched her he noticed that she looked different. Her face, usually such a stern mask, had softened and she appeared to be giggling, an action that was accompanied by the feminine and slightly self-conscious gesture of covering her mouth with her hand. Davis was surprised. Seeing Maureen act coy was like seeing an elderly couple French kiss, or like hearing an intelligent remark from the mouth of a Republican—not completely out of the realm of the possible, but certainly rare and unexpected.

The line progressed, and as it did the reason for Maureen's personality shift came into view. It was a man—a man whose luggage was also tagged with the wild-eyed penguin. A man who had what one of Davis's elderly aunts referred to as "matinee idol" looks, and the sight of him left Davis appropriately dazed and starry-eyed. So much so that the woman in line behind Davis had to tap him on the shoulder so he could close the ten-foot gap that had opened between him and the person in front of him. Davis moved dutifully forward, but kept his eyes on the man, who was at least as tall as, if not even an inch or two taller than, Davis himself, and of inverse proportions. Whereas Davis's torso was pear-shaped, the man walking next to Maureen was the opposite: an inverted pear, with broad shoulders that tapered into a narrow waist. The sleeves of his shirt were rolled up, exposing tanned, muscular forearms and enormous hands, accented by silver rings and a silver and turquoise bracelet. Davis was attracted to him, yes, but in that curious twinned and conflicting way that attraction so often afflicts gay men, making them both desire and desire to be the one they are attracted to.

Just then, Davis's attention, and the attention of most of the others waiting in line, was directed toward a scene playing out a few steps ahead at one of the security checkpoints.

"No!" a nasally voice shouted. "Fucking no! Goddamned fascists. You're only picking on me because of how I'm dressed. Do I look like a fucking terrorist?"

The man yelling, evidently in response to the transit police demanding that he empty the contents of his backpack, was the antithesis of the matinee idol: short, skinny, with shoulders that drooped forward, making his chest almost concave. He had a large hooked nose, which was not, Davis would later reflect, unattractive, but seemed out of proportion to the delicate and tiny pair of wire-framed glasses perched upon it. His hair was a coarse mess of blond dreadlocks. In the center was a round, egg-like dome of premature baldness that provided an odd contrast to the sparse, pubescent-looking down on his face that he seemed to be urging unsuccessfully into a beard. His rust-colored work pants, the pockets of which he was in the process of violently emptying into a plastic tub, were worn and faded, and when he removed his jacket, the back of his T-shirt exclaimed: *Burn oil executives, not fossil fuels!*

"Go ahead, make me take off my shoes, take my toothpaste, my shampoo, pull out all my condoms and my girlfriend's tampons, put our rubber sex toys on display for all the world to see! Go ahead!"

"Sir, step to the side!"

"You see what's happening here, people?" he cried, looking up and down the line of hostile passengers stacking up behind him. "Do you see?! It's not just a search; it's the erosion of your civil rights!"

"Sir!" the guard barked. "I'm not going to ask you again. Move to the side!" She took her radio from its holster and summoned reinforcements. With exaggerated gestures the man began emptying the contents of his backpack and pitching them into a plastic tub. When he was done he turned the bag upside down and shook it several times to prove it was empty. Then he tossed it over to a table, where another overweight, rubber-gloved transit agent was trying to keep from smiling.

"Level orange, my ass!" he shouted. "The whole goddamned rainbow system is just an excuse by the government to whip up fear and make us swallow all of their police-state tactics!"

"Sir, your shoes," the woman demanded, pointing to the tray that held a pair of fetid hiking boots, the toes duct-taped to the soles, each boot containing a sock that had probably once been white.

"You wanted 'em off a me," the man cried. "You can carry 'em over!"

Reluctantly, the woman picked up the plastic tote tray and carried it at arm's length, handing it off to the smiling man behind the table, who accepted it with equally outstretched arms, holding his head back and to the side, to avoid the stench.

"Today it's the airport," he yelled, turning back to the crowd now watching him, his eyes as big as a frog's behind the lenses of his glasses, "tomorrow it'll be your blessed shopping malls, next week they'll be rooting around in your homes—if they're not there already!"

He was yanked into a Plexiglas room, his rant muffled by the circle of fat-assed transit police.

The line started moving again. Davis approached the screening station, grabbed a plastic tub, and commenced the public striptease known as Airport Security. As he was waiting to go through the metal detector, he caught glimpses of the grubby man through the circle of blue-uniforms and watched as he ripped off his T-shirt and theatrically tossed it in the air.

"There!" Davis heard him say. "Happy? No? Then how 'bout now?" And in one quick movement he stood up, dropped his pants to the ground and stood, arms outstretched, in a pair of red boxers, his pale chest and skinny legs covered, like his chin, with downy hair.

"Wand me!" he cried. "Just fucking wand me!"

As Davis emerged and began dressing and re-packing his bag, he noticed the man's backpack, filthy, forlorn and empty on a chair. Attached to one of the many loops was a green plastic tag, the penguin's smile seeming even more menacing and maniacal.

The flight to Dallas was comparatively uneventful, touching down around 6:00 P.M. Since the boarding time for the flight to Santiago wasn't scheduled until almost 10:00, Davis decided to pass the time in one of the airport lounges. He had just finished his first beer and ordered a second when he glanced down the bar, past all the upturned faces gazing at some sports spectacle playing out on TV, and noticed the grubby, dreadlocked tantrum thrower sitting by himself, a glass of white wine in front of him, his nose in a book.

While waiting for his second beer to arrive, Davis watched the man. His eyes were the only thing visible over the top of the book and they went back and forth, following the thread of the text, like a cat following a piece of string. Davis paid for his drink and walked down to where the man was sitting.

"Glad to see you made it through security," Davis said.

The man looked up, suspicious. "Who're you?"

Davis offered a hand and introduced himself. "I'm a tech writer." He then lifted up his carry-on and showed him the green tag. "I think we're headed to the same place."

"Name's Worm," the man said, referring to himself but offering no explanation, and making no motion to shake Davis's hand. "You don't look familiar to me. This your first time down?"

"To the boat?" Davis asked. "Yes. First time."

"A tech writer, eh? What are you gonna write about?"

Davis hesitated. "I, I'm updating documentation. That, and getting familiarized with the ship."

"Let's hope you do better than that last idiot. And what happened to that one chick?" he asked. "The one that used to do it?"

"Sarah?"

"I guess." He shrugged.

"She had twins. A boy and a girl. I'm what you might call 'the new Sarah,'" Davis joked, but the joke fell flat. Worm looked at him and frowned.

"I don't know why they think we need a tech writer at all. It's not like you guys even know any of the work we do down there."

Davis opened his mouth, ready to recite the well-rehearsed story about the out-of-control truck and the careless pedestrian, or the fortunate lotto winner retired to a tropical beach, but was not given the opportunity.

"They wouldn't need you guys at all," Worm continued, his tone growing more heated, "if they'd just hire people who had some smarts. It's not like they aren't out there. I mean, look at me. I've got the technical skills—and I know how to write my own documentation."

"And what do you do?" Davis asked.

"I'm an ET."

"Ahh," Davis said, feigning familiarity with the term.

"You don't even know what that is."

"You're right," Davis said, and Worm seemed to appreciate his honesty.

"Electronics technician."

"Ahh," Davis repeated.

"You still don't know what that is, do you."

"What are you drinking?" Davis asked, summoning the bartender.

"Pinot grigio."

"Good. I do know what that is."

He ordered them both another round. The bar was getting crowded, so when their drinks arrived Davis proposed that they move out onto the balcony overlooking the concourse.

"First time going down to the vessel?" Worm asked.

"Yes."

"You get seasick?"

"No."

"You seem pretty sure about that."

"I've been warned."

Worm gave him a questioning look. Davis held up his hand and shook his head, indicating he did not wish to discuss it. Worm returned his attention to the concourse.

"It'll probably happen," he said. "It happens to everyone on some level. Just don't be stupid like that last guy and not tell anyone about it."

Again Davis attempted a subject change: "So, what's it like, the place we're headed to in Chile?"

"Punta Arenas? Windy. Lots of bars, lots of whorehouses. It's where the Chilean navy used to post all the recruits with 'problematic behavior,' if that tells you anything. Not a bad place—if you like scrappy little port towns."

"And what about the others, the people on the boat?"

"The ship's crew and the captain are cool. The PSS folks are pretty good right now, although there are a few who're total shore whores."

Davis, unfamiliar with the term, raised an eyebrow. Worm explained:

"Dudes who took the job mostly so they could get away from their wives and screw around during the port call. Then they go to sea and spend most of their time trying to bang a coed. And then, of course, you've got all the . . . beak . . . ers . . ."

Worm's stream of invective trailed off, his attention hooked by something down below. Davis followed his gaze and saw Maureen, flipping her hair and then pulling on the hem of her shirt so that it was smooth and tight in the front. She walked, shoulders back, breasts pushed forward, to where the Matinee Idol stood, flipping through a magazine. She touched his sleeve, he turned, her face ex panded into a grin. And again she was flipping her hair and giggling into the back of her hand.

What she was doing was so transparent and obvious to Davis that it crossed the line into being clumsy. "Just look at her," he said, his voice dripping with scorn. Worm did not respond, so Davis turned to look at him, sure that Worm's facial expression would be as sour as Davis's comment. But it was not. Worm's head was cocked to one side, his forehead had relaxed, and his mouth had dropped open. It was that glazed, euphoric expression that people got when they were mesmerized by a beautiful display of fireworks, or maybe an Amazonian waterfall—or after they've shot some really high-quality drugs.

"Isn't she . . . awesome," Worm sighed.

Again, Davis followed the line of Worm's gaze down to the concourse, unable to believe they were looking at the same person. Right off the top of his head, Davis could think of many, *many* different adjectives he might use to describe Maureen, but "awesome" was not one of them, unless it served as an adjective to modify a noun like "bitch," "harpy," or "shrew," but he restrained himself from editorializing and instead asked: "You really think so?" Worm didn't respond.

"How well do you know her?" Davis asked.

"Maureen?"

"Yes."

"Oh, you know, pretty well," Worm said, trying to sound vague and disinterested. "I mean, we've sailed together a couple times."

His answer could have been much more specific, even mathematically precise, for in his head he had catalogued the statistics: He had sailed with Maureen exactly seven times in the past two and a half years; the total amount of time they had been embarked together had been five months and twenty-six days. It had been exactly seventy-two days since he had last seen her—from the 04 deck of the boat in Lyttelton, New Zealand. The ship had docked in that

delightful inlet at the end of a sixty-day cruise, and as soon as it arrived, Worm had spent almost two hours on the phone with the airline trying (and ultimately failing) to change his return ticket to
correspond with Maureen's. She departed a day ahead of him and
he was left standing alone on the deck in the rain, feeling sad, forlorn, and a bit hungover, as she descended the gangway to an
awaiting taxi. He stood there hoping, without any reason to hope,
that she might turn, gaze up from under her yellow umbrella and
acknowledge him, maybe even wave (God, just imagine!), but she
got into the taxi without a backward glance. Before closing the
door she twirled the umbrella a few times to scatter the raindrops
and then collapsed its skeleton and pulled it into the taxi with her.
The door shut and she sat, erect and motionless, while the driver
settled in, started the car, and then sped in a straight line down the
dock, pausing for a moment (an excruciating moment in which she
still did not turn and wave) while the security gate swung open, allowing the car to pass through. Worm's eyes followed the car and
its precious cargo as it traveled perpendicular to the dock and then
threaded its way up into the winding streets of the town before disappearing into a tunnel.

The shyness! The damn shyness! Two months at sea together
and he'd barely said a word to her! If he could just have said something—anything. If he could just have come up with some stupid
small talk, or have spat out a compliment or two, but it took concerted effort for him to speak to her on work-related topics without
stumbling over his sentences, so the thought of complimenting her
appearance, or even asking her how she'd liked her meal, seemed
stuck in the realm of the impossible. So, that last time at sea, like all
the other times they'd sailed together, he'd had to content himself
with admiring her in secret, usually from the safety of his lair inside
the computer racks, watching, as she sat, composed and erect, at
her terminal, developing some elaborate program or script, solving
problems with her high-tech sorcery, occasionally pulling her ponytail over her shoulder and weaving it through her fingers.

He knew all about her reputation for brusque brutality, knew
she was a colossal snob who looked down, imperious and condescending, on all the mere mortals beneath her, and yet that did
nothing to change his feelings. Her effect on him was chemical,

deeply psychological, existing on a subterranean level, like some primordial rock. Even the mere sense of her presence in a room was enough to accelerate his pulse, cause his hands to go cold, and confuse the synapses in his brain so that when he did try to speak, his words collided in his throat and were propelled from his mouth in a series of broken fragments.

And then, of course, there was her scent, wholly unique, and yet somehow familiar. It came from her hair, he knew, and it trailed behind her like delicate eddies in a wake, swirling through the air as she strode around the ship each morning, tossing her mane from side to side, letting it dry naturally before hiding it away beneath that damn baseball cap. He loved the scent of Maureen in the morning, and whenever he caught a trace of it lingering in the air, his mind would immediately abandon the task it had been focused on and wander after her, like a cartoon bear, still deep in hibernation but levitated from its slumber by the wafting aroma of a fresh-baked pie. Her scent was so soft, so feminine, that it belied her façade of steely sophistication and made her seem, to Worm at least, approachable, almost beckoning. And yet every time he saw her, a barbed-wire fence quickly encircled his vocal cords.

It was with frustration, but no real embarrassment, that he remembered an afternoon, several months back, when he had spent an hour in a Portland drugstore, uncapping, sniffing the contents, and then recapping bottle after bottle of shampoo, trying to find a close approximation of Her. Failing in that attempt, he had summoned the courage to cross town and enter the cosmetics department of one of the high-end department stores—all gleaming glass and chrome display cases, magnified mirrors, and Orwellian placards featuring bored, indifferent eyes staring out from flawless faces with inflated lips and haystacks of carefully coiffed hair. He had gone there, a place more alien to him than the moon, in further hope of finding the bottle that held her particular scent. To that end he was assisted by a woman with well-practiced patience. She stood behind the counter, lab-coated, her skin concealed under an exceeding amount of, well, concealer, her eyes and lips made up like a clown's. He spoke to her, in all-too-vague terms, about what he was looking for and she selected several tester bottles, arrayed them on the counter, and then instructed him to stand, eyes closed, his large nose alert and ready, as she sprayed, first one, then another, and another atomized cloud onto a piece of white cardboard and waved it in the air in front of him. She did this fourteen times, but never was he able to recapture the scent. It was a scent that he didn't have the vocabulary to describe and so reverted to the only adjectives he knew—those used to characterize wine. Words like "sparkling, tannic, tea-like, herbaceous, oaky," throwing in the odd phrase "with subtle hints of nutmeg," or "an essence of sea spray," but none of it was quite right.

"Whatever it is," the weary sales lady told him, "it's probably affinitized by, like, the essential oils in her own skin. A woman has those, you know, and they'll react to any perfume and make it, for each woman, uniquely her own."

So that was it, then, he concluded, his shoulders drooping and his sinuses burning: Maureen could not be bottled. And since he was not willing to make do with an inaccurate facsimile, he left the store, purchasing nothing, frustrated in his search for olfactory pornography.

Now here she was below him again, not looking up, just as she had not been looking up that rainy day in Lyttelton.

"Yes, I guess we've sailed together a few times," he said, wistfully returning to the conversation with Davis. "She's a very smart girl."

"She sure doesn't look it now," Davis mumbled into his glass, watching as she stood, one hand on her hip, deliberately positioning herself so that the air-conditioning emerging from one of the concourse stores acted as a wind machine on her hair.

"She's . . . like . . . a living Botticelli!" Worm exclaimed, and then blushed, embarrassed that he'd allowed some of his inner magma to bubble up through his crusty façade.

As the two continued to gaze down at her, opposing emotions welling up in each of them, the Matinee Idol entered the scene carrying two bottles of water. He handed one to Maureen; she accepted it with a coy nod of thanks, and together they turned and walked away, luggage rolling behind them like a set of obedient pets. When they were almost out of view, the right arm of the Matinee Idol snaked its way around Maureen's back and came to rest on her ass.

"Artaud," Worm growled and then downed the rest of his wine.
"Is that her boyfriend?" Davis asked.
"No," Worm said, without conviction. "She wouldn't stoop to that goddamn beaker."
"Goddamn . . . what?" Davis asked.
"Beaker. It's a stupid little name that someone came up with for the scientists. That one," he said, pointing with his nose to his masculine rival, "is the chief scientist on our cruise, although I don't know why that arrogant prick even needs a boat since he seems to think he can walk on water. And I'll tell you something else," Worm said, shaking his empty glass at Davis, "the dude's not even that smart. Seriously. He gets all these other people—students, assistants, technicians—to do all the grunt work. Then he comes along and stamps his name on the finished product."

Which was not, Davis silently reflected, much different from what he himself was being sent down there to do.

"Is the flight very full?" Davis asked, handing the gate attendant his boarding pass.
"I'm afraid so," she said, tilting her head to one side and giving a plastic smile.
As he plodded down the gangway, then down the aisle to his seat, he allowed himself to imagine the luxury of a row of seats to himself, but that was not to be. When he got close enough to discern his row, his hope deflated. He was in the center bank of three seats. The other two were already occupied by a woman and a small male toddler. And not just any toddler, but one who spoke only high-pitched Spanish and had evidently been given a fistful of amphetamines prior to boarding the plane. His mother, on the other hand, must have ingested a tranquilizer, because less than a minute after takeoff she fell fast asleep, leaving the task of entertaining the spastic brat to Davis. The child, like a highly caffeinated, sticky-fingered Helen Keller, wanted to touch everything, including Davis's head, which the boy delighted in covering and uncovering with the gauzy blanket, again and again and again, in a seemingly endless game of peek-a-boo, erupting in a fit of squeals each time he whipped the blanket away. Davis played along for a while but then decided to do something to calm him down. He collected a

stack of paper airsickness bags, got a pencil from his carry-on and, fortifying himself with several doll-sized bottles of $5.00 bourbon, stepped into the role of in-flight Scheherazade.

The inspiration for the story he told came to him on the fly, so to speak, because trapped with all of the passengers in the cramped coach section was a large, bewildered housefly, pestering everyone with its panicked meanderings and inability to discover a way out of the tubular prison. Davis drew a picture of a fly, a big cartoon smile on his face, his little fly hands rubbing together, and before he'd put the final touches on the drawing he was pleased to discover that the boy recognized the thing, and pointed excitedly from the paper to the insect circling overhead.

Davis gave the cartoon fly a name, Mick, and, turning over the airsickness bag, depicted him as a young, newly hatched maggot, lying in a big four-poster bed with all of his brother and sister maggots, being served, by their apron-clad fly mother, bottles of whatever unspeakable stuff it is that maggots eat. The next panel showed the maggots transformed into baby flies, a change Davis illustrated by having them all stand next to their discarded blankets and do that little head-grooming thing that flies do with their front legs. The boy was quiet, his attention hooked, and thus, through a combination of pantomime, drawing, and pidgin Spanish, the story developed.

Little Mick grew and was so full of energy, so curious about the wide world around him that he ignored his mother's warning to stick close to home and instead followed his nose and appetite to the exotic scents emanating from a field of cows. This particular cow field just happened to be near the airport, so little Mick, who also had a short attention span, flew away from the field and into the terminal. Once there, he followed a little boy (here Davis drew his sticky-fingered seat mate) who was eating a bag of candy.

The boy shrieked when he recognized his cartoon self, and then turned to rouse his mother, repeatedly stabbing her in the ribs with his index finger. She sat up, groggy-eyed, looked at the picture, and smiled.

"Es mi, mama! Es mi!"

"*Sí,*" she said, and gave Davis a wink and an appreciative smile.

Now he had an audience of two, and he returned to the story

with renewed vigor, drawing the boy and Mick boarding the plane, and even providing some theatrical sound effects to indicate the plane door closing and the engines revving for takeoff. The little boy and his mother followed the story, she helping to interpret what was happening, as Davis drew little Mick buzzing around all the passengers, taking quick little nibbles from the food on their plates, before being shushed away by gigantic hands. But once the plates were cleared away and the cabin got dark, Mick remembered his mother and his brothers and sisters and, thinking he had better head back home, looked for a way out of the plane. He tried to escape out of the small square windows, but kept bumping up against the glass. He flew around and around and around the plane, but couldn't find an exit. Finally, exhausted, and his head aching from all the window bumping, he glued his feet to the ceiling (since that is, of course, the safest place for flies to sleep) and fell fast asleep upside down, cartoon Zs streaming from his head.

Davis looked over and saw that his little friend was asleep, too.

The mother silently mouthed a *"gracias"* and tucked the blanket around him.

Unable to sleep himself, Davis got up and decided to trek back to the bathroom to brush his teeth and wash his face. On the way, he caught a whiff of that unmistakable footy smell and, following his nose, saw Worm, shoeless, his tiny body curled, pupa-like, into two seats and his head bent back, exposing a stubble-covered Adam's apple.

A few rows behind he saw Maureen, erect in her seat, her body shrouded in a blanket, the seat belt fastened on the outside of the blanket, per airline regulations, so that the flight attendants would not need to wake her. She wore a blue satin eye mask and her head was held in place by an inflatable pillow encircling her neck. She looked like someone's idea of Hostage Barbie.

On his way back from the bathroom Davis peered through the curtain separating the first-class section and caught sight of Artaud's silver-braceleted forearm and the giant hand attached to it. The hand was holding a tiny champagne flute that was being refilled by a rapt and giddy male flight attendant.

Davis returned to his row, eager for sleep, but still sleep would not come. He was too large to fit in the seat, and the armrests were digging uncomfortably into his spare tire. He tried to find a position that wasn't miserable, but then gave it up and just sat there, sipping the watery dregs of his bourbon and meditatively crunching the ice. He took the airsickness story boards and the pencil from the seat pocket in front of him and looked back through the story. Granted, he was drunk, but it didn't seem half-bad. It had many elements that a good children's story needed: an offbeat and yet identifiable character, a journey, the themes of homesickness and fear of new things, and it had the potential for a whole cast of supporting characters. He would write up a synopsis and send it and some sketches to his agent, Estelle. He took his pencil and continued with the plot and sketches:

When Mick awoke, the people were all standing up and walking toward the open door of the airplane. Mick followed, buzzing around their heads, asking, "Where are we? Where are we?" But the people just swatted him away. He finally made it out of the plane, escaped through a gap in the tunnel covering the gangway, and was free, once again in the blue sky and sunshine. And it was warm! Very warm. Warmer than he could ever remember having felt. He flew around the tarmac, in and around the parked planes, their bodies so similar in form and function to his own, and then he flew out into the countryside to try and find his way home. He looked for the cows in the field first, but they were no longer there, nor was the field!

Davis worked all through the night until his attention was drawn away by the smell of bacon wafting through the fuselage. He looked up and noticed that the dark squares of the windows had turned to pink and the sun was about to burst through the clouds.

Chapter 12

The arrival in Santiago was a blur. Davis, Maureen, and Worm emerged from the plane, bleary-eyed and irritable, and were greeted by a group of rotund, jovial, middle-aged Chilean men who quickly shepherded them through the concourse to the baggage claim and then on to the domestic terminal. There, the bags were checked again and they were given their seat assignments and were ordered to run to the gate to avoid missing their southbound flight.

While not as modern or sleek as the aircraft run by American Airlines, the Chilean airline was infinitely more pleasant. The flight attendants were as young and eager to please as puppies, which was, to say the least, a stark contrast to the bitter, frustrated cougars pushing that cart of Sisyphus up and down the aisle, dispensing soda in eye-dropper portions and offering child-sized cocktails with the barked command, "That'll be five dollars. *Five dollars. Five dollars!* And no, I don't have change."

Then, too, there was the fiendish delight the American attendants seemed to take in roaming the aircraft after the lights had dimmed and shaking people awake because they could not see whether their seat belt was fastened or because their carry-on was not properly stowed in the overhead bin but was, instead, resting on the vacant seat next to them, in blatant violation of TSA rules.

"Sir, if we encounter unexpected turbulence, that bag could become a lethal missile!"

To which Davis longed to reply, "Ma'am, your waking me up qualifies as 'unexpected turbulence.' "

But the thing that annoyed Davis the most was how the American harpies forced the vast majority of people on the flight (those flying coach) to use only the two bathrooms in the rear of the aircraft, even though that left two bathrooms in the middle and one up front for the sparsely populated regions of business and first class. He knew the world was full of iniquities, knew the benefits that a first- or business-class ticket entitled one to—and that didn't bother him. What bothered him was that they forbade people in the cheap seats from using the middle and front bathrooms under the gauzy guise of "security."

Security, security, security! If there was anything that made Davis mad enough to charge the cockpit, it was the euphemism of security as a reason for excluding people from the bathroom.

By contrast, there was no business or first class on the Chilean airline, only a vast egalitarian sea of cramped seats and the liberty to use any bathroom you chose. And no sooner had Davis settled into his seat than he was given (yes, *given*) a glass of wine and given (yes, *given*) a headset. In this pleasant, relaxed environment, a slight wine buzz going, melodious Spanish guitar strumming from the speakers overhead, the sun warming his face as he gazed down at the serrated peaks of the Andes, the S-shaped glaciers, and the cobalt blue lakes shimmering at their base, Davis was soon dozing, content, at ease.

This is the usual order of things: 1) you are conscious, 2) you are struck in the head with a blunt object, 3) you go unconscious. For Davis it was the reverse: 1) he was fast asleep, 2) he was struck in the head with a blunt object (in this case a duty-free bottle of gin that had not been properly stowed in the overhead compartment), 3) he was immediately and painfully conscious.

There wasn't time to dwell on the pain, however, as the plane then did what felt to Davis like an evasive move to the right and then immediately did an over-compensatory roll to the left. The Fasten Seat Belt sign flashed and was accompanied by an incongruously soft doorbell ping as flight attendants stumbled down the aisle, collecting as many wineglasses and trays as they could before strapping themselves into the jump seats. Two of them were facing the passengers and they looked calm and unconcerned, even though the plane was being tossed around like a toy. Davis gripped the armrests and stole glances out the window at the bouncing wing, wondering how much strain the rivets could stand before they popped out.

"Relax," a voice said, and before Davis could look to see who the voice belonged to he felt the pressure of someone's hand tapping on his thigh. He turned and was surprised to see Artaud, now strapped into the seat next to him and looking over his shoulder out the window. "It's always like this flying into PA," he said, his voice level and calm. Davis, still looking at the wing through the window, studied Artaud's face, reflected in the glass. His eyes were large and wide-set, the lashes so long they looked like they belonged on a child. His eyebrows, like his hair, were flecked with gray and the space between his nose and his upper lip was large and expansive, giving him an almost chimp-like appearance that was somehow not unattractive. On the contrary, his features conveyed an almost exaggerated masculinity.

That Artaud was in the seat next to Davis was odd, but that he had patted his thigh with his enormous hand bordered (at least in Davis's mind) on the scandalous. And yet the thing Davis wished for the most at that moment was an exemption from the rule that they have their seat backs in the upright position because if he were able to recline, even just an inch or two, Maureen, who was seated directly behind him to the left, could have seen the spectacle and been jealous.

Davis glanced over at the hand, now dangling over the edge of the armrest. A hand that was, in turn, attached to a muscled forearm; a forearm that Davis felt certain must bulge into biceps, triceps, deltoids, lats, and pectorals. In short, a hand that was attached to a body that was perfect in just about every way, including that scar on his lip, the evidence of some bar fight or industrial accident, perhaps. A scar that Davis could imagine contemplating for hours while the man's dozing head rested on a pillow next to his.

These thoughts were interrupted by another roll to the right and then another violent correction, and soon Davis's erotic imaginings were subsumed by the fear of his life being extinguished in a disintegrating crash. This went on for another forty minutes, at which time the plane bounced on the runway and the reverse thrusters started to roar. As they taxied toward the terminal, Artaud got up and returned to his seat. Davis exhaled, for what felt like the first time in an hour, and wiped the sweat off his forehead and upper lip. He waited until almost all of the passengers had disembarked before getting up, collecting his carry-on, and exiting the plane. Then he wandered, in an exhausted daze, through the terminal.

It was a small airport, as airports go—about the size of two large barns—and had only one baggage carousel, around which all of the passengers were eagerly assembled, their empty carts waiting to be filled. Suspended from the ceiling was a transparent Plexiglas sculpture of a whale, much like the whale skeletons that are suspended from the ceilings of many natural history museums, and while Davis was contemplating it, a woman approached and tapped him on the shoulder.

"You are Davis?" she asked.

"Yes."

"I'm Maria, the agent. I'll take you to your hotel. Do you have all of your bags?"

He nodded.

"Good, you give me please your passport."

Davis did so, and she handed him a plastic card in a small white envelope.

"You need the card to get to the boat. Don't lose it, okay?"

Again, he nodded and put the card in his pocket.

"We wait for a few more people," Maria said, tapping on her clipboard with a pen and eyeing the baggage claim area. "Ahh," she said, with a distinct descending tone in her voice, "there is the Maureen. And there is Worm. Also," she said, looking through the pages attached to her clipboard, "we are supposed to have Señor Artaud."

Maureen came out, followed shortly by Worm. She greeted Maria with a nod, which Maria politely returned. Then Maria retreated a step, as if Maureen, and not Worm, were giving off an offensive odor. Maria smiled and winked at Worm, which had the effect of making his face turn a color as tomato-ey as that of the iconic Che, emblazoned on his T-shirt. They stood waiting until the baggage claim cleared out, Maria and Worm occupying the time with small talk in pidgin Spanish, until eventually Artaud emerged, looking fresh and composed. As soon as Maria saw him she abandoned her veneer of professionalism and ran toward him. He caught her in an embrace, lifted her off the ground, spun her in a circle, and then gently set her down, planting a kiss on each of her cheeks.

Maureen set her jaw and lowered her sunglasses. Worm scowled.

As soon as they stepped outside, Davis understood why the flight had been so rough. From inside the airport, there was nothing to give the indication of the ferocity of the wind. The sun was shining, the sky was blue and cloudless, and there was almost no vegetation to give a visual cue as to the force of the gale, but forceful it was, nearly ripping their hair from its roots. Only with extreme effort were they able to cross the parking lot to an awaiting van. There, the driver stacked their luggage in the back and acted as usher as they all piled in.

Once out of the airport grounds, the van sped off down a road that ran parallel to the sea. There were a few low trees along the route, growing at a severe slant, like giant bonsais, but other than that, the landscape was mostly flat and carpeted with low yellow grasses. As all new cities are when one arrives by car, Punta Arenas was mazelike and dizzying. Davis wanted to stay awake to absorb the new sights and impressions, but the wine and the long hours of stressful travel, combined with the gentle hum and rock of the van, lulled him to sleep. When he was elbowed awake by Maureen, they were the only two left in the van.

"This is us," she said, sliding open the door, her hair subsequently sucked up and out as if by a giant vacuum. Davis roused himself and emerged, stiffly, from the van. They were parked on the side of a busy street next to a wide sidewalk. The sidewalk was crowded with people, most of whom were hunched over and leaning into the wind. Davis collected his luggage from the back of the van and then waited on the sidewalk with Maureen while Maria went into the hotel to check them in.

Although constructed completely of concrete, the Hotel José

Nogueira is one of the more ornate buildings in Punta Arenas. The concrete was cast, quite effectively, to resemble stone blocks, and the blocks were then assembled in imitation of some Baroque castle somewhere in the world, complete with columns and pediments, arches and entablature. The exterior wooden window frames were varnished instead of painted, giving them a warm, honey color, and the building was topped by a mansard roof of black slate. Its best feature, however, is an iron-framed glass dining room, almost like a Victorian hothouse, inside of which, protected from the wind and cold, is an arbor of grapevines. Davis hardly had time to admire any of it before he was pulled along by Maria. She returned his passport, along with his room card, and said, "Okay, Mr. Davees, you're all set." He thanked her, said good-bye, and then rushed to catch the elevator, which Maureen, although she saw him, made no attempt to hold. He caught it, parted the reluctant doors, and squeezed his ample self and his luggage into the tiny space. Maureen emitted an impatient sigh and jabbed at the Close button with her mannish index finger. Once they were ascending she spoke:

"I suppose I'll have to be the one to show you the way to the vessel. Be in the lobby in fifteen minutes."

Before Davis could protest, or even question her, the door opened to her floor and she exited.

Fifteen minutes! Davis was hungover, jet-lagged, and desperately needed to shit. All he wanted was a shower, a toothbrush, a chance to lie down—horizontally—and shut his eyes, but what choice did he have? He had no idea which direction the pier was, had no idea how he was to get there. He was totally dependent on Maureen and, he suspected, she knew it.

The elevator arrived at his floor and he towed his suitcase down the high-ceilinged hallway to his room. Once inside, he looked longingly at the large bed, at the heavy, red velvet curtains that would, he knew, so effectively darken the room, but he didn't allow himself the luxury of sitting down. Instead, he hoisted his suitcase onto the luggage rack, took out his toiletry case, and headed to the bathroom. He stood looking at his puffy, windblown reflection in the mirror and considered the distance he had traveled. He was almost at the southernmost tip of South America, seven thousand miles from where he'd started, and there was still farther to go.

Why had they even brought him to a hotel if he immediately had to leave it? Why not just take him to the ship? Surely this was just some sadistic tactic of Maureen's. The others were probably tucking themselves in right now.

When he arrived in the lobby, Maureen was already there, showered and in a change of clothes. Her wet hair was mostly hidden under a baseball cap, the length of it twisted into a ponytail and threaded through the hole in the back. Her eyes were hidden behind sunglasses, making her expression inscrutable, but there was no mistaking the impatient glance she shot at her watch when she saw him. He approached and was about to say "hello," but before he could speak she had turned and exited the hotel. He followed her, taking large strides to catch up, but she sped down the sidewalk, leaning into the wind. She walked about half a block before she was stopped by traffic at the corner. Davis caught up to her there.

"What's that?" he asked, pointing to the park-like area across the street from them.

"A square."

"It's beautiful," Davis said, ignoring her moodiness. He was about to inquire about the large statue in the center when his attention was distracted by a small dog rubbing up against his leg. It was then that Davis noticed there were dogs everywhere. In fact, there were more dogs than people on the streets. While they waited for the light to change, Davis reached down to scratch the greasy neck of one of the mongrels nuzzling against him. The creature responded with a look of ecstasy and leaned into him. When Davis looked up again, Maureen was already across the street. He stood up and followed her, again struggling to catch up, a small pack of dogs trotting along behind him. They passed the statue, an enormous bronze, mounted on a stone pedestal, obviously something of historical significance, but Maureen offered no comment on it. Instead, as they exited the square and headed down the hill toward the water, she said, "There's a supermarket next to the pier. Stock up on any toiletries or snacks you might want before we leave port. There is food on board, of course, but if you want anything special, you better get it there."

When they emerged from the protection of the buildings, the

wind hit them like a wall and nearly knocked Maureen down. Davis caught her arm and righted her but she offered no thanks, just shook herself free and shouted, "You have to be careful!" as if Davis, and not she, had been the one who stumbled. "There have been people blown off this pier before. Their bodies were never found." For a moment Davis wasn't sure if that bit of information was meant as a caution or a threat.

When they reached the security checkpoint, they removed their plastic cards from the tiny envelopes and swiped them to release the turnstile. Once through, they were on the pier, a quarter-mile-long strip of concrete extending out into the water. There were ships of various sizes tethered to it, and the waves crashed into the vessels on the windward side, splashing water high into the air where it was frozen by the wind and descended in an icy mist. The Antarctic ship was easily identifiable at the end of the pier. It was tall, painted primary yellow, with a rounded bow and an American flag whipping from the mast. Davis and Maureen stumbled toward it like a pair of drunks, each fighting to keep themselves upright and ambulatory while at the same time trying to avoid even the appearance of needing support or assistance. This was easier for Davis, who noticed the advantage of his bulk even as he felt the frigid wind penetrate his fleece jacket and pull his pant legs tight against his skin. His eyes watered and his head ached from the cold, but he was so intrigued and fascinated by the variety of vessels that he hardly noticed. There were brightly painted wooden fishing boats, their bobbing crew struggling to unload plastic crates of spiny crabs; dull gray Chilean navy ships with the polished brass motto *Vencer o morir* mounted above the gangplank; large Japanese fish factory ships craning on provisions for their next outing; and even a towering cruise ship, through the windows of which elderly passengers could be seen eating breakfast.

Although the wind was loud, it did nothing to lessen the pitch of the wolf whistles that came from the men on the crab boats. Whistles that were directed, of course, at Maureen, who pretended not to hear them.

When they arrived at their destination, there was a tiny building, about the size of a child's playhouse, really nothing more than a single room with three windowed walls, a door, and a peaked roof. Its yellow paint color indicated that it belonged to the ship they were to board, so Davis followed Maureen as she entered. Inside, an Asian man was sitting in a chair with his feet crossed at the ankles resting on a desk. He was singing in time with a song on a small tape player next to him, and although he acknowledged them with a slight nod when they entered, he did not get up and did not stop his singing. Maureen, offering no greeting and no instruction to Davis, signed her name in a book, took a badge from the wall, and then left the shack and disappeared up the gangway. The man followed her with his eyes until she had disappeared. Once gone, he turned to Davis and asked: "She sailing?" Davis nodded. The man shook his head. "Going to be a long trip." Then, focusing on Davis, he asked, "Where you from? I haven't seen you before."

"From Denver. From the office," Davis said, and then introduced himself. The man did the same, giving his name as Renaldo, adding "but everyone call me Ronnie."

"Ronnie. Listen," Davis said, holding the pen as if it were some foreign object. "I'm not sure what I'm supposed to do here."

Ronnie sat up and swung his legs to the floor. He pointed at an empty space in the book. "You sign in here when you get here, and sign out here when you leave. Put the time in and time out next to your name. Even if you just go to warehouse, you have to sign. I give you a badge. Supposed to wear it all the time but people don't. Just don't lose it."

Davis signed, took a badge, and then went back out into the wind. The gangway, which looked to Davis like a slanted railroad track studded with metal teeth, was difficult to climb and he gripped the railing as he ascended, feeling the whole thing bounce and bow under his weight. When he got inside the ship, it took his eyes a moment to adjust, but it was a relief to be out of the wind. He heard the low hum of the engines idling, but the rest of the place seemed lifeless and quiet. He saw no sign of Maureen, no sign of anyone, so he walked tentatively down the hall. On either side of him there was a series of solid green doors, each numbered like a hotel. Davis assumed that these were the cabins. He looked at his watch. It was just after noon. He paced up and down the hall, wondering if he should knock on one of the doors, maybe take the stairs down to one of the lower levels. As he stood trying to decide, a door swung open and three men, identically dressed in rust-colored work clothes, each wearing a hard hat and sunglasses, came up a staircase from a lower level. Two of them were arguing with each other while the other—the one in the lead—spoke into a radio.

"We need to onload the rest of that plywood before three today!" the radio holder said, and then bustled past Davis as if he were invisible. The two others followed.

"You just have to do it," one of them was saying.

"I know, I know, but—"

"No, just do it! And quit whining about it."

They all exited the door that Davis had just entered, and it closed with a bang. A second later, it was opened again. The man with the radio poked his head around the corner, raised his sunglasses and squinted at Davis.

"You the tech writer?"

Davis nodded.

"Give me five minutes and I'll be right with you." Before Davis could respond, the man had disappeared again, the door slamming behind him.

While he waited, Davis looked at the framed pictures lining the hallway. Most of them were posters created by past science parties, usually a group photo of the participants posed on the bow, sometimes superimposed over a map of the area they'd traveled to. Others were historical pictures of Antarctic explorers dressed in fur parkas, their beards crusted with ice and snow and their eyes hidden behind round, dark goggles. There were also a few pictures of the boat itself, silhouetted against an iceberg by either the morning or evening sun (Davis couldn't tell which), and one of the boat being christened with a champagne bottle by a buxom blond woman dressed like a pole dancer. That she was surrounded by geeky men in suits who were all ogling her made the image seem even more perverse.

The vessel, the *Hamilton,* Davis would later learn, had been named after Henry Hamilton, the captain of a nineteenth-century American sealing boat. A man who was believed, errantly so as it turned out, to have been the first person to sail into Antarctic waters. In truth he had set sail from his home in Nantucket on a voyage of such distance and duration in order to avoid allegations that his missing wife had actually been the victim of foul play. Unprepared for such an endeavor, he had sailed his vessel too far south, gotten hopelessly lost, and his ship had blown apart in a storm. The captain and two of his crew had miraculously survived for thirty-eight days in a lifeboat, a heroic fact that was tainted by rumors that there had originally been five in the boat but that two had been eaten by the other three.

The door at the end of the hallway creaked open and then slammed shut. Davis turned and saw the radio talker approaching. "I'm Martin, the MPC. I do most of the goat-roping here," he said, removing a work glove and offering Davis a hand. "Jake told me to keep an eye out for you. How is that old boozer?"

"He's fine."

"Did you just get in?"

"Yes," Davis said, "Maureen brought me down to the ship."

Martin raised his eyebrows. "She must be softening in her old age. Did she show you around?" Davis shook his head.

"That sounds more like her. Listen, I don't have a lot of time but I'll give you a quick tour. You can scope out a place to work and then tomorrow we'll get you moved onto the ship. Sound good?"

Davis nodded. His eyes were stinging from fatigue and he could imagine just how stoned he must look. And in truth, he felt stoned, but somehow he made it through the thirty-minute tour of the ship. He didn't really take much in but did manage to learn that MPC was an acronym for Marine Projects Coordinator. After that, things blurred together. This lab was for this, that lab was for that, this was where you were allowed to eat and drink, this was where you weren't, these were the hours when the galley was open, this was the place you could go to smoke, these were the areas where you were forbidden to go without a float coat and a hard hat, this was up, this was down, any questions?

No.

"Okay then," Martin said, giving him a slap on the back. "I guess you can set up your little tech writing station anywhere you can find space."

"Thanks."

Martin was almost to the end of the hall when he turned around and came back.

"Oh, I almost forgot," he said, "Jake said you've got some sort of policy or presentation to give to the techs. . . ."

"Yes," Davis said, not wanting to elaborate. "It shouldn't take long."

"PowerPoint?"

Davis nodded.

"And it's just for the techs, not the science party. . . ."

"Yes."

"Then you can probably do it during the crossing. Maybe wait a day or two for everyone to get settled and into a routine, then I'll round them all up for you."

"Great, thanks."

There was, Martin had explained, a four-day turnover between one cruise and the next, and that time was spent offloading cargo and samples from the incoming cruise while simultaneously onloading and unpacking cargo and supplies for the outgoing cruise. With all that activity and bustle, Davis found that no matter where he went on the ship he was mostly just in the way. Many of the technicians and scientists around him were as bewildered as he was as to why he was there at all, but he just repeated the same mantra that had often been repeated to him: "I'm here to update some documentation and get familiar with the ship."

Sarah had recommended that he set up his laptop in a place called the Hydro Lab, if there was a table and some space. Davis found the lab and went in. There wasn't anyone there, so he installed himself at one of the lab tables. The table was under a porthole looking out at the pier. He unpacked his laptop, his notebooks, his package of colored highlighters, the rainbow-colored Post-it Notes, the discs and printed manuals—all the accessories that a busy tech writer needed to, uh, write technically. He had just taken a seat, plugged a network cord into the back of his laptop, and turned it on when the door connecting the Hydro Lab and the Electronics Lab burst open and Maureen appeared, hands on her hips.

"What are you doing?" she demanded, her tone weary and annoyed.

Davis was not quite sure how to answer, so he stared at her dumbly.

"You can't be in here," she said, her tone indicating that, of course, he should have known better. "This space is reserved for the science party."

"Oh."

"They arrive tomorrow. Until then, I'm using this as my staging area for some new monitors, so you'll have to pack up and find another space for yourself."

"I see," Davis said, shutting down his computer and collecting his belongings.

"And has that laptop been screened?"

". . . what . . . do you mean?"

"I mean what I said, has it been screened? You took the training!" she screeched. "You're supposed to know about that."

Ah, yes, *the* training. How could he have forgotten? There had only been seventeen different trainings. How could he have forgotten *the* training?

"It's a requirement if you're going to connect an outside laptop to the ship's network. Give it to me," she said, crossing the lab and yanking out the network cord. She then snatched up the laptop and disappeared with it into the E-Lab. Davis watched her go but was too timid—and too tired—to follow.

He stood waiting for what seemed like a very long time. He needed to move to avoid falling asleep, so he began exploring the Hydro Lab, opening empty drawers and cupboards, examining the contents of the spill-response and first-aid kits, playing with the bidet-like eye-wash attachments on the sinks, wondering all the while how long until Maureen would return with his laptop, how long until he could leave and find another place, how long until he could return to the hotel and collapse? He wasn't even sure what day it was, not that it mattered much since he was now required to begin the twelve hours a day, seven days a week schedule, but still, it would be nice to know.

He allowed himself to sit down and close his eyes for a moment. He dozed off and awakened when his chin fell off his palm. He rubbed his eyes, looked around, and noticed that the ship had suddenly grown quiet. No one was hustling boxes up and down the hallway, no music came from the radio in the other lab. Davis got up, poked his head into the hallway, but saw no one. He walked across to the adjacent labs and looked through the little glass panes, laced with chicken wire, but the rooms were empty. He was not sure if everyone had left for the day or if there was some meeting he was supposed to be attending. Fearing the latter, he walked back to the Hydro Lab and gingerly poked his head into the Electronics Lab, half expecting Maureen to lob something at him for having the audacity to cross into her realm, but the room was empty. He looked at the racks of blinking computer equipment, listened to the whir of their tiny fans, and then noticed his laptop standing open on what looked like a chart table in the center of the room. There were several desktop computer stations lining the walls, each with a different brand and size of PC, but they had all gone into sleep mode. Davis was almost frightened by the silence and emptiness. This was like the pre-climax scene of a horror movie, or like some apocalyptic science fiction story where everyone—except him—had been simultaneously sucked off the face of the earth. He went over to one of the portholes and looked out. Ronnie was still lounging in the guard shack, still singing along with his cassette player. Davis was relieved to see him and was just about to go out and ask him where everyone had gone when the door opened and Martin thrust in his head.

"Hey, man, it's Chicken Time."

Davis gave him a blank look.

Martin mimed shoveling food into his mouth. "Everything pretty much comes to a stop about now. C'mon."

Davis followed him down the corridor to the galley, which was full of people, the air thick with the greasy smell of fried food. He lifted a tray from the stack, took silverware from the cylindrical containers, and got in line behind Martin.

"Why's it called Chicken Time?" Davis asked.

"Because nine times out of ten, that's what you're gonna get. And trust me, that's a good thing, because if it's not chicken, there's no telling what it is."

Since Davis's ultimate solace for anxiety these days consisted of eating or drinking, he loaded up his plate with the standard "school lunch" fare: chicken nuggets, disintegrating broccoli crowns that had had all of the green boiled out of them, mashed potatoes from a box, rolls from a tube, and a vat of mucousy coleslaw, all to be washed down with orange or purple sugar water, gurgling side by side in clear plastic tanks. Once his tray was full, Davis wandered over to the tables, trying to assess the seating arrangement before committing to a spot.

There were four sets of tables in the galley and they seemed to be oddly segregated by race and rank. All of the Filipino deck hands were at one table, chatting away in Tagalog; the vessel crew, mostly Cajuns from Louisiana, were at another, speaking their own hybrid tongue, punctuated by gut-busting laughs; the Polar Support Services staff, which that day consisted of Worm, Maureen, Martin, Davis, and a few random others, occupied a third table. There was one table that was empty, and when Davis asked about it, Martin informed him that it was usually occupied by the science party, which would not come on board until the next day. The whole situation seemed to Davis a little too similar to a Birmingham lunch counter or like some bizarre form of cultural apartheid but, being new, and not wanting, as the saying goes, to rock the boat, he went along with it without question, taking the only empty seat at the PSS table, which happened to be next to Maureen. She remained seated for mere seconds after Davis sat down, then jumped up exclaiming, "Lots of work to do."

After lunch, Davis returned to the Hydro Lab, where his laptop was waiting for him. Since he'd been banished from that room, he walked across the hallway to one labeled the Bio Lab, which was empty. He installed himself in one of the far corners, had just booted up his computer and was about to unpack his accessories again when a man tumbled into the room, his face hidden behind the stack of boxes he was carrying. He had tripped over the raised threshold and he and the boxes tumbled to the floor. He lay on his stomach, dazed, trying to determine if he was hurt or not. The fall had knocked his glasses off his face, and from the way he was groping around the floor, he was blind without them. Davis got up, retrieved the glasses, and handed them to him.

"Oh, thank you," he said, fumbling them into position on his face. He looked up at Davis and seemed relieved to see a stranger. "Thank you," he added again, and took the hand that Davis offered to help pull him up. Without introducing himself or inquiring who Davis was, the man turned and began picking up the boxes, one by one, and placing them on the lab tables. As Davis watched him, he noticed that he was one of those long-torsoed, short-legged men who seem to be always running when, in fact, they are just having to take twice as many steps to keep up. His hair was cut in a businessman's style, but was overgrown and bushy, almost indistinct from the hair on his face, which was, in turn, indistinct from the hair on his neck, back, and arms. In fact, he seemed more animal than man, except for the glasses, which looked like two black-framed monitors mounted to his face.

He waddled back out into the hallway and began bringing in more boxes, one at a time, pausing after depositing each load to examine Davis. It was clear that he wanted to say something or ask some question, but each time he seemed about to speak, he would disappear into the hallway again and get another load. Finally, Davis offered to help him with the boxes.

"That'd be great," he wheezed. "Thanks."

"Are you . . . You're not Andrew, are you?" the man asked.

"No, I'm Davis."

"Are you sailing?"

"Yes."

"Oh," he said, and in his tone Davis sensed some suspicion.

"And you are . . . ?" Davis asked.

"What do you mean?" the man demanded. Then, realizing the innocent nature of the question, he replied, "I'm Jerry. I'm with Artaud."

"You weren't on the flight this morning, were you?"

"No, I've been here a while. My girl's here."

"Oh, you have a daughter?" Davis asked.

"Something like that."

"Where do you want these?" Davis asked, looking over the top edge of the box he was holding.

"Over there's fine," Jerry replied, pointing to where Davis had set up shop. "You're not . . . one of Artaud's?"

"No," Davis replied. "I'm from the office, but let me guess: You need this space."

Jerry nodded, adding, "If you don't, that is. I mean, I don't know what it is you're doing here. I mean what your role is . . ."

Davis concurred, but thought it best not to advertise his lack of direction. "No, it's no problem," he said, trying to sound agreeable. "I can work anywhere. I'll help you get these unloaded and then move out of your way."

Jerry thanked him and they got back to work. Since he could not lie down and go to sleep, Davis was actually glad to be doing something productive, or at least something that would keep his blood pumping and his eyes open. When the last box had been unloaded and the man began unpacking, Davis did the opposite with his belongings, exited the Bio Lab, and moved farther aft along the hallway to a door labeled Wet Lab. He looked through another chicken-wire-laced pane of glass and, seeing no one inside, pushed open the heavy door. The room had a large, empty table in the center that Davis hoped he might claim, but as he approached it he heard a loud knocking coming from below. He walked around the table and saw Worm, the upper half of his body submerged, upside down, in a hole in the floor, his legs spread wide to anchor him, one foot braced against a wall, the other hooked on a table leg.

"Dude," he said, gazing up from the cavern, his face obscured by the light from his headlamp. "How's it goin'?"

"It's not. But let me guess, you're going to be using this lab."

"That I am. You looking for a place to set up?"

"That I am."

"Hang on," he said, arching himself up and out of the hole "I've got just the spot." He stood up, replaced the metal floor cover, switched off his headlamp, and led Davis back down the hallway toward the galley.

"The spot," as Worm had called it, turned out to be a narrow, slope-ceilinged, windowless space (nothing more than a closet, really) under the stairs. For some reason it was referred to as the Environmental Room, which seemed to Davis someone's idea of an ironic joke since there was not a room on board the boat that was more insulated from the environment than this one. One entire wall of "the spot" consisted of floor-to-ceiling cabinetry, broken only by a miniscule niche of countertop, in which, Worm indicated, Davis could set up his computer. That was all fine and good except for the fact that there was no recessed area beneath the counter to put his legs, so when he was seated in his chair, his choice was either to spread them very wide, which, given his girth and lack of flexibility, he could not easily do, or to sit with his legs swiveled off to one side, his torso facing the counter. Either way was fine—for a while—but not for twelve hours a day, and not once the boat left the dock and started moving. But Davis, then far too tired to argue, took "the spot" without comment or complaint, although after Worm had left he waited several minutes, almost half an hour, actually, before unpacking his computer and setting up his desk for fear that someone else would come and kick him out.

A few hours and about forty solitaire games later, Worm appeared in the doorway again and said, "C'mon, let's go get drunk."

The rest of the evening was a blur. A large group of his shipmates wandered en masse up the pier, and then up the hill to the lovely grapevined bar at the Nogueira for a few rounds of Pisco Sours. That was not a problem. Davis, as has been shown, loved to drink. The problem was that whenever he was nervous or ill at ease, the ability to sip cocktails abandoned him and he found himself inhaling them. And this particular cocktail, a tart, pale green confection composed of sugar, lime juice, egg whites, and the South American variety of brandy known as Pisco, was served in a dainty, long-stemmed, harmless-looking cordial glass. Trouble was the drink had a kick. Davis drank the first one, felt nothing, ordered another. He drank that one, felt a little of the tension ebb from his shoulders, and ordered another. They were, after all, small, and half of the glass was just harmless meringue from the shaken egg whites—what could be the danger? Halfway through his fourth, he noticed that when he turned his head it took a few moments for his eyes to follow.

"Dude, you better be careful," Worm cautioned. "This shit's potent."

And indeed it was, for when he awakened, hours later, fully clothed on his bed, he had no recollection of how he had gotten there. He went in the bathroom, downed glass after glass of water, and went back to bed. He awoke the next morning and his tongue felt like a desiccated whale, beached on the rocks of his teeth. His head pulsed and he felt sure that he was suffering an aneurysm. He showered, dressed, ate a quick breakfast in the hotel lobby, choked down the best over-the-counter hangover cure known to man—a massive tablet of vitamin B—and then set out again to battle the wind, arriving at the boat around 8:30. Breakfast was just finishing up and several people emerging from the galley grinned when they saw Davis and asked something along the lines of "How you doin' this morning?" "How's the head?" occasionally punctuating their queries with a wink or a playful sock in the arm.

Chapter 13

Picture an old vaudeville act: a skinny man in a suit and a straw hat doing an exaggerated dance from one side of the stage to the other, his perma-grin always facing the crowd, a cane held laterally, which he raises up and down in contrast to his steps from side to side. Now picture that same act but with a man about 140 pounds heavier, wearing rust-colored canvas work pants and a flannel shirt. On his head? One of those South American alpaca hats with tasseled earflaps, the tassels swinging to and fro as he stumbles from one side of the stage to the other, and instead of a cane, he holds in his hand a laser pointer, for which he cannot find the off switch.

The performer in this second scenario was, of course, Davis, who was standing at the front of a conference room, ready to give his BM presentation to the yawning crowd of marine techs. The conference room was four decks up from the draft line of the boat, and the boat was then lumbering across twenty-foot seas, which made the feeling of being on the fourth deck akin to clinging to the uppermost point on a metronome.

Nearly all of the grantees and most of the other PSS contractors, who were hitching a ride to Palmer Station, were in their bunks on the lower decks, down with seasickness, which was why Martin had proposed that Davis give his presentation during the crossing: "That way they won't be bothering us and you can have the conference room to yourself." The technicians were presumably seasoned sailors, used to rough crossings like this and thus immune to seasickness. Soon after he began the presentation, Davis looked out at the audience. They looked sick, all right, but it wasn't from the sea.

There were six technicians in total, including Worm, all clad in the same rust-colored canvas work clothes and flannel shirts. Davis clicked the next slide, looked up at the screen. The boat crested a wave and Davis lost his balance. He did a lateral cartoonworthy shuffle to the right, which was arrested when he slammed into a wall-mounted bookcase. There was a pause, long enough to allow him to regain his footing, but then the ship rose up on another wave and Davis did the same dance but in the other direction, his momentum stopped this time by a wall-mounted desk.

"When avian/vessel collisions occur," he began, reading from his PowerPoint, "do the following: Record all birds, dead and alive, found on deck; Treat and release injured birds; Euthanize birds that are beyond help, and freeze and package their bodies for transport to CONUS."

"You want us to what?"

Davis turned back to the screen and read again from the top: "Record . . . all birds, dea—"

"You want us to kill the birds?"

"Euthanize," Davis corrected.

"Dude, seriously?"

Davis looked at the faces, all registering the same disbelief. Then he turned back to the screen and clicked into the next screen and read the details on how to collect, categorize, and count the birds; how to shelter those that were disoriented and allow them to dry out their feathers; and then how and when to release them.

He turned to see if there were any questions. Then he hesitated, swaying from side to side, before clicking the next screen into view. The groans and exclamations were instantaneous. He didn't turn around but read, in a deep baritone, from the heading.

"Preferred methods: The preferred method of euthanasia is thoracic compression," he said.

"You want us to squeeze them to death?"

"Compress their thoraxes," Davis corrected. "Done correctly, death is almost instantaneous."

"Sick!"

The audience was facing him, arrayed in a semicircle. They were seated in low, flat-bottomed upholstered chairs that looked like bumper cars, just heavy enough to keep them from bouncing around or sliding. Six of the chairs were occupied by the techs. The seventh (and the one that Davis had hoped to reserve for himself so that he could avoid the side-to-side dance) was occupied by Maureen, who had been summoned to the conference room to provide technical support when Davis had been unable to get what he saw on his laptop to display on the larger screen. He had hoped she'd leave once she got him set up, but she didn't. Instead, she scooted her chair (which was to have been Davis's chair) back behind the main group, and sat, legs stretched out in front of her, arms up and hands locked behind her head. The others were interested in his talk, but Maureen seemed to be the only one really enjoying herself. Unfortunately for Davis, what she was enjoying was the sight of him stumbling around like a drunk as he clicked through slide after slide of some man in Alabama strangling a pigeon.

He went on: "This is the aspect of the job that will require discretion on the part of the euthanasian."

"The what? Is that even a word?"

Davis had been afraid of that. There hadn't been time to look up the correct term before he'd left Denver. The one dictionary on board, a decades-old paperback missing several pages, offered no guidance. He continued:

"In general, it is best to work in private—"

Laughter and dismissive hisses.

"You have got to be kidding."

"If a crowd has gathered," Davis continued, "ask them to leave, or move the animal to a more discreet location before euthanizing it. If you must kill an animal in front of others, first explain what you are doing and why."

"Just tell 'em it's what's for dinner."

He clicked on to the next screen.

"For larger birds, skuas, gulls, and albatrosses, the preferred method is cervical dislocation."

"Dude, wait. Did you really just say you want us to kill albatross?"

"And then what? Wear it around our necks?"

Davis was suddenly transported back to a sophomore English class. Crap! How could he have forgotten that?

"Yes, yes, I know." He nodded as if he'd expected that. "But you're technicians and scientists, not poets, so you don't need to worry about those superstitions." He turned back to the screen, inwardly cursing his stupidity.

"This technique is commonly referred to as 'breaking the neck' but is more accurately described as 'snapping the spine.'"

"That is twisted!"

"Actually, it's more of a stretch and separate combination move, followed by a rapid twisting," Davis corrected.

"No way am I doing that."

"The goal is to quickly separate the spinal cord from the brain to provide a fast and painless death."

As he was saying this last part, the ship took a roll and Davis fell backward; his legs got tangled in the cords and pulled the laptop onto the floor. Fortunately the table was low and the floor carpeted so no damage was done. The projector, tethered to the laptop, teetered on the precipice of the table, two of its four rubber feet hanging over the edge. Davis saw it, pulled himself quickly up onto his knees, and was able to grab it before it fell. There was laughter as he picked up the laptop, set it back on the conference table, and then waited for a break in the rolling to stand up. The pointer had been dropped and rolled back and forth under the table, projecting a chaotic beam at the ankles of the audience. He ignored it, turned back to the screen, clicked the next slide into view.

Like the pointer, the presentation rolled on, Davis shuffling from side to side, his little earmuff tassels gyrating next to his cheeks, his right shoulder and left thigh smarting from his collision with the bookcase and desk, but neither smarting half as much as his ego.

When it was over, they all filed out of the conference room and Davis was left alone, feeling nauseous and exhausted. He turned off the computer and the projector and began winding up the cords. From the shadows, Maureen emerged. She approached, took the projector from him with an exasperated sigh and, without saying a word, unwound the cord Davis had wound clockwise around the rubber feet and, once it was unwound, proceeded to wind it again, but this time counterclockwise.

"Does that make a difference?" he asked.

"This is the way it goes," she said.

"Is that in the manual?"

She gave him a look of mild malice and repeated: "This is the way it goes."

Davis shrugged. He closed his laptop and collapsed backward into one of the bumper-car chairs. Maureen remained standing, projector under her arm, her body swaying with the ship. She had that same snotty smile on her face. He took off his itchy wool hat and rubbed the bump on his head inflicted from the flying gin bottle, wishing that the headache and nausea would go away, wishing that *she* would go away.

"How is it you're here?" she asked. Davis continued rubbing the painful spot. "It's clear you're not qualified for the position. How did you get it? I mean, really, I'm dying to know."

The fact that she could ask such a question (of anybody, let alone of someone as low on the totem pole as Davis) during the era of George W. Bush's presidency struck Davis as ironic, and he longed to reply with something like *It's not what you know, but who you know* or *It helps to have friends in high places* or even *It helps to have friends, period.* He longed to say those things but then he remembered the meds, and the insurance, and Jake's warning to watch what he said around "The Fourth Branch," and instead he just looked up at her and smiled. A synthetic smile, granted, but one that conveyed very clearly that he knew just what she meant by her question but that he had no intention of answering it.

After she'd gone, he got up and went back down to the Bio Lab. He felt like he was wearing a rusty suit of armor, and each step he took was labored in spite of the fact that he was descending. He got back down to the 01 deck, and it took him a moment to adjust to the transition from the metronome of the upper deck to the pendulum motion of the lower. He passed by the E-Lab, saw Maureen typing away at her terminal, but other than that, the deck seemed deserted. He returned to the Environmental Room, plugged in his laptop, and sat down, watching the Reality Detection Device as he waited for his computer to boot up. When it did, he opened another game of solitaire. There were other games, of course, but none as mindless or plodding as solitaire. He played one game, lost; played another, this time with his leaden head resting on the palm of his left hand, but that didn't work since he needed to hang on with one hand or he would tip out of the chair. He sat up, gripped the edge of the desk with his left hand, and moused cards with his right. He shut his eyes, just for a moment, and when he woke up it was not quite in time to stop himself and his chair from falling to the floor. He landed on his elbow and it took a second for the pain to register. When it did, he got up, cursing. Then he lashed his laptop to the desk with a bungee cord, wrapped another around the back of the chair, lashing it to the desk, and went to the bathroom, where he vomited, flushed, rinsed out his mouth, and then unwrapped a fresh roll of toilet paper, turned out the light, and lay down on his back.

Minutes, hours, days later (who knew how long?), Davis was awakened by a deep thud. Afraid that someone was knocking on the bathroom door, he sat up. The initial thud was followed by another, and another, but their frequency was different than a knock. Thud! There it was again, dull, heavy, coming from outside the ship. Davis stood up and turned on the light. The ship was no longer heaving. The engines were still humming, the sonar still chirping away, but he realized that he could stand without having to hang on to something.

He flipped on the light, straightened his hair, returned his toilet paper pillow to the roll, and then flushed the toilet and washed his hands—just in case anyone might have been outside wondering just what he had been doing in there for, well, however long he'd been napping. He checked his appearance once more in the mirror. Satisfied, he opened the door and walked out into the hallway. Again the thud, followed by another, and another. He walked up the stairs to the main level and then out on to the deck. The air was biting, but the wind had died down. There were several people outside, all leaning on the rail. Davis feared that it might be some sort of mass vomiting but then one of them turned and he saw that her face was no longer green. He approached the rail and looked over.

Ice! Small bits of it floating all around the boat. Then he looked up. Off in the distance, like a chaotic, oddly shaped armada of white ships, were icebergs. Beyond that, barely visible in the distance, was what appeared to be land. Not much of it, granted, but every so often the blanket of snow was penetrated by an outcrop of jagged brown rocks. Worm came up behind him and patted him on the back.

"Welcome to the seventh continent!"

Chapter 14

E-mail was transmitted to and from the vessel twice a day via satellite. The times of those transmissions were only vaguely fixed (around breakfast and sometime after dinner), and were largely at the whim of the network administrator, a title that was assigned, on this particular cruise, to Maureen. There was a whiteboard hanging in the hallway outside of the E-Lab and, once the e-mail had been sent and received, Maureen would write the time and date of the transmission in red marker. She knew how much power this task carried, and she relished it, often waiting an hour or even two after breakfast to run the script and bring in the mail and news from the outside world. There was nothing quite so delicious to her as when some lovesick young undergrad, dying the death of a thousand cuts because he or she had not heard from little Mr. or Miss Significant Other, would timidly approach her desk and ask, "Um, have you had a chance to run e-mail yet?"

At those times, she would emit an exasperated, overworked sigh, swivel her chair around, and effectively disintegrate them with an acidic glare. She loved it when she could do this nonverbally, just turn around and communicate all of her displeasure, all of her annoyance, with the narrowing of her eyes.

Then, too, she relished the times when, eager to hear about the triumph or defeat of some stupid sports team, or who had won the Academy Award for best acting, the masses were huddled in anticipation, waiting for her to download the electronic version of the newspaper. Her glee at watching them squirm was almost sadistic, as they whispered together and formed mini committees to decide who would be assigned the onerous task of approaching her and asking about it. Even more than watching them squirm however, she enjoyed the opportunity their query provided for her to deliver an aside on how busy she was, or to remind them that the real purpose of this trip was collecting data for the scientists, not wasting time on personal correspondence or following the superfluous high jinks of some vapid Hollywood starlet or college sports team. Then, once they'd been shamed, once her integrity had been boldly established and underscored, she would disappear with a sigh behind the computer racks and begin downloading the transmission, making it seem like one of the labors of Hercules, when really it was nothing more than entering a series of keystrokes. Keystrokes she had entered so many times in the past that she could type them in without thinking, the whole process, start to finish, taking less than thirty seconds.

Since Maureen rarely received any e-mail that wasn't work related, it should surprise no one that she did not know the value of personal correspondence. Or maybe she did, for there was, in her torturous withholding of it from her shipmates, an undeniable layer of envy. Envy she dealt with in the way envy was so often dealt with—by belittling the thing one was envious of and convincing oneself that what the others had was not really worth having at all. In this case, persuading herself that electronic missives from loved ones were trivial, banal, a waste of bandwidth. This self-deception was usually quite easy for her. Usually.

All e-mail came to the vessel as a compressed file, which Maureen then had to run a script to decompress. Once that was done, she parsed it out for delivery to the individual e-mail accounts. There was rarely any cause for her to read any of the incoming or outgoing messages, exceptions being when a particular e-mail was cluttered with attachments too large to send—a common occurrence with a boatload of shutterbug students on their first trip south, who were all so eager to send photos of their first sighting of an iceberg or penguin that they routinely forgot to resize their photos. That was one acceptable instance. Another might be to allay suspicions about someone, a scientist or student, say, who had been given permission to send data in excess of the seventy-five kilobyte per day limit, provided that what they were sending was project related. If she had reason to suspect the content was not project related, that it was, perhaps, an overdue term paper or some other nonauthorized correspondence, then she was justified in digging deeper. But even those cases could be checked without actually reading the e-mail by merely scanning the title of the attachment and looking for suspicious words or phrases like "Man vs. Nature in Stephen Crane's *The Open Boat*" or "Blog entry 744: Antarctica!" or "Penguin Pics!"

In those cases the standard procedure was to bounce the e-mail back to the sender with a terse, one-line reminder about personal e-mail size restrictions.

Although there was rarely, if ever, cause for her to actually read the contents of the e-mail, that was often precisely what she did, especially if she happened to be the only network admin sailing, as was the case on this particular cruise.

Reading other people's e-mail was, for her, an endlessly entertaining vice, and it did help buttress her occasionally sagging feelings of superiority. What better way to banish any encroaching insecurities and reestablish power (at least in your own mind) than to smugly eavesdrop on the insipid electronic correspondence of silly undergrads? But more than anything (although she would never admit it, not even to herself) her voyeurism provided her an anonymous way to peer through the window at other lives less lonely than her own.

On this cruise, her interest was focused on Artaud. Not specifically on his correspondence, since she still held him on a pedestal and thus did not want to diminish or sully her pure feelings for him by prying into his personal e-mail, but into the correspondence of the three little sprites—two female and one male—who had accompanied him on this trip and who were, clearly (clearly, at least to her), hot for teacher. She began by opening their outgoing e-mail.

* * *

From: Meghan.Johnson@HAH.pss.gov
Sent: Wednesday, October 26, 2005 7:50 PM
To: KJohnsons2@MSN.com
Subject: I'm here!!!
Hi Mom & Dad,
I can't believe I'm actually out here!!! I got a little seasick at first, but I've got my sea legs now and am doing much better. We saw our first iceberg today and I've taken a ton of pictures (thanks again for the new camera!!!) but we haven't really done much yet. So far the food is gross, the beds are lumpy, and my roommate (also from BC State) is cool but snores a lot at night. Dr. Artaud has been awesome!!! And I can't wait until we get to the study site and start doing some science. I'll write more later!!!
Love you guys!!!
Meghan

Maureen made a mental note of the girl's name. That part about Artaud being "just awesome" was a red flag. She'd have to watch her closer.

From: Kristi.Leukens@HAH.pss.gov
Sent: Wednesday, October 26, 2005 9:18 PM
To: J_Dude@add.com
Subject: Re: Miss you, Babe
Hey babe,
I made it down here fine (looooonnng flight). Was sick as a dog during the crossing, which made me panic because, well, you know. But I got it this morning (finally!) so we can both breathe a little easier now. Not that I wouldn't like to have a baby with you someday—I SOOOO would—but I think it would be better if we finished school first ;-)

The rest of the e-mail was a detailed rehashing of their good-bye lovemaking and a disgustingly vivid description of an oral technique she hoped to practice on him when she returned home. Maureen moved on.

From: Andrew.Martin@HAH.pss.gov
Sent: Thursday, October 27, 2005 12:02 AM
To: PLGroove@Cnet.com
Subject: Last Friday
Pookie,

I haven't had a chance to write because we've been so busy since I got here. The seismic gear is in the water and I've got to monitor it pretty much all the time that I'm awake, but I've got a minute now so I thought I'd drop my main man a line, and tell him how much I miss him :)

What a liar, Maureen thought, shaking her head. The science for this cruise had not even begun yet and the seismic gear was still tightly packed away in a shipping container on the back deck. What's more, this Andrew had not been working at all, unless you counted sprawling on the couch in the lounge watching movies as work. The little conniver was just the type who might go after Artaud. She read on.

I'm really sorry about what went down last Friday night. Devon means nothing to me. We were just dancing. Really! He's always had a little crush on me but you're the only one, Pete. Really.

She closed that one without reading the gritty details. It was the kind of message her father would have sent to her mother—full of prevarication and pathetic rationalizations, all designed to make the woman (or in this case, the man) second-guess what she had clearly seen with her own eyes. Men, she concluded somewhat tritely, were pigs.

Since she didn't have anything pressing to do, she popped open an outbound message from Artaud's assistant, Jerry. Artaud had confided to her that Jerry was leaving his wife for a girl he'd met at a whorehouse in PA. She hoped his message might provide some dramatic entertainment, and she was not disappointed.

From: Jerry.Tetlock@HAH.pss.gov
Sent: Thursday, October 27, 2005 6:34 AM

To: CelianaGomez@netmail.ch.com
Subject: ATM and Visa

celiana,
i can't do anything now about money. i thought i gave you enough before i left. i have to be careful how much i withdraw or maryanne gets suspicious. there won't be any more deposited in your account until my paycheck comes next week. should be wednesday. i wish you'd waited to buy the tv. i know we talked about that. i only left you the visa card only for emergencies only. i know things are tight now but after the divorce is finished everything will be better and we won't have to be so careful with money. you deserve so much. i'll make sure you get it soon! besos. jerry.

She scanned the rest of the outgoing mail and, seeing nothing else of interest, closed up the files and typed in the script to transfer the packet. Then she waited, staring vacantly out the porthole at the leaden sky, as the outgoing ones and zeros traded places with the incoming.

When the incoming transmission was complete, she scanned it for anything addressed to Artaud. There were three total. The first two were technical in nature, relating to the functioning of the equipment they were going to use, and the third was from the marine manager, Jake. She hesitated, remembering her vow to not pry into his personal e-mail, but curiosity got the best of her and she popped it open, figuring if it was from the marine manager, it probably wouldn't be classified as personal, even though she knew they were friends.

From: Jake.Mason@pss.gov
Sent: Monday, October 24, 2005 2:50 PM
To: Edourd.Artaud@HAH.PSS.gov
Subject: Welcome!
Dr. Artaud,
On behalf of all the Marine staff, I'd like to welcome you aboard the RV/IB Henry A. Hamilton. . . .

Blah, blah, blah, boilerplate form letter. But at the bottom, in a slightly different font, there was a personal message:

> I tried to assemble a crew of pretty girls for your cruise but remembered that you usually travel with your own harem of nubile undergrads. And of course you've always got Maria and Maureen to fawn over you. Remember, you can rock the boat but don't tip the boat over ;—)
> Happy sailing!
> Jake

Maureen fumed over that for a few minutes, annoyed that her attraction to Artaud was apparently so obvious, but more annoyed by the fact that Maria, just as she'd suspected, had her sights set on him as well. Then with a self satisfied grin she reflected on how she, and not Maria, had spent last night in the chief scientist's cabin, and how she, and not Maria, would have an entire month alone with him.

She then idly perused some of the other incoming e-mail before distributing them, only slightly molested, to their rightful and intended recipients.

When the e-mail did finally make it through the Maureen filter, Davis was thrilled to see that he had three messages in his in-box. The first was from his brother, asking how he was doing, telling him about the latest drama with his niece and nephews, and then asking the usual questions about how the journey had been, had he seen any penguins, etc. At the bottom of the message, his nephew, Bryce, had painstakingly typed the following:

> Hi, uncle Davis! we learnd about Ant Artica today in school and I got to tell them about you being there. Please please please send some pictures of some seals. Try to get one of a lepperd seal! They eat other seals and penguins. Here's a joke we learnd. How does a penguin make pancakes? With its flippers!
> Love Bryce

The other two messages were from his agent, Estelle, and from Jake.

He opened the one from Jake first.

From: Jake.Mason@pss.gov
Sent: Monday, October 24, 2005 2:50 PM
To: Davis.Garner@HAH.pss.gov
Subject: Ahoy!
Hey there, friend,
How was the trip down? Your Pisco exploits are already making their way around the office. I expected better from a liver like yours—one that I have personally trained and nurtured over the years. Ah, well, you'll get a break from the sauce soon enough. Thirty days at sea on a dry ship is like nautical rehab. Just watch out when you get to station. People tend to go a little crazy.

How are you liking it so far? Are you finding things to do? How did the bird presentation go?

Davis groaned and then started composing a reply.

From: Davis.Garner@HAH.pss.gov
Sent: Friday, October 28, 2005 12:24 PM
To: Jake.Mason@PSS.gov
Subject: Re: Ahoy!
Hello,
Yes, I made it here. The presentation went okay. I'm still not sure what I'm supposed to be doing.

Davis stopped typing. He had always confided in his friend, but now that his friend was also his boss, he hesitated and felt the need to omit many of the facts. What could he say? That the promised workload had never materialized? That the consistent responses he got whenever he asked technicians to review some documentation were rolled eyes and a dismissive wave? That he felt, justly so, that he was in the way? That he probably should not ever have taken this job since the stress of trying to dig up things to do was more exhausting than any work he could imagine?

In the end he wrote a vague, simple e-mail answering Jake's immediate questions and promising to write more later. Then he hit Send. But as soon as he'd done so, he felt regret. Regret that he seemed to have crossed a threshold and was now communicating with his friend in a manner that was less than honest.

He moved on to the next e-mail. He looked at the sealed envelope icon blinking in his in-box. It was from his agent, Estelle, and Davis tried to think how she could have found him. Who could have given her his ship address? She must have rooted it out from someone, probably his father or Jake. The woman really should have been a detective instead of a literary agent since she was excellent at the former and only so-so at the latter. He looked at her message, and could tell from the subject line

Davis, what in the hell are you doing dow—

that it was not going to be a lighthearted missive. Estelle had the habit of beginning her e-mail messages in the subject line and then continuing them down below, a few words of her message inevitably lost in the jump. It seemed she was too impatient to say what she had to say to bother with the conventions of the form. Reluctantly he double-clicked on the icon.

From: EstelleWillBookem@aol.com
Sent: Tuesday, October 25, 2005 11:07 PM
To: Davis.Garner@HAH.pss.gov
Subject: Davis, what in the hell are you doing dowere, but I can't believe it. You? *Antarctica?!* Really? I know you're wanting to avoid me AND Frank, AND that waaaaay overdue deadline, but don't you think you're taking the avoidance strategy a bit too far?

Actually, no, Davis thought as he closed the e-mail, leaving the bulk of it unread. On the contrary, Antarctica suddenly didn't seem far enough away. Maybe he should have shot himself into space or dug an underground bunker. She was justified, he supposed, in having tracked him down. She wanted her cut of the money. Money that would not be paid out until he delivered the manuscript. He had, so far, missed two deadlines, with a third set to pass while he was at sea. But more than the money, he knew, what Estelle really wanted was to preserve her good relations with the publisher. Writers? They were a dime a dozen, but establishing a good rapport with a publisher? Well, that was something much more rare.

Feeling masochistic, Davis opened her e-mail again and began reading where he'd left off.

I don't need to remind you of the due date but I will tell you that Frank has been calling nonstop and is insistent this time. He really wants something from you, or else!

Or else what? Really, what could they do? Sue him? For what? And how would they get the money? Garnish his wages? They'd have to get in line behind the credit card collection agencies.

Davis knew all that and yet there was something inside him, some small sprout of ethical morality, that just would not wither and die. His writing was all that he had—the one thing in his life that was remotely genuine—and he still wanted to deliver something good, something that he himself could be proud of, or at least something that didn't make him cringe six months after it came out in print. But as much as he wanted that, he found himself unable to move forward on the manuscript. The reasons for this were many but basically came down to the fact that his resolve consisted of one part perfectionism, one part insecurity, and several dashes of laziness—a paralyzing cocktail that made him unable to just sit down and tap out prose. Instead he had to obsess and agonize about it, had to start and stop the project at least fifty times before even getting a hint of a story he could live with. And in between the stopping and starting there was the pacing—from one end of the room to the other—the consumption of pot after pot of coffee, the filling of the ashtray with cigarette butts. Then, once he had the basic story, he would move on to the drawings—hundreds of them— reams of drawings he would commit to paper and then dispose of before finally settling on characters and settings that fit the scenario he had laid out. Even with his last book, the one with Edgar, the collie, and that idiotic cat, he had spent months toying around with those characters in his head, months trying to get the drawings in sync with the story he had written, and in the end he had not so much finished as just given up and decided to just stop poking at it.

For this latest book, he had nothing to even fret over, had been stuck in a period of creative constipation for so long that he began to have real anxiety about sitting down at the computer, utter dread at the thought of picking up his sketch pad. And so acute were these feelings that he instinctively avoided the computer and sketch pad just as one would avoid the flame on a hot stove, or eating food that smelled rotten.

But here again was Estelle, having tracked him to the bottom of the earth, demanding to know when he'd deliver something. He tried to calculate how far away from him she actually was. He could picture her clearly, seated behind her desk in her one-room office in New York. She was not a beautiful woman. She had an enormous ass and legs and tried to counteract their bulk by wearing blazers with large shoulder pads. This had the unintended effect of making her look like a linebacker—albeit a linebacker with a fondness for glittery mocha eye shadow and maroon lip liner.

Estelle had once been a writer herself, of romance novels, or so she had told Davis over lunch one day, years ago, when they'd gone out to celebrate the signing of his first contract.

"I got interested in books," she told him, "when I was a teen and discovered Harlequin romances. I was a happy child, had married parents who loved each other, stable, middle-class home. You know, idyllic American childhood."

But then puberty came and she, like Davis, had morphed into something almost freakish. Neither of her parents were unattractive, but somehow she had managed to get the worst aspects of each of them: her mother's birdlike upper body and her father's rugby player legs and ass.

"I wasn't entirely ugly, but boys weren't attracted to me and girls liked me only as a friend who wasn't a threat. Sort of like a Girl Friday they could confide in."

Nevertheless, hormones raged within Estelle and the only outlet she found for them was reading romance novels.

"Trouble was, I was a smart girl, and soon I saw through their formulas."

And what she saw was that although the characters, settings, and outfits might be different, the premises were always the same: A rich haughty woman was brought to her knees by passion for a man, usually one who was lower on the socioeconomic scale. Or, inversely, a poor, virtuous woman met a rich powerful man who elevated her away from her humble life. Regardless of the scenario, the two always ended up embarking on a marital adventure together that would, the reader assumed, last forever.

"It was always one or the other," she told Davis, "never the way life really is, where two boring, mediocre people meet when they're drunk at a bar, or at an office Christmas party, date for a while, and then marry because the condom broke or because they realize they're getting old and don't think anyone better will come along."

Shortly after Estelle discovered the Romance Novel Formula, she found that she could concoct it as well as anyone else and began writing and peddling her own stories. She wrote several books, sold them all, but soon realized that in that particular genre she was not going to make enough money to support herself. Nor was she talented enough to make the jump from genre fiction out into something larger and more legitimate, so, having read enough to be able to distinguish trash from treasure and realizing she would never produce the latter, she decided to become an agent.

"Most fiction," she told Davis, "I don't care if it's children's, young adult, horror, or romance, will follow a formula. Once you figure that out, the rest is easy and you can start cranking it out like a factory."

But for Davis, that had not been the case. He did discover that much of children's fiction was, indeed, formulaic, but for him the formula was never so easy to follow. He was never able to "crank it out," as Estelle had said, and for that reason he was, he knew, a disappointment to her. After all, she was in the business to make money, and she had not done so with him. He had hoped that she might just give up and leave him alone, but no such luck. She seemed determined to collect on all the money due to her, or at least not have to pay any of it back if Davis failed to deliver. And with those anxieties swirling in his mind, he wrote a short synopsis of the Mick story and e-mailed it off to her.

Her response was, like any good blow to the head, swift and hard, arriving with the next day's e-mail:

A fly who goes around eating cow poop? A bed full of maggots? That's just what a mother wants to read to her child before tucking him in. Come on, Davis! What were you thinking? I sell books for children. What parent is going to buy their kid a book about maggots? I just can't see something like that under the tree at Christmas. You're a dog author, and a dog-gone good one. Stick with what you know and don't waste our time on things I can't sell.

Our time, he loved that. Don't waste *our* time. It made it sound so inclusive, so like they were playing on the same team. Christ!

Chapter 15

The approach to Palmer Station through the Gerlache Strait and Neumayer Channel offers some of the most surrealistically beautiful scenery in the world. If the sun is out and the water is calm, as they were the day the *Hamilton* first transported Davis to the station, it is like sailing on a sea of mercury. The jutting, snow-covered peaks, floating icebergs, and cerulean sky were reflected, almost seamlessly, on the water, disrupted only by the plumes of steam from spouting whales, and by flocks of penguins making splashing arcs as they repeatedly pierced the thin membrane separating their dual worlds.

From the way people in the office raved about Palmer Station, usually with the poetic descriptors "marvelous," "spectacular," or "awe-inspiring," Davis half expected to see a collection of half-timbered Alpine villas or something like the tsar's Winter Palace. What he saw instead, when the boat steamed into Arthur Harbour was, well, nothing like that. What he saw—a cluster of blue tin shacks—looked more like a mining camp or a prison colony than some glittering outpost devoted to the noble pursuit of science. Granted, the approach to the station was marvelous, spectacular, and awe-inspiring as the boat meandered through bobbing bergs and past huge walls of crumbling sapphire ice, but then those visions of loveliness were intruded upon by the sight of the prefabricated sheet-metal buildings, rusting shipping containers, and the muddy tracks and gray fumes that trailed behind the tractors and forklifts. There were flags flying in front of the place but, like the flags at some rural Wyoming post office, they seemed obligatory rather than festive.

In spite of that negative first impression of Antarctica's man-made structures, Davis was excited by the arrival, although most of that excitement was, he realized, due to his desire to escape from the bobbing metal puke bucket in which he'd been encased for the better part of the past week and to once again feel terra firma beneath his feet. His excitement was stifled, however, for once the vessel approached the tiny pier, all of the passengers were ordered back inside to avoid interfering with the tying up. Most of those who were disembarking returned to their cabins or remained talking in the hall. Davis went back to his desk and began another game of solitaire.

After his third losing game, he wandered down to the galley. He grabbed a handful of cookies and ate them absently, staring out one of the portholes. Outside, there were orange-suited men and women looping the thick, frost-covered mooring lines to the bollards. Behind them was a small crowd of similarly orange-suited people gathered on the pier. Davis finished the cookies and went up to the main deck. There were still people waiting, their luggage and duffel bags lining the hallway. They all stood, listening to the engines and the crane, no one speaking. Finally, one of the Filipinos opened the door, nodded okay, and they all filed out onto the deck. Davis remained behind until the last of the station personnel had gone. Once the gangway was clear, he descended, bouncing along until his feet were finally touching solid ground. Images of the pope landing at a foreign airport and then dropping to his hands and knees to kiss the tarmac came into Davis's mind, although he didn't really consider doing so himself. Instead, he bent down and discreetly picked up a small stone, a gray and black speckled piece of granite, and marveled at the fact of it being a part of a place where so few had ever set foot. Although he had learned in one of the tedious trainings that it was a violation of the Antarctic Treaty to pick up any rocks, bones, shells, or feathers as souvenirs, he slipped the stone in his pocket and then looked around to see if the action had been observed. It had not, so he continued walking toward a network of wooden boardwalks connecting the various buildings.

Only later would he learn that the rock he had picked up from the pier was not actually a piece of Antarctica but was, instead, from a quarry in Chile and had been shipped to Palmer Station on the same vessel that had brought Davis. The rocks were deposited, by the ton, into the thick, sheet-metal pen that constituted the Palmer Station pier. The tide gradually washed these rocks away from below, so on each trip a new shipping container of rock was unloaded to replace those that had washed away.

People moved around the pier in a manic frenzy, but Davis, as usual, had nothing to do, so he stood off to the side, toying with the faux-contraband rock in his pocket and watching. Despite his size and the fluorescent orange jumpsuit he was wearing, no one seemed to notice him. He was like a smooth, round stone in the middle of a stream around which the water flowed without effort. Since everyone seemed occupied unloading cargo and greeting old acquaintances, Davis took the opportunity provided by their inattention to enter one of the station buildings. Once inside, and once his eyes had adjusted to the change in light, he found himself in a place that had all the charm and character of a state school dormitory—indoor/outdoor carpeting, off-white walls, fluorescent lighting, fiberglass ceiling tiles. He walked down one hallway and passed several vacant rooms. The doors were open. Each bedroom contained a bunk bed, a desk, and a chair, but no personal effects. These were, Davis assumed, rooms recently vacated by departing personnel, soon to be occupied by the recent arrivals.

At the end of the hallway was a high-ceilinged room containing a kitchen and galley area with the same institutional feel as the one on the ship (although instead of having the tables and chairs bolted to the floor, these were picnic-table contraptions that could fold up and be pushed flush against a wall if, say, the galley space was needed for square dancing, or musical chairs, or some other community event that Davis could only imagine). Farther along, he found an exercise room, with its various pieces of equipment standing mute and motionless, like a museum display of instruments of torture. He rounded another corner and entered a room with several overstuffed reclining couches arranged in a druidic semicircle in front of a giant, flat-screen TV. The walls were lined with bookshelves, but instead of books there were rows of DVDs. Davis walked across this room to a set of double doors. He tried the handles, found them locked, so he peered through the slender gap between them. The room on the other side was sunny and dominated by a central pool table. Off to the side, he could just discern a few wooden stools facing a bar.

Bored with the mundanity of the place, Davis headed outdoors again. He trudged along on the hard-packed snow toward an outcrop of rocks, from which he thought he might get some pictures of the boat with a giant blue glacier in the background. His feet had not taken thirty steps when he heard footsteps running after him and an authoritative voice cried out, "Can I help you with something?"

Davis spun around to face his inquisitor, a man, orange-suited like himself, but with sunglasses and a stocking cap.

"No," Davis said, turning and squinting at the man. "I'm just looking around."

"Ah, well, we can't really have you doing that. Are you from the vessel?"

"Yes."

"Do you have authorization to be here?"

"I didn't know I needed it. I just got off the ship to, you know, walk around . . ."

"Yes, well, this is a scientific station. We can't just have people walking around. There are restricted areas, scientific experiments, ecologically sensitive zones, not to mention the inherent dangers of a crevasse, or even the possibility of a slip and fall."

And thus Davis discovered what most visitors to Antarctica inevitably discover: The ironic inaccessibility of the place. Ironic because it is, in theory, a place that is accessible to all, owned by no one, governed loosely. But once there, you are usually confined to a station, where there are many, many rules and where movement is highly restricted. There is no place to rent a car or any other sort of vehicle because there are, outside of the stations, no roads. There are no quaint picnic spots, and you cannot just go walk around on your own because of the very real threats of getting lost and freezing to death or the aforementioned possibilities of falling into a crevasse or disturbing some scientist's delicate experiment. At Palmer Station, the chief means of physical activity consists of ascending and then descending a snow-covered hill behind the station, referred to as the Glacier. And, of course, drinking and sleeping with your coworkers.

Back on the ship, Davis had an appointment with one of the young marine science technicians, to whom he hoped to "farm out" some documentation. The girl was, by at least a decade, Davis's junior, and yet was so obviously his intellectual superior that in less than five minutes she accurately deduced that his professional veneer was just that. Without saying a word, she flipped through the document. When she reached the end, she closed the notebook. "Well," she said, "it certainly needs updating." Davis nodded. And then they sat, for what seemed, to Davis, like an eternity, the sound of the engines rumbling beneath them, as each waited for the other to speak. Davis cracked first:

"I was hoping you might have time during this trip to, you know, go through it." She picked up the document again and looked down at it, her lips pulled tight across her teeth.

"So, how is this supposed to work?" she asked. "I cross out what's outdated, make all the content changes, make sure everything is current, and then you do . . . What? Make it pretty?" Her tone wasn't sarcastic, merely inquisitive, which made it even more difficult for Davis to reply.

"Well, basically, yes. Of course, there's a lot more to it than that." He chuckled, realizing as he did so that there really wasn't; he cleaned up the text, put it in the right template, regenerated the table of contents, and occasionally labeled and arranged the pictures. That was it. So, yes, essentially he was making the documents pretty, although when worded like that, it made it sound like his job consisted of cutting little strips of pink and white gingham with a pair of pinking shears and then tying them into bows.

In the end, she took the manual and left. Davis, chastened and ashamed, decided to delve back into the manuals he had and try again to make some sense of them. These were operation manuals on various pieces of shipboard instrumentation that Sarah or one of Sarah's predecessors had written. She and Jake had suggested that he read through some of them to get a feel for the types of instrumentation available and the types of documentation he would need to provide. He printed up hard copies of manuals on the Gravity Meter, the Proton Precession Magnetometer, the Multi-Channel Seismic Streamer, and then retrieved them and returned to his little sidesaddle excuse for a desk in the Environmental Room, determined to read and study until he understood the contents. He should also have printed up another manual he'd noticed, one on something called a Depth Sensor, because less than five minutes into his attempted study it became glaringly obvious that he was way out of his. He held his head in his hands and tried to focus on the words, tried to make sense of what it was that the machines did, but soon he was lost again in a thick bamboo forest of unfamiliar vocabulary and technical jargon. It wasn't so much the complex nature of the equipment that baffled him as the convoluted language used to describe it, the polysyllabic words hyphenated onto other words and thus made into undecipherable phrases: There was *the manometric flow inhibition system* in one document, *the knurled cone on the tube-cap-extruder bar* in another, and then, of course, *the insertion device for the headspace air recirculation preventer pin.*

The reading was, for Davis, more difficult than trying to decipher the vocabulary in *Beowulf,* more boring than reading one of Shakespeare's history plays, more tedious to follow than a dense, highly mannered eighteenth-century English novel in which paragraphs stretch on, unbroken, page after page. Nevertheless, there Davis sat, head held in his hands, the manual on the desk before him, his bloodstream coursing with caffeine, fingers plugged into his ears to block out any external auditory distractions. There he sat, trying, really genuinely trying, to focus on the text before him, reading line after line, climbing the mountains of nouns, verbs, adjectives, and adverbs (in his own language, no less) all printed so clearly on the page, but before he reached the end of even a single paragraph he'd realize that his attention had stopped along the trail and was no longer with him, forcing him to turn back to the beginning and start again. And again. And again. He tried mouthing the words, as if verbalizing the gibberish might give it some familiarity, but always he'd lose focus somewhere between the left and right margin, his brain like a whiteboard on which he was trying to write with a dried-up marker.

And then, from behind the foggy foothills, the insecurities would reemerge. Trouble was, they were no longer hidden. In the months since Davis had taken the job, they'd been on the move and had now set up camp out in the open, where they had been busy unpacking their previously covered wagons and spreading out all of his many fears and inadequacies for all passersby to inspect.

As Davis sat there trying—and failing—to mentally ingest the interstices of the various pieces of marine science equipment, his mind wandered back to the idea of his innate stupidity, to the fact that he had no business being out there. And yet out there he most definitely was. And out there he most definitely needed to be. To remind himself of the reason, he reached in his pocket and brought out the two zeppelin-shaped pills, one orange, the other yellow, and set them on the table. Together, they constituted a one-day supply, the retail value of which was $120.00. Multiply that times the number of days in the year, and then times the number of years in, say, a decade (although his math skills were not developed enough to enable him to crunch such numbers without the aid of a calculator), and the motivation for keeping the job again became vivid. So, in spite of the anxiety it caused him, he realized that he'd better figure out a way to pull it off, had better figure out a way to push the settlers back into the foothills or at least pretend they were not there. And yet, how to do that? And if successful, how long could his insecurities possibly be contained? There were already people like Maureen and Worm and the marine science technician he'd just been dealing with who saw through him. How long until they did something about it? How long until one of them exposed him to someone with some real power?

He looked again at the pills. Failure was not an option. How did the line from Macbeth go? . . . *screw your courage to the sticking place, and we'll not fail.*

Great.

Words of comfort from one doomed, fraudulent queen to another.

Chapter 16

After dinner that evening, Worm again poked his head into Davis's
cubicle. "C'mon dude, let's get drunk." Davis minimized his solitaire screen and followed Worm up the stairs. The caption on the
back of Worm's shirt: *Nobody died when Clinton lied.* They both
went back to their respective cabins, grabbed jackets, and then ren-
dezvoused again by the door. Worm went out on deck first, Davis
followed. The sky was clear and a brisk wind bit into them.

"You got any cash?" Worm asked as they descended the gangway. Davis instinctively felt for his wallet, which he still carried in
his pocket, along with his car keys and cell phone, even though all
three items had become useless the minute they'd left port.

"Yeah, I've got some cash."

"Good, because you have to buy whatever you want to drink
from the little souvenir shop and it closes in five minutes."

With that as incentive, the two hurried along the pier and up the
snowy hillside to the station entrance. Inside, Davis followed
Worm through the maze of hallways until they reached a small
closet. The walls were lined with shelves of liquor and wine, cartons of cigarettes, baseball caps, T-shirts, and postcards. At a table
in the corner sat a girl who, by the look of her bored and put out
expression, Davis could only conclude had drawn the short straw
and was working there against her will. She wore a heavy fleece

jacket and a long stocking cap. She was busy knitting and did not raise her head when they entered.

Davis selected a fifth of bourbon and a baseball cap emblazoned with the station name, paid for them, and then stood looking at postcards while Worm lingered over the selection of Chilean wines. They paid for the items in American currency and, purchases in hand, ascended a staircase to the second level and found themselves in the TV room Davis had visited earlier that day. A movie was playing on the flat screen and several people were lounging around drinking beer and, curiously enough, knitting. Worm and Davis walked toward the double bar doors, which were now unlocked, swung them open, and entered.

Inside, a pool game was going on, two of the Filipinos playing against two of the ship's crew. From somewhere unseen, a speaker was blaring Lynyrd Skynyrd. Over in one corner, gathered around Maureen, was the science party from the cruise.

Worm went behind the bar and got a corkscrew and some glasses. He filled the glasses with ice and handed one to Davis. They both poured themselves hefty tumblers of their respective alcohols. Davis drank his down before the ice even had a chance to cool the liquid. Then he poured another, twirled the contents with his index finger, and took a look around. The surroundings were similar to any number of American dive bars Davis had visited in his thirty-four years on the planet. So similar that he had to periodically remind himself where he was. Such reminders came often, since any time someone opened the door to the balcony, where they were forced to go in order to smoke, a blast of Antarctic air flooded the bar and caused all conversation to momentarily cease.

Davis followed Worm over to a corner of the bar where a group from the vessel had congregated. Perched on a stool in the center was Artaud. Around him were his three undergrads, the hairy troll man with the picture-tube glasses, and Maureen, who was drinking what looked to Davis's trained eye like a glass full of scotch.

It was her second scotch, actually. Technically some might call it her fourth, since in just about any bar anywhere the amount she'd poured into her highball glass would have been considered a double. Unlike most people, however, alcohol didn't fuzz Maureen's perceptions. On the contrary, drinking seemed to heighten them, made her more aware, almost acutely so, of the underlying motivations of the other human beings around her. She referred to this mental state brought on by the rapid consumption of alcohol as her sixth sense. Most other people would probably call it something else (delusional paranoia comes to mind), but when Maureen drank scotch, it was, to her, as if all the clouds had been blown out of the way and she could finally see the mountain range she needed to conquer. Best of all, with enough scotch in her system, she felt fearless, bold, focused. And it was in that frame of mind, drink in hand, standing in that bar on the bottom of the world, that she fixed her gaze on what she perceived to be the competition: the two girls and one fey boy who were then gazing at Artaud with the adoring eyes that children their age usually reserved for pop stars. She looked at the blonde, Kristi, the one with the freckled nose, a nose that wrinkled up like a pig's snout whenever she laughed. The one who had not, Maureen now knew, been impregnated by a boy known as J_Dude. It should have been comforting to Maureen to know that the girl had a boyfriend at home but it was not, for if there was one thing that she had learned in all of her years as one of the Frozen Chosen it was that Antarctica was like a high-latitude Las Vegas: What happened South of 60° (and plenty did) stayed South of 60°. For that reason she knew that in spite of Kristi's "feelings" for J_Dude, in spite of her brush with accidental pregnancy, the little slut would probably have no qualms whatsoever about jumping into bed with Artaud or anyone else she took a liking to. She was probably just out of her teens, barely legal, as they say, yet already she knew just how to use those juvenile tits to her advantage. And then there was the way she tilted her hips out to the left, cocked her head to the right, and pulled down her pouty lower lip with her index finger. So coy, such a vulgar move, and yet one that Maureen felt oddly envious of, wishing that she herself had known about it and could have employed it when she'd been that age. Instead, she'd spent her youthful Friday and Saturday evenings in the campus computer lab honing her skills and providing masturbation fodder for all the geeky, pimple-faced TAs. Damn it! Even just looking at the girl made Maureen feel irritated—like she had a poppy seed caught in her teeth and no toothpick, or like she'd swallowed a pill sideways without the aid of water and it had become lodged in her esophagus. But worst of all, looking at nubile young Kristi made Maureen feel, well, old.

She shifted her gaze to Meghan, the heavier of the two girls: Nothing to worry about there. Why, she wondered, did girls like that insist on wearing low-rise jeans, and with thong underwear, no less? Had there not been a mirror in the dressing room when she'd tried them on? Her guts were cascading over the waistband, and one could only imagine how deep that butt floss was wedged up into her crack. Too disgusting to think about, and yet once the image became embedded in Maureen's brain, she found it difficult to banish.

She shook her head, took another drink of scotch, and looked at the boy. The boy who, she knew, had a justifiably suspicious and jealous boyfriend back home. He was attractive, no denying that, with those smooth Italian features, the biceps he was obviously proud of and felt compelled, in spite of the fact that it was fourteen degrees below zero, to display in a tight, short-sleeved shirt. And yet why was he a threat? When Artaud was with her, he was a very convincing heterosexual. In fact, just that afternoon, when they had both been able to sneak away for half an hour while the others were at Chicken Time, she had been given cause to remark on the skill of his technique, so different from all the other men she had been with, so considerate of her needs, of what made her feel good. His needs were almost secondary and, indeed, she could not recall him having climaxed. Instead, he seemed to derive immense pleasure from seeing just how much pleasure he could coax from her. It was selfless, and yet also somehow incredibly self-centered.

She felt a hand circle around her back. She looked over at Artaud and he gave her a little wink.

"You look deep in thought," he said, and his comment made her immediately self-conscious, afraid of seeming broodish and moody. Again, she shook her head, forced a smile, and said, "Oh, no, not at all! I was just thinking of some jokes I'd heard."

"Jokes?" Artaud said, surprise evident in his voice. "Solemn Nordic types like you don't tell jokes!"

The remark stung. Solemn? Did she really come off like that? And what did he mean calling her a Nordic type? That meant depressing. That meant she was tall and mannish, didn't it? Suddenly aware that her brow had pinched together in the middle, she took a breath and consciously tried to relax it. *There. Relax. Be fun! He likes you when you're fun.*

"Oh, I know lots of jokes!" she exclaimed, a bit too eagerly. "You'd be surprised at all the jokes I know."

He laughed and patted her on the shoulder. It was a friendly, almost condescending pat and it stung as much as his earlier remark. *Okay,* she said to herself, stepping into the role of life coach. *You're okay, Maureen. Relax. Be funny. You are a lighthearted gal. You are full of mirth!* She took another gulp of scotch, flipped back her hair in a demonstration of how carefree and fun she was, and then scrolled through the files of her memory, eventually retrieving her jokes. "Okay," she said, "okay, I've got it. Are you ready?"

He nodded. She looked around at the small group, pleased to see that all eyes were on her.

"Okay. How does a penguin make pancakes?"

There was a pause as they waited for the punch line.

"With its flippers! Get it? Flippers! Like little spatulas."

"Ugh," said Artaud, but he was smiling.

"That's baaaad," said Andrew.

Kristi was doing that thing with her lip and her index finger again. Disgusting.

"What?" said Meghan, a bewildered expression on her moon face. "I don't get it."

That made everyone laugh more than the punch line so, without hesitation, Maureen popped out another one:

"What did the sea say to the iceberg?"

They all thought for a minute. Kristi stuck the finger in, knuckle deep; Artaud stroked his chin; Meghan shrugged.

"Nothing," Maureen said, "it just waved."

Silence. None of them got it.

"It didn't *say* anything," Maureen added, "it just *waved*. Get it? The sea *waved*."

"Ohhhh," Artaud groaned, and the groan was soon echoed by his minions.

"I think," Artaud said, effortlessly removing his left arm from Maureen's hip and encircling his right around Meghan's, "we've either had too much to drink, or not enough." Then, turning to

Meghan, he whispered: "Why don't we open a few more bottles of wine." The girl blushed and gave an eager nod, the kind of nod an obese cocker spaniel might give were a treat attached to a string to be bounced in front of its nose.

"A round for all of us!" Worm called after them, hoping to keep Artaud away even longer and thus allow him unobstructed access to Maureen. He turned, his heart racing, and attempted a smile, but she was not looking at him; her attention was focused somewhere on the floor next to him. For a moment the group was silent. Two pool balls clacked together and then one clattered into a pocket. A depressing and depressingly familiar Eagle's song (one that was surely playing simultaneously in any number of other cheap American bars in the world) whined on from the unseen speaker. The large window showed the white haze of an illuminated blizzard.

Maureen's gaze followed the planks of the wood floor from her feet to the bar, where Meghan and Artaud were standing. Her eyes traveled up their legs and focused, laser-like, on Artaud's arm, still fastened around that mass of Meghan's back fat. The sight made her feel as if a capsule filled with poison had just burst open inside her. She knew it was lethal, but she knew of no antidote to stop it from coursing through her veins.

Worm and Davis had approached just as the punch line of Maureen's second joke had been delivered. They hadn't heard it, but they had heard enough to realize that it had fallen flat. Everyone in the group—Maureen, Kristi, that devastatingly handsome Andrew—already had that rosy-cheeked look of inebriation, and the attention of all seemed to have followed Artaud and Meghan to the bar. The conversation flagged.

"I've got a joke," said Davis, eager to break the ice that was rapidly forming over the group since his arrival. And he did have a joke; he had several of them—and all coincidentally related to Antarctica. They were, of course, the idiotic jokes his nephew had e-mailed to him that morning. They were groaners, granted, the kind appreciated only by children and the very drunk, so it seemed he had the perfect audience.

"Okay," Davis began: "How does a penguin make pancakes?"

Kristi removed her finger from her mouth with a pop and rolled her eyes. Maureen swallowed the last of her scotch. Her voice hoarse and lifeless, she said, "With its flippers."

Only Worm laughed. "That's good!" he said, beaming at Maureen. "Stupid, but good."

"We, like, just heard that one two seconds ago," Kristi said, shifting her weight from one hip to the other. "And it wasn't even that funny the first time."

"Well, how about this one," Davis said, launching into the one about the sea and the wave. Again, they stopped him before he could even get out the first sentence.

Artaud and Meghan returned with an open bottle and began filling everyone's glasses. They all clinked the cups together and then Artaud, slipping his arm back around Maureen's waist, said, "Tell us another, my little ice goddess."

Her eyelids fluttered drunkenly. "How," she purred, "do penguins drink?"

Davis knew the answer, and was about to shout it out, but Maureen was faster.

"Out of beakers," she said. "Get it, beak-ers?"

"Brilliant!" Worm said, laughing out of all proportion to the joke.

Maureen went on:

What's a penguin's favorite salad?

Why did the penguin cross the road?

Who's the penguin's favorite aunt?

Each joke was more stupid than the one preceding it, but they all laughed and groaned. All but Davis, that is, who had read each and every one of those jokes—and in just the same order of delivery—in the e-mail from his nephew. It was coincidental, no doubt, and Davis thought nothing of it. The planet was shrinking, news traveled fast, and how many jokes about Antarctica could there be? Maybe Maureen also liked to read *Highlights* or the *Mini Page,* one of which had obviously been the source of the humor. Mildly defeated, he zipped up his jacket, pulled on his hood, and went out onto the balcony to smoke.

After Davis left, the jokey group dissolved. Artaud walked over to schmooze with the captain, Kristi and Andrew teamed up for a hopelessly lopsided game of pool against the far superior Filipinos, and that left Maureen standing with Meghan, who was busy feeding from a bag of potato chips. The crunching sound of Meghan's drunken, open-mouthed mastication, combined with the crinkle of the cellophane bag each time she poked her plump mitt into it, irritated Maureen, and she glared at the girl. Tipsy Meghan, crumbs descending from her mouth onto her ample bosom, misinterpreted Maureen's glare as a look of hunger and offered her the open bag. Maureen declined with a dismissive wave of disgust and then, quite needlessly and without provocation, or even a conscious desire on her part to be intentionally cruel, said, "Do you really think you need those?"

Meghan stopped crunching, her mouth open.

"I mean really, those jeans seem a little tight already."

Before she could turn away, a single, mascara-infused tear pendulously swelled in the corner of Meghan's left eye. A moment later it succumbed to the force of gravity, which was still the same, somehow, even at the bottom of the world, and rolled down her plump cheek, leaving behind a narrow skid mark. This single black tear was followed by many, many more—twin rivers of petroleum sludge—but Maureen didn't have a chance to see them because as soon as Meghan recovered from the initial shock of Maureen's words, she dropped the bag of chips and ran, coatless, out on to the balcony, where another soul, who was also familiar with medicating his feelings of inadequacy by ingesting large amounts of carbohydrates, stood silently smoking in the bitter night air.

Davis had been watching the snow silently fall to the accompaniment of the gentle hum of the ship's motor when the peace of the night was shattered by Meghan's weepy entrance. She ran to the rail of the balcony, gripped it with both hands, and stood sobbing, her shoulders heaving. At first, she didn't notice Davis, who was standing farther down along the rail, but then she must have smelled the smoke because she turned and, seeing a friend in fatness, ran to him and began sobbing on his chest. At first, he held his arms out, Christ-like, but, unlike Christ, he knew not what to do with either the lit cigarette or her unfettered emotions. WWJD? Davis wondered, and then pitched his cigarette butt (in flagrant violation of the Antarctic Treaty) over the balcony edge and put his arms around the shivering girl.

"Why is she su-su-such a *bitch?*" Meghan sobbed. Davis did not need to ask which *she* Meghan was referring to. No, all he wondered was what *she* could have said to provoke such a response.

"I know I'm not *skinny!* An, an, and... *blond!* And won't ever be as smart or pretty, but *whhyyy?!*"

Her sobs, whether from the cold or from an overdose of drunken melodrama, were becoming convulsive, so Davis unzipped the front of his Carhartt jacket and, as foreign, distasteful, and just plain inappropriate as it felt, let her snuggle herself inside, her enormous breasts compressing against his stomach as her plump arms encircled his torso.

"I, I can't go back inside!" she cried. "I just can't!"

Davis looked down at her raccoon eyes and nodded. "C'mon," he said, and together they went out into the blizzard and descended the icy balcony stairs.

Chapter 17

Some people enjoy flossing their teeth. Very few, however, enjoy flossing the teeth of others. This is because if the floss is not extracted at just the right angle, spit, bits of food, and who knows what all can come flying back at the face of the flossee. But more about that in a minute. . . .

She lay on her side and stared at his profile as he slept; the circular canyon of his ear, the stubble-covered jawline; and beneath the stubble, only visible if you were as close as she was then, the faint line of a scar, accented on either side by small, almost imperceptible pink dots where the surgeon's needle and thread had gone in and come out. She followed the stubble up the side of his face as it lengthened into his hair—thick, black, low on his forehead, forming a widow's peak above his left eye, his eyeballs gently rolling beneath their lids. Continuing her visual descent, she focused on his nose, large and crooked, probably broken at the same time he got the scar. And then to his lips, slightly parted, admitting and then expelling air.

She inventoried his face—eyes, ears, nose, chin, stubble, scar, lips—and assigned a value to each part, hoping to determine the total sum, a quantifiable reason for her attraction to him, but it just didn't add up. There was, as they say, no accounting for it, and that irritated her. He was handsome (a fact diluted by his vanity), intelligent and respected in his field (although undeniably arrogant, and not very innovative), and liberal in his distribution of compliments to her (although some of them were not quite as practiced or convincing as they might have been). She knew all of those parenthetical shortcomings, and yet none of them made any difference. She was hooked, and the hook was barbed and set painfully deep; she could not wriggle free.

Never one to dwell on emotions, she sought to explain her infatuation through science, and to that end she had two disciplines to choose from: biology and psychology. Biology defined her behavior with the word *instinct*. A fixed action pattern that magnetically pulled her toward strong, healthy, and wealthy looking providers who could, if things were to progress that far, pass on to any of their potential offspring a genetic dowry of broad shoulders, a square jaw, muscular forearms, and above-average intelligence. The biological tug, primal and yet entirely alien to her on anything other than an academic level, was heightened by an image that reappeared in her mind more and more as time passed—the image of her desiccating ovaries. She wasn't young, granted, but she certainly wasn't past childbearing years, and it annoyed her that she gave so much attention to the life span of her womb. After all, she was just what her mother had planned for her to be—independent, well off, self-confident—why, then, did she feel she needed someone to complete her? And why, of all people, did she want it to be the one whose profile she was then gazing at?

Those questions were answered, at least in part, by the other, more troubling branch of science—the science of Freud. The science that, in spite of her mother's conditioning (or perhaps because of it), made her attracted to him because he resembled her father.

From the age of four Maureen had been taught to distrust men. She had been taught this by her mother, an embittered woman who, as a young student at St. Mary's Academy for girls, conceived Maureen on the less-than-immaculate carpeting of her English teacher's apartment, a place she had gone, ostensibly, to discuss her essay on *Silas Marner*. Once there, it had taken only twenty-five minutes and a small gin and tonic to lower both her inhibitions and her panties, and to seal her fate.

After Maureen's birth her parents had lived together in relative harmony. Of course, it had been a rocky start. There had been the inevitable legal threats when the pregnancy first came to light, but once those died down, and once the English teacher's broken nose (courtesy of his future father-in-law) had healed, Maureen's parents had, in fact, married and settled down into a tidy domestic situation: Her father continued to teach English and her mother stayed home and raised Maureen.

That all changed one autumn day when Maureen was retrieved from preschool by a large dowager neighbor (an unusual circumstance) who drove her home in her lilac-scented Buick. When they arrived, Maureen found her mother inconsolable, her father gone, and her grandfather pacing the apartment punching his fist into his palm.

In the ensuing months Maureen's mother was forced, by her palm-punching father, to do the sensible thing (sensible for an uneducated single mother in the mid-1970s) and become a dental hygienist, which, after a few months of study, she did.

The subsequent years—years spent peering into gaping caverns of steaming halitosis; cleaning, polishing and yes, flossing, the human stalactites and stalagmites more commonly known as teeth—were hard years indeed. And Maureen's mother never forgot, as she was pelted with tiny bits of broccoli and strands of partially digested chicken, that it was a man who was responsible for her situation. A man she had trusted and loved, a man for whom she had sacrificed her education and youth. The injustice of it, and the anger she felt toward herself for her own youthful gullibility, grated on her day after day as she ruthlessly chipped away at the tartar on someone else's teeth.

Seeing no way to remedy her situation, Maureen's mother figured the best thing she could do—the best way she could take revenge on her errant husband and strike out at all errant men—was to raise her blond beautiful daughter, the pearl in the muck of her life, to be wholly self-sufficient, to not need a man; to be, justifiably or not, suspicious and wary of all members of the masculine sex.

And to construct such an independent being, she had developed a plan. A plan that involved strict adherence to the following rules:

- No school dances or parties.
- No fraternizing with other girls unless they were members of the math or science club.
- Mandatory participation in individual sports (tennis, swimming, golf) to foster competitiveness.
- No grade below an A.
- No cutting her hair, and only minimal use of cosmetics (usually chosen and applied by her mother).
- No off-campus "conferences" with male staff members.

In addition, Maureen was taught to believe that all the usual things that girls reveled in, namely boys and talking on the phone with other girls *about* boys, were so far beneath her as to not even merit consideration.

Her mother's goal was to mold her daughter into a beautiful, perfect, and completely inaccessible monument, something to be placed on a pedestal, something to be worshipped from afar but never touched. And the plan was largely successful . . but, like Dr. Frankenstein and his monster, what she succeeded in creating was a little different than what she'd imagined. Oh, Maureen did become successful in her career and was financially independent, so that part of the experiment was a success, but the girl was also a confused hybrid of brutality, inexperience, and suppressed neediness.

She looked again at Artaud in profile and wondered about her father. The similarities between the two men were obvious—both academics, both seductive, both emotionally distant—and those common traits only made the one next to her now all the more attractive. And it was that knowledge—the knowledge that she was being pulled around on an instinctual leash instead of by something mathematically rational—that she feared more than anything else.

Chapter 18

Davis couldn't remember where he had been when it happened, most likely in the galley on one of his bi-hourly snack breaks, or on an aimless yet determined-looking walk around the decks, but wherever it was, he had left his desk without locking his computer screen. Worse, he had not closed or even minimized the file that had been open, which was the official-looking template he filled with his own personal writing.

Shortly after he'd arrived on the vessel, Davis had developed a system to write his book. This system involved taking an existing document for, say, the bottle arrangement on the Conductivity Temperature Depth Rosette, or the instructions for sonobuoy deployment, and deleting all of the body text from it but leaving the pictures and the headings. He then put his own writing where the body text had been and in that way looked hard at work on Official Marine Science Documentation and no one was the wiser.

Sometimes Davis's text consisted of long e-mail messages he wanted to send, sometimes they were just rambling journal entries or stream-of-consciousness dialogues with himself, but this time he had actually been working on his book. Not the actual book, per se, but rather a protracted documentation of the agonizing thrashing about and self-flagellation that preceded any actual writing. What he had was a messy page of possible plot avenues, so numerous and twisting that they were more like cloverleaf freeways, and line after quotation-enclosed line of his futile attempts at dialogue. Although, if one were to be a stickler about such things, it should be referred to as *dogalogue,* since his creative resolve had again collapsed into laziness and he'd returned to characters of the canine variety. What made the document even more bizarre was the fact that it was punctuated with pictures of marine science equipment and would randomly change from block text to, say, a numbered list or a flowchart.

The reason that he had felt the need to develop his elaborate system was mostly because of Maureen, who would appear behind him, ghost-like, several times a day in the Environmental Room, hovering around his little workspace, always under the guise of looking for something in one of the cabinets. While looking, she'd make seemingly idle inquiries about what, exactly, he was working on, and would then watch him squirm as he tried to come up with an answer. Davis knew that she knew he didn't have anything to do, knew that she knew he wasn't qualified for his job, knew that she took a fiendish delight in quizzing him about his science background and work history, often in the presence of other crew members or science personnel. He knew that it was all a cruel ploy to humiliate him, to let him know that she was on to him. And Davis had to hand it to her, she was better at it than any junior high bully he had ever encountered.

Returning to his Environmental Room hovel, cookies in hand, Davis turned the corner and saw Artaud, leaning over the computer screen, examining what was displayed there. It was one of those moments in life that demanded one of two possible responses: 1) complete nonchalance (indicating that he had nothing to hide), or 2) indignant anger at the obvious violation of his personal space. Instead, Davis chose a third option: Like a burglar caught in the sudden blaze of electric light from an overhead chandelier as he attempted to stuff silver candlesticks into his little black burglar's bag, Davis froze. It was a response that cemented his guilt.

"You're a writer?" Artaud asked, his mouth curved in a devious grin. It seemed remarkable to Davis that the man had no qualms about having been caught reading something that was clearly not intended for his eyes. Davis remained frozen. Better, he figured, to stay silent and not further incriminate himself.

"This," Artaud said, pointing to the screen, "this is not a manual."

Again, no response from Davis, just a smile, a smile as inscrutable as the Buddha's.

Artaud pressed on: "So it's a book?"

"It's supposed to be." Davis sighed, leaning back into the hall to see if anyone else might be listening.

"If that's the case," Artaud said, his voice containing trace amounts of sarcasm, "I think there might be some issues with the formatting."

"I'll put it away," Davis said, moving into the room and closing the laptop. "I had some free time while I was waiting for some documentation to be reviewed, so I thought I'd do a little writing of my own while I was waiting."

"I see."

Artaud was still grinning, but only just, and what that grin meant, Davis could not tell. "I'm a bit of a lapsed wordsmith myself," Artaud confessed. "Nothing serious, just some Antarctic thrillers that are stuffed in a drawer somewhere and are probably better off staying there. Ever been published?" he asked, inclining his head toward the laptop. "That looks pretty serious."

"It is serious," Davis said. "The situation, I mean. The book's more than a year overdue."

"So it will be published?"

"If I finish it, which is a big 'if' at this point."

"Have you published anything else?"

Davis always hated this question because it forced him to bring up the ridiculous titles (which were never of his choosing but, rather, the choice of the publisher and sales department) and try to spit them out without sounding like a pretentious ass. With that in mind, Davis gave his stock answer:

"Nothing you would have heard of."

"Try me," Artaud said, folding his arms across his chest. "I read a lot."

Davis sighed and mentioned some of the titles in his literary canon.

"Kids' books?"

"The preferred term is children's literature, but yes."

"Did you write that other one, oh, what was it called? The one with the pug and the collie?"

"Reigning Cats and Dogs."

"Yes! That's it!"

Dead is the author who doesn't feel at least a small egotistical thrill on hearing that one of his books has actually been read. Davis was so excited that he wanted to throw his arms around Artaud and kiss him on both cheeks. The feeling was short-lived, however, and was soon replaced by suspicion. He wanted to believe it, but the coincidence was extreme, and thus extremely unbelievable. . . . Wasn't it? Things like that happened often in nineteenth-century novels and B-grade movies, but not usually in situations like his.

"I bought that book for my kids last Christmas."

"Oh?" Davis said, his skepticism thawing somewhat.

"They loved it. And I did too. I found it a really effective method of introducing children to science."

Davis squirmed. He loved the praise but was unable to bear it. It was like being tickled—pleasurable at first, but then quickly crossing the line into agony.

"Wow," Artaud said, his awe seemingly genuine. "I can't believe you wrote that." Davis felt sweat emerging from his hairline, and he knew his face had turned red.

"Really. You're very talented. I'm not quite sure why you're here. . . ."

The tone of that last statement was startlingly similar to Maureen's, and it immediately reignited Davis's suspicions. "How do you mean?" he asked.

"I mean writing manuals on a research vessel doesn't seem the place for an author—and a published one, at that."

"Well, those credit card companies do seem to like their monthly payments."

"Ahh," Artaud concurred, "the curse of economic necessity."

"Yes."

"But I would think being published—and having so many books out there—well, I'd think that you'd be making money from it."

"Yeah, you'd think so," Davis said, "but you'd be incorrect in your thinking."

Davis had long ago ceased to be surprised at how the published were viewed by the unpublished—as people who had finally reached a pinnacle of fame and success where money was no longer a problem. Such people had read only the headlines about big advances given to a few, usually already famous, authors or had heard about someone inking a six-figure deal for the film rights, never realizing that the vast majority of published writers processed their words in nearly complete obscurity, making little more than a third-world wage, if, in fact, they made anything at all. Then there were those writers like Davis, with little or no royalties coming in, for whom writing actually cost money. Writing in the red, so to speak; an expensive hobby.

"Someone with your talent," Artaud continued, "shouldn't squander it writing technical manuals, that's for sure."

Would he never *stop?* Davis squirmed. Would he never *shut up?* The embarrassment was unbearable.

"I hope you'll be able to find the time to work on your art while you're out here. And don't worry," he said, putting an arm around Davis's shoulder and pointing at the computer. "Your secret's safe with me."

Chapter 19

Davis was just about to experience one of those rare occasions in the world of online gaming, a winning hand of solitaire, when Worm entered the Environmental Room, forcing Davis to close the window and abandon the game.

"I went through this seismic document," Worm said, dropping the stack of papers on Davis's desk. "And it's fucked."

Davis, who was unsure what exactly the word "seismic" meant, nodded in agreement, his attention still focused on the abandoned game.

"I've fixed most of the text," Worm went on, "but the pictures are crap. We could use some new ones."

Again, Davis nodded, although at this point his nods were as automatic as one of those toy dashboard dogs whose head bobs in time with the motion of the car.

"You've got a camera, right?"

Nod, nod, nod.

"Then I'm thinking you should be out on the back deck taking some pictures when we're deploying the gear. You should probably do the same thing when we bring it back on board and take it apart."

"Okay," Davis said, his enthusiasm elevating somewhat at the thought of actually having something to do.

"I already took some pictures while the guys and I were putting the guns together, but we'll all be working our asses off getting the shit in and out of the water so it'd be better if you could be out there taking pics, *comprende?*"

"Sure."

"Cool. We should start putting it out after Chicken Time, probably around fourteen hundred. I'll give you a heads up a few minutes before so you can get suited up."

Worm turned to leave but then had another thought and returned.

"Do you . . . know what this equipment does?" he asked.

Again, what to say? If he said yes, the lie would be transparent, obvious. If he said no, he would further reveal his incompetence. The head of the dashboard dog made a circular, non-committal motion.

"Yeah, I kind of thought that might be the case. You want me to give you a little walk-through before we do this?" Worm asked. "So you've got some idea what we need pictures of?"

"That would be helpful," Davis said, managing to sound only somewhat desperate.

"C'mon, then," Worm said, "I'll take you back now and we can walk through it."

Davis put on his fleece and hat and followed Worm, who was still clad in nothing but a T-shirt, down the hallway, past the labs, through the Aquarium Room, to the door of the back deck. There, they put on hard hats and orange float coats and stepped outside. The sky was pale blue and the sea an appropriate navy blue, but the air between them was filled with the gaseous smell of the ship's exhaust that cascaded down from the smokestacks. Standing out there, the entire platform undulating beneath him, waves washing over the deck, Davis felt much more exposed and vulnerable, and realized that were he to fall overboard, the thin little float coat he was wearing would provide about as much protection from the icy water as one of Worm's T-shirts.

Worm, whose sea legs were more developed than Davis's, pranced across the tilting deck to a series of Y-shaped poles, spaced about ten feet apart from each other. Hanging from these, like a giant boa constrictor, was a thick, black rubber hose with a series of stainless steel cylinders dangling from its low points.

"These are the guns," Worm said, knocking on one of the cylinders with his fist.

"They look more like cans," Davis said. "Why're they called guns?"

"Because once they're in the water, compressed air gets fed into them through the air lines inside this rubber tube, called an umbilical. When the air pressure builds up to a certain level, a trigger goes off and the air fires out like a shot—or like a giant burp or a fart. In the old days they used to use dynamite instead of compressed air, but that got too dangerous. Anyway, it still makes a big boom this way."

"Why?"

Worm looked at Davis the way most parents would regard an inquisitive two-year-old. Davis had seen the look on his brother's face numerous times, and it was usually provoked by some baffling question like "Why is dirt brown?" A question to which there is an answer, just not one that can be easily understood by a two-year-old.

"O-kay," Worm sighed, pausing to compose his answer. "The air, when it explodes in the water, sends sound waves down through the water column. Some of these are of such a frequency that they'll even go into the ocean floor. You following?"

"Yes."

"Okay. Good. Once it hits the bottom it gets reflected back up, sort of like an echo. Got it?"

The dog nodded. And it was making sense to Davis; he just wondered how much Worm was dumbing it down for his benefit.

"Good, then that takes us over to the next part," he said, and led Davis over to something that looked like a giant fly-fishing reel. It was yellow, about the size of a tractor tire, and had a bright orange rubber hose wound around it.

"This here," Worm said, giving the hose a pat, "is the streamer. So called because it trails off behind the boat like, well, a streamer. Or like the tail of a kite. Inside this baby," he said, giving the hose another pat, "are a bunch of tiny hydrophones. They capture the echoes bouncing back up from the shot. The amount of time it takes for the echo to come back up tells the structure of the rock and sediment that's down there."

Worm must have sensed Davis's confusion at that last part because he made a wiping motion with his hands, as if trying to erase it, adding, "Never mind about that last part. Okay, so we got the echoes coming back and getting recorded by the hydrophones, right?"

Nod, nod.

"Okay, good. Then those recordings go from the hydrophones back to the lab, where they get processed and the results get printed out."

"Like a picture?" Davis asked.

"Sort of. More like an x-ray because it shows what's underneath the seafloor, too. And that could be anything from a different type of rock, to layers of sediment, or even oil and gas deposits."

"What's Artaud looking for?"

"Jesus, who the fuck knows. Probably his brain. Or his dick," Worm muttered, but then arrested his editorializing and returned to the topic. "So anyway, those x-ray-like pictures are used by geologists to map what's down there and to help them figure out how old certain areas of the earth are, which areas of the earth are expanding, how fast they're expanding, and how to locate the best places to drill for oil."

Davis nodded his comprehension and the tutorial then shifted away from marine geophysics to the comparably abstract explanation of how to operate the digital camera. Once Davis was sufficiently enlightened, he was shown exactly where to stand later that afternoon in order to get the best pictures.

The midday Chicken Time came and went, and shortly thereafter Davis took his position on the helo deck, camera in hand, ready to photograph the excitement that was then unfolding on the crowded back deck. Artaud and all of his orange-suited crew were there, along with all of the MTs, most of the ETs, and even some of the vessel crew. Since it was November and they were in the extreme Southern Ocean, there was no telling what time it was. The sun made a slow circular orbit throughout the night and day but never rose and never set. It was, Davis imagined, what the light would be like in purgatory.

To further confuse the concept of time, there were five Chicken Times per day to accommodate the 24/7 work schedule. For Davis, that meant he was expected to be working from noon to midnight, each and every day. Others did a midnight to noon shift, and still others worked from 6:00 A.M. to 6:00 P.M., or vice versa, thus ensuring an almost uninterrupted movement of people in and out of the galley, some eating breakfast, others eating dinner, and still others, lunch.

"What I want you to do," Worm shouted as he and Davis stood in the howling wind looking down at the frenzy of people below, "is stand up here and take as many pictures as you can."

As usual, Davis nodded. Worm had already told him all this twice.

"And if you see any wildlife," he said, "seals, whales, dolphins, penguins—anything other than fish—I want you to switch over to video and get some footage, all right?"

"Yes."

"And make sure you get both the animal and the seismic gear in there, okay?"

"Okay."

"And if you can," he said with a wink, "get Artaud in the frame, too."

"Okay."

"Cool beans," Worm said, and then slid sideways down the metal railing to the back deck, his pointy knit cap making him look even more elfin than usual.

At the time, none of Worm's instructions struck Davis as unusual. He had gone so long on this trip without any guidance that finally having someone assign him something specific to do came as a relief, if for no other reason than it would give him something to put in his weekly report. With that in mind, he happily snapped away, taking picture after picture of the students and crew as they struggled to get the massive rubber umbilical and its sagging metal teats into the water. The process was slow, and Davis, growing bored and cold, yawned repeatedly. They seemed to be having some problems getting the guns to fire correctly and so kept test-firing them on deck, barking commands into the radios and then firing them again. Shortly after they gave the signal, there was a hiss followed by a loud pop. Davis was far enough away that he felt the explosion more than he heard it—like when the drummer in an orchestra thumped on a kettle drum with one of those giant Q-tips— and as soon as it was done the people on deck removed their earplugs, talked back and forth via radio with the people in the lab, and then, tools in hand, approached the dangling guns and made more adjustments.

The ship was holding station, meaning that the engines were alternately thrusting backward and forward in order to keep the boat in roughly the same spot. Small bergs floated by on the starboard side. On one of them, a group of penguins stood, staring dumbly up at the giant yellow boat, unsure whether or not to be afraid. Unlike most birds, penguins seem fearless of humans. Their primary predators—leopard seals, killer whales, etc., are in the water, so they are unaccustomed to feeling threatened from anything on land. Davis took the opportunity provided by their ignorance of basic human nature and snapped several pictures of them as they floated past. While he was thus occupied, there was, coming from the port side, a sudden loud hiss, almost like one of the air lines had burst. Davis jumped, gave a startled cry, and dropped the camera. He whipped around and his eyes went to the source of the sound. A plume of steam and mist shot up from the water, followed by a slithering gray mass, roughly the size of a bus, that emerged and made an arc on the surface of the water. The smooth arc was briefly interrupted by an erect fin and followed a moment later by an unmistakable fan-shaped tail. Davis picked up the camera and continued to stare gape-mouthed at the water, but the animal did not reappear. The enormity of the thing had been frightening, and he noticed that although he no longer felt cold, the hair on his body was standing on end.

As he continued to stare out at the water, hoping for another sighting, all Davis could think was how what he had seen had been so much more incredible than anything he'd ever seen on TV. Usually real life was a pale facsimile of the version that was created, packaged, and sold by Hollywood. But this whale had been the opposite of that: It had been one of those increasingly rare occasions in life when what you see and experience far surpasses any of your preconceived notions.

The whale surfaced again a little farther off, and this time Davis had the camera ready. He snapped several pictures and even managed to get some video (mostly, he would later find out, of empty ocean). After five minutes without any more sightings, Davis turned his lens once again on the seismic setup on the back deck. He noticed Jerry, Artaud's hairy little assistant, staring up at him. Davis pointed the camera at Jerry, gave him a friendly wave, and snapped his picture, thinking it might be nice for the poor ugly guy to have an action shot for his online dating profile, if, indeed, he had one. But when Davis looked at the image on screen he saw that Jerry had not been smiling. In fact, Jerry had been doing the opposite of smiling, and now, armed with the same sour expression—mouth turned down, eyes narrowed—he was lumbering up the stairs toward Davis. When he reached the top step, Jerry stood teetering for a moment, trying to catch his breath, his hands on the handrail and his eyes on the camera.

"What are you ... doing?" he wheezed, trying to make himself heard over the engines and the roar of the wind.

"I'm taking pictures," Davis yelled, pointing with his mittened hand at the camera.

"Why?"

"For the documentation."

"We don't need this documented!" Jerry shouted.

"But it's my job," Davis said, and then wondered if he should recite the list of reasons for documentation—the beer truck, the lotto winnings, all that.

Jerry unclipped the radio attached to his belt and spoke into it: "Artaud, do you copy? Artaud. Over."

"This is Artaud. Over."

"I think you better come up to the helo deck. Over."

"We're kind of busy down here, Jer." His voice betrayed his annoyance. "Over."

"You better come up here. Over."

A few seconds later Artaud materialized at the top of the steps, a wrench clenched in his fist. His eyes were hidden behind dark sunglasses, the rest of his face was expressionless.

"What's up?" he asked, looking from Jerry to Davis. Davis decided to let Jerry speak since Jerry was the one who seemed to have a problem. Jerry led Artaud a few steps away and they stood with their backs to Davis so he could not hear what was being said. Jerry spoke and Artaud nodded occasionally, the two turned back once to look at Davis and his camera. Artaud then sent Jerry back down to the 01 deck. When he was gone, Artaud approached Davis, put an arm around his shoulder and led him back toward the helo hangar. They went inside and closed the door. This protected them from the wind but increased the engine noise, so although they no longer needed to shout, they still had to speak in loud theatrical tones.

"Listen," Artaud said, removing his sunglasses and looking Davis in the eyes, his face softening. "I don't know that this picture taking is such a good idea."

Again Davis thought of the careless pedestrian, the lotto winner, the caught-in-the-act office porn surfer. . . . "It's for the documentation," he said. "So that the next time they use this equipment they'll have some pictures to guide them on how it's done."

"Yes, yes, I understand. But there are people like me, and like Jerry, who always sail on these cruises, and we're very familiar with the equipment and how it works. It never really changes that much, so there's no real reason for you to spend your time out here. How's the book coming along?" he asked, again draping a congenial arm around Davis's shoulder and leading him across the helo hangar toward the door to the hallway.

The door from the deck creaked open and then slammed, both men turned. Worm entered and was striding toward them.

"What's going on?" he demanded, ripping his sunglasses from his face. Then he seemed to reconsider his tone, and in a softer voice added, "I mean, we're all ready to go. You two should be out on deck."

Davis looked from one to the other, confused.

"Nothing's going on," Artaud said. "Davis is going inside to do some work."

"Oh," Worm said, nodding and trying to appear nonchalant. "I'd asked him to take some pictures out back. For documentation."

There was an awkward moment of silence as the two men stared at one another.

"I don't think Davis needs to be out there," Artaud said, managing to sound diplomatic but firm.

"Hmmm," Worm hummed, placing his thumb on his chin and tapping his upper lip with his index finger. "And why not?"

"Just look at it out there—the sea's getting rough, he's up high. I'm not sure that it's the safest place for him to stand. Also, we've got too much going on as it is. Having another person to keep track of just seems to heighten the risk."

Worm nodded, clenching his jaw and looking from Davis to Artaud. "I think he'll be fine. It's stable enough out there. He's got the railing to hang on to and we can always tie him off, if need be. Besides, we need some pictures for the seismic manual, and that's pretty much why he was sent down here."

That was the first time Davis had heard that particular reason given for his presence on board and he cocked his head to the side, pug-like, trying to remember if Sarah or Jake had specified that as a reason or if something else was going on here.

"Understood," Artaud said. "Understood. I just . . . it's just that I would rather he not be out there taking pictures while we're getting the gear in the water."

Now Worm cocked his own head to the side, bewildered. "I don't get it. Why not?"

"Because I don't want him there," Artaud snapped, "and since I'm the chief scientist, I think I can call this one."

Davis wobbled between the two men, unsure what to do. They continued volleying the issue back and forth for a few moments, but then Artaud picked up his radio and summoned Martin, the MPC.

The conversation ceased while they waited for him to arrive. Artaud crossed his arms on his chest and stared up at a spot on the ceiling. Worm paced back and forth, staring at the floor. Davis stood, not knowing what to do or say, wishing he weren't caught in the middle of whatever was going on.

"What's the trouble?" Martin asked, entering the helo hangar and removing his sunglasses. He looked from one to the other.

Worm and Artaud started speaking over each other, making them both unintelligible.

"Whoa! Whoa!" Martin said. "One at a time." He pointed to Artaud and held an outstretched palm to Worm.

"It's really nothing major," Artaud said. "I just happen to prefer that photographs not be taken while we're deploying the seismic gear."

Worm rolled his eyes.

"O-kay," Martin said, not quite sure what the problem was. "Any reason why not? And who was taking pictures?"

Worm and Artaud both pointed at Davis.

"It's for the documentation!" Worm shouted, his tone shrill and agitated, the elfin hat doing nothing for his credibility. "You know how complicated and dangerous this shit is. We need to document the correct procedure to deploy and retrieve it. We have to have pictures! And that's what we have the tech writer here for, right?"

Davis remembered their first conversation in the Dallas airport. The conversation where Worm had dismissed tech writers as "not needed."

"No," Artaud countered, shaking his head, "I will always be here when we're doing seismic. And if I'm not here, Jerry will be here."

"You're not the only group doing seismic," Worm said.

"Precisely!" said Artaud, emphasizing the point by pounding his right fist into his left palm. "The world of academic science is highly, *highly* competitive, and some of our methods are proprietary and are designed to advance our research—*our* research, not someone else's, and I don't want pictures of what we're doing and how we're doing it distributed to the world." He then looked to Martin and said, "Surely you'll agree I'm not out of line here."

They all stood in silence while Martin thought the thing over.

"He's got a point," Martin said to Worm.

"Oh, Christ! He also knows how controversial this work is," Worm said.

"That has nothing to do with it!" Artaud fired back.

"*Riiight*. Just ask those whales floating tits up in the Gulf of California, or the ones drying out on the beaches in the Bahamas and Canary Islands."

"Nothing's been proven there and you know it. We've been doing seismic down here for years—with no problems at all—until people like you decide to throw gasoline on something that was never anything more than a spark."

"People like me? What's that supposed to mean?"

"Okay, okay," Martin said, silencing them both. "Let's take this to the MPC office."

The three marched out of the helo hangar, leaving Davis bewildered and by himself. He waited for about five minutes, but when they did not return he wandered back outside onto the helo deck and peered over the edge. All work had stopped. The orange-suited students and technicians stood in small groups, talking and rubbing their hands together, the deck rising and falling with the swells.

Since there are few things more exciting than engaging in a forbidden activity, Davis took the camera out of his coat pocket and snapped a few random pictures. He could see nothing that seemed proprietary, or even very interesting, but he snapped away nonetheless, imagining himself as a spy or a member of the paparazzi.

Soon, however, he felt that he wasn't alone and turned to see Jerry standing a few feet behind him. His eyes, too, were hidden from the relentless sunlight by a pair of dark glasses, but Davis knew that behind those lenses Jerry's eyes were not twinkling with glee at the sight of what Davis was doing, so he discreetly returned the camera to his coat pocket and walked over to the port side of the deck, pretending to gaze out at the sea.

A few minutes later, the door to the helo hangar swung open again and Davis turned to see the three men, Artaud, Worm, and Martin, marching across the helo deck. Artaud snapped his fingers to get Jerry's attention and then pointed down to the back deck. The two descended with Worm following close behind. A moment later, Davis heard the air compressor start up. Martin stood next to Davis and they watched as the orange suits once again became active.

"Maybe you better not take any more pictures," Martin said.

"Okay," Davis said, putting his hands in his pants pockets.

"I don't know why, exactly, but we're out here to do some science, and we better get it done. If those two have some private axe to grind, I don't want to get in the middle of it."

"Yes," Davis said, and wondered if Maureen had really been the subtext of their argument.

"But we better do what Artaud wants, since he is the chief scientist."

"Okay."

"I gotta go down and help out," Martin said. "You're welcome to stay up here and watch. Just don't let them catch you with that camera."

The puppy nodded. Martin turned and descended the stairs to the back deck. Davis lingered for a few minutes but then grew bored waiting for something to happen. He was also cold from so much inactivity and, since his services were no longer needed, he returned inside.

On his way back to his lair under the stairs, he stopped outside the Dry Lab and saw Maureen and the rest of the science party staring intently at the blinking lights and screens in the computer racks. He watched them for a moment through the small pane of chicken-wire glass. Then, figuring he would just be in the way again, he continued on to his desk. With his index finger, he tapped the laptop screen back to life and opened a new game of solitaire. After five minutes, his eyes were crossing, so he retreated once again to the head. He longed to go back to his room, maybe lie on the bunk and read a book, but it was his roommate's time in the room and Davis knew better than to intrude.

In the narrow bathroom, Davis reclined into corpse pose on the floor, toilet paper pillow beneath his head. But he was not really tired, just bored, so after a few minutes he got back up, sat on the toilet, and thumbed through the magazines in the rack. He'd forgotten to grab a book when he'd left his room that morning, and the selection of magazines in the head was limited, to say the least. Occasionally there was a back issue of *Maxim* or some other teenage, testosterone-charged rag, the pages disgustingly stiff and stuck together, but usually there were only the really riveting reads like *Physics Quarterly, Diesel Trends,* or *Rod and Reel.* More often than not Davis ended up practicing his Spanish by reading the text printed on the toilet paper wrapper or on the back of the always-empty can of air freshener. He picked up this last item, shook it, found that it was, indeed, empty, and examined it. The label was similar to most air freshener labels the world over: a dewy meadow scene dotted with clumps of purple crocus and yellow daffodils, superimposed over a background of fluffy white clouds hovering in an impossibly blue sky. This particular brand of spray was called, strangely enough, Poett, which left Davis wondering if the word had an extra "t" in Spanish, or if this had just been some odd marketing ploy. If the meaning of the word was the same as in English, what, he wondered, would Poett smell like? Cigarettes and BO? Cheap scotch? Failure? He sniffed at the nozzle and realized that it was lilac.

Funny thing about lilacs: to Davis they always brought to mind the scent of old ladies. This was probably because, in his suburban existence, his first olfactory hit of "lilac" had come not from the flower itself but from some septuagenarian's hand lotion. Only when he was in his teens, or maybe even his twenties, did he smell it from its actual botanical source, and when he did it was oddly disconcerting since, in his mind, the proverbial cart had been put before the horse, and so the flower smelled like the old lady instead of the other way around.

After a while (who knew how long?), Davis got up, flushed the empty toilet, ran the water in the sink, and then hit the button on the air dryer, all for the benefit of someone who might be listening outside, which was ridiculous since everyone was either working on the seismic gear or asleep in their cabins.

He left the head and walked down the hall to the galley, which was, he was relieved to see, empty. He perused the dessert counter, scooped up several cookies, and then sat at one of the tables and began eating. Before he'd finished the first, he noticed a can of vanilla cake frosting on one of the shelves. He got up, retrieved it, and with the aid of a plastic knife, meticulously frosted each cookie before shoving it in his mouth. As he chewed, he remembered the camera in his pocket. He took it out and scrolled through the pictures, skipping over most of the equipment shots and lingering over the two he'd taken of the whale. The shutter had not quite opened in time so the first picture showed nothing more than a small segment of tail; the second, only the splash after the animal dove—nothing all that impressive, but he marveled at them nonetheless.

The door to the galley swung open and chubby Meghan walked in. She smiled when she saw Davis and waddled over, her movements hampered by her bulky orange Mustang suit. As she approached, Davis noticed that one of the knees on her suit was torn, revealing the white inner stuffing.

"That looks soooo good!" she exclaimed, eyeing one of Davis's half-eaten frosted confections on the table. "I'm starving!"

"Sit down and let me fix one for you."

As Davis carefully frosted a cookie for her, he reflected on how happy he was that one of the side effects of extreme drunkenness is the amnesia commonly known as the alcoholic blackout. This had evidently affected Meghan, as she seemed to have no recollection of (or at the least no shame about) having sobbed down the front of Davis's shirt two evenings before on the balcony at Palmer Station, nor any remembrance of having slid her icy hands beneath the waistband of his underwear, the thought of which still gave him a chill even days after the event. It wasn't that Davis disliked women, just that he was so far at the homosexual end of the spectrum that the thought of having intimate relations with a woman was as foreign to him as, say, the thought of eating the box instead of the cereal.

And yet, in spite of his Martha Stewart skill at frosting cookies, Meghan was oblivious to the rainbow signals emanating from him, and she plopped her hefty bottom into the seat right next to Davis's and leaned into him, cooing, "I'm freezing!" Indicating, of course, that she hoped he might help warm her up. Davis handed her the cookie and leaned back.

"What happened to your knee?"

"Oh, that," she said, looking down at the torn fabric of her Mustang suit. "I tripped over the umbilical and hit the deck. I was watching that whale on the port side. Did you see it?"

"Yes!"

"That so rocked!" she said, shaking her head in amazement. "I mean, a whale! I can't even believe it."

"So why are you back inside?"

She pointed to the torn knee and rolled her eyes. "When I

tripped, my foot snagged a bunch of wires and pulled them out of something important that I can't remember the name of. Jerry lost it. He's kind of fed up with me anyways. I was helping him put together the guns yesterday and he, like, expects me to know all this stuff. I mean, I'm like, this is my first time on a boat. I know all this seismic; I mean, we learned about the theory in class, but not all about the mechanics of putting the stuff together. Artaud's a good teacher," she said, cramming her mouth with cookie, "but Jerry's just creepy. And a jerk."

As if on cue, Maureen swept into the galley. The two eaters immediately lowered their heads, this time less like dashboard puppies than, say, guilty puppies who've just been caught digging in the trash.

Maureen sighed as she glared at them. *There they are again, lined up at the trough,* she thought as she stood refilling her mug with scalding water. She wondered if they were sleeping together yet. And if so . . . how? It must be like two elephant seals mating. The thought amused her, and as she returned to the Dry Lab, there was a wicked smile on her face.

Chapter 20

Later that evening, when the guns were finally in the water, blasting away; when the streamer was trailing off behind the boat, recording the little echoes coming up from the fathomable depths; when the clusters of tiny wires inside the streamer were busy transmitting their coded electrons from the back deck to the lab, where a suite of computers decoded and then recoded them into the form of a picture, which a printer steadily printed out on a spooled sheet of paper that was then respooled, making a sort of scroll. Yes, once all of *that* was functioning on its own, the exhausted humans responsible for it—the technicians, the scientists, the students—amassed once again in the mess hall to refortify themselves with the hearty sustenance of yet another Chicken Time. This time, however, the steaming metal vats did not contain chicken. Instead they were filled with row after row of brown meat, each piece molded into a cylindrical shape that was identical in size, consistency, and temperature to a human turd.

Using a pair of metal tongs, Maureen lifted first one and then another of the gravy-covered logs onto her plate and offered this appetizing comment: "I can't help but wonder if someone hasn't already eaten this."

Hearing that, most of those queued up behind her decided to bypass the meat, opting instead for the side dishes or the salad bar.

And that was probably just as well because Maureen, once she had taken her meat, did not move. Instead, she stood, tray in hand, scowling through the rising screen of steam at the young Chilean girl on the other side. The girl, Pilar, was facing Maureen but pretended not to notice her. She rested her pert little ass (clad in a pair of too-tight chef's whites) against the counter and examined her fingernails, which were long and painted the same obnoxious yellow as the boat.

For several reasons, Maureen disliked Pilar. First, because she was young, her skin as taut and elastic as an inflated balloon. Second, because she was dark and exotic in a way that Maureen herself would never be. Third, and most acutely at that moment, she disliked Pilar because the girl was not a cook but a whore who had been hired for her oral skills (renowned among members of the crew) instead of her culinary skills, which were also renowned, but for the opposite reason. Pilar had been plucked from one of the seedier Punta Arenas establishments by a mate who had sampled her wares and thought she might be nice to have along on board for longer journeys. However, since the *Hamilton* was a government-contracted vessel, the girl needed to be given something semi-legitimate to do in order to justify her presence. So, they gave her a hairnet and some chef's whites and put her to work in the galley. All of her paperwork was in order, so there was nothing the contractors or scientists could do—other than complain, which they did, often, vociferously, but without effect.

Once seated at their respective tables, those who had already taken the brown lumps (which had, as an unfortunate side dish, corn), poked at them with their forks, but very few ventured to actually put the things in their mouths. Soon they, too, rose from their seats and formed a line at the salad bar or next to the small under-counter refrigerator, in which there were a few bagged rectangles of sliced white bread, bottles of yellow and white condiments, and some disturbing lunch meats—disturbing because of their shapes, which had obviously been designed to appeal to children: The beef was in the shape of a cow, the pork in the shape of a pig, and the chicken . . . well, you get the idea. It was as if those animals had been miniaturized and then hunted down with a steam roller. Still, the barnyard shapes would eventually be concealed between the two slices of spongy bread, so one had only to look at them while the sandwich was being constructed. And any mental trauma that their shapes might have caused was infinitely less than sitting down to a plate of turds and corn.

The salad bar held its own perils. The aluminum tub of rusty-at-the-edges iceberg lettuce was usually safe, although with about as much nutritional value as a glass of water, but the real danger lay in the dressings—bottle after gluey bottle, never refrigerated, corralled on a shelf above the vat of lettuce. All of the opaque grotesques from bygone decades were represented, their euphemistic names invoking romantic, vaguely Mediterranean places: Green Goddess, Thousand Island, French, Roquefort, and then, of course, that perennial staple of the American palate, Ranch. There was no vinegar, no oil (that being reserved for the deep-fryer), just bottle after sticky bottle of gluey goop.

One of the more optimistic MTs took a seat at the table with his heaping plate of salad and said, "At least she put out some olives and capers for the salad." Maureen leaned over and examined his plate. "Capers," she said. "Those aren't capers; they're just bugs that escaped from her hair net."

This comment pushed the last few people in the chow line to the third and final option: a bowl of cereal.

"I wonder what she'll come up with for dessert?" one of the techs muttered, motioning with his head to Pilar. A deadpan Maureen replied: "If we're lucky it'll be antacids."

Silence fell over the galley as they all poked at their meals. A few attempts at conversations were launched, floated in the air for a moment, but then evaporated. For some reason Davis decided to make an attempt, tossing out an offhand and completely innocent question, one designed to move their collective attention away from the slop on their plates and toward something more interesting. Addressing his comments to no one and everyone, Davis asked, "So what's this seismic stuff supposed to do to the whales anyway?"

What followed can be described using any number of clichés: an awkward silence, the calm before the storm, the anticipation of the blow, but whichever one is chosen, it is important to note that, by and large, the people in the galley divided into two opposing camps, and Davis could tell who was in the same camp by the knowing looks they shot at one another.

"There really is no big deal," Jerry called over from his table. "Just a lot of hype." Worm, whose back was to Jerry, put his hands on the table and leaned back, pushing out his chest. Another of the MTs made a dismissive hiss and shook her head.

"That's not true," Worm said, looking at Davis and then glancing around the table to see who was with him. "There have been incidents," he said, his tone low and modulated, "some might even call them crimes."

"And some," countered Jerry, who had risen from his table, "might say there's no science to back that up. And that is what we're here to study, right? Science."

As Worm had done, Jerry then looked from person to person around the PSS table. Most kept their heads down, pretending to focus on their dinner. Davis looked at Maureen, swirling the poo and corn around on her plate, seemingly oblivious. He looked at Artaud, who sat at the science table with his arms across his chest, listening but making no jump into the fray.

"Look, man," Worm said, rising from the table and turning to face Jerry. "That's your opinion. You're entitled to it. But there have been incidents."

"Most involving sonar," Jerry countered, "not seismic."

"Most," Worm concurred, "but not all."

"They're two totally different things."

"Maybe, but they both blast sound into the water. And they've both caused strandings."

"That's enough," Jerry shouted, pounding a fist on the table with such force that it made the plates bounce. "We're the science party! You're the contractor. We've been funded to do this research, you're paid to support it. End of story."

"End of ethics, maybe, but not end of story."

The argument went on, but most of the diners were too tired from the day's work to engage in it. Others, just having come on shift, were still waiting for their coffee to kick in. All of them were disappointed with the meal they'd been given and were in no mood for philosophical jousting. One by one, they exited the mess hall. Soon the audience for Jerry and Worm's performance consisted only of Davis, Artaud, and Pilar, although the latter was busy behind the counter grinding up the significant amount of leftover brown meat, which would, with the addition of some tomato sauce and a few powdered spices, debut at the next Chicken Time as spaghetti sauce.

Jerry and Worm were both standing, facing each other across the table, lobbing points back and forth, their volume increasing with each volley. Davis watched and thought how similar their argument sounded to the political arguments of his cube mates back in the office. Both left him feeling like a disinterested line judge in a lengthy tennis match, or like a child trapped in a car with bickering parents, so when Artaud got up and motioned for Davis to follow him, Davis did not hesitate.

Once out in the hallway, Artaud spoke: "Guess they both have pretty strong feelings on the subject."

"Yeah, I'm sorry I brought it up."

"Oh, no, no, no! Don't be! Discussion is healthy. Questions like yours are what spur people on to make discoveries—and force them to back up their positions with evidence."

"I guess." Davis shrugged, although he was thinking of the number of times he'd been in "discussions" like that, most notably with his father or with Mark the Meteorologist, and how he had, without hesitation, grabbed whatever argumentative weapon was close at hand that would enable him to win, regardless of whether or not he could back it up with any supporting evidence.

"Hey, I've got an idea," Artaud said, bringing a finger up to his temple. "I'm giving a science talk tomorrow in the conference room—nothing fancy, just a PowerPoint explaining what I'm studying and why. It's open for anyone who's interested. Usually some of the crew and technicians attend. Why don't you come?"

The tone of the invitation was odd and stilted, and Davis found himself both flattered and wary—flattered because Artaud had personally invited him and had seemed almost shy doing so, wary because of the word "PowerPoint," which brought to mind both the Denver trainings and his own disastrous foray into the medium with his Bird Murder presentation.

"Do come," Artaud said. "It will better explain what we're doing out on the back deck, and give some of the reasons why. It will also answer a lot of the questions those two are yelling about in there, but in a less hostile manner."

Artaud told him the time; and, Davis, wanting to get away, agreed to attend.

Later that evening, Davis was struggling with an e-mail to his niece, trying to give his descriptions a scale that she might understand.

> I am traveling in a big yellow boat with black trim. It looks like that gigantic bumblebee that stung your Aunt Debbie last summer when we were at the cabin. Imagine that bee, but much, much bigger—the size of 20 schoolbuses! A very big bee! And if you close your eyes and imagine what it would sound like riding inside a big buzzing bee like that, you'll know what it sounds like to be inside this ship with the engines running. And it gets even louder when we're traveling through the ice. Do you want to know how loud? Tomorrow, when you eat your Cheerios for breakfast, close your eyes and listen to the crunching sound. That's the same sound we hear when the boat is breaking through the sea ice. Really loud!
>
> Today I was out on the back deck of the boat and there were lots of penguins floating by on icebergs. They can't fly like other birds but they swim very fast and shoot up and out of the water like little black and white missiles. I also saw something amazing! A whale! It was—

Worm stuck his head into the Environmental Room. "Hey," he whispered, cupping a hand around his mouth. "You got those pictures?"

Davis, reverting to professional mode, minimized the e-mail window and looked up slowly, as if he'd been in the middle of solving some complicated equation.

"From out on deck?"

"Yeah."

Davis nodded.

"Cool. Can I make some copies?"

Davis opened the desk drawer and retrieved the camera. He took it out of its case, pushed a little button on its underside, and the memory card popped out. He handed it to Worm, with some hesitation. "You sure this is okay?"

"Oh, hell yeah," he said. "You worried about them losing their shit about it on deck today?"

Davis nodded.

"Fuck 'em. It's not even their equipment. I've been working on this boat almost four years and I've never had anyone say 'don't take pictures.' That's just bullshit."

Before he could agree or disagree, Worm had taken the memory card and disappeared back into the hallway. Davis went back to composing his e-mail.

I also saw something amazing! A whale! It looked like a giant dinosaur and blew a big plume of water and steam into the air out of its nose, which is really just a big hole on the top of its head. I got one picture, but it moved fast and was only partly out of the water for a few seconds. By the time I got the camera up, it was already back under the water. You can just see its tail in the picture. I don't know if it was a boy whale or a girl whale, but I think it was a type of whale called a minke, which rhymes with pinky, which is funny because your pinky is so little and the whale was so big!

Worm returned. "Wrong card, dude."

Davis, still typing: "That's the only card."

"There's nothing on it."

He stopped typing and looked at Worm to see if he was kidding. Worm handed him the card. "See for yourself."

Davis put the card back in the camera, turned it on, fumbled a minute with the tiny black buttons, trying to remember how to get the screen to display the contents of the card, finally figured it out, and got a black screen with orange lettering that said *Nothing on card*.

"Nooooo," he said, his tone descending several notes. He was sure that he himself had somehow inadvertently erased it, probably when he was showing the pictures to Meghan in the mess hall.

"You sure there isn't another card? Maybe you downloaded 'em to your laptop?"

Davis shook his head. "I never took the card out of the camera until you asked for it."

"Dude, what'd you do?"

"I don't know!" Davis whined.

"What do you mean you don't know?"

"I mean, I still don't really know how to work the camera. I thought I did. I must have done . . . something."

"Great," Worm said, rolling his eyes, "Goddamned spectacular!"

Davis kept poking the buttons, trying to make the pictures appear, upset himself at the loss of the whale photo.

"I guess it doesn't really matter. Probably nothing all that good on the card anyway. No offense, but I doubt you even got any good snaps of them doing anything bad. I was down there doing the setup, so I would've seen it myself. It just pisses me off that they go out there and swing their nuts around like that. I really only wanted the pictures because Jerry and Artaud don't want me to have them."

"Here," Worm said, taking the camera from Davis and pulling up a chair next to him. "Let's figure this thing out so you don't go losing anything else."

The two then spent the next twenty minutes rehashing the camera's capabilities, Worm again showing Davis what it could do, but this time quizzing him on it afterward. When Worm first started explaining it, Davis stifled his yawns and wondered how long he would have to listen to him ramble on before he could get back to his e-mail writing, but Worm's teaching methods were not boring and soon Davis found himself asking questions and feeling appreciative of his patience.

"There," Worm said, holding the camera an inch from Davis's face and snapping a picture, blinding him with the flash. "Now you should know how to work it."

"Thank you," Davis said, blinking away the blue-green shadows. He took the camera, put it back in its case and then back in the drawer.

"And another thing . . ."

Davis sighed and waited for him to continue.

"Your bird presentation sucked ass."

"Oh, please," Davis said, "that had at least as much to do with the subject matter as it did with the presentation."

"Maybe, but nobody's going to squash a little bird in their bare hands. Or wring its neck."

"Well, I can't blame them, and with any luck there won't be an incident where we'll need to test the policy."

"Oh, it'll happen, all right," Worm said. "Maybe not while you're here, but one of these trips, it'll happen. And when it does, the techs are gonna keep right on doing what they've always done: scooping 'em off the deck with the snow shovels and pitching them over the side."

Davis shrugged and then started reciting a version of what Sarah had told him: "I'm not here to make policy or execute it. My job is to make sure it's available in a clear and conci—"

"Yeah, yeah," Worm said, waving a hand. "I don't care about all that. What I'm saying is if you want to change things, you gotta go about it in a different way. How I see it is like this: Your first goal is to get the dazed birds off the deck, get 'em warmed up and back into the wild. Right?"

"Right."

"Your second goal is to humanely kill the ones that are gonna die anyway. Yes?"

"Yes."

"Then you're fine as far as the first goal, but you gotta find some less sicko methods for the second."

"Such as?"

Before Davis had time to protest, he was being led down the hallway, camera in hand, to the MT shop. The walls were covered with tools, each hanging from an individual hook. Outlines had been traced around each wrench, hammer, clamp, and what-all, so that it could be easily returned to its hook after use. Davis saw the tool tracings not because there were tools missing from their spots but because as the ship moved, the tools swung from side to side, revealing their ghostly negatives.

Worm disappeared and returned a minute later bearing a large plastic cooler, the kind with a flip-up top that a large family might take camping, so large it could almost double as a bench. He set the cooler on the deck in front of Davis and disappeared again, returning a minute later with a cordless drill. He pulled out a few drawers and examined some small metal fittings, trying several before finding one that slid over the bit. He put the fitting in his pocket, closed the drawer, and moved on to another, from which he removed a large spool of small-diameter rubber tubing. He measured out three arm lengths of it and cut it with a knife he had attached to his belt. Then he closed the knife, closed up the lockers, and returned to the cooler. He started drilling a hole through the plastic on one side. "How's your Holocaust history?"

Davis shrugged. "Pretty good, I guess. Why?"

"'Cause what we're gonna make here," Worm said, retrieving the metal fitting from his pocket and pushing it through the hole in the cooler, "is a little birdy gas chamber."

"Ahh," Davis exclaimed, rubbing his hands together. Worm attached one end of the rubber hose to the fitting and stood up.

"Now all you'll have to do," Worm explained, gleefully pantomiming his actions as he went, "is put the injured birds in the box, put the lid on, probably duct tape it shut so they don't flap their way out, and then hook the other end of this hose to one of the CO_2 tanks."

Davis leaned forward and clapped his hands.

"They sit in there for, say, ten minutes, and then," Worm said, lifting the lid, closing his eyes and sniffing at the air, "Petrel Time!"

Chapter 21

The next day, Davis was again in the 03 Conference Room, but this time as part of the audience instead of the presenter. He had arrived too late to get one of the bumper-car chairs, so he took a seat on the floor, propping his back against the bookcase. Artaud stood at the front of the room, as erect and stationary as a ship's mast. Since they were traveling through ice, the sea was calm and there was none of the side-to-side motion that had plagued Davis's presentation.

"Thank you all for coming," Artaud said, making eye contact with select members of the audience. "I've sailed with many of you before, so I'm sure most of you probably know what we're doing out here and why we're doing it, but for those of you who don't," he looked at Worm and then at Davis, "and those of you for whom this is your first trip to sea, I hope this presentation will enlighten you somewhat to what we're studying and what we hope to discover."

He made a slight inclination to Maureen. Obediently, she got up, turned off the lights and then sat back down. Artaud clicked the first slide. A colorful painting of a tropical scene came into view. Exotic palms, lush ferns, dinosaurs, and in the background, a puffing volcano.

"Welcome to Antarctica during the Cretaceous era. Or at least what scientists like to theorize it looked like back then. A lot has changed, eh? Definitely wouldn't need any ECW gear for a trip back then."

This elicited polite smatterings of laughter and set the tone for the rest of the slide show, which seemed, to Davis at least, more intent on amusing the audience than on imparting any real information. There were stories about the bad weather on previous cruises, stories about the days when they used dynamite instead of compressed air to do seismic profiling, stories about colorful characters from past trips, anecdotes about teaching, but the topic of the science was brought up only briefly, and then consisted of a recitation of the party line: "What we hope to learn by studying the sedimentary record is to help model past climate change."

Climate change.

Davis had been in The Program only a very short time and yet he was already aware of the game the scientists had to play in order to get funded. Climate change was the hot topic (pun intended) and, as such, had to be included somewhere in any proposal that hoped to get funded. Biology, geology, oceanography, glaciology, whatever. If the proposed science wasn't, in some way or another, studying the impact of climate change, it rarely made it past the first round of reviews.

And since he was an experienced player, Artaud did mention climate change in his talk—how he studied the greenhouse gases that were trapped in sediment cores; how the recent collapse of the Larsen Ice Shelf provided heretofore unavailable opportunities to study the recently exposed seafloor. He went on and on about those things and more, but it seemed he would just touch on a topic and then move on to another, leaving the audience short on specifics. To Davis, Artaud's theories seemed slippery and elusive, like trying to get a piece of shell out of a bowl of eggs. Soon, Davis found his attention wandering and again his neck began to feel boneless.

"My belief is that this was . . . a cataclysmic catastrophe that would have resulted in significant biological die-off . . . what my team is hoping to prove is that . . . in order to study the deep sedimentary layers from the Cretaceous era . . . past fluctuations in climate . . . using a bundle with anywhere from two to six

five-hundred-cubic-inch seismic sound sources . . . advanced pro-
cessing methods allow deeper resolution than we'd ever thought
possible."

Although unable to mentally ingest the content of the presentation, Davis could, as a visual artist, appreciate the production values. Artaud had, Davis surmised, hired someone to help illustrate
his theories and methods, and in that he had succeeded in making
the presentation visually stimulating, if not actually comprehensi-
ble to laypeople. On the screen there was a cross-section view of
the ocean, much like you'd see if you were looking at someone's
home aquarium, only much more elaborate and without any fish.
There was the gently undulating surface of the water with a tiny
yellow boat, looking very much like the one in which they were
then sailing, serenely floating above a transparent water column.
Beneath that were the sedimentary layers of the ocean floor, represented by variegated shades of brown, and beneath that, a solid
black layer labeled "basement." As Davis watched, the tiny yellow
boat skimmed across the ocean surface, emitting a tiny little trail of
smoke from its teeny little smokestack. Artaud clicked the remote
and mini air guns and a streamer appeared, trailing behind the
boat. He paused to let everyone appreciate the artistry and then he
clicked the remote again and the guns emitted little flashing Xs, followed by a diagonal line, representing the subsequent sound wave
descending to the bottom of the ocean, down through the sedimentary layers to the basement, and then bouncing back up at an
angle toward the surface, forming a V-shape in the water column.
The boat continued to move forward, the gun emitted another X,
another line shot down and then up, just crossing over the previous
line, forming a W. This continued on, each W fading away as another emerged to take its place. It was, Davis reflected, like watching a more elaborate version of the old video game Pong, but with
the sound waves representing the path of the tennis ball.

"Lower frequencies," Artaud said, "allow deeper penetration
into the strata, which is our focus area. If we were looking at the
upper sedimentary layer, we would use a higher-frequency sound
source."

Soon after this point, Artaud's speech plunged to depths that
were totally beyond Davis's comprehension, so he turned his focus

from what was happening on stage and looked instead at the audience. They were all—even Worm—paying close attention. It was clear to Davis that Artaud had a certain passion for his subject matter—a passion that, combined with his good looks, infected his listeners and provoked their enthusiasm and interest. Not able to understand the science, Davis found himself instead studying the method of presentation, which was, undeniably, slick. And yet for all that slickness, there was something about it that was not quite right. Something (what exactly, he didn't know) that was ringing false. The presentation seemed, to Davis, more style than substance. He shrugged off this feeling by reminding himself of his own ignorance: "I just don't understand. I'm stupid. I'm the DCD." A belief that was reinforced when he again looked back at the smart, capable group of students and technicians, all listening, none of their faces showing even a trace of incomprehension. He scolded himself for his stupidity, resolved to try harder, and turned once again to face the screen.

In the time he'd been looking away, the cross-section aquarium scene had vanished and been replaced by a screen of equations. This stayed in place for a very long time and was not, as far as Davis could tell, much referred to. Instead, it seemed to act as a backdrop for Artaud—an academic curtain in front of which he stood and did his routine. And it really did dissolve again into a routine, as he pitched softball questions to his students, made little jokes, told long, rambling sidebar anecdotes about mishaps, triumphs, and just plain funny events that had occurred on previous Antarctic adventures. It seemed, to Davis, like he was doing some sort of one-man show. Like he was an old actor or an elder statesman, or maybe an old actor playing an elder statesman, giving an amusing account of his vast past experience.

In spite of his resolve, Davis's mind wandered yet again. He looked at the bookshelf opposite, trying to make out the titles. Soon the spines began to rotate and spin and the next thing he knew he was awakened by the sound of applause. The lights were on. Artaud was smiling, mouthing the words "Thank you," bowing slightly to the audience. The applause subsided and people stood and stretched, making their way toward the door. Davis pulled himself up and followed.

When he was halfway across the conference room, he heard Artaud call his name and he turned.

"Did the presentation help?" he asked.

"Oh, yes!"

"Good. That's good, because you seemed to be getting a case of the head bobs toward the end."

"No," Davis protested. "No, no, no. Just nodding my agreement. It was great. Really! It was a little bit over my head when you got into the math, so maybe I did tune out just a little, but the presentation was very informative. Fun."

"Thank you."

"Yes."

Artaud continued to hold his gaze. Davis wondered if it was acceptable for him to leave, or if Artaud had more that he wanted to say.

"So you understand what we're doing and why?" Artaud asked.

"Sure."

"Because if you have any questions, I'd be glad to answer them."

"Sure. Thanks," Davis said. He gave an awkward wave and backed toward the door.

The rest of the cruise was comparatively uneventful. They traveled up and down the Peninsula, mapping the seafloor and collecting seismic data, pausing occasionally to collect sediment samples. Once this sea mud was brought on board, the undergrads were kept busy examining, cataloguing, and then packaging it up in sample containers to be shipped back to their university.

Davis? Well, Davis still had very little to do. There were no vessel/seabird collisions that would test his policy, and the few "farmed out" pieces of documentation that had come back from the techs usually took him no longer than an hour or so to "make pretty" and repost to the ship's intranet. He mentioned his availability to the technicians and to the science party, hoping they might have some task he might be able to assist with, but they just waved him away with a look that seemed to say *If you don't have anything to do, why are you here?* Even bovine Meghan had lost interest in him, her attention now focused on documenting the striations in seafloor mud.

So, once again, Davis retreated to his lair under the stairs where he watched the Reality Detection Device dangle, invented and refined the content for his weekly reports, wrote countless e-mails, played game after game after game of solitaire, and walked up and down the stairs to the bridge and back deck. Then, when all of those diversions had been exhausted, he sat down again and tried to come up with a synopsis for Estelle.

His latest story involved, not surprisingly, a baby albatross, which he, for some reason, christened Brad. Brad left the nest one day and got lost at sea during a storm. He saw some bright lights off in the distance and, thinking they might be some sort of cozy oasis, flew toward them. The lights were not a cozy oasis but (also not surprising) a ship and, predictably, he collided with it, injuring his wing. During the dark, cold night that followed, Brad lay on deck, nearly freezing to death, but when dawn came he was rescued by a flock of friendly humans who brought him inside, dried out his feathers, put a splint on his wing, and then did not, of course, snap his spine, crush his chest, or lock him in a picnic cooler and gas him to death with CO_2, but nursed him back to health and then released him from cupped hands to fly free back into the wild blue Antarctic.

He typed up this treatment as succinctly as he could and then sent it off to Estelle. Her reply was equally succinct, arriving with the next morning's e-mail:

From: EstelleWillBookem@aol.com
Sent: Sunday, October 04, 2003 11:07 PM
To: Davis.Garner@HAH.pss.gov

Subject: Yaaawwn! What is that shit supposed to be? *Jonathan Livingston Albatross?* Try again. And hurry!

All my best,
Estelle

But Davis did not have much time to fret about her rejection, for just as they were about to leave the relatively calm waters surrounding the peninsula, they hit bad weather. Bad weather that was again preceded by Maureen, in Chicken Little mode, going from lab to lab shouting, "The barometer is falling! The barometer is falling!" Davis hoped she was wrong, but began ingesting meclizine, Sudafed, and oyster crackers as a precaution. And he was glad he had done so because the storm they entered six hours later was as bad as, if not worse than, the one they'd sailed through during their southern crossing.

After about a day and a half, the motion settled down enough that Davis was able to venture out of his cabin. The lower decks were deserted, so he went up to the bridge. The captain and a few mates were there, smoking, talking, seemingly at ease. Davis looked out at the panoramic scene provided by the bridge windows. The storm had passed, but a few low clouds zipped across the sky like clusters of seeds blown off a dandelion. The waves were still a foamy white, their caps turning to mist as soon as they crested, but off to the right Davis saw land. Most of it was snow covered, but there were exposed patches of rugged brown rock.

"What's that?" Davis asked.

The captain approached, exhaling a plume of smoke. He pointed with his cigarette. "That there's Deception."

Davis thought this might be some sort of riddle or joke and he waited for the punch line. When it was not forthcoming he asked for clarification.

"Deception Island," the captain said. "We're holding in the lee until this wind lets up."

"Why's it called Deception?" Davis asked. Instead of answering, the captain motioned him over to the chart table.

"That there's Deception," he said, pointing down to a round, hollow formation on the map. "From the outside, it looks like a solid island, but there's one little channel right here." He pointed to a narrow gap in the circle labeled "Neptune's Bellows." "You go through there and it opens up big inside, a collapsed volcano. Used to be a big whaling station for the Norwegians. Abandoned now. Last time it erupted was . . . Any you guys know how long ago?" They shook their heads and shrugged. "Anyways, been abandoned since it erupted. We're still ahead of schedule, so if this wind calms down, we might be able to sail in and take a look-see. That is, if we can talk Artaud into making a little morale-boosting diversion."

In the end, the decision was not made by Artaud, but by the weather, which offered a gap in fierceness only long enough to allow them to shoot across the Drake before the next band of low pressure descended.

As soon as the ship hit the dock in Punta Arenas, Artaud flew to Santiago, leaving Maureen and the rest of the crew to clean up the mess from the crossing. It had only been two days since he'd gone, but in that time her imagination had led her into a maze of agony as she imagined him being eye-raped in a coffee shop or bar by one of that city's numerous, leggy bachelorettes, all olive skinned and minkish, with their dark, baby-harp-seal eyes and freshly waxed everything. She knew Santiago well, knew from her own experience as a tall, somewhat busty blonde how ardent the attentions of that town's male inhabitants could be, and naturally assumed, without reason, that the female natives would be equally, if not more, ardent and predatory.

Santiago was a place where many people coming off stints on the vessel or at station took off their mantles of propriety and left them in a locker at the airport, claiming them only right before boarding their flight north. And as much as she tried to act like she was made of marble, Maureen was actually made of flesh, and her flesh had, more than a few times, proven weak. It didn't happen often, usually after one of the longer, sixty-day cruises, when she'd been deprived of contact and attention. Then she would schedule a brief layover in Santiago, giving herself just enough time to dip her toe into the illicit bath of weekend passion and succumb to the relentless fervor and flattery of Andean men.

It was with fondness, and some embarrassment at her moxie, that she recalled a scene from the previous February when she had fled to Santiago, abandoned her Carhartts and baseball cap for a scooped-back sundress, high heels, dark glasses, and yes, even white gloves. Thus costumed, she had taken a taxi to the park at Santa Lucía, where she played tourist, slowly strolling up the winding path, fanning herself with a map until, breathless and perspiring, she arrived at the top and stood on the small platform, gloved hands clinging to the railing, while she surveyed not the city below, not the jagged Andes surrounding her, seen vaguely through the carbon monoxide haze, but rather, the crowd of men who had followed her and were then gazing up at her from the numerous niches below. She was, at that moment, Princess Grace benevolently acknowledging her horde of adoring Monégasques; Eva Perón surveying the *descamisados* from the balcony of the Casa Rosada; a Top 10 songstress performing for a sea of blue-balled troops in Iraq or Afghanistan; she was the pearl in the oyster, the one egg toward which all the sperm were swimming.

She remembered those stalked strolls in Santa Lucía as she stood trapped in prosaic Punta Arenas. She thought of Artaud off in Santiago, similarly stalked, and her blood pressure spiked, for she knew that if she—the ice princess, the Nordic beauty, the frigid bitch (she was aware of all the pseudonyms, both public and private, that had been applied to her)—if even she had been capable of surrendering to Santiago lust, then the chances of Artaud remaining faithful to her while he was there were slim to none.

She stood, staring out one of the round portholes, as impenetrable and confining to her as the barred window of a prison, and imagined him involved in all manner of entanglements. Entanglement. What a perfect word, for he was a man who looked best swaddled in sheets, bedecked in bedding. Bed became him.

Book 4

Easter Island, Kingston, Jamaica, the Denver office

Chapter 22

On the flight from Punta Arenas to Santiago, Davis pulled out his notebook and tried to formulate a plot and some dialogue. From Santiago to Dallas, he put the notebook away and slept, but the next morning, on the short flight from Dallas to Denver, he took out the notebook again and continued plotting, mouthing the dialogue he'd written. None of this had anything to do with his book, but rather, with the story he was going to tell Sarah and Jake about what he had accomplished over the past two months.

In the eight weeks he was at sea, he'd composed eight separate works of fiction—in the form of weekly reports. This was something required of every company employee sailing on the cruise and was collected and e-mailed back to the office each week. It didn't have to be much; usually just a bulleted list of the tasks you'd accomplished during the week so that your supervisor could tell that you were doing something, but for Davis it proved one of the more challenging tasks of his week and, almost as soon as he e-mailed his weekly on Saturday night, he again started to worry about how he could come up with content for the coming week. Not that it mattered all that much, since there wasn't anyone in the office paying much attention to what he did or did not do. Nevertheless, he did need to come up with something.

Sitting across the aisle from Maureen on the flight to Santiago, he had fretted about what she might report back about him to others in the office, but she seemed preoccupied, lost in her own thoughts, uninterested in terrorizing him. Once they got to Santiago, she (and most of the others who had disembarked) did not follow him into the international terminal but raced to catch domestic connections to various Chilean vacation destinations. Davis's hope was that her vacation might blur the edges of her memory regarding him, although he doubted that would be the case. Regardless, her delay would buy him some time to convince Sarah and Jake that he had, in fact, been a busy little worker bee.

As he rode in the taxi from the airport to his brother's house, he pulled a list of his tasking that he'd printed before he'd left the ship:

- Reviewed documentation to determine the need for updates (*a partial lie*)
- Familiarized self with the labs (meaning he had walked around and looked at them)
- Familiarized self with the seismic equipment (*another partial lie*)
- Familiarized self with the coring equipment (*outright lie; he hadn't even seen it*)
- Took pictures of equipment for use in future documentation (*true, until he was ordered not to do so*)
- Familiarized self with sonar equipment (*outright lie #2*)
- Reformatted documentation (yes, most certainly yes; he had beautified the documentation)

There were eight weeks of reports, most of them repeating the same information but in a slightly different way. Sometimes instead of *updated documentation* he would attempt the more formal-sounding passive voice: *documentation was updated* or *necessary updates to documentation were undertaken and completed,* but that usually had the effect of making it sound like someone else had done it, which was, unintentionally, more accurate. Regardless of the tense, he always made sure to change the order of the bulleted items so that sometimes the things he had familiarized himself with preceded the documentation he had updated. Also, from week to week he changed the font, alternating between the businesslike 10 point Arial and Courier New to the more familiar and pedestrian 12 point Times New Roman. Toward the end he even started to spice things up by venturing into the new terrain of 11 point Baskerville Old Face and Lucida Console.

He arrived at his brother's house around noon. The place was empty except for the ecstatic Edgar, who, despite his age and arthritis, managed an enthusiastic welcome. Davis lavished him with attention and treats and then headed for the shower. He emerged fifteen minutes later and was just settling down on the couch in the afternoon sun when his phone beeped. It was a text message from Jake:

Drinks 2nite. 6. My place. Dinner after.

Davis's stomach did a little flip and he hesitated before replying, afraid that the grilling was going to begin. Since it had to start sometime, he figured it might as well start with someone he knew who might be a more sympathetic audience on which to practice his well-rehearsed elaborations.

OK, he typed **CU@6**. Then he turned off the phone and dozed, the dog snoring next to him.

When he arrived at Jake's later that evening, Jake opened the door, looked behind Davis to see if anyone had followed him, and then pulled him into the house, locking the door behind him. He had a cocktail shaker in hand and he shook it as he walked past the living room and returned to the kitchen.

In the two months he'd been gone, Jake's house had undergone a radical transformation. Gone was all the mission furniture, the lamps with their amber shades, the eclectic clutter collected during his years of world travel. In its place was a landscape of magazine minimalism: rigid chairs, glass end tables on fragile legs, a narrow, low-backed sofa, arranged with mathematical precision around a red lacquer coffee table, in the center of which was a square vase containing a spray of tiny orchids. On the walls there were huge canvases, some white with large black brushstrokes, others black with large white brushstrokes, and all lit by retina-piercing halogen lights suspended from a network of wires stretched across the ceiling. Davis stared at the room, awestruck, until Jake returned and pulled him by the sleeve into the kitchen. There, on the counter, two glasses awaited, into which Jake carefully dispensed the cloudy yellow liquid.

"Sazeracs," he said, handing a cocktail to Davis and clinking their glasses. "We have to hurry. Before Nabil gets home."

The two downed the cocktails like shots, and Jake quickly dispensed another round.

"What's the hurry?" Davis asked.

"He'll be here any minute," Jake said, as if that were explanation enough. "He's going to dinner with us. Hope you like Thai food, because that's about all we eat anymore. It's better than eating here, though, because then it's all macrobiotic. Nasty stuff. I never know if I should eat it or step over it."

"But why are we drinking so fast?" Davis asked.

"Because."

"Because . . . ?"

"Because drinking's not in the plan."

"What plan?"

"There are several," Jake replied wearily. "Just drink up, because all we'll be allowed to have with dinner are a few thimbles of sake."

"I hope the sex is good."

"Oh, man, maybe the best ever!"

They downed their second cocktail as fast as their first, and then the dreaded question arose:

"So, tell me about the cruise. How'd it go? How'd you do?"

Davis replied with a stream of generalities. He spoke of the boat, of the rough seas, the seeming success of the science mission (although for all he knew it could have been a dismal failure), the food, how he managed his seasickness . . .

"Yes, but how did *you* do?" Jake asked. "With the work, I mean?"

The door opened and in strode Nabil, portfolio in one hand, cell phone in the other, his cowboy boots making ominous thuds on the hardwood floor as he approached. Davis and Jake immediately switched roles, Davis becoming more relaxed now that the conversation had been interrupted and Jake at nervous attention, trying to nudge the cocktail shaker so it would be out of view behind the blender.

Nabil came into the kitchen still talking on his phone. He mouthed "hello" to Davis, and managed to wave at him with his pinky. He approached Jake, leaned in for a kiss, but then recoiled like a cobra when he caught the undeniable scent of alcohol. His eyes narrowed. Jake responded with an appropriately contrite expression—head down, eyes on the floor, then turned his head to the side and winked at Davis.

"Listen," Nabil said to the caller on the line, "I've *got* to go. Yes, I must. I *will* call later. I promise."

Dinner went well, largely because Davis was successful in his attempts to deflect the conversation away from himself, which was not at all difficult with someone like Nabil at the table. Davis asked about the new decorating scheme, about Nabil's upcoming art opening, about the health benefits of organic flax seeds (which provoked a lengthy, detailed, and impassioned response, and led somehow to the topic of colonic cleansing), and Davis would probably have made it safely through the entire evening had it not been for Nabil's phone, which received incoming text messages at least once every four minutes. When that happened he would cease talking, glance down at the thing, apologize to Jake and Davis, and then focus his attention on hastily thumbing in a response. In these intervals, Jake would resume questioning Davis about the cruise. Questions to which Davis would vaguely reply, all the while keeping one anxious eye on Nabil, hoping he would end his messaging, reenter the conversation, and reorient it, like an errant compass, back to himself. Davis always knew when Nabil had finished texting by the cessation of his manic thumbs, but also because before returning the phone to his pocket he would hold it up to his face and use its reflective screen as a mirror to check the status of his face and hair.

At the end of the evening, as Davis was getting into his car and Jake and Nabil were going into the house, Jake called out: "You'll be at the office tomorrow?" Davis nodded.

"I've got meetings all morning but we'll talk in the afternoon. There's a lot we need to discuss."

After that remark, and in spite of his jet lag and fatigue, Davis knew he would have difficulty falling asleep.

* * *

Although most certainly on terra firma the morning of his return to the office, Davis felt the now-familiar rumblings of seasickness in his stomach as he walked across the parking lot to the building, again fearing some sort of confrontation from his coworkers about how little he had accomplished during his trip. But to his surprise, that confrontation never came. He rounded the corner to the tech-writer cubicle and found them all—Gordon, Tom, Janet—pretty much as he had left them, still facing into their respective corners, still with the atmosphere of volatile contempt hanging in the air.

They greeted Davis and shook his hand, made polite inquiries about his cruise and the flight home, but then swiveled back into their corners and began click-clacking away. Davis plugged in his laptop, eased himself back into his own corner, logged into his e-mail account, and started wading through two months' worth of e-mail. After about twenty minutes, it was like he'd never been away.

Almost none of his e-mail was important. In spite of all the network security and impenetrable firewalls that the IT Department never tired of boasting about, a whole lot of junk managed to make it through to his in-box. Nigerian scams, Viagra solicitations, ads for penile enlargement cream, and links to the latest pop starlet sex tape. Once those had been deleted, he found himself reading, with pathetic interest, the numerous messages sent out over the past two months from the office manager, RE: the car in the south parking lot with its lights on, RE: the lone earring found on the bathroom counter (call to identify and claim), RE: the men's room toilet backing up (again), RE: the schedule for the lunchroom refrigerator cleaning (anything not out by 3:00 P.M. Friday will be tossed!), RE: the day (three weeks past) on which the Girl Scouts would be in the lobby selling cookies. Interspersed with all that junk was the daily emphatic: *Your mailbox is over its size limit.*

Since he was wading through the e-mail chronologically, he did not get to Sarah's message from that morning until after he had returned from lunch.

"Please call me as soon as you get in. Something I want to touch base with you about."

His bounced his right leg up and down with the speed and regularity of a sewing machine needle. Tears of perspiration dripped down the sides of his torso. Davis didn't know much about baseball, but when you "touched base" with someone, didn't that make one of you out? That was it, of course. He was out. She was either coming back from her maternity leave or she was so disappointed in his poor performance on the cruise that she was going to replace him. And then what would he do? How would he pay for his pills? His pulse throbbed in his head. What was he going to do? Where would he go? He could stay with his brother for a while longer, that was no worry, but how would he get *those pills?* He agonized over that for a minute more and then picked up the receiver. With unsteady hands, he punched in Sarah's number. It rang once and then he heard the three ascending notes followed by "We're sorry, the number you have called is no longer in service. If you feel you have reached this recording in erro—"

He hung up, took a deep breath, and looked at the number in the e-mail again. He tapped it in again, slowly, deliberately. While he listened to the ring, he thought about building a Reality Detection Device for his desk. Something simple, stationary, that would reassure him of stability.

"Hello."

"Sarah? It's Davis."

"Oh, hi! Welcome back!"

"Thanks, thanks. It's good to be back. How're the twins?" Deflection #1.

"Oh, they're still kicking. And screaming. But they're awesome, really, and each is developing his own little personality."

As so many people who spend their days focused on one thing, or in this case, two things, she did not require much prodding to talk about them, and gladly went on and on about their length, their weight percentile, their conflicting sleep times, the funny thing one does with his feet when it's bath time . . . and again Davis found himself nodding replies, making empathetic little expressions, which, of course, she could not see. When that spinning topic finally lost momentum and slowed to a stop, she turned the questioning to him:

"So how was the cruise?"

"Oh, it went well. I think. I mean as far as I can tell. I was busy, you know. What with the bird mitigation policy, updating the seismic documentation, and um . . ."

He paused and consulted the bulleted list he'd printed up.

"Um, familiarizing myself with the . . . equipment and, um, well, the general workings of the ship. I've got a list of the things I worked on. If you want it, I mean. Or I could just tell it to you over the phone. Whichever."

"No, don't worry about that. I'm on the distribution list for the weeklies. Sounds like you found plenty to keep you busy. And you weren't sick, right?"

"Right."

"Good, good. Then there's something else I need to touch base with you about."

He braced himself for the blow.

"I didn't think this was going to be a big deal or I would have said something about it before the last cruise, but now the shit has hit the fan and the higher-ups are freaking out."

All the blood raced away from Davis's hands, and yet somehow they were perspiring so much he could barely keep a grip on the phone. He pictured the Reality Detection Device swinging off the chart, going all the way up and around like a dial. This was it. This was the base she wanted to touch. They'd found out about his being HIV+ and wanted him out. That was it.

"I see," he said, his voice neutral.

"One of the techs sent an e-mail complaining about it and, well, they're worried about the PR if we don't do something. And, of course, well, there are safety concerns."

Fuck. Why hadn't Jake mentioned any of this last night? Probably because Davis hadn't allowed him to speak, at least not about anything that didn't have to do with Nabil, and certainly not about anything that was work related, but about something like *this?* He would have expected Jake to tell him right away, maybe even before the first cocktail.

"There's no risk," Davis said. "Unless I'm bleeding and, you know, someone else is bleeding."

"What?!"

It occurred to him then that maybe they weren't talking about the same thing.

"Nothing. Sorry. I was talking to someone else. They're rounding up people for a blood drive today. You were saying?"

"I was saying they should not have stopped you from taking pictures of the seismic equipment. One of the techs contacted NSF about it and made some veiled threat about going to Greenpeace, and now the whole thing's blown up."

Davis felt the sweat break and his shoulders relaxed.

"I'm coming to the office to talk to Jake about it early next week. You should probably be there. We've got to figure out what to do."

The conversation went on a while longer, but Davis was no longer paying attention. After he hung up he wiped his forehead on his sleeve. Janet's head rose up and she rested her arm on the partition.

"The blood drive was last week."

Chapter 23

The two wore plastic coats to protect themselves, but the rat-a-tat-tat of rain on their hoods was so loud and insistent that neither could hear what the other was saying. They held hands and were silent and walked along the rows of elongated stone heads, so ubiquitous in advertising, comic strips, and souvenir stands that once you saw them in the flesh, so to speak, it was a bit anticlimactic. The heads, called "moai," were big, yes, and impressive, but the stabbing rain made Maureen indifferent to their charms and not at all curious about the people who made them or the sophisticated engineering they must have used to drag them from the quarry.

They ate an unremarkable dinner of cold fried fish at a little café in Hanga Roa, washed it down with a few bottles of the local beer (its label emblazoned with yet another artistic rendering of a moai), and then shared a chocolate bar on their way back to the hotel. There, with nothing else to do, they engaged in sex that was as unremarkable and perfunctory as their dinner, and Artaud fell asleep while Maureen sat up in bed watching a Hindi soap opera on satellite TV.

Three days before, after she'd finished her work and been allowed to leave Punta Arenas, she had flown to Santiago and met Artaud at the airport. They'd rushed to catch a flight to Easter Island, where they'd been ever since, in the wind and the rain. There were four days to go on this little post-cruise holiday and already she was bored. She kept telling herself that she should be happy (he seemed happy), she had him all to herself, no more slutty under-grads or Chilean temptresses to worry about, but long after they had turned off the TV she lay awake in the dark, watching the or-biting blades of the ceiling fan. She tried to convince herself that this trip was an expression of his love for her, perhaps the precur-sor to a proposal, but even she could not be that delusional. This trip was meant as her reward, her payoff, for in his suitcase were six tapes of seismic data. Data that had been acquired by another sci-entist and that Maureen had copied and brought to him. The other scientist was female and had, at one time, been Mrs. Artaud, a fact that had somehow made the task of copying the data easier for Maureen to rationalize. Still, since handing the tapes over to him, some emotional sand had shifted within her and things were not as they had been before—for either one of them. There was a forced cheerfulness in his conversations with her and she had the sense that his mind was always off somewhere else. This was most appar-ent in their sexual relations, during which either the lights were out or he had kept his eyes tightly shut, as if he needed it that way for the cinematic reels featuring some starlet or student to play in his head and enable him to perform. And it was a performance, like the kind put on by an amateur suburban theater troupe, full of wooden monologues, clumsy blocking, and timing that was always just a bit off.

She did not sleep well that night; her mind never quieted down. She kept scrolling through a number of different scenarios for the coming day, the coming weeks, months, the next year, etc. None of it was very clear or defined, and it became even less so as she plunged in and out of sleep. She awoke at one point, again con-scious of the fan still whirring overhead, then the sound of his feet compressing the thick carpeting as he walked to the window. She opened her eyes and saw his body silhouetted in the gray light. He'd stuck his head through the curtains, so all she could see was the dark shadow of his broad shoulders and back tapering down to his narrow waist. He was shaped like a heart, or an inverted spade, or a stingray—broad upper body and skinny legs, so skinny they looked almost like a tail. He never did any leg work in the gym, it was always bench presses, shoulder shrugs, biceps curls, sometimes a set of lunges to firm up his ass. Such a nice ass . . .

The next thing was the smell of coffee, then the brightness. Tentatively, she opened her eyes, squinting against the sunlight. Artaud was sitting next to the bed in a chair, showered, shaved, wrapped in a white robe, his hands cupped around a steaming mug.

She sat up, looked at the window, and saw full blue sky, the blue swimming pool, and beyond that, the ocean itself, wavelets lapping at the cobble-studded beach.

"What time is it?"

"Time doesn't matter," he said. "This is vacation."

From the angle of the sun she gauged it to be late morning. How had she slept so late? She *never* slept late. He ordered breakfast to be sent up. She sat, cloudy-headed, on the terrace, sipping her coffee. There was still a slight breeze, but it died down as they ate and by noon it was quite warm. After breakfast, Artaud wanted to go lie out by the pool, so he suited up in his square-cut trunks and headed down with a towel under his arm. Maureen joined him for a while but then grew restless, couldn't relax, so she went down to the beach. She put on her goggles and swam out into the chill, doing laps in the calm sea, and then swam farther out, peering down at the small crabs and the waving sea grass; her eyes followed the sandy shelf as it sloped down into deeper, darker water. She dove, but soon it was too dark and murky to see and, frightened, she surfaced and swam quickly back to shore, scolding herself for her silliness as she emerged unsteadily into the sun. There was only one other person on the beach, a barrel-shaped man with his swim trunks pulled up nearly to his nipples. The other hotel patrons were clustered around the manicured concrete of the patio and pool area with its continuously cycling waterfall. Not really wanting to be social, and feeling awkward with Artaud, she remained on the beach, gazing out at the ocean.

Their hotel was on the northwest side of the island on Anakena beach. There were, of course, moai there, too, but these, she learned, were faux moai, having been molded from concrete sometime in the 1980s and arranged in an almost perfect semicircle around the beach—a beach which also boasted some of the island's few palm trees—also impostors, having been imported from the South American mainland.

"You want the real moai," the barrel-shaped man told her after he'd ignored her obvious body language and introduced himself anyway, "you should go to Rano Raraku. Many more there. You will like."

She gave him a cool nod and returned to the pool area, where she told Artaud about the place the man had recommended and asked if he wanted to go.

"Mmmmm, I think I'm good here for a while," he said, not opening his eyes. "But you go. Take the car."

She nodded, waited for a while hoping he might change his mind, but then she heard him snoring. She looked over and saw his mouth open and his head drooped to one side. She wondered if he'd applied sunscreen. Should she wake him and ask? No, too mothering. He wouldn't like that.

Back in the room, she showered, combed out her hair, and changed into shorts and a white button-down shirt. Then she sat on the bed, her eyes moving from her own reflection to Artaud's suitcase, which sat unlocked and partially open on the luggage stand. The case was polished aluminum with rounded edges and reminded Maureen of a giant waffle iron. She got up, went to the window, and looked down at the pool.

Still there, still asleep.

She closed the curtains, turned, went over to the suitcase, and lifted the lid. There were the seven tapes, just resting on top of his clothes. She walked over to the door and locked it. She emptied her shoulder bag on the bed and selected from the pile her wallet, passport, airline ticket, and keys to the rental car, all of which she returned to the bag. The rest of the stuff—magazines, makeup, beach towel, and ball cap—she pushed onto the floor and then under the bed. Then she returned to the suitcase, stuffed all seven of the tapes into her bag, and stood in the middle of the room, unsure what to do next. Resolve came to her and she found herself in the breezeway, sunglasses lowered, bag on her shoulder, walking to the end of the shaded corridor. There was a balcony there. She looked down at the pool, the beach beyond, back at the pool.

Still there, still asleep.

She went down to the car, backed it out of the garage, and followed the signs to the airport.

Twenty minutes and several pulverizing potholes later, she arrived, not at the airport, but at the ruins of the quarry the man on the beach had suggested. She didn't know what she was doing, why she was there, but she knew she needed to be away from Artaud for a while. She stopped the car along the side of the road. Off in the distance was the sloping edge of a dead volcano. The landscape was littered with moai, and partially carved moai, some having sunk at odd angles into the earth. She saw a few tourists, maybe three or four, up around the rim of the caldera, but she was essentially alone. She took the bag and walked up the slope, passing the enormous stone heads, some the size of upended RVs, as she went. She knew from her guidebook that the statues had once had eyes, the whites made of coral and the pupils carved from black obsidian. These had long ago fallen out or perhaps had never been put in place, leaving them with the empty-socketed visages that were now a part of the world's collective unconscious. Seeing them up close, the eye sockets were disconcerting because regardless of which way she went, they seemed like the eyes of a portrait in a cheap horror movie—never moving but always following her. They gazed down their long, sloping noses, their thick Polynesian lips seamed together in an arcane line. It gave her the creeps.

"Maureen?"

Startled at hearing her name, she spun around and in the process tripped over one of the volcanic stones partially embedded in the ground and fell backward. It was Worm.

"Are you all right?" he asked, running toward her and kneeling down.

"What are you doing here?" She was wide-eyed and scooted back from him, still feeling like she was in the low-budget horror film.

Worm looked back over his own shoulder, sure there must be someone else behind him responsible for her terror. Seeing no one, he faced her again and said, somewhat defensively, "I, I just came here for a vacation. You know, like a holiday."

"You didn't follow us?" she demanded.

His shoulders dropped when he heard the "us." So she was with him. It figured.

"No," he said, his dejected eyes scanning the stony panorama.

"Oh," she said, pulling herself up from the ground. "It's just . . . I'm just . . . so surprised to see you is all." She smiled, brushed the dirt off her jeans, tried to reapply her notorious air of casual indifference. "You know, when you're used to seeing someone in one place and then you see them in another place. A place where you don't usually see them." Her shoulder bag had slipped off when she fell and it still lay on the ground. Worm, seeing an opportunity for chivalry, bent down to retrieve it. Maureen, seeing him move toward it, and aware of what it still contained, tried to beat him to it. In their dual descents their heads knocked together like two coconuts. They retreated in mutual pain, each squinting and rubbing their respective points of contact. Then again, each for his and her own motive, they turned and both reached for the bag, this time narrowly averting yet another collision but each grabbing a separate end of the strap. Worm, seeing that she had it, let go of his end.

"I just wanted to—"

"No, it was my fault."

"Is your head okay?"

"Fine," she said, lifting the bag back over her head and letting the strap settle between her breasts. She reached behind her head with one arm and flipped her hair out from under the strap. Worm's eyes involuntarily gravitated to her chest, and his nostrils flared at the sudden presence in the salty breeze of that long-elusive scent.

They both looked around, scanning the ridge of the volcano and the plains leading off to the sea, but they were quite alone. It was the perfect setting for the cover of a romance novel, and Worm found himself wishing that he could transform himself into one of those large-pectoraled, long-haired fantasy men to whose slender waist beautiful damsels would yearn to cling. He was, of course, aware that he was not such a man, but nevertheless the setting seemed ideal, that scent was in the air, and his inner turmoil so suited to the melodramatic plot that he forgot he was not physically appropriate for the role and made his move, grabbing Maureen's upper arms, closing his eyes, and pulling her toward him, his lips almost making contact with hers, but hitting a little too far up and to the right. He felt her mouth open but didn't know how to interpret it. Was it from shock and surprise, or was it a welcoming invitation? Regardless, he kept his grasp on her arms, kept his lips pressed to her face. Her body was rigid at first but then started to quake. The quaking increased to a degree that seemed to him almost orgasmic, and she let her head fall backward. She was laughing! Worm opened his eyes and let go of her arms.

"So *that's* it." She giggled, her head rolling to one side.

Worm stepped back, unsure what she meant, but pretty sure it wasn't what he'd hoped. She continued laughing, her head drooping forward, hair curtaining her face. Gradually, she composed herself, sat back down on the large rock she'd tripped over, and swept the hair back from her eyes, which were teary with relieved amusement.

"I'm sorry," she said, although there was nothing whatsoever apologetic in her demeanor. Worm, feeling helpless and exposed, felt true fury toward the long-dead indigenous assholes, whoever they had been, who had felled the last tree on Easter Island and in so doing left him no place to hide his shame. The trees were gone, but in their place were the forests of towering stone faces whose eyes all seemed focused on him, their mouths, like Maureen's, barely containing their amusement. In a rage, he turned and began marching back up the swale of the volcano, his hands scrunched into fists.

Maureen's heart, which did, in spite of rumors to the contrary, exist, felt pity for Worm's embarrassment, so she got up and followed, a few paces behind, pursuing him for what she told herself were purely altruistic reasons, to make sure he was going to be okay and not do something rash, like, well, whatever one did at the rim of a dead volcano.

"Wait!" she called, but he continued up, opening his stride. As he crested the ridge, he paused to catch his breath, the sun blinding him. She was taller and in better shape so she reached him easily, and yet when she got to him and looked down at the gentle valley on the other side, the crater filled with tranquil water (so unlike the precipice she'd imagined him hurling himself off), she realized she needn't have worried. The most he could have done to himself was maybe stub a toe.

She stood there, arms at her sides, hair like seaweed around her head, unsure of what to say or do. And she shouldn't have been unsure. Situations like this were not new to her. She was often pursued by men she deemed undesirable, often had to convey to them, usually with brutal clarity, that she was not interested in what they had to offer, but this one had been such a surprise, so out of context. She'd known him (in the same peripheral and indifferent way that she'd known most of her coworkers) for years but had never had any indication that he saw her as anything other than a colleague. And then, of course, there were the tapes, the theft of which she had assumed, with the insane paranoia that often afflicts the guilty, that he had somehow discovered and had thus flown five hours to this remote wind-blasted island in the middle of nowhere to confront her about.

"Leave me alone!" he said, still trying to catch his breath and walking away from her down into the crater. But again, she did not leave him alone.

"Would you like to go get a beer?" she asked.

"No! Go away," he said, kicking at the dirt with his boot, his eyes fixed on the ground.

"Look, we all do stupid things, it's no big deal."

"Fuck you," he said, and resumed his march. She followed.

"Look, I know what it's like—to do stupid things, I mean."

He stopped, turned, and faced her, appalled by the callousness and arrogance of what she was saying but thrilled nonetheless that she had followed him. They stood in the wind and the sun as the shadows of the clouds made shifting patterns on the cobble-studded lawn stretching off in all directions. She let the bag with the tapes slip from her shoulder to the ground and approached. Taking his head in her hands, she kissed him. How long it lasted neither one could say. When she released him, she glanced around at the vacant scenery and, seeing that they were alone, reached down and undid the buckle of his belt. His face reddened. He waited to affirm that she was doing what he thought she was doing, and when he was assured, he let his hands come alive and move up and under her shirt, along her back until they reached her shoulder blades. Then, with a strength she found surprising, he pulled her toward him, but with such force that it knocked him down and pulled her on top of him. All outside light was dimmed by the aromatic blond tent of her hair. Their eyes met and locked as they struggled with straps and snaps. Fabric ripped, a shoe slipped off and tumbled down the hill as they rode and thrust on the grass. In less than five minutes, it was over. She rolled off him and they lay next to each other on their backs, staring up at the clouds forming and disintegrating.

Then she was up, pulling down her bra, buttoning her shirt, avoiding his eyes. He watched her for a moment but made no attempt to stop her. He knew it had been too good, too perfect. Nothing like that could stay. She found the bag, got it back over her shoulder, and again flipped her mane free. Fully dressed again, she extended a hand, not to help him up, but as a warped sort of good-bye. In response he sat up and slapped her hand away. He stood, pulled his pants up, and looked down the hill where her car was parked. "Just go," he said. And without another word, she did, heading back to the hotel, arriving just in time to replace the tapes in the suitcase before Artaud emerged from the shower.

Chapter 24

The discussion started when the admin brought over a fax for Janet. Janet, in turn, gave the woman what seemed, to Davis at least, an innocent compliment on her T-shirt. The shirt featured a picture of a large angel cradling the earth. Underneath the picture, in gothic script, were the words "Angels are my security system." Such accoutrements were not at all out of the ordinary with this admin, who was—whether from real religious conviction or merely as a theme for her collecting—obsessed with the winged immortals. Peering down from her computer monitor and from the ledges of her bookcase were several giddy ceramic cherubim, as well as a few of the more dour and rigid Catholic variety. On the wall behind her desk there was a pale blue plastic wall clock that every hour chimed out the first few bars of a different angel-themed song: "Angel Eyes," "Angel Baby," "Hark the Herald Angels Sing," "Heaven Must Be Missing An Angel," etc., and her battered Chevrolet was easily identifiable in the office parking lot by its bumper sticker, posted in the center of the rear window, proclaiming *Never drive faster than your angels can fly*.

The discussion started well after the angel admin had flitted back to her own desk. Gordon's conversational Tourette's kicked in and he said, seemingly apropos of nothing, "How absurd," but then did not elaborate. A few seconds elapsed before Tom took the bait:

"What's absurd?"

"The idea," Gordon proclaimed, "that wings like that mounted on the back of an average hundred-sixty-pound homo sapiens male could lift him into the air. Physically impossible."

Janet looked up; her chair moved ninety degrees. "You've got to be kidding me. You didn't just say that."

"Of course I did. Such wings would need to span at least twice the width of the human body. Not to mention the huge network of back muscles and the reinforced skeletal structure that would be required to support and operate them."

"There's such a thing as faith," Janet barked. "Divine mystery."

"What's the difference between faith," Tom asked, swiveling around to enter the fray, "and say, a magic show?"

"Exactly." Gordon nodded. "There's always some rational explanation for the rabbit coming out of the hat, or the woman sawed in half. I've seen a TV show about it, that one where they tell all of a magician's secrets. Enlightening."

"And if God, or Jesus, or whoever, wanted people to fly," Tom said, warming to the topic, "why did he have to give them avian characteristics? Couldn't they just float on their own without having to sprout feathers?"

"Don't worry," Janet sneered. "Where you two are headed, you won't be needing wings."

It was into the midst of this discussion that Sarah descended. In the three months since Davis had seen her, she had, of course, become much thinner but, by contrast, her breasts seemed inordinately large and were compressed into a Western shirt, whose mother-of-pearl snaps strained to contain them. She wore jeans, rolled up to just below the knee, and a pair of white canvas tennis shoes. She had also grown out her hair, although it was artlessly concealed beneath a red bandana. The only thing missing from her outfit was a long blade of prairie grass clenched between her teeth. As usual, however, her appearance belied her professionalism and, after making a polite round of greetings and then displaying the numerous photos of her tiny, and quite vocal, progeny, she pulled a chair up to Davis's desk, sat down, and flipped open a folder.

"First of all, here is your offer for permanent employment. Congratulations. Read it over and if you find the terms acceptable, sign all the paperwork and return it to HR."

Davis was stunned. And by the sound of the chairs swiveling around behind him, so were his colleagues.

"You're not coming back?" Tom asked.

Sarah rolled her eyes and swiveled her own chair around to face them.

"Not full-time," she said. "And the way my life is right now, I certainly can't deploy for months at a time. Not that a break like that wouldn't be nice! But I think it would end my marriage. I've accepted a consultant position. It's a fraction of the pay, but I'll be able to work from home."

"How nice for you," Gordon said.

"Yes," Janet agreed. "Betcha won't miss that traffic every day. Day in and day out."

"Or all the meetings and trainings."

"Oh, I'll have to dial in to most of the meetings," she said. "And I'll still be required to complete the online modules."

"But still . . ." Tom said.

Davis's eyes went from the paperwork to Sarah, then back to the paperwork. This was the absolute opposite of what he'd expected to happen. So much so that he didn't know how to react. The pills would be paid for, that was a relief, but what about his writing? What did this mean? It was all moving too fast. He turned and looked at the embittered faces of Tom, Gordon, and Janet. Did this mean he was . . . one of them? The thought sent an involuntary shudder through his body. Before he had a chance to digest the idea of himself as a full-timer, Sarah turned back to the desk, closed the file with the employment paperwork, and opened a notebook.

"This is what you'll need to work on next," she said. "It's essentially the same as the bird mitigation policy, but this one involves marine mammals."

"What?" Davis cried. "No!"

Sarah was surprised by his reaction, and a little annoyed.

"Yes. The same."

"But . . . not in the same way . . ." Davis replied.

She looked confused for a moment, but then realized the reason for his trepidation. "Oh, no." She chuckled. "No, no, no. No blood, no mess. In fact, it will probably bore you to tears since it will involve a whole lot of standing around and doing nothing."

He nodded. Nothing. That he could most certainly do. Sarah went on:

"Here's the deal: There's controversy surrounding the use of seismic. Biologists and geologists don't see eye to eye on much of anything, and on this topic they really disagree. Also, there's pressure from some environmentalist groups who claim tha—"

No sooner had the words "environmentalist groups" left her mouth than three chairs swiveled around and three sets of ears went on the alert. Davis knew it was only a matter of seconds before one of them began editorializing. Sarah knew it, too, and with a sigh and another roll of her eyes, she closed the notebook, leaned close to Davis, and whispered, "Why don't we go see if there's an available conference room."

Davis nodded. He and Sarah rose and left the cubicle. When they were a safe distance away she said, "I forgot that those walls have ears. And mouths."

"Yes." Davis agreed, and then filled her in on that morning's angelic discussion.

"You think that's bad? There was one day last summer when they argued for almost a week on whether Ronald Reagan should be added to Mount Rushmore."

They found an empty room, went in, and shut the door. "You'll have to research this some more on your own," Sarah said, taking a seat and setting the notebook on the table, "but here's the background. There have been a few instances, mostly involving sonar, but a few implicating seismic, that have been linked to whale strandings."

Davis recalled the outline of the discussion from the Worm/ Jerry fight in the galley, but again he was tripped up by some vocabulary.

"Strandings?"

"Whales beaching themselves."

"Oh."

"Not just whales—dolphins, porpoises, those sorts of critters.

Most of the higher-profile cases have involved Navy sonar, low frequency, used to detect submarines. There was one notable case in the Bahamas that they pretty much admitted causing. And again, most of this has to do with sonar—not seismic—but now biologists and environmentalist groups are going after anything that makes noise in the water. And that's not to say they shouldn't. There have been a few cases off Baja where seismic has been linked to strandings. We knew we were going to have to come up with some mitigation policy sooner or later, we just hoped it would be later. Unfortunately, Artaud had to raise the red flag and make it look all suspicious by forbidding photography, so now we've got to do something."

"But he said he did it because he didn't wan—"

"Oh, I know all about what he wants and doesn't want. Believe me. We had several teleconferences on the subject while you were at sea. And I've sailed with him a lot in the past. I even had the pleasure of being on the cruise when his marriage broke up. And let me tell you, those brawls make your little cubicle tussles seem like a game of Go Fish.

"The point is, NSF knows what he did and they don't like it. You have to think of them like an elderly aunt who's easily scandalized. They don't like anything with even the whiff of controversy, and if—"

"How did they find out?"

Sarah shrugged. "That doesn't matter. What matters is that it made things look suspicious. And if the NRDC or Greenpeace or, God forbid, Sea Shepherd were to get wind of it, well . . . there might be unpleasantness."

"What do I need to do?" Davis asked, dreading what was coming next.

Sarah opened the notebook and scooted it over to him.

"Like I said, you've got to come up with a mitigation policy for dealing with this—a way to make it seem like we're protecting marine mammals while at the same time allowing seismic operations to continue. They liked your Bird/Light Mitigation presentation, so you've got some credibility."

Whoever "they" were, Davis was certain that "they" had not

been in the audience for his shipboard PowerPoint performance. Could it be, he wondered, that Sarah had not heard the details about that?

"I printed up some of the e-mail traffic that came through on the topic while you were deployed. As you'll see, the higher-ups got a little panicked. Read through these first," she said, sliding the thick notebook over to him, "and you'll get an idea about who the players are, who you might go to for information and, most important, who you'll want to avoid.

"Other research institutions use seismic all the time, and so does the oil and gas industry, so I'm sure they're taking heat about this, too. Find out what they're doing and see if you can follow their lead on any of it."

Davis contemplated the subtext of Sarah's phrase "follow their lead." Did she mean *follow their lead* in the same way that he had followed the lead of the Alabama exterminator? Had she never wondered where he'd obtained the graphic graphics? She had seen them—and signed off on the presentation—before he went to sea. Surely she didn't think they were his own creations. Was she tacitly telling him to do the same thing here?

As he considered this, the spectral forms of that multiethnic, sexually balanced cast of characters Anne, Ernesto, Tyrone, and Cheng (each clad in appropriate business attire) drifted into Davis's mind like some Shakespearian ghosts, whispering their ominous ethical message, *What if?*

"Any questions?"

"Yes."

"Shoot."

"Well, if this is so important . . ." Davis trailed off.

"Then why is it falling in your lap?"

"Yes."

"Frankly, because no one else wants it, and because you're now the marine tech writer. You've been on a seismic trip. You know the basics of how the equipment works. Who else would do it?"

Davis raised one side of his mouth; the pathetic approximation of a smile. Sarah patted him on the thigh.

"And, to be honest, you don't seem to have an agenda."

"What does that mean?"

"It means you're not on one side of the fence or the other," she said, but then sighed and added: "At least not yet."

While he was considering what *that* meant, she continued:

"Fundamentally, this is just another CYA policy. It is very important, of course, but it doesn't have to be perfect, m'kay? The goal is to show that we're doing something, even if it's a not very effective something."

"Okay."

"Ideally, we need this before Artaud's next seismic cruise in January."

"That soon."

"Yes. You'll be sailing to instruct them on the policy and to conduct some trainings."

"I will?"

"Yes, you will."

It burned, on the lips, in the mouth, as it slowly descended the esophagus, even for a few seconds before it was absorbed by the acid in the stomach. Vodka, gin, shaken with ice, served up, no garnish. The White Angel. It was the signature drink at Joe Bell's Bar. Many people tried it once, but only the foolish or desperately alcoholic drank it a second time. Both Davis (who did not have a reputation for learning from his mistakes) and Jake (for whom twelve steps meant nothing more than the distance from the bar stool to the urinal) had so far consumed three rounds of the beverage. They had met after work so that Jake could indulge his vice without having to endure the not-so-silent disapproval of his teetotaling boyfriend, and so that Davis could question Jake about Sarah's assignment. They had ordered White Angels because to Davis, it seemed almost divinely coincidental, given that morning's cubicle discussion. Jake appreciated it because it was economically alcoholic: not gunked up with a mixer, but more classy and refined than a shot.

"It's stupid," Jake said, "but we have to do it."

"Why stupid?" Davis asked, sipping from his drink and feeling the burn go up into his sinuses.

"Oh, because there's no proof seismic does shit to whales."

"Then why didn't he want the pictures taken?"

"Search me. The guy's an ass. And he's got that assistant . . . that . . ."

"Jerry?"

"Yeah."

"What about him?"

"Smart, but strange. An oil-and-gas guy. He's supposed to replace the brains that Madeleine took with her when she left, but he's not doing such a great job."

"Madeleine?"

"The ex-wife. They made a great team for a while, collaborated on all their research, but the guy just couldn't keep his dick in his pants. Now he's the one scrambling for tenure and funding and she's getting published in all the science journals."

"I wondered where his kids came from."

"Madeleine Burroughs Artaud," Jake said, enunciating all the syllables in her name. "She wanted to go back to her maiden name but figured she better hang on to his so that he doesn't steal the credit for the work they did together. She's twice the scientist he is—and knows it. She's also the queen bee ball buster."

"He must like them that way."

"Either that or he makes them that way."

"I won't be sailing with her, with Madeleine, right?"

"Right. She's doing work in the Arctic for the next few years. They barely even speak to each other anymore. You'll be with Artaud and his crew again. Probably all the same players, but on the other side."

"Of the peninsula?"

"Of the continent. In the Ross Sea. You leave from New Zealand instead of Chile. You'll love it! No gentle straits to go through to let you get your sea legs. As soon as you leave the harbor—BOOM! You're in open ocean. Reserve yourself a space at the cough trough."

Chapter 25

The black sunglasses were so large they made his face look like a hornet. He stood fanning himself with a sign in the shape of an auction paddle. On one side was the logo of the car company, on the other, in heavy black ink he'd written *William Oliver Radley III*. The sign was an adequate fan and had, so far, kept the sweat from dripping onto the collar of his crisp linen shirt. There was air-conditioning in the terminal, but most of it poured out into the tropic heat through large automatic doors that almost never had a chance to shut due to the steady in-and-out stream of human traffic.

The driver had been paid in advance by Mr. and Mrs. William Oliver Radley Jr. to pick up their son when his flight landed. When the boy arrived, the driver had been instructed to apologize to him and to tell him his parents would have come themselves but they were hosting a dinner party and could not get away. The driver was told to drop "Bill" at a hotel in Kingston where they would meet him for breakfast the next morning.

The doors from customs and immigration swung open and people spilled out, pushing metal carts overloaded with luggage. The driver stopped fanning himself and held up the sign so the name was visible. He was busy scanning the crowd so was surprised when he felt a tap on his arm, followed by "I'm him."

He looked down and did not conceal his skepticism. This man, dressed in an old T-shirt, the sole of one boot held on with silver tape, his long hair uncombed, looked more like one of the drunkards who lived on the beach, or like some of the poor student tourists who wandered around stoned and disheveled in the mornings trying to find a Starbucks. The driver lowered his sunglasses and looked at the man more intently. There was, in the size of the ears, the receding hairline, and the overall elephantine expression of the face, a resemblance to the old man who had paid him. He'd thought those were just the traits of old age, but now he realized that the old man had probably looked that way most of his life.

Again he pushed his sunglasses up and looked down at the duffel bag, lying filthy on the floor between them. He was just bending over to retrieve it, trying to think how he could carry it without dirtying his pants, when Worm hoisted it onto his shoulder and said, "Don't worry. I got it."

From the windows of the refrigerated car, views of the cardboard and tin shanty towns soon gave way to manicured gardens and wedding cake villas. Tableau after tableau of watercolor-worthy scenery presented itself to the passenger in the car, but he saw none of it. His head was thrust back and he stared blankly at the velour ceiling. He was already depressed and now he had the even more depressing prospect of Christmas with his parents unrolling before him. The house would be filled with all the trappings from a more northerly clime: the pine tree; the stockings; the heavy smells of roast beef, Yorkshire pudding, and pecan pie; the cinnamon- and pine-scented candles that would burn nonstop the entire week, giving off their cozy cabin glow while outside it was eighty-seven degrees in the shade. There would be tennis and cocktail parties, cocktail parties and golf, and his mother would be dressed incongruously in her holiday sweater and lampshade tennis skirt, applauding from the cart as he and his father meandered their way through the course, his father talking on and on about the family business and how he hoped he wouldn't be forced to sell it off "to strangers."

Thank God, Worm thought, for their dinner party and the night at a hotel. It would give him more time to mentally prepare himself.

Worm was an only child and he dutifully loved his parents. What he didn't love, however, was how much they fussed over him whenever he was around, how they never quite managed, despite their valiant efforts, to conceal their disappointment in his choice of work, his failure to find a wife and provide them with grandchildren. They had always encouraged him to pursue his own life, had spared no expense on his education or travel opportunities, but were surprised when his ideals and values turned out to be so different from their own.

In the course of the coming week, Worm knew, his parents would ask 1) how long he intended to work on that boat and 2) if he was seeing anyone. Hearing "I don't know" and "No, no one special," they would then proceed to update him on the intricate and expanding lives of the friends and neighbors he'd grown up with. With painful recollection he replayed some of the conversations they'd had during his last Christmas visit:

"That Chuck Green," his mother said, "you remember him, don't you, Bill? He was in your grade, lived over on Alder Circle in that house with the tire swing out front. Anyway, he and his second wife just had triplets. Can you believe it? That's in addition to the two he's got from his first marriage, and the one the second wife had on her own. They sure will have a brood!"

The only memory Worm had of Chuck Green was when he and three other boys had held him down and stapled the sleeves of his shirt to the table in shop class.

"Your mother's in a book club," his father had said one day while they were making lunch. "Tell him about it, Peg."

"Oh, he's not interested in that."

He wasn't, but he played along. "Sure I am, Mom. Let's hear it."

"Well, all right then. It's through the library downtown. Gwen Tomkins told me about it, so I read a few of the books they'd chosen and just started going."

"Good for you."

"Yes, it's been so . . . refreshing, I guess you'd say, to meet with people who are younger. Such interesting perspectives you all have. And the facilitator is just great!"

A glance between the parents, almost imperceptible but caught by their son.

"I think you know her . . . Lori Brewer? She told me she went to school with you, was just fascinated when I told her what you were doing, really, just so curious about it, would love to have you give a talk or slide show sometime at the library. She does so much outreach to seniors and students. Such an angel. And smart! And time certainly has been on her side. She still looks just like her yearbook picture."

And here his mother, in a burst of schoolgirl enthusiasm, disappeared into one of the bedrooms and returned a moment later bearing his high school yearbook, a Post-it Note marking the page with Lori Brewer's picture.

"You brought my yearbook to Jamaica?"

"See how pretty she was? And now that I look at her again I can say she looks even better now. Her skin's cleared up and she doesn't have that frizzy perm, although for some reason that I can't for the life of me figure out she wears an earring in her nose. Can't imagine how a girl like that is still single."

But the worst conversation had come on Christmas Eve, right before they were to have dinner.

"Got one of your buddies, Jim Wilbury, working for our sales team," his father had said. There was silence after this remark, during which the elder Bill stirred his highball with his knobby index finger and avoided looking at his wife, who was sitting on the couch, a pen in one hand and a crossword puzzle in the other. She did not look up, looked as though she was trying to keep from crying. His father cleared his throat and continued. "Jim says to tell you hello, by the way. Jim does. He's really proven himself, always hitting his quota. Helluva guy, that Jim. Helluva guy."

He stirred his drink once more, and then took a large sip. His mother tapped the pen on her lips and gazed intently, almost too intently, at her puzzle.

"Brought his, uh, partner to the company picnic," his father added, and then paused for the significance of the comment to sink in. Worm closed his eyes and prayed to a God he did not really believe in that the conversation was not headed where he feared it was heading.

"That raised some eyebrows," his father said, "I can tell you. But not as many as you might think. Most folks these days are okay with . . . that sort of thing."

Another pause.

"Your mother and I are okay with it."

"We certainly are," she said, her face still locked onto the puzzle. "However people can find happiness in this crazy world these days is A-OK with us."

The rest of that visit had been taken up with his attempt to persuade his parents that he was not gay, that he did like girls, was, in fact hoping, someday, to find the right member of the female sex to settle down with and raise a family. And the truth was he did want that, did hope that someday he'd have someone to bring home to them, some announcement to make, someone who would help him gain enough momentum to finally spin out of their parental orbit and create a solar system of his own. But here he was, a year later, thirty-six years old and still alone, still too shy to cross the threshold anywhere other than in his imagination. Always falling in love with beautiful women he was too shy to approach.

As he stared at the roof of the taxi he recalled the recent, but no less embarrassing scene on the volcano with Maureen, and self-pity rose like a gas bubble in his throat. He made several concerted and evidently vocal swallows to push it back down.

"You all right, my friend?"

Worm sat up straight. The hornet glasses were reflected in the rearview mirror.

"Yes," he said. "I'm all right."

"Do you need to stop somewhere before the hotel?"

Worm gave him a questioning look. In response, the driver took one hand from the wheel and first pantomimed guzzling a bottle, and then smoking a joint.

"I can get you some of the finest."

"Thanks. No."

"What about a girl?"

"Thanks," Worm said, "but I'm all right."

"That's not the look of all right, I'm tellin' you."

"You got a family?" Worm asked. The man lowered the visor, took down a plastic envelope, and handed it over his shoulder to the backseat. Worm leaned forward and took it. The envelope accordioned out to reveal several pages of photos.

"Six girls, two boys, one more coming soon."

Worm examined the photos: smiling faces at birthday parties, jubilant soccer victories, first communions.

"They make you happy?" he asked, folding the case and handing it back over the seat.

The driver shrugged. "Happy, sad, angry . . . Depends on the day, my friend. You always make your parents happy?"

Worm shook his head.

"That's not the job of children. These kids, I bring them into the world, try to show them how to live, but I'm just their father, I am not God. Some days they are like a band of devils. On those days it is good to have someone on your side. On those days you are grateful for a wife. Then you almost always have an ally." He paused for a moment and repeated the qualifier: "Almost always."

They traveled on, the gardens and white walls gradually giving way to the high-rises and apartment blocks of the city.

"You have a girl?" the driver asked.

"Me? No," Worm said. Then, after a moment: "I mean, there's one that I want."

"I thought so."

"Why?"

"I can tell. Not interested in drink or smoke or women. It was either some girl or you like the boys."

"That might be easier."

"So you love this one?"

Worm thought about that. It seemed a new concept to him. All the time he'd spent thinking about her, all the time he'd spent in that stupid department store tracking down her scent, the way he'd replayed in his head that bitter scene with her on the volcano and could, in fact, remember very little else from the entire week-long trip. The slightly nauseous, amusement park feeling he had in his stomach when he heard her voice. Was that it? Was that love?

"I think maybe I do," he said.

"She married?"

"What? No. But there's someone else. Someone not good for her."

"Ahh, competition."

"Yeah, whatever," Worm said, turning to look out the window, annoyed by all this talk.

"She smart, this girl?"

"Yeah, she's smart."

"If he's no good, she'll maybe figure it out."

"Can we . . . just not talk about it anymore?" Worm said.

"Sure, sure."

They drove in silence the rest of the way. When they got to the hotel, Worm got out and walked to the back of the car. The driver popped the trunk and both reached for the duffel bag.

"You don't have to," Worm said. "I know it's dirty." He set the bag on the pavement and reached for his wallet, pulling out a bill and handing it to the driver. When he was almost to the revolving door of the hotel, the driver called out.

"And a tip for you, my friend."

Worm turned and squinted at the man, his hand held up as a visor.

"You say he's not good for her, this competitor. I wonder if she is good for you."

Chapter 26

Davis closed the binder and stared at the gray screen of his monitor. He didn't know where or how to begin so he did what any desk-bound bewildered person would do and typed the words "seismic and marine mammals" into Google and hit Enter. The screen was instantly populated with a dizzying array of options. Davis clicked on the first one and was taken to a website for an oil and gas company. A fog of artificial clouds disintegrated, revealing an aerial shot of a brightly painted oil drilling platform in the middle of a calm ocean. A gleaming tanker was docked next to the platform, presumably onloading crude oil, although looking as if it had just dropped by for a visit. Off to one side, just visible beneath the surface, were a large whale and her calf, calmly swimming, unfazed by the human and mechanical activity in their backyard. As Davis watched, the clouds magically reformed themselves, but this time into the company's name and logo, and then into the phrase:

Responsible Energy Development—Because the World
Belongs to Us All.

There were similar sites from other energy companies, and one massive site from the Navy, all featuring aerial shots of undisturbed whales or dolphins frolicking in and around various vessels and installations, all with similar catchphrases:

To Provide and Protect—for Future Generations
Oil Exploration *and* Environmental Conservation?
Yes We Can!
At (insert company name here), we take stewardship of
the environment seriously.
Meeting the energy demands of our generation without
sacrificing our legacy to the next. That's the (insert
company name here) way of doing business.

Although slick in appearance, and with Madison Avenue phrasing for their message, the tone of these websites was just ever so slightly off. Something about needing to have a website explicitly designed to reassure the public that what you were doing was not harmful or unethical somehow made you more suspect rather than less.

Whereas those sites were subtle and defensive, the opposing side was, appropriately enough, explicit and offensive. Their websites featured grainy crime-scene photos of beaches littered with desiccating whale and dolphin carcasses, or whaling vessels hauling in their catch from a crimson sea. They referred to the ships conducting seismic operations as Whale Harassment Vessels (WHVs) and called the crew manning them Sonic Butchers. Their banner headings (never materializing out of the mist) were imperative demands expressed in primary-colored block capitals:

NO BLOOD FOR OIL!
STOP THE KILLING!
WASN'T ONE HOLOCAUST ENOUGH?
IS IT REALLY WORTH IT?

After just half an hour of hopping from site to site, visiting first one, then the other of two apparently alternate universes, Davis was as familiar with the two distinct sides as he would ever be. There were those who claimed seismic was perfectly safe, and those who claimed it was a deadly weapon; those who said that it was our patriotic duty to explore for offshore oil in order to free ourselves from the Arab yoke, and those who said that by doing so we were destroying the world we purported to defend. What began as semi-rational discussions usually escalated into screaming hyperbole and one-sided exercises in discrediting the argument of the opponent.

One side would describe the sound emitted by "seismic sound sources" in almost quaint, old-timey terms, as being equivalent to listening to soft music while standing three feet away from a radio. Others described shots fired from "seismic guns" and compared them to the deafening blast of standing next to a rocket during lift-off.

One said it was a harmless sound emitted into the water that the animals might possibly notice but would probably not be bothered by. The other talked of bleating dolphins with bleeding ears.

The arguments were, fundamentally, no different than the arguments he listened to every day in his cubicle; were, in fact, a reflection of the cubicle, the country, and probably the world. Draw a line in the sand between two people and each will, often without any real reason, assert that the side he's on is best, not out of a desire to speak the truth so much as a desire to prevail and thus belittle the opponent. Alas, it seemed that humankind never really advanced beyond adolescence.

To confirm this hypothesis, Davis attempted a social experiment with his coworkers. He disconnected the cord of his desk phone from the wall and pretended to have the following conversation:

"Yes, hello. My name is Davis Garner and I work for the Marine division of Polar Support Services. I sent you an e-mail about the seismic/marine mammal mitigation plan I'm working on. Is now a good time to talk? . . . Great. I was told you might be a good person to speak to since your institution has dealt with the topic in the past."

No discernible reaction from his coworkers. He cleared his throat to get their attention and continued:

"I see," he said. "Yes . . . Uh-huh . . . Interesting . . . Dead? On the beach? . . . That many? . . . Wow."

Behind him, Davis heard the rhythmic click and clack of typing fingers slow and then cease altogether. He envisaged hands held aloft, heads lifted, ears on the alert. He was curious to see whose interest had been piqued first, but he had seen enough old movies to know that he needed to stay focused on his monologue and feign obliviousness to anything going on in the background.

"So, if I'm hearing you correctly, your thought is that the noise from the seismic operations is causing the whales to beach themselves."

The dull sound of plastic casters rolling over plastic carpet protector as a chair was eased back away from the desk; then the pitter-patter of little steps as the chair was swiveled around.

"Uh-huh . . . uh-huh . . . Terrible . . . So sad. But I guess there's not much we can do about it."

One more swivel.

"Burden of proof . . . Uh-huh . . . Uh-huh . . . It is science, after all."

More pitter-pattering.

"Uh-huh . . . Yes, well, that's understandable. Everything has a cost, I suppose. Sometimes it's money, sometimes it's a pound of flesh."

A hermit crab scuttled away from its protective desk toward the center of the room.

"Thank you for your time, it's been very informative. Yes, you too. Bye now."

Janet: You really buy into that crap?

Davis pretended to be writing on a legal pad.

Janet: That "Save the Whales" nonsense?

Davis turned, as if he were suddenly aware he was not alone. His expression was blank and he said nothing. He didn't need to. He'd said enough.

Gordon: Ensonification of the seas is not nonsense.

Janet: Ensoni-what?

Gordon and Tom (in chorus): Ensonification!

Gordon (alone): Contaminating the ocean with sound.

Janet: You've got to be fucking kidding me.

Tom: Noise pollution is no joke.

Janet: Give me a break. You think whales never hurled

themselves onto the beach until they started using seismic? They're no different than birds flying into windows, or like those idiots who need a tennis ball on a string hanging from the ceiling of their garage to tell them when to stop. Plain stupid.

Tom (shaking his head): That's really ignorant.

Gordon: Appalling. Not surprising, but still appalling.

Janet: Oh, please. I'll tell you what's appalling: What's appalling is the environmentalist nuts who've got this country by the balls. What's appalling is having to pay foreigners for gas when we've got plenty of our own to tap into on the homeland. What's appalling is protecting a fish over a human!

Tom: Not fish, Janet, mammals, just like us. Although as cold-blooded as your argument is, I'm beginning to think you might be amphibian.

Janet: What's appalling is enemy subs invading our waters and the terrorists storming our beaches because we can't use sonar to detect them—all because we might hurt a few whales.

Tom: What's appalling is the eradication from our planet, by us, of yet another species.

Gordon: What kind of world will we leave for our children?

Janet: You don't have children. You can't even get laid.

Tom: And all so that people can drive their SUVs to the mall to buy some more crap they don't need.

Gordon: Precisely.

Janet: You won't need to worry about any of that once the terrorists get into this country and put IEDs all over those malls. You'll be happy then.

The argument went on for some time, and Davis sat on the sidelines, taking it all in, making note of the points on each side. The discussion ended when Janet's phone rang.

"What? . . . Yes. I'll tell him."

She hung up and narrowed her eyes at Davis.

"That was your little friend Jake," she said. "He wants you to come over to his office. Said he's been trying to call you but your *phone* isn't working."

Davis turned back to his desk, pretended to check the connections of his phone and in the process clicked the cord back into it. The click was, unfortunately, audible, and when he turned around again, there were three sets of narrowed eyes.

"Funny," he said, holding the receiver in front of his face and listening to the dull buzz of the dial tone. "Seems to be working now."

Chapter 27

The telephone as an instrument of torture was without rival. E-mail came close to stealing the crown, especially if your significant other happened to break up with you via that medium, but then texting piggybacked onto the telephone and firmly established it as the sovereign of misery.

For Maureen, back in the office after her vacation on Easter Island, her telephone became a sort of ringing, vibrating ball and chain. She had parted from Artaud at the airport in Dallas and called him later that night, just to tell him she'd arrived home safely, to say that she hoped his flight home had been pleasant, and maybe add that she missed him, although maybe not. Nothing major. Polite niceties. Protocol. Manners. Common decency. Her call had gone directly to voice mail and she'd left a message inviting him to call her back, saying, "I'll be up late."

A week passed; no call. During the days and nights that she waited, the phone went everywhere with her, even into the bathroom.

The following Monday she came up with a work-related pretext and called him from her desk phone. Again, she got his voice mail.

"Hello. It's me. Maureen. I was editing some of your bottom mapping data and I was wondering which, if any, filters you might want applied to it. You can call me back at this number, or on my cell," and she recited her cell number, careful to enunciate each digit. He responded the next day via e-mail with the information she had requested and a few businesslike niceties tacked on at the end. She read his response, three sentences in total, over and over and over, analyzing each word with the fervor of a CIA operative intercepting a message from Al Qaeda.

For all the paroxysms of inner agony this message caused her, she still managed to present a normal façade to the outside world. Oh, she was a bit more short-tempered than usual with some of her coworkers, but nothing that anyone would think was too out of the ordinary.

Her obsession with the phone, however, and the mental distraction it caused her was more of a problem, and there were a few times during the week when she was asked a direct question by her boss and had to quickly swim up from the depths of her tormented thoughts, break the surface, and ask for the question to be repeated. Since her job largely consisted of doing the same things over and over again, she almost always had an answer she could automatically recite. But that was both a blessing and a curse, since the repetitive and mindless nature of her work left vast tracts of fertile gray matter open to paranoid development.

Throughout the day she asked herself a series of pointless questions and inevitably thought up the worst possible answers: Why wasn't he calling? (He hated her.) What was he doing? (Screwing a pert young student, no doubt.) What had she done to alienate him? (Been too clingy? Bitchy? Available?) She contemplated all the possible scenarios (car accident, new mistress, reconciliation with his wife, grand mal seizure) that might be behind his failure to dial her number. She set the cell phone on her desk and often called it from her desk phone just to confirm it got reception in the building (it did).

The second week, she summoned the courage to call again. Expecting to get voice mail, she had a well-rehearsed speech in her head, the delivery of which he ruined by answering. When she heard his voice, the anger that had inflated her sails, pushing her toward this very point of longitude and latitude, vanished, and she was able to sputter nothing but generalities and platitudes: *How are things going?* Great. You? *Great. Not too much going on here. It's been sunny.* Really? We've had rain.

To make the conversation even worse, it was punctuated by a series of pauses, during which she could hear him typing and shuffling papers.

You sound busy. *I am a bit.* I should call back later. *Yes.* Or you can call me. When you're free, I mean. You know, like, whenever you have a free moment. *I'll do that.*

After that, she stopped calling. She did not, of course, stop waiting for his call, and during her waking hours she consulted her cell phone every quarter hour. The tormented imaginings recommenced. The same paranoia she'd felt in Punta Arenas when he'd gone on without her to Santiago was resurrected, only now instead of imagining him in the clutches of a Latina temptress, she saw him with a sophisticated colleague—one with mannish wire-rimmed glasses and an off-the-rack pantsuit, her hair held up in a bun during the day—a tight, controlled woman who loosened up in the evening after a few glasses of something classy and unpronounceable. One who shook out her hair and emerged from the bedroom (where she had gone, of course, to slip into something more comfortable) looking like Rita Hayworth in *Gilda*. Those were the thoughts that tormented her. All clichés, she knew, but could there be any bigger cliché than a woman anxiously awaiting a phone call from her indifferent lover?

The irony and hypocrisy of her mania did not escape her; the fact that she, not he, had been the infidel—and during their vacation, no less. But in her mind, that wasn't the issue. The issue, as she saw it, was that she had done something unethical and illegal for him, and now that he had what he wanted, he was ignoring her. It was unconscionable, scandalous, outrageous! But above all it was an ego bruise.

During the third week, she only texted once (ending her inane message with a winking emoticon, the recollection of which would later cause her visceral pain) and then called twice. Both times he answered but couldn't talk. He was apologetic but was on his way out the door to a meeting (probably at a motel or some cheap off-campus apartment) or a dinner engagement (candlelit, no doubt, with two glasses and a bottle of that chalky Chianti he was so fond of using to loosen up the fairer sex). And always he ended their conversations by saying, "I'd love to talk more, babe, but I've really got to go. People are waiting."

After the first call, she hung up, set the phone down on the desk, and scowled at it. Was she not *people?* Was she not *fucking waiting?*

After the second call, she hung up and pitched the phone at the sofa. It bounced back and hit her in the shin, whereupon she snatched it up in a rage and hurled it at the wall, silencing it permanently. Remorse rose up in her almost immediately. Afraid that she might miss a call, she collected the pieces of the shattered device, got her coat and purse, and left the house to procure a replacement, making sure that the salesman of the new device understood the importance of obtaining any messages, voice or text, that might have come through in the interim. Sadly, there were none.

Very much later that night, her nerves settled and her courage fortified by very many glasses of scotch, she telephoned him on her new phone, determined to confront him about his neglect. Of course, her call went to voice mail, but the message she left must have been potent, because the next morning at work her desk phone rang and it was him.

"How's your head?"

"Fine," she lied, trying to sound perky. "Artaud?"

"Yes. You sound surprised to hear from me."

"A little."

Another of those awful pauses, in which the details of her drunken dialing leeched back into her consciousness.

"Are you there?" she asked.

"I'm here," he said, "but this needs to stop. I won't tolerate messages like the one last night."

She pressed her fingertips hard on her eyelids and tried to think. She remembered dialing, remembered hearing the ring and his voice-mail message, but the rest . . .

His voice was terse: "If you've got something to say to me," he said, "then have the courage to say it to me directly, not in some liquor-fueled tirade on voice mail."

"I'm sorry," she whined. "I'm really sorry."

Her simpering tone combined with the two words she so rarely uttered together were so shocking to her coworker on the other side of the cubicle that he rose and peeked over the top to see if it was really her.

"Listen," Artaud said, the gentleness she so loved returning to his voice, "maybe we should take a breather for a while." A cactus-spined panic rolled up her back when she heard that.

"What do you mean?" she asked.

"Nothing major. Just a little space until the next cruise. Give us each some time to think things over, see how we feel."

She wanted to scream. She didn't need time to think! She knew how she felt. She felt sad, rejected, unloved; she felt a yearning for him that was so strong it made her dizzy—and all those feelings were enlarged and amplified by his weeks of silence and her throbbing hangover. *Time to think?* What she needed was an end to the thinking! An end to the tormenting speculation!

What she said was: "Well, if you really think so. I mean, if you think that's what's best."

"Babe, I do. I really do."

Chapter 28

Over the next few weeks, Davis immersed himself in all things whale, dolphin, and porpoise, and attempted to make some sense of the bewildering science of acoustics. In spite of the difficulties, he was, for the first time, really interested in what he was doing. And the more interested he became, the more intrusive and annoying the ensonification of his cubicle became. His initial efforts to tune out the squabbling of his coworkers involved stuffing his ears with wadded-up bits of Kleenex. When that wasn't enough, he went to a drugstore and bought some squishy, expandable earplugs. Those were more effective, but Gordon's voice was of such a pitch and frequency that rumblings of it still managed to penetrate. What finally did it, what finally brought Davis the desired bliss of near-total silence—the silence that blocked out all exterior noise and made him suddenly aware of the inward hiss and gurgle of his own breathing and swallowing—was a set of noise-canceling headphones. They were large, obviously visible (fitting over his ears like two hamburger buns), and were, therefore, a hostile statement of antisocial behavior toward his cube mates, but he found them necessary roughly 60 percent of the time he was at work and he found it easy to ignore the snub his wearing them implied.

So interested was he in what he was researching, so transfused with purpose, that he even forgot about toilet napping. In fact, there were many times that month when he was so mesmerized by what he was reading that he found himself crossing his legs and swinging his feet, not wanting to interrupt his concentration with even a quick trip to the urinal.

There were still, of course, the mandatory, drool-inducing Marine Staff Meetings and the Company All Hands Meetings to sit through, still the Online Ethics Modules and the Six Sigma Practicums to endure. None of that tedium was new or surprising to Davis; he had been required to do the same, or at least very similar things, during his last stint in the office, but the difference was that now those meetings and modules and practicums were intruding on his doing real work, and he was surprised how much he resented it. It seemed that he would just get into a mental groove, just have stumbled upon something really interesting and useful when a meeting reminder pop-up would flash on his screen giving him the five-minute warning for the Internet Rules of Behavior (IRoB) Meeting: attendance mandatory.

Of course, Davis being Davis, the part of the research he loved the most was the accumulation of information that was base, trivial, and, for his purposes, ultimately useless. Perhaps it was due to his landlocked upbringing, perhaps it was simply the excuse to surf the web without feeling guilty, but he found the information about whales—both the sublime and the ridiculous—fascinating.

First, there was the basic, common knowledge, known to everyone, it seemed, except Davis: that whales are mammals, not fish, and thus must surface to breathe since they don't have gills. From there, he learned that whales, like humans, have a four-chambered heart. That some of them hunt in groups, often using complicated and sophisticated methods, creating swirling nets out of bubbles to ensnare and confuse their prey. That the smallest had teeth and chewed their food, while the largest, the baleen whales, took big gulps of seawater and then filtered it through a fence of bristles, eating anything and everything that was trapped therein, existing mostly on flea-sized shrimp called krill. That unlike humans and most other land-dwelling mammals, whales decide when to take a breath. For that reason they cannot, like Davis when seated in the bathroom stall or watching a PowerPoint presentation, fall into an unconscious state for too long, since they need to be conscious in order to breathe. Therefore, only one hemisphere of their brain sleeps at a time, and only one eye is closed at a time. That way they never completely go to sleep but still get the rest they need.

He learned that many whales navigate in the same way as a bat, by making low-frequency sounds that are transmitted hundreds of miles through the ocean. They are thought to use these noises more as a means to map underwater features, much the same way seismic and sonar do, in order to help them navigate and orient themselves.

Moving onto acoustics, he learned that the sounds of some whales are of such a pitch and frequency that they resemble bird chirps. So much so that Arctic sailors in the wooden-hulled ships of yesteryear were able to hear, when they were below deck, the songs of beluga whales and gave them the nickname "sea canaries." Then there were humpback whales, which, again like birds, produce songs with repeating patterns. But unlike birds, the songs of humpbacks may last from five to thirty minutes, and like a child on a long car trip, they will sing the same song over and over for hours on end. Killer whales, on the other hand, have a vocabulary for communication. They live in groups, and each group has its own dialect, much like someone from England might have a different dialect from someone living in the United States. And like people from those two countries, killer whales from one pod will maintain the characteristics of their dialect even when they intermingle with another, foreign, pod.

He learned that at a certain depth the sea is so dark that a man (if he could stand the pressure) could not see his own hand held in front of his face. At such depths, whales and dolphins, whose eyes are no better than humans', can't see either, so they use echolocation to hunt their prey. To do this they produce a sound that projects forward and bounces off the squid or fish they are going after. The whale or dolphin then detects this returning echo and determines the location of its prey. Dolphins are especially good at this, able to identify an object four hundred feet away that is no bigger than a baseball. What's more, dolphins can tell if the object is dead or alive and whether it is friendly or aggressive. If it is alive, and they want to eat it, dolphins and sperm whales fire off a high-intensity shot of sound that stuns and sometimes even kills their prey.

Moby Dick aside, there were the cultural legends, most of which held whales in high esteem, as good omens and things to be respected. The Greeks, for instance, believed that dolphins were the friends and helpers of humans and that killing one was as morally wrong as killing a human. Farther north, the Vikings believed that certain whales would drive fish into their nets—so long as the fishermen did not quarrel with one another, and to the Vietnamese, whales were actually believed to be divine, sent by the god of the waters to protect sailors and to carry shipwrecked mariners on their backs to safety. They believed that every time a whale died, the rain would pour and the winds would howl for three days. In the Amazon, too, river dolphins were considered sacred and thought of as the protectors of people. A person would never attempt to capture a dolphin or eat its flesh. Or at least so said one website. Another, however, did not paint such a nice picture of the Amazonians and said they often killed the river dolphins and wore their eyes and penises as amulets.

This then led into Davis's favorite vein: the ridiculous, predominately phallic, but no less fascinating whale stories that were good for little other than cocktail party trivia:

The male species of an arctic whale called the narwhal has a single enormous tusk, sometimes as long as nine feet, jutting out from its upper lip. The existence of the narwhal was kept a secret among sailors, at least as far back as the Middle Ages, so that sailors returning home could pass the tusks off as unicorn horns and thus make enormous profit.

By some estimates, the penis of a blue whale can measure up to sixteen feet long and its testicles weigh in at around twenty-five pounds apiece.

A large male whale can emit five gallons of ejaculate at a time. (Davis chuckled when he imagined the wad of tissues that would be needed to clean up that mess. He chuckled even harder when he imagined Edgar's delight on finding those tissues.)

And finally, when Jacqueline Kennedy Onassis sat her patrician ass on one of the bar stools in her second husband's yacht, the *Christina,* she was sitting on leather made from the testicles of a whale.

In addition to the whales, Davis, of course, researched mitigation plans. And his searches were fruitful, returning complete plans from several governments, militaries, energy companies, and research institutions. Since their plans were already in place and operational, they were only too happy to post them on the public sections of their websites in order to prove that they were taking positive steps toward responsible stewardship of marine living resources and thus would avoid, or so they hoped, the attention and wrath of environmentalists.

Davis grazed over these policies, chewing and swallowing elements that were useful for his purposes and then, from his grazings, regurgitating the cud of his own procedure. When it was done, he e-mailed it to Sarah along with a list of items he determined he would need: two sets of binoculars for daytime marine mammal observations, two sets of night-vision goggles for nighttime observations, a notebook to hold all of the many forms (because, as Davis was learning, the sign of any good policy was the amount of paperwork it generated), and lastly, a small but sophisticated-looking listening device that would be lowered over the side of the vessel to listen for the underwater sounds of marine mammals prior to starting up the seismic equipment.

While he waited for Sarah to review the policy, Davis again found himself with nothing to do, which was fine because he was not quite ready to move on from his research. The whales in particular held an odd fascination for him. He was in awe of their size, their power and slow grace, their mystery. He read on and on about them, often remaining in his cubicle corner long after the other tech writers had gone home.

As is the case with many successful artistic endeavors, he didn't embark on it consciously. It was what a cook who has misread a recipe and been thrilled with the errant result might call "a happy accident." Indeed, for Davis the idea of using whales as the subject matter for a new children's book was such an accident that he didn't even recognize it as such until many weeks later. It came to his mind in fits and starts, beginning with nothing more than doodles in the margins of his research notes. Soon these progressed into page-sized illustrations, used mostly to assist in the narration of his research to his niece and nephews in the evenings. That their attention and interest in the subject was retained night after night was apparent only to their parents, who commented on it one evening to Davis.

"I don't know if it's you," his sister-in-law said, "or what you're talking about, but I've never seen them so . . ." She was at a loss for words to describe their behavior. Her husband, however, was not:

"Quiet. Well-behaved. Not throwing tantrums when we ask them to put their pajamas on and brush their teeth."

"Yes! It's like you've drugged them, or replaced our children with the idealized ones from some fifties TV show. I actually have time to decompress in the evenings. It's wonderful."

"And you know that the drawings you give them are pretty much all they take for show-and-tell anymore. It's great stuff."

Davis gladly accepted the praise but still thought nothing of it in a professional sense. Indeed, he continued routinely waking up in a middle-of-the night panic over what he could possibly deliver to Estelle.

Sarah returned the policy to him early the following week with a few minor grammatical changes and the vague comment "looks good." She directed him to talk it over with Jake to see if he could get the necessary equipment in time for Artaud's cruise. Davis dutifully incorporated her changes, printed up copies of the procedure, its many related forms, and the list of items he wanted to purchase, put them in a file folder, and placed it in Jake's in-box.

As he was headed back down the narrow hallway to his cubicle, he saw Maureen coming toward him. He was trapped. There was no doorway to duck into, and, having just dropped off his pile of papers, his hands were empty, so he couldn't pretend to be reading something while he walked. He decided he'd better at least make eye contact with her, give a polite nod, but though her eyes met his, she seemed to see right through him and kept on walking.

Book 5

Deployment #2: The Ross Sea

HAMLET: Do you see yonder cloud that's almost in shape of a camel?
POLONIUS: By the mass, and 'tis like a camel indeed.
HAMLET: Methinks it is like a weasel.
POLONIUS: It is backed like a weasel.
HAMLET: Or like a whale?
POLONIUS: Very like a whale.

—*Hamlet,* Act 3, Scene ii

Chapter 29

In terms of hours aloft there are more miserable flights than Los Angeles to Auckland, but not many. Invariably it is a night flight, implying that you should enjoy a meal, recline into a restful slumber to the accompaniment of the muffled hiss of jet engines, and arrive bright-eyed and refreshed the next morning, ready for business.

What happens if you are Davis is that you sit semi-erect watching a movie you would never pay to see in a theater, you probably drink too much alcohol and not enough water, and then you stagger off the plane into the harsh morning sunlight, eyes stinging, hands digging in your carry-on for an ever-elusive pen to fill out the customs paperwork while waiting in the interminable immigration line, all with one eye on the clock as it ticks ever closer to the departure time for your connecting flight south to Christchurch.

Christchurch, the south island town that is the jumping-off point for all flights headed to the two larger U.S. Antarctic stations, McMurdo and Amundsen-Scott South Pole. At the beginning of the austral summer season in October, the population of Christchurch swells with Antarctic-bound American contractors and scientists, who are given their flight assignments, outfitted with their extreme cold weather gear, and then usually go out and try to get drunk or laid (usually both) before they begin their stint in the minimum security-prisons/kindergartens/frat houses known as the U.S. Antarctic stations. Places where everyone wears the same clothes, everyone eats at the same place and at roughly the same times, where the walls are lined with coat hooks and hand-washing stations, where one's movements in and outside the station are tracked and restricted, where the bunkhouses are given charming and frighteningly appropriate names like Hotel California.

Since flying to Antarctica can be almost as perilous as sailing there, flights often boomerang, making it halfway across the Southern Ocean before bad weather sends them back to Christchurch to try again the next day. Sometimes flights will be canceled before they even leave the ground. Those lucky passengers are then given an extra day, sometimes as much as an extra week, on stand-by in leafy green New Zealand.

In January, when Davis was headed to Christchurch, most of the people scheduled to work on the ice had already passed through the city months ago, so the only other person on Davis's flight whose luggage sported the familiar green rubber tag was, of course, Maureen, who, of course, ignored him. He had expected to see Worm or some of the other technicians, but many of them had arrived days before and were, most likely, already embarked on the vessel.

Ideally the science party was to arrive only a few days, sometime even a day, before scheduled departure, leaving the technicians time to prepare and set up equipment. Davis and Maureen had intended to arrive sooner as well but, due to a snowstorm in Denver, their outgoing flight had been delayed. In the end, their late arrival didn't matter since the vessel itself, which had been slowly transiting the South Pacific from Chile to New Zealand, had itself been delayed. A fact that was relayed to Davis and Maureen by the New Zealand agent when they emerged from customs. The agent, a whiskey-voiced, clipboard-clutching woman named Dora, saw their rubber tags and waved, like someone trying to fend off a wasp, to get their attention. "The vessel hasn't arrived yet," she told them as they followed her out of the terminal into the summer heat, "so it looks like you'll have an extra day in Christchurch."

Dora ushered them to a van that would shuttle them to their hotels. A burly Maori driver loaded their luggage in the back while

Dora stood, clipboard in hand, holding the sliding door of the van open for them. They climbed in; Dora slid the door shut and then climbed in the front seat next to the driver.

"You're scheduled to go to the CDC tomorrow. We'll pick you up around eleven. Please be ready in the lobby."

"What's the CDC?" Davis asked. Maureen clicked her tongue, presumably at his ignorance, yet made no attempt to explain.

"The clothing distribution center. It's where you go to get your ECW gear."

"Ahh. And what's ECW?"

"Extreme Cold Weather, stupid."

"Coats, hats, gloves—those kinds of things."

"Has any of the science party arrived yet?" Maureen asked, trying to sound unconcerned.

"Not yet, ducks," Dora said with a wink. "Not yet. You got a sweetie you're expecting?"

Maureen ignored the remark. Davis turned to the window to conceal his grin but Dora caught it and gave him another wink in the rearview mirror. She lit a cigarette and the smoke cascaded into the back of the van. The back windows did not open, so Maureen made a passive-aggressive show of waving the smoke away with her folded itinerary. When that failed to have any effect, she made another annoyed click of her tongue, tapped on the back of Dora's seat and said, "Do you *mind?*"

Dora nodded, took one last hearty drag, and then stubbed out the cigarette in the ashtray.

"A flight came in yesterday with a few of your people on it," she said. "Most are at B-and-Bs or hostels. You can probably meet up with them tonight at Bailies. There're lots of tourists this time of year, but not a lot of you ice folks."

Although Davis and Maureen had been traveling together since Denver, any outside observer would never have suspected they even knew each other. Davis, behind her at the ticket counter in Denver, had given her a polite nod of recognition when she turned and headed toward the gate. To his surprise, the nod had been acknowledged, but he knew better than to interpret that as an indication of a potential thaw in their icy relations. And, just as expected, she did not communicate with him or even acknowledge his presence for the eighteen hours that it took to cover the eight thousand miles between Point A and Point B. Their mutual disregard continued during the ride to the hotel, on into the lobby as they checked in, and in the elevator as they both ascended to the eleventh floor, each exiting and disappearing behind their respective doors. There was no mention of going to get dinner or a drink, no offer from Maureen to show Davis around, and no request from him for her to do so. He knew how she was.

Unlike his last trip to Chile, when he had been ordered to report to the boat with no time to rest, he relished the fact that the vessel was delayed and the chance it afforded him to indulge in the amenities offered by a high-end hotel—the big bathtub, the white terry cloth robe, the room service and snacks from the minibar, the semi-exotic cable television shows, with their news and celebrities he knew nothing about. Since it was late afternoon he indulged in all of them, then, as evening approached, he popped his pills, crawled between the sheets, and slept the sleep of the dead. When he awoke the next morning, it was nearly 9:00 and he could hear traffic in the square below. He got up, stepped out onto his balcony, and looked down. The white van was there again and next to it the peroxided head of clipboard-clutching Dora. As Davis watched, the science party—Meghan, Andrew, Jerry, Kristi, and Artaud—emerged, stiff and yawning, from the van. Out of the corner of his eye, Davis sensed movement. He looked to the right. Two balconies away was Maureen, bathrobe-clad like Davis, holding a coffee cup in her hands and peering over the railing at the van. She sensed Davis looking at her and for a moment seemed embarrassed to have been caught. Then she scowled and retreated to her room.

Two hours later, the two were dressed and seated side by side in the white van headed to the CDC.

"The vessel should get in tonight. We'll shuttle you over to Lyttelton tomorrow morning at nine."

"What's Lyttelton?" Davis asked. Maureen gave an exasperated hiss to the window, but offered no explanation to dispel his ignorance.

"Lyttelton's the port for Christchurch," Dora explained. The land around Christchurch is muddy and shallow, so ships have to go to Lyttelton. It's on the other side of the Port Hills. Beautiful little gem, Lyttelton is."

"Will the scientists be going tomorrow, too?" Davis asked.

"Yes, we'll do one trip with the people, one trip with the luggage."

Since Maureen obviously wasn't going to supply him with any information, Davis pretended she wasn't there and spoke over her to Dora, who seemed to be chain-smoking more to irritate Maureen than for any pleasure she derived from it.

"I slept all afternoon," Davis said, "so I didn't do any sightseeing yesterday. Is there anything you'd recommend I do with just one day?"

She told him about the Botanic Gardens and the art museum, and when they got to the CDC she gave him a map showing places to shop for souvenirs. They stood talking beside the van while she marked a few more things she thought Davis might like and then handed him the map. Davis thanked her and together they walked into the building.

"She's not very friendly, is she?" Dora said, making a stabbing motion at Maureen's back with her pen.

"Not really."

"I remember her from the last time. It's a pity; people like that don't tend to get happier as they age."

Chapter 30

"Isn't that the fat tech-writer dude?"

The voice had an American accent, was barely more than a whisper, but the air was humid and still, so Davis had heard it. He turned to where the sound had come from and saw a group of people lying on the grass, surrounded by beer cans. It was the vessel techs. Davis waved, but kept on walking. He would have to spend the next two months with those people and wanted to enjoy his last few hours of privacy, but Worm's head popped up out of the group. "Hey!" he called, rising from the lawn and brushing the grass out of his hair. "You just get here?"

"Yesterday," Davis said.

"Same flight as Maureen?"

"Yes, she's here. We're both at the Heritage, but I haven't seen her since this morning."

"Cool, cool," Worm said, leading Davis over to the supine group and falling back into his spot. "Have a beer."

Davis dropped his bag and sat down. There were a few groans, a few heads were lifted in greeting, but then they lay back down and were quiet.

"We've been here a couple days already," Worm said. "You heard about the boat being delayed?"

"Yes,"

"It better get here soon," Worm said, kicking an empty beer can to the side, "because I don't think I can handle many more days and nights with these dudes."

While Davis drank his beer, Worm and the others gave a detailed account of their nights of debauchery.

"We're all going for drinks and dinner later," Worm said. "You should come."

Davis nodded, but then cringed as he remembered his last pre-cruise Pisco hangover in Chile.

"Cool. We'll meet up for some cocktails at Bailies around seven and then head out from there."

"Sounds good," Davis said, getting up and waving good-bye, eager to continue his walk. To his surprise, Worm got up and followed, walking beside him.

"So," Worm said. "I hear you're the new marine mammal guy."

"Yes," Davis said, "but don't worry, there's no strangulation or gassing involved."

"Maybe not of animals, but word on the street is Artaud's mad as hell about the whole thing."

"Greaaaat," Davis groaned.

"*I* think it is!" Worm said, slapping his thigh. "Dude deserves it, if you ask me."

"It's a pretty sketchy policy," Davis said. "There's not all that much to get upset about."

"We heard you got all sorts of fancy equipment."

Davis thought back to the suitcase full of "fancy equipment." The cheap binoculars, the single pair of night-vision goggles Janet had picked up for him at some military surplus store, the hydrophone that looked more like one of those cheap metal detectors old men wander around with in parks looking for lost suburban treasure.

"I think you'll be underwhelmed by most of it."

"Still, it's good that somebody's doing something," Worm said, turning and heading back to the group. "Bailies at seven."

At the bar that night it was like a cast reunion from the previous cruise: the same technicians, the same science party—everyone was there except the vessel crew. They all stood in small groups around the bar, segregated as usual, Maureen being the only one who broke ranks, standing on the periphery of the science party, a highball in one hand, her other hand at her side, the pinky interlocked with Artaud's index finger.

They all had a few drinks at the bar and then set off, en masse, down Colombo Street toward an Indian restaurant. It was good food, there just wasn't much of it, especially in relation to the amount of alcohol they had consumed, and by the end of the meal most everyone was drunk. Davis, having anticipated the direction the evening would be headed, and wanting to avoid a repeat of his Pisco port call, had paced himself, and when they left the restaurant he felt loose, but not nearly as far gone as his shipmates, most of whom were engaging in a bruising competition of parking meter leapfrog. Davis used his large and relatively sober body as a barrier between the contestants and the traffic whizzing by in the street, and had, by his accounting, prevented at least two potential fatalities.

When they reached the corner of Lichfield and Colombo, the group dispersed somewhat; a group of guys headed off to a strip club while another group headed back to Bailies. Davis had hoped to round out his evening at a gay bar he had looked up online but was pulled along by Meghan and Worm. They rounded the corner into Cathedral Square, and both Worm and Meghan came to a halt. Davis, whose arms were locked in theirs, was forced to stop as well. He looked from one to the other and saw that the mirth had drained from their faces. He followed the direction of their gazes to the large, conical statue in the middle of the square, at the base of which were the clear silhouettes of Artaud and Maureen engaged in a kiss.

Davis resisted the urge to affect a Transylvanian accent and say something like, "She's gone weeks without human blood; she's got to feed!" or to make some wry comment about bitches in heat, but instead tried to gently lead his lovelorn charges away from the scene, as from an accident or a street fight.

"C'mon," Davis said to Worm. "I'll buy you a glass of wine. A whole bottle, if you want."

"No. I—I think I'm just going to head back to my place,"

Worm said, and without another word he turned and walked the other direction, hands in his pockets.

Davis thought about following him but then figured it might be better to just let him go. It was a shame to see him get so upset over *her*.

As Davis and Meghan walked, she kept turning back to look at the two, still joined at the mouth.

"C'mon," he said, his stride more insistent. "I feel the need to cleanse my palate."

Two minutes later they were seated on bar stools drinking Irish Car Bombs.

"Why does he hafta like her?" Meghan whined. "I mean, of all the girls, why her?"

"People like what they like."

They did another round, which seemed to buoy her spirits, and soon she was off the stool and standing next to Kristi, who was sucking her finger and twirling her hair to the evident delight of a group of rugby players. Andrew, who, if he was anything like the majority of other gay men, found nothing more ego inflating than bagging a straight man, was deeply involved in a game of pool with one who looked to be just about at the tipping point.

Davis smiled, turned back to the bar, and was shocked when he caught sight of himself in a mirror behind the bartender. He looked old in comparison to Andrew and the others, and he felt old. Old, and stupid, and drunk. Just drunk enough to allow himself to indulge in feelings of self-pity and its conjoined twin, resentment. He resented that he wasn't young, that he wasn't good-looking and muscular, and that he didn't have a promising future in science or academics in front of him. But most of all, he resented the fact of his infection, and the fact that it had pulled him out of the casual sex game that everyone seemed to be so feverishly pursuing that evening. And he couldn't blame them. They were all trying to satisfy their libidos before those libidos were, so to speak, put on ice for two months. He, on the other hand, had a handful of pills to look forward to, and then, well, probably a date with that same hand. He paid the bartender and headed across the street to his hotel.

When he got to the elevators Artaud was there waiting, trying to support Maureen, who was very drunk. He had one arm around her back and with the other was trying to push the elevator button.

"Let me give you a hand," Davis said, swooping in and pushing the button.

"Thanks."

Maureen's arm fell and her purse slid off onto the floor. Davis picked it up and held it awkwardly.

"She's had too much to drink. I-wou-would you mind helping me?"

Davis got under one of her arms and put it around his shoulder. Her head rolled back and her hair was in Davis's face. He couldn't move it out of the way because one of his hands was holding her hand to keep her arm around his shoulder, and the other was holding her purse, so he blew and puffed the strands out of the way.

"I'm fine," she said, eyes rolling in their sockets. "I be fiiine!"

"Shh, shh, shh. Sure you will, babe. Let's just get you upstairs."

"What did she drink?" Davis whispered, still spitting blond tresses out of his mouth.

"Anything. Everything. I don't think she ate much."

The elevator opened and they shuffled in. The toe of one of Maureen's sandals snagged in the gap. Davis, still holding her and her purse, bent down and tried to get an arm around her calf to push it forward. In so doing, the purse tipped upside down and the contents spilled out.

"I'll get it," Artaud said, letting go of Maureen and bending down to collect the rolling bits of feminine debris. As he chased a lipstick into the hall, the doors closed and the elevator began ascending.

"Shit!" Davis hissed, leaning forward and attempting to hit the Stop button. Maureen's dead weight leaned into him, pushing him into the panel and illuminating all the buttons. They then proceeded to stop at each and every floor on their way up to the eleventh, which was where, Davis assumed, she would be going.

When, after ten opening and closings, the doors finally parted on the eleventh floor, Davis dragged her out and down the hallway to her door. He eased her down and propped her up against the wall, like some enormous ventriloquist's dummy. There wasn't much else he could do. Her room card had been in her purse, and the contents of her purse were with Artaud. Nevertheless, he shook the empty purse upside down just to make sure. He then sat down next to her in the empty hallway, and the thought of the ventriloquist's dummy came back into his mind. He reached over and gave her face a gentle slap. No reaction. He gave her another, a bit harder. Nothing. This was great! He picked up one of her lifeless hands and stuck the middle finger in her nose. She winced slightly but was powerless to remove it. The sight was so comical to Davis that he snapped a picture of it with his phone, laughing so hard that he could barely keep the phone still. Oh, if only he had a felt tip pen, or even a tube of lipstick! As he was imagining the graphic possibilities—and how much Meghan, Dora, Ronnie, Jake, and, well, just about anyone she had ever been in contact with would enjoy seeing the pictures—the elevator emitted a soft ping and Artaud stepped out, his hands cupping her wallet, passport, various cosmetics and unmentionables. Davis quickly pulled her hand away from her face, but could not stop laughing; was, in fact, almost crying with delight.

"Do you have the card for the door?" he managed to ask. Artaud nodded and then motioned for Davis to open the purse so that he could deposit her belongings. Once his hands were free he reached in his back pocket and took out the room card, swiped it, and the door clicked open. Artaud turned on the light and then held the door open with his foot while he and Davis dragged Maureen in and got her onto the bed. Artaud folded the bedspread over her and then stood back and ran his fingers through his hair.

"We should probably prop her up," Davis said. Artaud cocked his head.

"So she doesn't, you know, choke." Davis laughed. He tried to regain his composure but then remembered the sight of her with her finger up her nose and completely lost it, falling onto the floor and clutching his stomach.

"What's so funny?" Artaud asked, himself now smiling.

"I'm sorry," Davis whimpered, his eyes tearing up. "Sorry."

Artaud pulled back the bedspread. "We should probably get her shoes off." He removed her sandals. Davis got up and propped some pillows under her back and neck so that she was in a semisitting position and then Artaud covered her again. Davis picked up the phone and dialed reception.

"What are you doing?"

Davis held up a finger. "Yes, hello. This is room 1157. I'd like to schedule a wake up call for 7:30 tomorrow. Great. Thanks." He hung up. "They're picking us up at nine. That should give her enough time, don't you think?"

"Yes. Good thinking."

Once they were back in the hallway, they both leaned against the wall. Davis was still having episodic fits of laughter but thought it prudent not to show the picture to Artaud.

"Thanks for your help," Artaud said. "How about I buy you a drink."

It was only about 10:30, but Davis didn't especially want to return to the sexual feeding frenzy that was probably still going on at Bailies.

"I think I'm going to pass," Davis said, looking at his wrist, which did not have a watch on it.

"Oh, c'mon," Artaud prodded. "I want to hear about your book."

He was a bad actor when it came to sounding sincere, but that didn't bother Davis. When a handsome, intelligent man expresses curiosity in a gay man's creative venture, the gay man's resistance is liable to fail, especially if said gay man has just consumed, in rapid succession, two toxic teenage drinks, so he nodded his assent.

"But let's not go back to Bailies," Artaud said. "I know a much better place. It's about a fifteen, twenty-minute cab ride but will definitely be worth the trip."

"It's not a titty bar or a whorehouse, is it?"

"What?!" Artaud asked, holding a palm to his chest, theatrically scandalized. "What kind of trash do you take me for?"

"No, seriously," Davis said. "I'm not taking any moral high ground. I'm just not up for watching some girl with bad teeth try to make her rent."

"Understood."

Five minutes later they were in a cab speeding through the deserted city streets and out into the suburbs. On the way, Artaud did not speak about Maureen or what had transpired between them over the course of the evening, nor did he talk about the upcoming cruise. Instead, he inquired pointedly about Davis's books.

"The last time we sailed together you were still trying to come up with a new story. How is that coming along?"

This line of inquiry made Davis uncomfortable. Not because Artaud had busted him working on his book during the last cruise, and not because it seemed, well, apropos of nothing. No, he was uncomfortable because the main character of the new story (a whale) was also the one topic he did not want to discuss with Artaud. Also, the plot was still developing in his mind, and Davis was superstitious about such things, his fear being that to talk about it when it was still in its embryonic stage might cause the idea to mutate or miscarry, and another creative stillbirth was not something he could then afford. Instead, he told him about the rejected *Mick the Maggot*, transfusing the corpse of that story with fresh details that he thought up on the fly, so to speak. He talked on and on, barely stopping to take a breath. Then the taxi entered a long tunnel—all white-tiled and illuminated like an operating room. Davis looked over at Artaud, saw that he wasn't paying any attention whatsoever to Davis's narrative, so he ended it abruptly, figuring that he couldn't really be offended by Artaud's lack of interest since the story had been filler anyway. To his surprise, the cab driver spoke up:

"That sounds like the perfect story to tell at the Wunderbar. You be sure to tell the bartender that one. He'll pay your bloody tab."

Hearing mention of their destination, Artaud's attention reoriented itself and he turned to Davis with a grin, "You're going to love this place."

And he was right. Davis did love it. The Wunderbar was a bar like no other, perched on top of a supermarket and reached only by climbing an Escher-esque metal staircase—a staircase that had, Davis imagined as he wheezed his way up, surely been the cause of numerous drunken falls. About halfway up, their access to the bar was impeded by a group of people, three men and a woman, all dressed in business attire, who were engaged in a heated contest to see who could walk farthest up the stairs while clenching a fifty-cent piece between their ass cheeks. They insisted that Davis and

Artaud play, too, which they did, Artaud going first. He made three failed attempts and then passed the highly unsanitary coin off to Davis, who effectively ended the game by gripping it between his ample cheeks, locking his legs together, and hopping up all three flights of steps. When he reached the top he released the coin and it dropped with a clink.

He didn't bask in his victory for long, however, because as soon as he looked up his attention was snagged by the toy-box interior of the bar, visible through a series of large plate-glass windows. The place was lit by several pendant light fixtures, all fashioned from the headless plastic torsos of female mannequins, each dressed in a frilly nightie and illuminated from within. Stuck to the wall of one side of the bar were hundreds of rubber doll heads, their vacant eyes staring out from their bald, decapitated heads. Other walls were made from panels of button-tufted red velvet upholstery, and there were several high-backed booths covered in the same. Random musical instruments—an accordion, a tuba, a ukulele with several snapped strings dangling—hung above the bar, which was itself a raft of bamboo poles, lashed together and turned on its side, the upper portion fringed with beaded curtains and tiny Mylar balls. For music, there was a turntable. Not a DJ station, just a single turntable, allowed to spin only one direction, from the beginning of Side A to the end, at which point the needle would levitate, move to the side, trip the mechanism to drop another 45 into place, and then move back in and skid into the groove. It was a turntable similar to one that Davis and his brother had had as kids—the kind that folded into the shape of a suitcase and had a red and black plaid cover. The needle on this particular model skipped any time the door slammed, or any time anyone bumped or smacked the bar, which gave the patrons the impression of being in a jump-cut edited movie. And the music itself, ranging from early Debbie Reynolds to late AC/DC, and chosen at whim from a milk crate sitting next to the record player, only added to that choppy feeling.

The bartender, when he appeared, was a middle-aged man so ghostly pale that he looked like he'd been living in a windowless vault since birth. The paleness was offset by black bangs cut in a severe horizontal line across his forehead and an absence of eyebrows. He was short, barely tall enough to rest his elbows on the bar, and while Davis and Artaud waited in line for a drink, Davis realized that the man was even shorter than he'd originally thought; a midget, in fact, who navigated the space behind the bar via a series of hidden stools and stepladders.

Davis was mesmerized, his senses overloaded.

"What do you think?" Artaud asked.

Davis let his eyes travel around the room. Insane places like this made him feel sane and happy, and he drank in all the intricate details of the space.

"I love it!" he said. Artaud handed him his drink and they sat on stools at the bar.

"So," Artaud began, placing both palms on his thighs. "Tell me about all this observer nonsense they've got you doing?"

"I don't know that it's nonsense..." Davis said. Artaud raised one side of his mouth in a wry smirk. A smirk that said *C'mon. It's just us. You don't need to pretend.*

Davis's confidence in his plan was shaky enough without Artaud pollinating his doubts. He knew Jake had sent Artaud a copy of the policy, and now Davis knew from Worm that Artaud wasn't at all happy about it, so he figured he'd better put on his professional mask and go on the defensive.

"As I think you read in the documentation," Davis began, "we'll be doing a half-hour watch for marine mammals before the seismic guns are fired up. If we don't see or hear anything in that half hour, or if we do see or hear mammals, and they appear to be swimming away from the boat, then we'll give the okay to slowly ramp—"

"Yeah, I know all that. And if you see a whale, or think you see one, while the guns are firing they'll have to be shut off and then the whole process will start over again."

"Yes."

"And I have to supply the observers from my own science party."

"Yes. But I'll be doing a lot of observing, too," Davis said, his codependency kicking in, "and we can ask some of the technicians to volunteer. I'll handle all the training and the paperwork."

Artaud shook his head. "Wow. This is really going to cause problems. You know that, right? It's going to eat into the time I have to do science."

Davis took a drink, then a deep breath and held it. The needle jumped and skipped over a violin-laden version of Lynn Anderson's "Rose Garden." The midget, annoyed by the repeated skipping, lifted the arm of the needle and Scotch-taped two coins to it. During the ensuing silence Artaud continued shaking his head and glared disappointment at Davis. Worst of all, Davis, the Nervous Imbiber, had an empty glass. He wanted to get up and buy another round but had spent all his Kiwi cash on dinner and hadn't stopped at an ATM. Instead he took off his professional mask and slipped into his "I'm just the messenger" role, reciting lines he'd heard Sarah and the other tech writers use:

"Hey, it's not like I want to do this," Davis said. He was lying, of course. He very much wanted to do it. For the first time since he'd had the job he felt like he was doing something vaguely useful and productive, and it was disheartening to hear Artaud dismiss it as nothing more than a roadblock to his science goals. Not to mention that it again sounded the bugle call for Davis's fears and insecurities to reemerge from behind the foggy foothills and cause him to question whether or not he knew what the hell he was doing.

"This is just what I've been assigned to do. It's a mandate from up above," Davis said, pointing up to the invisible powers on high, but then realized, as Artaud's eyes followed his finger, that what he was really pointing at was one of the lingerie-clad chandeliers.

The coins affixed, the bartender lowered the needle back on Lynn Anderson and the song resumed. The violins now sounded like violas and the voice, when it finally did come, was lugubrious and mannish. The bartender cursed, lifted the needle again, and began unwinding the tape.

"The thing that really gets me about this," Artaud said, "is that it's all driven by emotion, not by science. People like whales and dolphins, I understand that. I think they're cute, too, fucking adorable, but there's no science to the argument that seismic harms whales. The research just isn't there."

Artaud was looking at Davis like it was somehow his fault that the research wasn't there.

"Look," Davis said, trying to emphasize the positive, "they weren't going to let you shoot at night but I talked them out of that by getting the night-vision goggles."

"I don't see what good that's going to do," Artaud said with a laugh, "since we'll be so far south the sun probably won't even set."

"The point," Davis went on, "is that I'm on your side here."

"How so?"

"I'm trying to make this policy as amenable to your needs as possible."

It was difficult for Davis to argue his point, first, because he was slightly drunk; second, because he didn't really understand all of the science involved in it; and third, because he knew that the bulk of the plan was, in fact, useless. It dealt only with animals that were visible from the surface, and these were animals that spent 95 per cent of their time below the surface.

Davis stopped talking, wondered why he was even getting defensive. He was just there to implement the policy; he hadn't been the one to call for it. And if anything, Davis's version was much less restrictive than the policies of some other institutions. Davis tried to explain this but Artaud just shook his head. He downed his drink and banged his glass on the bar. The record skipped. The bartender glared. Davis stared at his empty glass and rolled the base of it in a circle.

"I'd offer to buy another round," Davis said, "but I don't have any cash."

"I got it," Artaud said. He ordered another round and then strode off toward the bathroom, the record skipping with each angry step he took. While he was gone Davis tried to think of another line of reasoning. When it was just him, alone in the office researching the plan, it had all seemed to make perfect sense. Now he was beginning to second-guess himself.

By the time Artaud returned, Davis had finished half of his drink and the record had changed. It was now emitting the shrieking violins of the soundtrack to *Psycho,* which was unsettling but did make the needle skips less noticeable.

Artaud frowned at the turntable. "Let's sit out on the balcony."

They picked up their drinks and went outside. The balcony was comparatively quiet, although the contest with the fifty-cent piece continued on the stairs and there were now more players, all trying to perfect Davis's hopping technique. Artaud leaned over the railing and looked down at the ships in the harbor.

"I'm sure it will work out fine," Davis said, trying to sound reassuring and feeling like some pathetic wife trying to get into good graces with her moody husband. "We'll work together. I'll try to keep the impact on your work as minimal as possible."

"I guess that's the best I can hope for," Artaud said, still wearing his annoyed expression. Davis hoped the annoyance was more from the music, which was now muffled and seemed more suitable as the soundtrack to a smothering than a stabbing.

"Look!" Artaud cried, rising out of his chair and pointing down at the ocean. Davis stood, his eyes following.

"It's the *Hamilton.*"

Even in the dark, the vessel was not hard to spot, lit up, as it always was, and looking like a giant lemon plying the waters. They stood without speaking, watching as tugs slowly maneuvered the boat into place along the pier. It was the same boat, but there was something odd about seeing it pull up right in front of them, there, halfway around the world from where they'd last seen it.

The game participants grew tired and winded and moved into the bar. The music was now a low rumble, punctuated by gaps of silence as the needle levitated, moved to the side, and one 45 dropped onto another. They finished their drinks. Artaud dropped his hand onto Davis's thigh and left it there.

"We should get a taxi back," he said. Davis looked down at the hand and at Artaud, making no move to get up. In the end, Davis stood, pretended to stretch and yawn, and walked over to the stairs. They found a cab near the bus stop and both got in the backseat. Again, there was the hand on Davis's thigh. Occasionally the thumb made a back-and-forth motion. More sober than he cared to be, Davis tried to make eye contact with Artaud, hoping to see some clue about what was going on, but his face was toward the window and his eyes were barely open.

Probably just drunk, Davis concluded, and tried his best to ignore the hand for the thirty minutes that it took to get back to the hotel, where, wanting to avoid what he saw as inevitable awkwardness and the possible necessity for disclosing his HIV status, he bolted for the door while Artaud was busy paying for the cab.

Chapter 31

The exodus from the hotels in Christchurch to the vessel the next morning was not pleasant. Due to the late arrival of the boat, there was a lot of work to be done in very little time. Cargo from the transit had to be offloaded; new cargo, food, and fuel for the outgoing cruise had to be onloaded; and cabins needed to be cleaned and prepared for the oncoming personnel, who were all, without exception, hungover from the night before. Tempers were short, snitty arguments were frequent, and to many, the day seemed unending.

Davis did not feel all that bad. He had a minor headache early on, but by the evening Chicken Time he and most of the other people were feeling better. That feeling was short-lived. The next morning, the vessel pulled away from the dock, left the sheltered calm of Lyttelton harbor and, just as Jake had warned, immediately got hammered by the gyrating waters of the South Pacific. Soon thereafter, most of the green-faced passengers left the labs and sought refuge in their cabins. It was at this time, when the vessel had been in open water for about ten hours, that Maureen approached Artaud. She didn't want to talk to him, didn't want to have to explain her blackout in Christchurch (especially since she herself couldn't understand it), didn't want a messy confrontation, but the biggest reason she wanted to avoid a discussion was because she knew that it was over between them, knew that he had only ever pursued her so that she would steal Madeleine's data. The evidence was clear. They'd had sex exactly once since she'd given him the tapes, he had avoided her phone calls and texts, had not come to her hotel room in Christchurch or even called when he'd arrived, in spite of the imploring message she'd left him. And then there had been their meeting in the bar the night before last—a meeting that only added to her mental muddle. It was the first time they'd seen each other since Easter Island, the first time she'd spoken to him since he'd chastised her for her drunken telephoning. Since then, there'd been no communication, good or bad, until she saw him at Bailies. She'd come down to the bar and found him more congenial than ever, buying her drinks, putting his arm around her and squeezing her ass, as if everything were all right. They had linked pinkies, for Christ's sake, he'd whispered in her ear how beautiful she looked and how much he'd missed her, as if all his neglect and all her tortured imaginings had been baseless and unfounded.

The rest of that night was fuzzy in her mind. She remembered walking to the Indian restaurant, remembered sitting next to Artaud, his leg resting against hers under the table, but after that she really couldn't remember much other than feeling tired and finding it harder and harder to walk as they headed back to the hotel. She knew she had drunk too much. It had not been more than she was used to, but coming so soon after her episode of drunk dialing, she began to worry that maybe she had a problem. Maybe she had a problem and it wasn't entirely due to him.

When she found him, he was alone at one of the computer stations in the E-Lab, composing an e-mail. She approached and stood just behind him to his right, her feet spread wide to brace herself against the movement of the boat. He didn't say anything, didn't stop his typing, but nodded to indicate he knew she was there.

"Could I . . . ?" she ventured. "I need to talk to you about something."

He did not turn around, kept his eyes on the screen. "Okay," he said. "I'm listening."

She took another step forward and held on to one of the workstations for support. She hesitated, silently reminding herself that she needed to do this, that it would be better once it was all out in the open.

"Listen," she said, lowering her voice and inclining toward him, "I don't know what is going on. With us, I mean, but I don't—I'm not comfortable doing this anymore."

There. It was out. Sort of.

"What do you mean?" he asked, his eyes still on the screen.

"*Madeleine's data,*" she whispered. "You—I—I know you've got problems with her, but I—"

He swiveled his chair around to face her and leaned forward, elbows on his knees. He reached out and took her hand in his. He was looking at her with that particular expression of his—eyes full of compassion, mouth turned down in a pouty frown, head nodding, as if to say "I understand." The overall effect was contrite, but something about it made her think back to the e-mail she'd intercepted on the last trip—the one that his student, Andrew, had written to his boyfriend, explaining away his dance-floor indiscretions by admitting a small degree of guilt but then pinning the blame for the majority of the spectacle on the other guy. She had immediately seen the phoniness in that e-mail, and she saw it now in Artaud. He wasn't contrite; he was just playing contrite.

His head stopped nodding and their eyes met. Usually, she could lose herself in those eyes, her focus shifting from one to the other, his pupils like the negative space of a black hole, whirlpooling her in. Now when she looked at them they held as much genuine expression as those of a taxidermied gazelle. But the worst part was that it did not make her yearn for him less. Indeed, his ethical lapses were part of what she found so intriguing; but now he was being unethical with her, and that made her sad and, again, angry with herself for still finding him attractive.

The courage to confront him had come from a place deep in her gut—an area of herself that, she now realized, had never quite relaxed around him. At first she had attributed it to nerves, the giddiness of new love, but now she realized that it had actually been more of a lighthouse flash warning her away from the rocks, or like someone playing a kazoo while she was trying to conduct a symphony. Yes, that was it. And when she first heard it, she had ignored it, not wanting to hear it, wanting to hear only the soaring violins. Later, when her suspicions became harder to ignore, she had soaked what she perceived as her oversensitive self in scotch, but even that had not worked. She had known all along that he was using her, that he didn't really love her, but it had been an undeveloped fact that hadn't fully articulated itself until, well, until that very moment.

He was still gazing at her, waiting for her to speak, but she knew that when she did—when she said what she knew she had to say— that she would lose him. She inhaled, looked down at her small hand enveloped in his, and in a cracking voice said, "I, I'm not going to help you anymore."

The swiftness of what followed surprised her, but it probably shouldn't have. He knew what she was talking about and there was no need for clarification or elaboration. He released her hand and sat up, rubbing his eyes with his fingers. Then he turned back to the computer screen. "Yes," he said, finding his place and resuming his typing, "you will."

She stood, arms at her sides, mouth open. Was he serious? He couldn't be serious. He hadn't heard her. She found her voice and said, "No, really, I'm not going to." And then added in a whisper: "I shouldn't have done it in the first pla—"

"You're right about that," he said, still looking at the screen, his voice just above a whisper. "But you did do it. And that's a mistake you're going to have to pay for."

She wobbled in place, uncertain whether her instability came from the sea or from the shock of his words. She knew exactly what he meant, knew that he had her right where he wanted her, had all the leverage he needed to keep her there. Worst of all, her fears were confirmed: He had used her, had never loved her.

Her sinuses stung and she thought she was going to sneeze but then something convulsed and tightened at the back of her throat and she knew she was about to cry. She turned and walked toward the door so he wouldn't see her. When she was almost out of the lab, he called her name. She stopped, but did not turn around. "We can talk about this more later," he said. "Or not. I'll leave it up to you. But you did put your things in your own cabin, right?"

She turned and gave him a questioning look, which he didn't see because he was still looking at the screen.

"I mean, you didn't put your things in my cabin. . . ."

There was a fire extinguisher mounted on the wall next to her and for a few seconds she rocked on her feet and considered picking it up and throwing it at him. Instead, she opted for a mundane exit: "No, I have my own cabin," she said, stumbling into the hallway.

Chapter 32

Not wanting to repeat the step-shuffle-step performance of his Bird Murder presentation, Davis made sure that this time there were plenty of chairs in the conference room so that he wouldn't have to fight against the sea in an attempt to stand. And unlike the last time, when he had sought to keep the audience's attention by having colorful words and phrases blink and cartwheel into the frame of his PowerPoint, the slides this time were much more elegant and subdued. A "just the facts, ma'am" presentation that was, predictably, boring.

He began by giving a synopsis of the history of the mammal/noise controversy, and that led into an inevitable bullet-pointed list of the reasons for the policy. His narration of these parts was repeatedly interrupted by the derogatory sniffs of Jerry, who sat, arms crossed, head shaking in disagreement. Davis ignored him and jumped right into explaining the policy and what was expected of them as the official marine mammal observers.

"Thirty minutes before we start up the guns, we'll do a pre-shooting search for any mammals. To do this, we'll turn on the hydrophone and put it in the water. It will transmit the sounds it receives to a transponder in the lab where one of you will be sitting, wearing headphones, listening for whale or mammal sounds. If you hear any, we will delay firing until the sounds have gone away."

That was vague, Davis knew, but since there didn't seem to be any objection to it, he went on:

"While the hydrophone listener is listening, there will be two of you on the bridge using binoculars to make repeated 360-degree visual scans of the ocean. If you don't see anything, and if the person listening in the lab hasn't heard anything, we'll then pull the hydrophone out of the water and move into the next thirty-minute period, during which the guns will be slowly ramped up to full power."

One of the technicians held up a hand. "What's the point of slowly ramping up the guns, why not just start firing with full power?"

"Good question," Davis said, and he was profoundly relieved to have an answer to it. "Ideally the slow ramp-up will give warning to any mammals in the vicinity and allow them to swim out of harm's way."

Artaud rolled his eyes.

"And what are we looking for during the visual search?" Meghan asked.

"Okay," Davis said, thumbing through the files in his head to find the correct response, lifted from some website or other, to recite. "What you're looking for are any signs of marine life within the two-hundred-meter 'safety zone' of the vessel. Sometimes all you'll see is a fin, or a fluke, or a spout. You're not usually going to see the whale breaching or flapping its tail. But if you see anything come up, keep your eye on it and have the other observer immediately radio down to the lab to stop the countdown. Once the animal has moved away, we will resume the countdown."

"But we won't have to go through the whole sixty-minute process to restart the guns. . . ." Jerry said.

"Not the whole process, no. Just another thirty minutes for the slow ramp-up."

"You're kidding!"

Davis shook his head. Jerry stood up and stamped his foot.

"This is crazy! How are we supposed to get any work done?" With his red beard, dwarfish features, and pointy stocking cap, he reminded Davis of an angry lawn gnome.

"I'm just the one tasked with implementing policy." Davis

sighed, giving his best diplomatic shrug. "I'm not the one who dictates the content."

"Christ."

"As I said," Davis resumed, "if you do see a mammal in the water, keep your eye on it because you'll need to record the type of mammal and its action and behavior."

"Meaning what?" Jerry asked.

"Meaning was it fleeing away from the vessel in obvious terror—"

"Oh, now c'mon," Artaud interjected, "I don't think we need to—"

"—or was it bobbing along contentedly, oblivious to the noise surrounding it."

"Should we try to identify the species?" Worm asked.

"If you can, that would be ideal, but usually, as I said, all you'll see is a fin or a fluke or a spout, so specific identification will be difficult. There is a marine mammal chart on the bridge, which I encourage you all to study—when you're not busy observing, that is."

This explanation was followed by an equally detailed but much more tedious and boring explanation of the numerous forms they were to fill out. Once that was done, Davis made a visual assessment of his audience. Artaud and Jerry were still fuming; Worm seemed intent and eager, but Kristi was asleep, head back and mouth open. Andrew, Meghan, and the three technicians wore that glazed look that was a mix of boredom and seasickness. And then there was Maureen. Her head was cocked to the side, her attention on the spines of the novels on the bookshelf. Davis wasn't even sure why she was there. He doubted that she would volunteer to stand watch. Probably she just wanted to add yet another bitchy arrow to her already full quiver of pointed verbal ammunition by witnessing his ridiculous attempt to sound authoritative on a subject about which he did not, by his own admission, know all that much.

"Gosh," Meghan sighed once the lights were turned back on. "That's a lot to remember."

"Don't worry about that now," Davis said. "The PowerPoint, and all associated paperwork, will be available on the ship's network and there will be hard copies of everything in the Marine

Mammal Observer's Handbook, a copy of which you'll all be given on your way out the door today. Also, I'll be up on the bridge several times during the day and night to answer any questions you may have, and to provide another set of eyes."

"I'm sure that won't be necessary," Artaud said, rising and heading toward the exit. "They're all smart kids. They'll see that it's done correctly."

"Still, I'll be up there most of the time—just to make sure."

What he wanted to make sure of was not so much that the procedure was being followed correctly but that it was being followed at all, and that they weren't, say, doing homework, writing e-mail, or reading magazines.

"I'll take on a shift or two," Worm offered.

"Yeah, I can do one, too," one of the other techs added.

"Great!" Davis said and produced a sign-up sheet. "Here's the schedule. We need to get all of these spaces filled, even the ones at night, so try to take on more than one shift if at all possible."

In practice, the observing proved even more tedious than in theory. Unless you actually saw something, which did not happen often, it was just a lot of staring at the same boring seascape: one-half sky, one-half water, occasionally an iceberg. Since all observing was done from the uppermost deck of the ship, the bobbing motion was more pronounced than on the lower decks and was further magnified and intensified by having to stare through binoculars. After fifteen minutes, most people had gone pale and were struggling to keep down their last meal. Even Davis, who was in danger of ODing on his Coast Guard Cocktail, occasionally lost it while on duty.

On the first day, Davis was on the bridge with Andrew and Meghan. Kristi was in one of the lower labs wearing headphones and listening to the transmission from the hydrophone.

The flaws in the plan became clear to Davis almost instantaneously. The first and most glaring was that Kristi had no real idea what whale calls sounded like and kept hearing the ship's engines and sonar, mistaking the rhythmic click of the latter for a dolphin. Her false reports, and the subsequent resetting of the thirty-minute clock, enraged Jerry and Artaud to the point that they started yelling at her, which caused her to break into tears, abandon her post, and lock herself in her cabin.

"Someone better get their ass down here," Jerry radioed up to Davis, "or we're going to fire up the guns and start shooting!"

Davis sighed. He gave some final instructions to Andrew and Meghan and then lumbered down the four flights of stairs to the lab, where he put on the headphones and took over the listening duties. It was then that he realized how useless the hydrophone was. He had listened to several whale calls on the Internet so he knew, vaguely, what he was listening for, but there was so much static coming through the headphones that it sounded like an AM radio caught between stations. Then, too, there was the background noise coming from the ship—a low rumbling punctuated at regular intervals by the chirp sonar, which was like having a sparrow nesting in your ear. But the most jarring aural assault came when the vessel smacked into a piece of ice and it subsequently scraped and screeched its way along the metal hull, like some giant, amplified fingernail on a chalkboard.

When, at the end of thirty minutes, Davis removed the headphones, his ears were ringing and the area behind his eyes felt bloated and achy. He radioed up to Andrew and Meghan to see if it was all clear from their vantage point. His call provoked no response.

"Andrew! Meghan! Copy!"

Nothing. In a huff, with his head feeling like someone was driving a pencil into each of his ears, he pulled himself up the stairs to the bridge where he found the two observers, one sound asleep in a chair, the other leaning on one of the counters, her large ass swaying with the motion of the ship as she flipped through the pages of a magazine.

"What are you doing?" Davis huffed, then leaned over, hands on his knees, and tried to catch his breath.

"Wha—?" Andrew woke up and rubbed his eyes. Meghan continued turning the pages, oblivious, and soon Davis realized that she was not swaying to the motion of the ship but to the song coming through the earbuds of her iPod. Pulse racing and lips pursed, Davis grabbed the neglected radio (which hadn't even been turned on) from the chart table and flew at Meghan, making a spectacular leap before Andrew had time to call out a warning. He landed, un-noticed, behind her and leaned in. When his mouth was about six inches from the back of her head, he screamed her name. She shrieked, spun around, wide-eyed and trembling, and yanked the buds from her ears.

"That's not funny!" she cried. "You scared the crap out of me!"

"What are you two doing?" Davis boomed, looking from one to the other. "You're supposed to be observing!"

"Dude, relax," Andrew said. "We watched for, like, almost the whole time. We didn't see anything."

"And c'mon, the captain is here," Meghan said, pointing to the enormous man at the helm. He tipped his hat and puffed his ciga-rette at the mention of his title.

"It's the captain's job to drive the boat. That's why he's called the captain and not the observer. You're the observers. And why did you turn the radio off?" Davis demanded, shaking it in their faces.

"It was off?" Andrew said, genuinely surprised.

"Yes, it was off! I've been radioing up to you trying to see if we can give them the okay to start the ramp-up."

Just then Davis's radio crackled to life.

"Davis, back deck here." It was the annoyed voice of Jerry. "What's the story? Copy."

Davis snarled at the two students and then spoke into his radio. "Back deck, bridge here. All clear to start the ramp-up."

"Roger that."

While the amused captain watched, Davis thrust a pair of binoculars into Meghan's hands and pulled her by the arm over to the starboard side of the bridge. "Now watch!" he ordered. "And do a 360-degree search of the water for the next thirty minutes." Then he turned, glared at Andrew, pointed to the port side, and yelled, "You! Over there!" Andrew skidded over to his spot and held the binoculars up to his eyes. Davis turned on their radio to full volume, lifted up Meghan's fleshy blubber, and clipped it onto her belt.

For the next half hour, while the guns were being ramped up, Davis played prison guard, goose-stepping back and forth between the fatty and the fag (allowing himself to silently refer to them thus since he was essentially a combination of them both). When something actually did appear in the water, it was not Meghan, Andrew, or Davis who spotted it, but the captain.

"You've got something right over there," he said, pointing to a spot in the water where Davis saw, well, nothing. He grabbed the binoculars still around Meghan's neck and brought them up to his eyes, pulling her face tight against his chest.

"But I don't see anything," Davis cried, more eager to sight a whale than most Mexican peasants were for a sighting of the Virgin of Guadalupe.

"Keep looking," the captain said, "it'll surface again. I've got the harpoon ready, ha, ha, ha!"

Davis kept looking and, sure enough, he saw a slight bump that looked, at first, like an old tire floating in the water. A faint puff of mist emerged and then the bump disappeared. His eyes focused on the horizontal reticle marks that were etched on the lenses of the binoculars and he determined that the whale, or whatever it had been, was well out of the safety zone and was swimming away from the vessel. He gave a disappointed sigh as he stared at the vacant water.

"Can you . . . let me . . . go," Meghan pleaded. Davis lowered the binoculars and handed them back to her. Andrew had approached and was still peering through the binoculars at the area of the sighting.

"It was too far out, right?" he said.

"Yes," Davis said. "Exactly. Good job. See, Meghan," Davis said, and made her look through the lenses. "If it's closer than the third line, you radio down to the back deck and tell them to stop the guns. That one was just over the fourth line and was headed away. Now keep looking! We've got ten minutes left."

Their interest invigorated by the sighting, the observers kept watch for the next ten minutes with minimal prodding from Davis. Once the time was up, he watched over their shoulders as they filled out the paperwork and then made them wait and continue watching until Kristi and one of the techs arrived for their shift.

Having shared Kristi's earsplitting experience with the hydrophone, Davis was much more patient and sympathetic with her than he had been with Meghan and Andrew, although it was difficult for him to contain his annoyance when, after ten minutes of looking through the binoculars, she ran to the bridge bathroom and vomited.

"She should be used to this by now," Davis said to the captain as he roamed around the bridge looking out each of the windows.

"Listen to you, Mr. Sympathetic. At least she'll stay thin. That last little girl you was yelling at could use a few puking episodes, if you know what I mean." Then he winked and added: "Wouldn't hurt you none either."

Chapter 33

Davis remained on the bridge until all of the observers had been through the drill at least once and therefore had no excuse to claim they did not know what was going on. There had been five sightings that first day and four calls to the back deck to shut down the guns. Each of the calls had been greeted with either a stream of bitter curses from Jerry or stony silence from Artaud.

Since the sun never set but just circled in the sky overhead, Davis didn't really notice the passage of time until, feeling tired, he looked at his watch and realized he had been on the bridge for over sixteen hours. He looked at the roster to see who was on duty next and realized that he had been wrong in thinking everyone had been trained. There was still one person who had not, and that person was Maureen. She was scheduled to work with Worm, who had arrived early and was already busy roaming the deck and scanning the sea. None of the techs were required to do any shifts since they already had twelve-hour days, but this was, nevertheless, Worm's second shift that day. Davis looked at his watch, yawned, and was just resigning himself to the fact that Maureen was not coming and that he would have to do another shift when he heard footsteps on the stairs and she rounded the corner.

"Ah, you're here," he said, his voice signaling both enthusiasm and relief.

She raised her lip in a sneer. "I signed up, didn't I?"

"Yes," Davis said, removing the binoculars from his neck and handing them to her. "So you did. Just step over here and I'll show you what you need to do."

"I went through the training," she said, snatching the binoculars and moving over to the starboard bridge wing.

"Okay . . . yes," Davis said, but then began reciting his spiel anyway: "You'll need to do a 360-degree visual sweep every five minutes an—"

"I've got it."

"Then let me show you the paperwork."

"I'm sure I can figure it out," she said, not lowering the binoculars.

"Yes, but—"

"I *said* I can figure it out."

Usually, Davis would have ignored her, but since he had spent the past sixteen hours wobbling around the bridge with an incessant headache, dealing with people who were alternately apathetic or hostile to what he was telling them to do, he gave into his fit of pique and fired back.

"Fine!" he snapped, his face hot, his hands squeezed into fists. "Then I've got just one question for you." Something, probably the hardness in his voice and its elevated tone, made her lower the binoculars, although she did not turn to face him.

"Do you have to make an effort to be such a snot," he said, his voice hoarse with the effort of containing his rage, "or is it just something you're hardwired to do?"

Maureen clenched her jaw and stared straight ahead. They were both aware that the captain and Worm were now their rapt audience. Slowly, Maureen raised the binoculars. Davis, feeling stupid and embarrassed, struggled to think of a suitable exit strategy. When nothing came to him, he slammed the notebook shut and headed to the door.

"Give me a call if someone doesn't show up for their shift," he called out, to no one in particular, but then gave a dismissive "what the hell" wave and went down the stairs. He stopped at the galley, grabbed a handful of cookies and a carton of milk, and was about to head up to his room to fill his emotional void when Artaud walked in.

"Milk?" he cried, making a sour expression at the box in Davis's hand. "Wouldn't you like something a little stronger than that?"

Davis looked down at the carton and shrugged. Artaud, still wearing his orange float coat, his sunglasses pushed up on his wool cap, went over to the carb counter and took a handful of cookies for himself.

"How about we eat these upstairs?" he said. Then, leaning in, he whispered, "And I might even have something a little stronger than milk to go with them. We can relax and talk."

Davis groaned. All he wanted to do was stuff his face and watch the dumb DVD he'd found in the ship's TV lounge. The last thing he wanted was another argument.

"Come on," Artaud said. "Give me five minutes to shower and change, and then another ten or fifteen minutes of your time. I'll make it worth your while," he said with a wink. Davis rubbed his eyes.

"Sure, okay," he said, figuring he might as well get it over with. "I'm gonna go shower myself. I'll come by after that."

"Sounds good," Artaud said, and gave him a playful sock in the arm.

When Davis arrived, Artaud answered the door in a pair of boxer shorts and a T-shirt.

"Come in, come in," he said and returned to the bathroom, "I'll be right with you. Would you like something to drink?" he asked, poking his head out of the bathroom.

"What . . . do you mean?" Davis asked, thinking maybe he had one of the cartons of sickly sweet fruit juice on hand. Artaud emerged from the bathroom and walked over to his bunk. He bent down, pulled out a pair of jeans and some socks, and then rummaging around deeper in the drawer his hand emerged clutching a bottle of bourbon. He set it on the bed, wedging it between the wall and the pillow so it wouldn't roll off, closed the drawer, stood, and got dressed. He pulled on a pair of slip-on boots that were sitting by the door. Then, signaling to Davis with his index finger that he would be right back, he went out into the hallway.

When he had gone, Davis walked over to the bed and picked up the bottle. Then a thought came to him and he set the bottle back down, fearing it might be some sort of setup. He knew it was probably stupid to be so paranoid, but the day's contention and strife had left his nerves on edge. All the more reason for him wanting a drink.

Artaud returned a few minutes later bearing two paper cups from the galley, each filled with ice. He handed them both to Davis and motioned him to sit on the couch. Davis did as he was told, obediently holding the cups aloft while Artaud decanted the amber liquid.

"This is illegal," Davis whispered, feeling like he had just raided his father's liquor cabinet or was trying to sneak beer into a movie theater.

"Many things are illegal," Artaud said, capping the bottle and taking one of the cups from Davis. "Few of them with good reason. Cheers." They tapped their cups together.

"What is the reason?" Davis asked.

Artaud paused, savoring the taste of his drink before swallowing. "For the ban on alcohol?"

"Yes."

Artaud rolled his eyes, "One drunk captain runs an oil tanker aground in Alaska and we're all supposed to suffer for it."

"That was it?"

"That, and the insurance costs. But since we're not the ones driving the ship, there's little reason to worry."

Davis drank, albeit tentatively, savoring the drink all the more because of the illicitness that went with it.

"So tell me," Artaud said, leaning back and kicking his feet up to the side so they could rest on the desk chair, "how do you think the first day went?"

Now it was Davis's turn to roll his eyes. "Fine," he said. "As well as can be expected, I suppose, given that it's a new policy and no one seems to take it very seriously."

"They did show up for their shifts, though, right?"

"Yes, they did. But sometimes it helps if you bring the brain along with the body."

"I see."

"Yes."

"It can't be very interesting work."

"No."

"And you do realize that there's no science to prove that seismic does any harm to whales or mammals?"

"Yeah," Davis sighed, leaning back into the sofa and taking a gulp of his bourbon. "So people keep telling me. But there's no proof that what you're doing *doesn't* harm whales."

Artaud laughed.

"No, really," Davis said, leaning forward, his energy reinvigorated by the drink and his annoyance with Artaud's arrogance. "You have to admit the possibility that the whales, dolphins, and what have you might just be down there suffering—or worse—every time you shoot off those guns."

"Okay."

"And that you know as little about what's going on under the surface as I do."

"As far as charismatic macrofauna are concerned, yes."

Davis ignored the comment and continued: "From what I've read, some scientists think that when marine mammals get spooked by loud noises, they swim away as fast as they can, and in the process they either dive too deep or surface too fast, which is almost as harmful to them as when a human diver does it. It puts little gas bubbles in their bloodstream and bursts their capillaries."

"Yes," Artaud sneered. "The bends theory. I know all about it. But again, there's no hard evidence backing that up."

Davis didn't reply. His argumentative gun had only one bullet, and he'd just fired it. Artaud was a scientist, Davis wasn't. But something about Artaud's easy dismissal of Davis's argument didn't feel right to him. After all, it wasn't like the calls to shut down the guns were stopping the science. The technicians shut them down just as often, if not more often, to make repairs or because they had frozen up. Granted, the shutdowns did eat into Artaud's time at sea to collect data, but not all that much. They were, after even just one day, acquiring data faster than his little undergrad minions could process it, so if this policy was somehow protecting some mammals (although even Davis had to admit that he really didn't believe it was), or even if it was just, as Sarah said, providing some good CYA for the company and the government, then what was the harm?

Davis's watch beeped, reminding him that it was time to take his HIV medication. He excused himself to Artaud's bathroom. Artaud's dirty clothes fell off the hook on the back of the door when he closed it. Davis bent down to pick them up and saw, at the bottom of the pile, one of the biggest brassieres he had ever seen. He picked it up, clutching it between his thumb and middle finger, and held it away from his face as if it might bite him. It seemed to have been designed for udders rather than breasts and he was amazed that Maureen, who seemed so slight and petite, could possess such a rack. Shaking his head, he returned it to the hook and turned back to the sink. He removed his pills from the zipper pocket of his fleece jacket, popped them in his mouth, and washed them down with scooped handfuls of water from the faucet. Once he'd swallowed, he stood up, looked at his face in the mirror, and a thought occurred to him. He went back out into the main room.

"Listen," Davis said, resuming his seat on the couch and picking up his glass, which, he was pleased to notice, had been refilled. "This is just like medical testing."

"What is?"

"This seismic."

"What are you talking about?"

Davis paused to formulate his idea, then proceeded: "Okay, think of a drug company—they can't just develop some drug and start selling it untested, right? Because if they do, the drug might harm somebody."

"Yes."

"Well, the same could be said about what you're doing. There's no proof that blasting those guns in the water causes harm, or distress, or even discomfort to whales, but shouldn't the burden of providing proof that it doesn't be on you, the one who's doing the blasting?"

"Whales are not human, my friend."

"No, they're not. But one thing that is uniquely human is the concept of public relations, and you, my friend," Davis said, echoing Artaud's snide tone, "are on the wrong side of it. People like whales. They're not cute or cuddly, but they're gentle and awe-inspiring. What's more, they've got one thing many people can appreciate—persecution. They've been hunted to the brink of ex-

328 • *Chris Kenry*

tinction, they get ensnared in fishing nets, hit by boats, harassed by
sonar and seismic . . . They're like the Jews of the sea."

"And so that makes me a Nazi, is that what you're saying?"

In response, Davis lifted a particularly annoying comeback
from one of his former therapists: "No, that's what *you're* saying.
All I'm saying is that by making such a stink about what I'm sent
down here to do, you're not making yourself look so good."

"How's the book coming?" Artaud asked. Davis was surprised
by the radical change of subject.

"Why?"

"Oh, I don't know. You were so hard at work on it on the last
cruise—to the exclusion of everything else—I was just wondering
if you'd finished, that's all."

"Oh."

"So?"

Davis gave a noncommittal shrug.

"Have you finished?"

"No."

"And do your bosses know—are they *aware,* I mean—that you
did nothing but work on your little artistic venture the last time you
were out here?"

A figurative wave crashed onto Davis, momentarily pinning
him, but in an instant it was gone and he was back up. He narrowed his eyes at Artaud. This was, Davis knew, a tacit threat, and
for a moment, he was afraid. But only for a moment. Then he realized the irony of it all. The irony that on this trip, unlike the last
one, he was actually doing the work he was sent down here to do.
And precisely *because* he was doing that work so thoroughly, the
threat to reveal his sloth on the last cruise was being lorded over
him. Now, of all times. Not before, when he was, admittedly, doing
nothing but taking up space, but now, when he was working harder
than he could ever remember working. He almost laughed.

"To be honest," Davis said, stretching out his legs and crossing
his arms behind his head, "I don't think they're too concerned
about what I was or wasn't doing on the last cruise. They sent me
down there to familiarize myself with the ship, which I did. Other
than that, their expectations weren't all that high."

"How 'bout another drink," Artaud said, retrieving the bottle and pouring more into their glasses.

"I don't know about this," Davis said, realizing that the drinking might be yet another way to blackmail him. "We could get in trouble."

"We could," Artaud agreed, and then sat down on the sofa next to him. Right next to him, the sides of their bodies touching. Artaud stuck his legs out and kicked off one, then the other boot. Davis stared at his feet, languidly stretching in their bright white socks, and he watched, as if it were happening in slow motion, as one foot crossed over the top of Davis's ankle and came to rest.

"Drink," Artaud commanded. The Nervous Imbiber obeyed, his eyes fixed on Artaud's foot. Then came the hand, up and over, hovering for a moment before coming to rest on Davis's thigh. Artaud leaned forward and set his cup on the floor. When he leaned back, he reached over, grabbed Davis's chin, and turned his head so that they were facing each other. Davis didn't offer much resistance, at least not at first. He was, for some reason, not shocked by what Artaud was doing, or maybe he was just too tired. He certainly wasn't drunk, that much he knew. His considerable girth, coupled with his years of drinking with Jake, had raised his tolerance of alcohol to a point where three small paper cups of bourbon had little effect on his resistance. And it wasn't that he didn't want to give in to what Artaud was evidently angling to do, because a part of him (namely the part between his legs that was now stirring from what seemed like a long hibernation) definitely did. But what made Davis pull away was the knowledge that before they did anything sexual, they would have to have the boner-deflating "conversation." The one about His Internal Visitor, the other Mrs. Rochester, or any of the hundred other euphemisms he'd come up with to tastefully explain away his infected bodily fluids. And again, he was sober enough to realize that this round of drinks and flirtation, coming, as it had, at the end of another attempt to convince Davis of the folly of his marine mammal observing, was just another attempt at manipulation. Davis stood up.

"Don't you want to suck me off?" Artaud asked.

This time the irony made Davis laugh. Here he was, the slut

from the apartment with the revolving bedroom door—the same slut who had indiscriminately admitted men, most of whom he wouldn't want to be seen talking to on the street, into his apartment for just such purposes—looking down at this Greek god of a man, his legs spread invitingly wide, and said, "No, thank you."

Although it was not impossible that someone so good-looking, someone so allegedly straight, would find Davis desirable, especially given the length of their journey and the relative isolation of their location (the meaning of the expression "any port in a storm" suddenly made sense), he knew, nevertheless, that the chance of Artaud being genuinely attracted to him was unlikely, and thus he knew there were other motivations for his advances.

"I think I'd better go," Davis said, setting his drink on the floor and rising from the couch. There was a first for everything, he supposed, and this was a first on two fronts: leaving a drink unfinished and turning down an obvious offer for sex. He went down the hallway to the stairs and went down to his cabin, chuckling to himself as he went.

Chapter 34

They stood at opposite ends of the bridge, forty feet apart. The captain stood between them, navigating the ship between bergs. Five minutes passed. Worm walked from the port to the starboard side until he stood just three feet away from her.

"Do you see something?" she asked, sensing his presence but not lowering her binoculars.

"No," he said, raising his and looking out to sea. She took a few steps aft. He followed and stood next to her. Leaning in, he whispered, "I need to talk to you." She lowered her binoculars and glanced over her shoulder at the captain, who was drinking coffee and smoking a cigarette. His attention seemed to be elsewhere. Worm nodded to the deck behind the bridge. "We should go out there," he said, loud enough for the captain to hear. "That way we'll be able to get a better all-around view."

They put on their coats, hats, and gloves, and Maureen undid the dog hinges on the door and pushed it open. The wind howled in and they stepped out quickly, slamming the door behind them. She walked to the starboard rail and resumed her observation. Worm stood a few steps away, his back to hers, his binoculars up.

Aside from public niceties in the galley, they hadn't spoken since their encounter on Easter Island, an encounter that had left Maureen physically satisfied but mentally embarrassed. Embarrassed both by the public spectacle of their act and by her fellow actor, about whom she had never before entertained any erotic ideas. Then there had been the guilt she had felt when she'd returned to the hotel and found Artaud waiting for her, and the nauseating way her guilt had caused her to simper and coo and do everything to make him avoid suspicion. What a waste it had all been! How stupid, especially given the fact that he had not slept with her again after he'd got hold of the tapes. And then, too, there was the way he had ignored her subsequent calls and e-mails, as if she'd been nothing more than a one-night stand. Bastard!

A disturbing thought then occurred to her and she lowered the binoculars. It was one of those thoughts that spills into one's consciousness only when the level of hypocrisy overflows the banks of plausibility. The thought was this: What Artaud had done to her, she had done to Worm. Just as she had called and e-mailed Artaud, Worm had called and e-mailed her. His last message (a tentative, inquiring, subtly pleading electronic missive) had, as the days and weeks rolled by, remained unanswered, until it descended out of sight in her in-box. She would, she had told herself, get to it, just as soon as she could craft a response. Of course, such a response had never been crafted, let alone seriously considered, and soon it went out of her mind completely. She remembered it then as she stood shivering on the deck with her back to Worm, and hoped that maybe it had gone out of his mind, too. Hoped that maybe he was one of those men her mother had warned her about—one who bagged, bragged, and moved on to the next one.

"I wanted to talk to you," he began, his voice almost a shout so that he could be heard over the wind, "about what happened." The wind was so cold it stung his face and his eyes teared up. "I don't know if it meant anything to you—" he began, then, thinking that sounded weak and desperate, changed course and asked, "Are you still seeing him?"

"No."

He was not sure which question she had answered, and was not sure how to ask for clarification. "Oh," was all he said, and then went back to looking out to sea. Minutes passed during which both shivered but neither one said anything. Maureen was the first to speak.

"I never thanked you," she said, regretting how stupid it sounded before the words were even out of her mouth.

"For what?"

She wondered if she really needed to clarify what she was saying.

"Oh, that," he said, blushing. "No thanks necessary. I mean, I liked it a lot, too. You were great, but I . . . Are you . . . ?"

"Still seeing him? No."

Worm felt a surge of adrenaline on hearing that word. No, she was not seeing him. Yes, there was hope. Then she surprised him, and herself, by asking, "Maybe we can do it again sometime?"

"You mean . . . ?"

She nodded.

"Oh, you bet," he said, nodding vigorously. "Yes. Anytime." Then the awkwardness returned and they both went back to observing.

"Now?" Maureen asked.

He lowered the binoculars and swallowed hard. "Now?"

"Yes," she said, her voice almost plaintive.

"Where?"

The ice tower was a small, windowed room, roughly four feet by five feet wide, that was above and slightly aft from the bridge. It was accessed via a metal ladder that led up to a trapdoor in the ceiling. It was the highest enclosed point on the vessel, and once inside, you were largely invisible to anyone else on the lower decks. In theory the ice tower existed to enable a ship's mate to spot fissures and cracks in the sea ice, or to see icebergs or other obstacles that might be a danger to the ship's progress. It was, due to advances in radar, a navigational redundancy but, like many redundancies, it now served an unintended purpose: as one of the few places on the vessel (aside from the bathroom) that afforded even a modicum of privacy. It was, thus, the preferred place for sexual assignations, hence its unofficial designation: "the stabbin' cabin."

"I'll go up first," Maureen explained, her voice low and excited. "You come up in a few minutes. The captain won't know. And if anyone else comes, we'll hear them climbing the stairs before they get to the ladder."

"Okay," Worm said, his voice cracking and his mind wondering how it was that she was so familiar with this particular protocol. Maureen walked back to the bridge and went inside. Trying to affect an air of nonchalance, she coughed to let the captain know she was there, walked to the port-side bridge wing, did a perfunctory scan of the surrounding ocean, and then turned and walked in front of the captain, who was not, to her chagrin, paying the least bit of attention but was instead focused on a crossword puzzle that lay on the chart table in front of him. She performed another perfunctory observation through the windows on the starboard side, drummed her fingers on the windowsill for a moment, and then in a matter-of-fact tone said, "If that tech writer, or anyone else comes looking, I'll be up in the ice tower." The captain tipped the bill of his cap; his eyes never left the puzzle.

Maureen went out into the hallway, closed the door to the bridge, and climbed up the ladder, her arms and legs tingling. She crawled up through the trapdoor, emerged into the room, and then looked down through the aft windows at Worm, still standing erect (so to speak), the binoculars up, looking out to sea. She waved and tried to get his attention, but he was still playing along with the observer charade, obediently waiting the "few minutes" she'd commanded.

Her motives for wanting him again were not, she knew, altogether pure. This time she wanted him partly because Meghan, her roommate, had, soon after they'd left Port Lyttelton, taken up residence in Artaud's cabin. A fact she had first realized when she saw the girl emerging from his lair, disheveled and sock-footed, one morning as she, Maureen, was coming off the night shift. It was a fact that everyone now knew, since gossip on board a ship spreads faster than a grease fire, and as much as she hated to admit it, the rejection and betrayal stung, and it brought to her mind the one person she was certain would not reject her. The one who could, she suspected, make her feel wanted and provide the full-throttle, thought-obliterating sex she now craved. The kind she'd expected and hoped for from Artaud but that had never really materialized.

Looking back, she had to admit that the sex with Artaud had always been, in spite of his good looks, bland—a mannered, overly scripted event devoid of any passion or spontaneity. He was often prepared with what Hollywood and Madison Avenue had taught him to believe a woman wanted: cold white wine, a Satie piano piece coming from a hidden speaker, schlocky comparisons of her beauty to the flight of doves or some such ridiculousness that more often than not left her blushing for him and wishing he would just shut up and do it already. But even when he finally did move on to the act, it was itself just another of his performances. There were smug demonstrations of his skill and technique, numerous facial expressions meant to convey his feelings of ecstasy, but it was all a bit too rehearsed and theatrical to be believable.

Her thoughts were interrupted by the sound of Worm's boots on the rungs of the ladder. She leaned back into a corner, her back against the glass, her hands on the windowsill.

Worm climbed up into the room, his eyes moving up her body as he ascended. Once in, he stood, looked her in the eyes for a few long seconds to confirm that she was serious, that she was not playing some game. Satisfied, he turned, bent down, and lowered the hatch, ensuring their privacy. Then he stood again, turned, and approached, standing inches away from her but seeming unsure how to proceed. He was just lifting his hands to her shoulders, reaching out to touch her hair when she leapt forward and grabbed his head, pulling his mouth to hers. There was a struggle with belts, buttons, zippers, and elastic, movements that were accompanied by rapid breathing and the smacking sounds of their mouths. His pants slid down his skinny legs and the belt buckle clattered on the metal deck. With her hands, and then with the aid of one foot, she lowered the waistband of his underwear so that he could shimmy it down around his ankles. Her frenzied hands had been inhibiting his own hands from removing her pants, so he grabbed her wrists and guided her hands up to his shoulders. She laced her fingers around the back of his neck and his hands returned to her waist, popping the snap, lowering the zipper, and then, in one deft movement, reaching around her and sliding under her waistband, cupping her ass. He lifted her, set her down on the narrow sill.

"Hold on to the window," he said, his voice low, their bodies swaying with the rolling of the ocean. She held herself awkwardly in place while he took a step back and lifted her legs, removing her shoes, then the legs of her pants, and finally, the small pink undergarment, which he paused to admire before tossing it behind him. Then he approached and she encircled him with her arms and legs, clinging to him like a monkey on a tree as he reached behind, placed his hands once again on her ass, and lifted her up. He spread his legs wide (or as wide as his bunched-up pants would allow) in order to steady himself, and for the next few anxious moments they both held their breaths as he blindly struggled to find the precise point of insertion, both exhaling when he hit the spot and lowered her into place. They held each other, sharing the burden of her weight, neither making any movement, but surrendering to the rock and sway, back and forth, side to side, the hum of the ship's engine traveling up through his legs and into her until she felt the frequency of the vibration increase until it was nothing but a high-pitched buzz. Wanting to be closer, have him deeper within her, she tightened her grip around his neck, locked her ankles, and squeezed him to her, thrusting her hips forward against his until the only part of her body left to squeeze him with was the part that he was in. She closed her eyes, gritted her teeth, narrowed the focus of her attentions to squeezing that one single part of her body tighter and tighter until finally her grip collapsed into a series of tremors that sent giddy waves of contraction through her torso and out into her limbs.

Worm, who had been struggling to contain his own orgasm, felt the grasping shudder, pulled back once, and then thrust up and into her, his legs rigid, his ass cheeks clenched, and his head filled with popping stars. He lost his balance, fell back into a wall, and was pushed down to the deck. She gave a sudden yelp as they went down but was unable to do anything to help and they landed with a thud.

As the endorphins dissipated into their bloodstreams, they became aware of themselves once more, and like their predecessors in that primordial garden, struggled to conceal their nakedness.

Once they were up and re-arrayed in their matching rust-colored work clothes, once her hair was again twisted and pulled back through her baseball cap, once their respective binoculars were back around their respective necks, Worm put a hand on her shoulder and turned her to face him. They were exactly the same height, so their eyes and noses and mouths were at the same level.

He kissed her mouth first, then her chin, then moved up to her cheek.

"We'd better get back down," she said, pushing her face to the side. He sensed her discomfort, saw her expression of distaste, and his shoulders dropped. He stepped back and looked out the bank of windows.

"I mean, I don't know how long we've been up here," she said. He looked at his watch.

"Seven minutes."

He opened the hatch, stood to the side, and motioned that she should descend. She did, and was surprised when he did not follow her down but instead lowered the hatch back into place. She stood staring up at it for a moment and then walked back to the bridge. The captain did not look up. She went over to the starboard side, lifted the binoculars, and gazed blankly at the sparkling sea, hoping she wouldn't see anything. She had, in fact, been instructed not to see anything, had been told to act as a blind observer whose lack of sightings would allow the seismic operation to continue uninterrupted. She had not wanted to do these shifts; she had been ordered to do them by Artaud.

As her thoughts were thus occupied she heard the rapid clang of boots on the ladder. The door to the bridge burst open and Worm entered.

"Okay," he said, "we've done this twice now and you've blown me off twice. I won't let it happen again. At least not without me saying something."

"Not here," she said, her voice firm and level. The captain, now looking up from his puzzle, gazed at them over the rims of his glasses.

She nodded toward the aft deck and walked toward it, putting on her hat and gloves as she went. He followed her out wearing only his T-shirt. The bridge sheltered them from the wind but he wanted to be far enough away to raise his voice, so he grabbed her by the wrist and led her down a set of stairs to the middle of the helo pad.

"I don't know what you think you're doing," he boomed, "but it's not very nice."

"Will you just stop," she said, emitting an annoyed sigh.

"I won't! Not this time. You're making me out to be some fuck-toy idiot, and I'm not. I don't know how you've worked it with other guys—"

"What other guys? I haven't worked it! I haven't done anything at all. I, you—You seemed to enjoy it as much as I did!"

"Yeah, I did. Because to me it actually meant something. It wasn't just another trip to the stabbin' cabin."

"That's disgusting," she said, turning and stomping back up the stairs.

"Not really," Worm said, following her, "but I'll tell you what is. What's disgusting is you pouncing on me like I'm the last man on earth and then not even having the courage to look me in the eyes. That's disgusting."

She was at the door of the bridge. He grabbed her arm and yanked her back around.

"I'm not finished."

His face and neck were red; his hair, animated by the wind, stuck out from his head in all directions, and his eyes were owl-like behind the lenses of his glasses.

"He dumped you, right?" Worm demanded. "He screwed around on you just like he did with Madeleine, and I'm just a way to get revenge? That's it, isn't it."

"Leave me alone!" she said, trying to pull her arm away.

"Or was he just a lousy lay? Is that why you've done this to me twice now? Is that it?"

"Let me go!" she cried, jerking her arm. He let go, expecting her to run away, but given her freedom, she did not leave, perhaps out of fear that he would follow and make another public scene. Instead she stood rubbing her arm and staring down at the deck.

"You can't just use people like that," he said, waving a hand at the ice tower. He was trembling. The wind and waves were so strong that it made standing up difficult, but though they swayed, neither one of them moved away.

"You're cold," she said, noticing his shivering arms. He shrugged, but his teeth were chattering.

"I'm sorry," she whispered, but her face was down and he had not heard her over the wind. God damn it, she would have to say it again. She took a step toward him, lifted up her head, and said it louder this time: "I'm sorry." But as soon as the words were out of her mouth she realized how snide and defensive they sounded, like she wasn't sorry at all, but was just saying so because she'd been forced to. He shook his head, crossed his arms on his chest, and kicked at the deck with the toe of his boot. She swallowed and tried again, this time without the edge in her voice.

"I'm . . . sorry." She tried to make eye contact with him when she said it, but he didn't look up. She went on: "I didn't think about how you felt. Please, I am sorry."

She stopped herself, scarcely able to believe those words had come from her own mouth. It was like she'd been possessed or hypnotized, and again she felt naked and embarrassed.

He took a step forward, hesitated, then put his arms around her. It was an awkward embrace. She stood rigid, their binoculars clattering together on their chests, but she let him hold her, did not pull away, and then slowly, tentatively, she let one of her hands come around his slender waist and move up and down his back. Then she pulled away, ran to the rail, and was sick.

"I don't know what's wrong with me," she said, once she'd recovered and he was leading her to her cabin. "I never get seasick."

"Maybe it's me," Worm said, only half joking.

They reached her cabin and went inside. She immediately ducked into the bathroom, closed the door behind her, and threw up again. When she emerged, pale and staggering, he led her over to the bunks.

"Which one is yours?" he asked. She pointed to the lower. He helped her climb in and tucked the comforter around her.

"Who's your roommate?" he asked, examining the untouched upper bunk.

"Meghan," she said.

"You're kidding."

"No."

One side of Worm's mouth went up in a wry grin. "That's funny."

"Jesus," Maureen sighed, turning her head to the wall. "Does everybody know about them?"

"Probably not everybody, but I had a personal interest in the topic, so I made a point of finding out. Anyway, I meant that it was funny in the ironic sense, although it is kind of funny ha ha, too."

"I guess," she said, turning back and producing a weak smile. "Maybe I'll appreciate the humor a little later. Or maybe it'll just give me another reason to puke."

"Sit tight," he said, kissing her forehead. "I'll be back in a few."

He left her and went down to the galley, a new spring in his step. He put some oyster crackers in a coffee cup and grabbed a bottle of soda water from one of the refrigerators. She was asleep when he returned, her body turned toward the wall, so he left the crackers and water on the desk, kissed the back of her head, and left.

As soon as she heard the door click shut she opened her eyes, rolled onto her back, and stared at the bunk above her. It wasn't that she'd wanted him to go—in fact, she had very much wanted him to stay—but the truth was that again she was troubled by an unsettling thought. A thought so unsettling that it made her stomach flip and caused her hands to come up to the sides of her face like that swirling specter in Munch's *The Scream*. She closed her eyes and did the math, trying to figure out just exactly how late she was.

"I can't be!" she cried, all too aware that she most certainly could. She had been careful, but not 100 percent careful, and the worst part was that she had not been 100 percent careful with either one of them.

Chapter 35

The following days fell into a steady rhythm. The seafloor mapping continued, the observing continued, and the guns were shut down, on average, six times a day due to marine mammal sightings. And whenever that happened Jerry would, without fail, march up the four flights of stairs from the back deck to the bridge to vent his anger at whoever had ordered the shutdown.

"What the hell do you think you're doing?" he'd demand. "We just get the gear in the water and you shut everything down."

"It's not me," Davis explained again (and again and again). "I'm just following policy."

"Screw your policy! I don't believe you're even seeing anything."

In confrontational situations like that, Davis could usually remain silent. He'd had years of exposure to the irrational tirades of his belligerent father and knew it was almost always useless to argue, but this time with Jerry he failed and spat back a sarcastic response:

"Right, you're right, Jerry, I'm just up here bobbing around to indulge my masochistic fetish for perpetual seasickness and being verbally lashed by elfin men in blaze orange jackets."

Jerry's face was now a similar color to his jacket. "You think you're pretty smart, you little smart-ass."

It was only Davis's size, he knew, that kept him from being punched. And his sarcasm was just another mask to conceal his near-crippling insecurity, for he knew he was not smart. He had misgivings and doubts almost every time he picked up the radio to make the call downstairs, misgivings that were all the more ridiculous because the job he was doing required patience but did not require much intellect. It took very little gray matter to stare at the ocean through binoculars for hours and hours each day looking for some little splash or fin, or plume of mist. It was a little more intellectually taxing than watching paint dry, but only just.

The confrontations with Jerry were bad enough, but in addition there were also the daily run-ins with Artaud, who, although less openly confrontational than Jerry, was still a thorny opponent. And Davis's heart sank whenever he heard Artaud's voice on the radio summoning him to the chief scientist's cabin to have what he liked to call "a powwow." Conversations that were little more than a riff on the discussion they'd had a few weeks before on the balcony of the Wunderbar; a riff on the discussion they'd had over drinks in Artaud's cabin; a riff on the discussions they'd had in the galley almost every day since then. Discussions in which Artaud argued that the observing was not really doing anything other than hindering the acquisition of data, and Davis argued that it was a policy he was assigned to develop and enforce, and that until he heard otherwise, that was what he was going to do.

The following evening, Davis did hear otherwise. He was radioed away from his observing duties to take a call on the satellite phone.

"Girl, how's it going out there?" It was Jake. "You're not getting seasick, are you?"

"No, I've been fine," Davis said, when the truth was that he had just become accustomed to feeling awful.

"Because I hear you've been spending a lot of time up on the bridge."

"I'm taking my pills," he said. "They're working." Davis suspected the reason for the call and the direction the conversation was headed—to yet another discussion about his frequent calls for shutdowns. Hoping to switch it onto another conversational track, he asked, "How's that artist of yours?"

"Nabil? Oh, fine. Why, what have you heard?"

"Nothing, why?" Davis asked, when in fact, he had heard quite a lot in an e-mail from a mutual friend of theirs and had decided that this call was as good a time as any to have them confirmed or denied by one of the drama's principal players. "What's happened?"

"Oh," Jake said, "nothing really. He had a little trouble."

Davis didn't ask. He didn't need to ask. The vacuum would be filled on its own.

"You sure you didn't hear about it?"

"About what?"

"It was really nothing. We're trying to move on."

"What happened?" Davis said, his voice low and even, more demanding of a response than requesting one.

"Oh, all right. He's got a temper, okay? He overheard some people trashing his work at one of his group openings and, well, he . . . sort of . . . went off on one of them and now he's out of a job."

"Was he drunk?"

"You know he doesn't drink. It's not in the plan, remember?"

"So, what's he doing for money?"

"What . . . ?" Jake asked, as if he hadn't understood the question. There was a pause, during which—in spite of the thousands of miles the conversation had to travel, up from Jake's telephone in the middle of the North American continent, up, up, up through the troposphere, stratosphere, mesosphere, and thermosphere to the tiny satellite circling the earth, and then back down, down, down, to the handset Davis was holding on a ship in the middle of the Ross Sea—Davis heard the unmistakable clink of ice cubes in a highball glass as Jake tapped the dregs of his evening cocktail into his mouth.

"He's . . . between jobs."

"Meaning you're supporting him."

"What was I supposed to do?" Jake demanded. "*Not* help him? And it's only for a little while. Just until he gets back on his feet. He's working on some new pieces, doing some work on my house, you know, that kind of stuff."

"Oh, Christ!" Davis said, but then stopped himself from going further, remembering that it had not been all that long ago that Jake had rescued him from even more dire straits.

"But that's not why I'm calling," Jake said, his tone turning officious. Davis sighed, knowing that it was now his turn to take a conversational beating.

"I'm calling because I've been getting calls and e-mails about your little marine mammal policy."

"From who?"

"Oh, come on, you can guess."

"Artaud? Jerry?"

"Yes and yes."

"What're they saying?"

"That you're making them shut down the guns every time the wind shifts direction, or whenever you spot a minnow a mile away."

"That's bullshit."

"I'm sure it may be. I'm just repeating what they've told me. Regardless, they're pissed off about the number of shutdowns you're calling for."

"What do they expect? As much as they'd like to think there's nothing down there but rocks and water, things do live in the ocean."

"Yeah, I realize that. But they need to get their work done."

Davis felt his pulse quicken and a tightening sensation around his throat. His voice when it came to him was both whiny and defensive.

"But I'm just doing what you told me to do! It's just the policy!"

"Calm down."

"I am calm! But what I'm getting shit for doing is just what you told me to do."

"Well, now I'm telling you to do something else."

"Meaning?"

"Meaning there's got to be some give and take."

"I don't get it. Either I'm doing my job or I'm not."

Jake sighed, and Davis had a mental image of him leaning on his elbows on his kitchen counter, holding the phone with one hand, rubbing his eyes with the other. Fundamentally, Jake's friendship was more important to Davis than the policy, but when he was out here, removed from the rest of the world, an alliance like that was easy to lose sight of. His perspective got skewed, and the policy (because it was all that he had) seemed like the most important thing he could imagine. He took a deep breath and asked: "What do you want me to do?"

"I want you to ignore the penguins and the seals."

"No, really?"

"Don't shut down the guns for anything but whales." Again Davis felt his blood pressure shoot up.

"So . . . what? They used to be worth protecting but now they're not?"

"Oh, Jesus."

"No, seriously. Where's the science behind that? Now a seal isn't a marine mammal? A flightless bird that spends half its life under the water is now exempt?"

"Will you stop."

The line went quiet. The passion of Davis's argument came, he realized, less from real concern for the welfare of the penguins and seals and more from a desire to prevail in his power struggle with Jerry and Artaud. For Davis, enforcing the policy was more about wanting to not look stupid, about wanting to not feel stupid, about wanting to have some relevance.

"You there?" Jake asked.

"Yes."

"I know this doesn't make sense to you, but just do it, okay? At the end of this cruise the science party has to write a review of how we did, and the services we provided, and if they don't get any science accomplished because of this policy, they're going to rake our asses over the coals."

"Then why did you tell me to do this in the first place?"

"Oh, Christ. Look, you get it from all sides in this job—in any job. People give conflicting orders and sometimes you have to make decisions and adapt. You try to placate both sides while not offending either one. It's an ass-licking balancing act, okay? It's not fair, it's confusing and contradictory, it leaves a foul taste in your mouth, but sometimes there's no way around it."

Another silence. Davis had no argument to make. He knew how

hard Jake worked, how much he'd risked professionally in hiring him, and, of course, Davis knew that he, himself, didn't have a scientific leg to stand on. Still, he felt the sting of wounded pride.

"They're breathing down my neck more than they're breathing down yours."

"I doubt that," Davis said, thinking of Jerry's Rumplestiltskin outbursts and Artaud's weird seduction attempt.

"I get calls every time someone calls for a shutdown—any time of the day or night. Just ease up a little bit. Make this one little compromise. Sometimes you have to ease these policies into place gradually."

"All right," Davis sighed. "I guess I don't really have a choice. No shutdowns will be ordered for penguins or seals."

"Thanks."

"Sure."

"And in the spirit of compromise, I'll say that if you happen to see a walrus or polar bear, well, you can shut down seismic for the rest of the trip, how's that sound?"

"Very funny."

"Not really, but it's the best I can do."

They spoke for a few minutes more, trading gossip about mutual friends, then Davis hung up and went back to his desk. He spent the next few hours modifying the policy and the forms to eliminate any mention of penguins and seals, and then composed and sent out a ship-wide e-mail alerting everyone to the change. He printed up several copies of the amended policy and the multicolor forms and then headed up the stairs to the bridge.

When he was three flights up, he realized he'd left his binoculars in the MPC office and went back to retrieve them. It was then well into the evening Chicken Time, so the hallways were deserted. The office door was still open, and as he approached he heard someone on the phone. It was Jerry, although his voice was hardly recognizable.

"I told you, baby, I just can't afford it this month. No. No. As soon as this cruise is over, I promise. No, really. I promise. Tell your daddy I promise. You know I'm not like the others. Tell your daddy that. You know I'm not. And baby, do you miss me? 'Cuz I sure miss you. I do. I sure do, baby. I'll be home soon and we'll go get it then. I promise. Love you, baby. Uh-huh, buh-bye."

"That was certainly a side of your personality that I've never seen." It was Artaud's voice. "What's the matter, daddy loading up the shotgun?"

Davis stood just outside the door, his back to the wall.

"No," Jerry said, "she just found some new portable karaoke machine she wants to buy. Wanted my credit card number."

"Ah, the cost of young love!"

"Tell me about it. Last week I call and she tells me she bought a puppy. I says, 'Honey, what're we gonna do with that when we move to the States?' "

"You gonna marry this one?"

"Don't have a choice. She's gonna have a kid."

"Please. Of course you've got a choice," Artaud said. "You even sure it's yours?"

There was a pause, followed by the sound of a chair being tipped over, papers scattering, heavy footsteps moving across the room. Davis turned and tiptoed back down the hall.

"All right!" Artaud said. "Relax! I'm sorry. I meant it as a joke."

"My fiancée is not a joke."

"Just calm down. And quiet down. Shut the door and make the call before it gets too late."

Davis heard the metal door click shut. He came back around the corner and reoccupied his former spot. There were loud beeps as they punched the number into the INMARSAT. He was eager to hear if they were calling Jake. Davis heard the phone ringing and figured they must have it on speaker. He heard a gravelly "hello," and then a string of conversation from Artaud, but the closed door was muffling the conversation and made the dialogue sound like it was being spoken through a long metal pipe. There was a quarter-inch gap between the door and the floor. Davis reached in his pocket, took out his room key, and held it in his hand, figuring that the pretense of having dropped it might provide the ruse he would need were he caught crawling around. He bent down slowly, trying to keep his knees from cracking, and put his face next to the floor, his ear close to the gap.

"Mr. Lopez?"

Mr. Lopez evidently responded, but Davis could not make out what he said as the connection was fuzzy and the sound further distorted by it being broadcast on speaker phone.

"Good, good," Artaud said. "The data is coming in fine. The weather's been cooperating, so if that continues we should get those cores."

This prompted a long, grinding sound, like a fork stuck in a garbage disposal.

"We're still working on that," Jerry said. This was followed by more grinding, but of an elevated pitch.

"Yes, still working on that, too."

"Not to worry," Artaud said, "If we can't get it, we should be able to get hold of the archived data and get it processed."

"...................."

"Yes, we can. . . . Trust me. We've got someone here working on that now. She does fine work."

"..........."

"We know, and we're getting as close as we can. There is a danger of calving, but we will try."

".........."

"We will try."

There were voices echoing up the stairwell. Davis got up and dusted off his knees and elbows. He started walking toward the stairs just as a group of techs emerged into the hallway. He greeted them with a nod and then continued on up to the bridge. When he got there, he opened the notebook, looked at the clock and, realizing there were only ten minutes left in the mid-rats service, closed the notebook and headed back down to the galley instead.

Pilar stood reading a Chilean soap opera magazine and twirling a strand of long black hair that had escaped from her hairnet. Since it was Friday, there was some sort of fried fish languishing in brownish green sauce. Pilar had been too lazy to fillet the fish, or even to cut off the heads, so the cooked eyeballs looked like dull white pearls. The carcasses were stacked pell-mell in the warming tray, giving the overall impression of a school of cataract-afflicted fish that had died in an evaporating pond. Using tongs, Davis lifted up the flank of one of the fish to make sure it had been gutted. Seeing that it had, he arranged a bed of white rice on his plate and then set one of the fish on top of it. He rounded out the meal with a peas-carrot-lima-bean medley that he knew would have the consistency of baby food, and then walked over to the tables. Worm was seated by himself with one plate in front of him and another covered in foil. Davis looked down at the fish, then up at Worm. "You can't be wanting seconds of this."

"What?"

Davis nodded toward the foil-covered plate.

"No, it's a sandwich. For Maureen."

"Ahh."

"She's got a touch of seasickness."

"Really?" Davis said with a smile. "Maureen?"

"Hey, it happens sometimes."

Davis didn't dispute that. It regularly happened to him, but Maureen? The irony delighted him. As if sensing this, Worm added: "It's probably just something she ate."

Davis changed the subject and told Worm about the change in the policy to exclude penguins and seals. His response was predictable:

"You've got to be fucking kidding me."

"No."

"Then what's the fucking point of doing it at all? Which bonehead made that decision?" Worm asked, rising from the table with his covered dish. Davis shrugged, not wanting to implicate Jake, but it was clear that Worm knew.

Once Worm had gone, Davis poked at the fish but could not bring himself to eat it. Maybe it *had* been something she ate. With that in mind, he scraped his uneaten meal into the trash and headed back up to the bridge.

Book 6

There are no facts, only interpretations.

—Friedrich Nietzsche

Chapter 36

Davis looked at the schedule. Artaud and Meghan were supposed to be observing but they were nowhere in sight. One pair of binoculars was on the counter, its strap neatly wound around its middle. He didn't even bother trying to hunt them down but instead put on the binoculars himself and held them up to his face, gazing through the twin portholes out at the sea and ice. Looking for whales was, he had to admit, tedious work. It was about as eventful as waiting for the artistic muse to visit him with ideas for his book, meaning that it involved a lot of hoping, wishing, and even some praying, but rarely, if ever, did anything appear when he was ready for it. A whale would inevitably breach, or spout, when his back was turned, or when he was all tangled up in the binocular cord—just as the prize-worthy literary idea would only materialize in his brain when he had no pen or paper.

He stared through the binoculars and thought more about his book. The book he'd begun (weeks ago) with such enthusiasm. The book that his niece and nephew were so looking forward to. The book that was supposed to redeem his career because it would be both entertaining and enlightening and might even have the "meaning and purpose" that had been lacking from his previous works.

That book.

It had been neglected, to say the least, and about that neglect Davis felt a mix of smug satisfaction and sadness. The satisfaction came from the fact he had spent so much time on this trip doing the work he'd actually been hired to do—his "little marine mammal policy," as Artaud referred to it—and hadn't had time to work on his "little writing project." The sadness came not from the fact that his endeavors, both artistic and professional, seemed always to be referred to with the diminutive (although that certainly was demoralizing), but from the fact that he was surprised how easy it had been for him to forget about the book, and how fast time seemed to be passing.

He had, of course, continued receiving the weekly e-mails from Estelle, wondering when she was going to see a manuscript and some drawings, but again, he had been too busy with the job at hand to worry much about his prior commitments and had, soon after the ship's departure, ignored her messages, figuring, as he had before, that given his location there was very little she could do about his missed deadline. He'd hoped to have something to give her by the end of the cruise, but as the halfway point loomed his confidence in his ability to deliver was waning. He did have several beautiful sketches, plenty of background information on whales and marine mammals, but they existed in a state of suspended animation, waiting to be assigned personalities and a plot to act out.

The vessel was traveling next to what looked to Davis like a wall of white ice, stretching off into the horizon. One of the mates was at the helm.

"Is that land?" Davis asked.

"That?" The mate asked, pointing to the wall. "No, that's just the ice shelf. Or what's left of it. Big old chunk of it broke off about this time last year."

"Global warming?"

The mate shrugged and lit a cigarette. "That's what Al Gore would say."

The sun, then at its lowest point during the day, cast a perfect silhouette of the ship on the shelf. Davis focused his binoculars on the area just ahead of the ship's shadow, and gazed at the numerous little waterfalls cascading down the ice and at the flocks of gliding seabirds.

"Why are we sailing so close?" Davis asked, but then immediately felt stupid for asking. Maybe it just seemed like they were close since the shelf was so large in comparison.

The mate nodded. "Seems a little risky with all the brash in the water, but they want to get a good map of the bottom here, so they're willing to risk fouling the gear."

Davis watched as a flock of penguins stomach-paddled down the sloping side of a berg and plopped one after another into the water, where, he reflected to himself, the poor things would probably be rendered deaf, or at least have the crap scared out of them, by the boom of the seismic guns. Maybe they would provide an easy meal for some leopard seals, provided that they, too, weren't stunned by the noise.

"Why do they want to map this area?" Davis asked.

"Never been mapped before," the mate said, "on account of it was under the shelf. Virgin territory, you might say."

It was 22:30. Artaud and Meghan should have been on shift for half an hour, but other than the missing binoculars there was no evidence that they'd been there at all. The hours around the noon and midnight shift changes were the most difficult to fill since everyone was either headed to bed or just getting out of it. Davis was part of the former group and longed to head down to his cabin and sleep. He leaned on the sill of the port-side windows and stared out at the shadow of the ship moving along the towering white mass.

It was alleged (by whom, Davis had no idea) that fire and water were the only two mesmerizing sights. Surely, he thought, this unbroken white wall could be added to that list. He was staring at it with such intent, slack-jawed vacantness that he almost didn't catch the strand of drool descending from his lower lip. He slurped, wiped his mouth with his sleeve and, while looking down, noticed two people sitting in the shadows, two decks below. They were huddled close together, gazing up like tourists at the shelf. Davis lifted the binoculars and brought the two figures into focus. The glow reflecting off the ice illuminated them enough for him to discern that they were Artaud and Meghan. At least, he sighed, they were observing something. It was clear that the two were huddled together for more than just warmth. He then remembered the enormous brassiere hanging from the hook on the back of the bathroom door in Artaud's cabin and suddenly the pieces fell into place and he saw the picture. The man had odd proclivities, that was certain: an ice queen, a fat homosexual . . . Hell, for all Davis knew, he was probably screwing Jerry, too. In that light, Artaud going after an overweight schoolgirl did not seem extraordinary. As Davis watched them, they turned their hooded faces toward each other and kissed. Then Meghan stood and approached the rail. With her mittened hand, she pointed at something out in the water. Artaud rose, looked, and then both turned their hooded heads and looked up at the bridge. Davis, feeling like a voyeur who'd been caught, lowered the binoculars and looked away.

"You got a pod of killers about forty degrees to starboard," the mate said, pointing at the same area Meghan had pointed. Davis raised the binoculars again and followed the mate's finger out over the surface of the bergy water until he saw them—the black fins jutting up out of the water, the black and white patches on their bodies, making them look like aquatic Holsteins. Again, Davis's thoughts on beholding such a majestic natural sight were clouded by his exposure to media. These whales were supposed to be jumping through flaming hoops in the turquoise pools of a Southern California theme park, not here, not hunting for penguins along an ice shelf. As soon as he recovered from that disconnect, he lowered the binoculars and picked up the radio.

"Back deck, bridge. Copy."

A few seconds later came the reply: "Bridge, back deck. Over."

"We've got whales within the safety zone. Shut down the guns. Repeat, shut down the guns."

"Roger that."

Davis noted the time, 23:42, and then went back to watching. There were at least three whales, two males and a female, the latter identifiable by her slightly curved dorsal fin, in contrast to the other two, whose fins stood erect, cutting through the water like knives. Soon, however, they were gone, invisible again under the water. Davis scanned the area for another five minutes but saw nothing. At any moment he expected an expletive-laden protest to come across the radio from Jerry, or to hear his heavy footsteps marching up the stairs, but nothing happened.

Meghan and Artaud were at the starboard rail and had been joined by several other red-parka-ed people, all pointing their cameras out to sea, hoping the whales might reappear. Seeing nothing, they soon trickled back inside.

The thirty-minute ramp-up of the guns went without incident, and before it was done Kristi and one of the vessel techs arrived to take over observing. Davis gladly relinquished his binoculars.

"Where's the sign-in sheet?" Kristi asked, flipping through the pages of the notebook.

"It's in there," Davis said. "That hasn't changed. Only the sighting reports have changed. Now we won't be shutting down for penguins or seals, only whales." Davis tapped his file folder. "I have the new paperwork here."

"There's no sign-in sheet," Kristi repeated. "There's nothing here but blank paper." She slid the notebook along the counter.

Davis flipped through it and saw that she was correct; all of the forms from the past three weeks were gone. He was confused but not alarmed. It was odd that someone would have taken the forms, but surely there was a reason for it. No one else was interested in them.

"I don't know what's happened here," Davis said, the fatigue of having been up for nineteen hours evident in his voice, "but here are the new sighting forms. I'll run down and print up some new sign-in sheets."

As he descended to the Environmental Room, he again tried to piece together a logical scenario for what might have happened but was too exhausted to think or worry about it. The forms would turn up. He went to his laptop, tapped the space bar to reanimate the screen, but nothing happened. He tapped it again, several times in succession, scoured the desktop with the mouse, but still nothing. He checked the power and network cords, saw that they were still connected, and then pushed the oval button to restart the machine. A tiny fan hidden somewhere in its depths stopped for a moment and then whirred to life again. While he waited for the reboot, Davis watched the Reality Detection Device. The boat was right up against the ice, and the sea was placid, so the little bolt tied onto the end of the string was, like the pendant of a necklace hemmed between two enormous female breasts, not moving much. He looked back at the computer. A single line of text appeared on the monitor.

"A problem has been detected and Windows has been shut down to prevent damage to your computer."

The Blue Screen of Death.

He rebooted again, hoping to make it go away, and again stared at the RDD while he waited. Back and forth, back and forth, back and forth. He looked back at the screen: again, the Blue Screen of Death. Feeling annoyed, but not really worried, Davis closed the laptop, unplugged the power cord and the mouse, and carried the machine to the E-Lab. There he found Maureen, sitting straight-backed at her workstation, the long blonde ponytail hanging, as ever, through the hole in the back of her baseball cap. Above her monitor she had mounted a small round rearview mirror, so before he was even halfway across the lab she had swiveled around to face him.

"This is hosed," Davis said, pointing to his laptop, which he held like a tray of rotten food on his palm.

"What's wrong with it?"

"How should I know?" he snapped, his fatigue and annoyance getting the best of him. "It won't start up. The screen says there's been some fatal error or something."

To his surprise, she did not retaliate to his sarcastic remark but instead turned back to her monitor, glanced at him briefly in the mirror, and said: "Just leave it there and I'll take a look at it. You're going off shift now, right?"

"Right, but I need to print up some of the forms that are in here," he said, tapping on the laptop.

"Well, that might have to wait. I've got a few disasters in line ahead of you, and I've got to run e-mail. I'll have it for you when you wake up."

Davis's eyes stung. He was too tired to argue, too tired to even think. He shrugged, set the laptop on the counter, and left. When he got back to his cabin he used the phone in his room to call up to the bridge and tell Kristi and the tech to keep track of their shift and sightings as best they could. He'd figure out the paperwork in the morning. He then lay down, fully clothed, on his bunk and did not stir until his alarm went off ten hours later.

Chapter 37

When Davis awoke, the forms were the first thing that came into his mind. Someone had probably just wanted to copy them, or use them for some sort of research, or . . . He didn't know what. He would send out a ship-wide e-mail and tell whoever had them to bring them back. No big deal. Then he remembered his laptop crashing.

He got undressed, showered, dressed again, and went down to the E-Lab, but Maureen was not at her desk. He turned and went to his hovel in the Environmental Room. The boat was turning hard to port so the Reality Detection Device was hanging sideways, hovering in midair. Davis's laptop was on the desk, lashed down with a bungee cord, a yellow Post-it Note stuck to the screen:

> Got it working. Couldn't save anything on desktop.
> Hope you had things backed up. —M

Davis groaned. As a technically challenged writer, he had lost enough of his work over the years to know the importance of backing things up, and, indeed, he was now in possession of a four-gigabyte memory stick on which his numerous furtive attempts at a book were dutifully stored. But the forms? Those silly little forms? Or any of the data they had held? Of course they hadn't been backed up. The forms were nothing special, just a few words and tables—nothing that couldn't be recreated in a few hours. But the hard-copy records of the animals that had been sighted, the records of how many times they'd shut down the seismic guns, the records of who had done the observing—those had all been actual words written on paper with a pen, and now they were gone.

The vessel banked up on a patch of hard ice and tilted hard to starboard. The RDD swung sharply to the right and, a second later, Davis followed, sticking his arm out to prevent himself from falling. The hair on that arm was standing up. Something . . . was strange about all this. Something . . . was not right. Something . . .

He plugged in the computer, turned it on, and waited as it slowly came to life. His laptop dying was not so strange, that sort of thing had happened to him several times, but that it happened at the same time the paperwork disappeared . . . ? He sat down and drummed his fingers on the desk, trying not to overreact, trying to persuade himself that someone, some curious student most likely, had just borrowed the forms to compile statistics or to document the negative impact of marine mammal observing on seismic research.

But as much as he tried, he couldn't convince himself. Something, something, something . . . *was rotten in the state of Denmark. Something wicked had this way come.*

He looked at the few standard icons on his otherwise blank screen. Blank. None of his old documents, none of his old folders, nothing. *Nothing . . . will come of nothing.*

The e-mail he sent out asking about the paperwork was, as he'd feared, no help at all, and in return he got only snotty remarks:

Artaud: "You're supposed to be the one taking care of this, right?"

Meghan: "Haven't you been making copies, or backing it up?"

Jerry: "Ha ha ha ha ha!"

Even Worm had harsh words for him: "Dude, what the fuck? You lost the paperwork?!"

"I didn't *lose* the paperwork," Davis protested. "Someone took it out of the folder." But as soon as he said that out loud, the self-doubt and second-guessing began. Maybe he had, inadvertently, taken out the old forms and misplaced them, or accidentally thrown them away when he'd gone to replace them. No, no, not possible . . . or was it? It was, he had to admit, slimly possible. He'd been so tired that the details were fragmented by his fatigue. He tried to replay the events from the night before: He remembered getting off the phone with Jake, making the new forms, and then heading up to the bridge to replace the old. Then he remembered traipsing back down the stairs to the galley. Could he have taken the forms that had been filled out and, what? Accidentally thrown them away? He got up and ran to the galley. Pilar was there, facing one of the stoves, idly stirring some steaming pot of mess. The large trash receptacle was mounted to the wall. Davis peered into its depths but saw only a few plastic forks and a half-empty coffee cup. The bag had recently been removed and replaced. Davis knocked on the metal counter top to get Pilar's attention. She turned and gave him a languid smile.

"When do they empty this trash can?" Davis inquired. Pilar stopped stirring, shrugged, then returned her attention to the pot.

"Who empties it?"

"The trashes?"

"Yes."

"The boys," she said, meaning the Filipinos.

"When?" Davis asked, "How often?"

"No sé." She shrugged. "Ronnie. Ask Ronnie."

Davis left the galley and went up to the 02 deck, to an area called the bosun's locker, which wasn't a locker at all but an unpainted room in the bow of the ship where the off-shift Filipinos sat on folding chairs and played cards. When Davis stuck his head in the room they all stopped talking and looked up at him.

"Hi, I was wondering about the galley trash," he said. "I mean, who empties it and where it goes?" This question provoked no response. He was sure they'd heard him but not sure they'd understood.

"I mean, I think I threw something away by mistake yesterday," he said, miming the act of wadding up paper and throwing it into a trash can. "I was wondering if there was any chance of getting it back."

There was some low talk in Tagalog, then one of them, Sam,

rose, started down the hallway and motioned for Davis to follow. The two went all the way to the stern of the ship and exited onto a catwalk leading to the aft control room.

"Here's trash," Sam said, pointing at a pile of black plastic bags. "But not yesterday's."

"Where's yesterday's?"

He gave a nod to a blue metal door, smudged with soot.

"What's that?"

Sam approached the door, touched it tentatively, and then turned the latch and opened it. Inside, Davis saw the orange flicker of fire.

"Burns stuff," Sam said.

"Incinerator?"

Sam nodded. Davis felt the rumblings of nervous diarrhea.

"The trash goes in there . . . every day?"

"Every day."

"So this is today's?" Davis asked, pointing at the pile of black garbage bags.

"Yes, today's. Maybe some from yesterday."

Davis sighed, knelt down on the frigid deck, and proceeded to unknot each bag and paw through it. Sam watched him for a minute but then turned and went back to his game.

Two of the bags contained galley scraps, which, when stewed together in the trash, were only slightly more grotesque than when they were served up on a plate. Davis sat down and, breathing solely through his mouth, poked through them for a freezing, fruitless half hour, but he found nothing. When he finished, he reknotted the bags and went inside. His arms were covered in garbage juice and stink. He wanted to go back to his room to shower and change his clothes but he knew he couldn't. His roommate was sleeping and it would be bad form to barge in and break the "your time is your time, my time is my time," rule that he himself had so emphatically stressed at the beginning of the cruise. Besides, they both knew what went on in that filthy shower, and if Davis were to run in, strip down, and frantically start bathing, it might, well, not look right. Instead, he went to one of the public bathrooms and cleaned up as best he could. He took off his shirt and washed the sleeves. Then he wrung them out and attempted to dry them under the hand dryer. While repeatedly hitting the silver button, he sat down on the toilet and tried to think.

When he emerged, his sleeves still damp but most of the smell masked by a few sprays from the can of lilac-scented Poett, he went to the MPC office, which was, thankfully, empty. He went in, closed the door, took the phone from its cradle, and punched in a number. Since it looked as though the forms were, in fact, gone, he figured he'd better tell Jake what had happened before his friend heard about it from someone else. Although Davis knew Jake very well, he had no idea what his reaction might be, especially since all the evidence for the loss pointed to Davis's own carelessness.

Jake answered the phone and Davis, skipping all pleasantries, quickly blurted out what had happened. His explanation was greeted with silence on the other end of the line. A silence that went on so long that Davis had to break it by asking, "You still there?"

"Yes," Jake said. "Still here. Just thinking. How could you—"

"I didn't do anything!" Davis whined. "The forms were in the notebook one evening and gone the next morning. I didn't do anything to them."

"Right. Well, they disappeared somehow. Christ, Davis, I've been getting flak from all sides about this policy. Artaud has screamed about it so much that now the NSF wants the environmental department to write up a report about it at the end of the cruise. And how are we supposed to do that without any fucking data? What am I supposed to tell them? How many people know that you lost the paperwork?"

"I didn't *lose* the paperwork," Davis growled, "it *disappeared!*"

"How many people know?" Jake demanded.

"Well, everybody. I sent out an e-mail telling them it was missing and asking whoever took it to bring it back."

"Shit."

"What?"

"I was gonna have you just try and make it up."

"Make it up?"

"Sure, why not?"

"Because, it's not . . . right."

"We don't have the luxury of doing what's right. We have to deliver some information and avoid looking like idiots. Here's what I want you to do: Print up a bunch of forms and fill them out from memory."

"Memory! It's almost a month's worth of information. I hadn't even looked through all of it. And we've had something like, I don't know, thirty shutdowns. How am I supposed to remember the details of each one."

"You're going to have to try."

"But everyone knows I los—" Davis stopped and corrected himself, "that the paperwork got lost."

"Tell them you found it," Jake said, matter-of-factly. "No need to give details. Just tell them you found it. Then start filling out new paperwork. Artaud's group hasn't been keeping track of the sightings or shutdowns, right?"

"No, not as far as I know, but—"

"Good, then there won't be any trouble. Just make sure you use different pens and maybe write some of the entries with your left hand so they don't all look the same. You think you can do that?"

"I suppose, but—"

"No buts. Just do it. God, Davis, this is not the kind of headache I need right now."

"I'm sorry, but—"

"Call me back when this is done. *Don't* e-mail me! Do you understand?"

Davis nodded, then remembered that he was on the phone where a physical response meant nothing and replied, "Yes, I understand."

After he'd hung up and was returning to the Environmental Room, he saw Worm coming up the hallway. Worm saw him, too, and beckoned him toward the E-Lab. Reluctantly, Davis obeyed, figuring he might as well start the lying with the person it would be most difficult to lie to.

"Listen," Worm said, taking him by the arm and leading him inside. "We got a backup system for you." The "we" he was referring to included Maureen, who was seated at her workstation, plotting points on an electronic map. She locked her screen, swiveled her chair around, and stood up.

"Close the door," she commanded. The heavy metal door, held open by a bungee cord wrapped around the handle and connected to a hook on the wall, was unleashed and allowed to slam.

"Okay," Worm said, nodding at Maureen, "tell him." She hesitated a moment and ran her tongue over her front teeth, which gave Davis the impression that there was some creature swimming around in her mouth. "Hang on to that," she said, handing him a small thumb drive on a lanyard. "Wear it around your neck under your shirt, and don't lose it." Davis took it and was about to tell her that he already had one of the devices, but she held up a hand to silence him.

"So that you don't lose anything else on this cruise, I'm going to show you how to scan your hard-copy forms into electronic format."

Then, going into exhaustive detail, she demonstrated the scanning functions of the copier, showing him where to insert the paper, which buttons to push to convert them to PDF, and where on the network to find the scanned files. When she was finished, Davis gave a synthetic smile and said, "This will all be really useful going forward, but I found what I thought was lost." Worm and Maureen looked stunned. "The paperwork, I mean," Davis clarified. "I didn't lose it after all. Stupid, I know, but I just had it in a file folder that got stuffed in with some other files. I didn't see it."

"You found it?" Worm exclaimed. Davis nodded, his eyes avoiding theirs. "That's awesome! What a relief! Dude, go get it. We can get it scanned in right away."

Now Davis was stunned. He had not prepared himself for that suggestion. He had to think fast.

"Oh, you don't need to help me," he said. "I'll take care of it. Maureen's explanation was very clear, as usual. I'll get it all scanned in this afternoon. And besides," he said, "it's time for my shift. I've got to get up to the bridge." And with that, Davis was out the door, almost sprinting down the hall. When he was halfway to the stairs, he made a sharp turn to the right and returned to the bathroom, closing and locking the door behind him.

He arranged his toilet paper pillow on the floor, lay down on his back and, swinging a leg into the air, kicked off the light switch with his toe. This room, once his refuge from extreme boredom, had now become a place to escape during moments of stress and anxiety—a place to close his eyes, regain his bearings, and plot out a plan to proceed. He crossed his arms on his chest and lay in the dark, thinking. He would do what Jake had said and recreate the forms. Then he would dutifully scan them as Maureen had instructed, and keep the electronic versions on the thumb drive she had given him.

Wait.

Stop.

He sat up. Again, something was not right. He understood why she had given him the thumb drive, but why tell him to keep it on a lanyard around his neck underneath his shirt? That seemed a bit excessive as a precautionary measure. But most of all, why would she even care?

Chapter 38

She closed the magazine, wedged it back in between the mattress and bulkhead, and stared up at the empty bunk above her. The only thing she could think of more pathetic than a woman scorned staring up at the empty bunk of her overweight rival was a probably pregnant woman scorned staring up at the empty bunk of her overweight rival, having just taken a quiz in a three-year-old issue of a women's magazine on how to determine if your man is cheating or not. The magazine quiz was especially pathetic since Artaud was not, and had never been, in spite of her delusions, her man. Even so, she still felt the sting of his having thrown her over for her bulbous roommate, not to mention the terror of his possibly being the father of the child she was possibly carrying.

At least, she thought to herself, I've got the lower bunk. It was poor compensation, all things considered, but it was something. The lower bunk on a ship was always more coveted than the upper since it was much easier to get in and out of, especially if, like Meghan, you had the body of a manatee. Also, the lower bunk offered slightly more headroom, so if you wanted to sit upright in bed and read a book or magazine (or just pop bolt upright in middle-of-the-night panic at the thought of your impending single motherhood), it was possible to do so without bumping your head. Maureen stared up at the horizontal wooden slats above her and was glad that the bed they supported was empty. Glad because on the one night that Meghan had actually slept in the upper bunk—presumably the night before she'd begun banging Artaud—Maureen had barely been able to sleep, listening to the slats creak and moan, as she imagined the bunk collapsing and sandwiching her underneath.

Now that Meghan was gone, there was no need to worry about that. They were on opposite shifts and were rarely, if ever, in the room at the same time. And even when it was Meghan's turn in the room, Maureen knew (by the way the girl's comforter and pillow were never disturbed) that she had not slept there, that she was using her assigned space as nothing more than a closet for all of her tent-sized clothes. The girl's fleece jacket and thermal underwear were, at that moment, hanging from hooks on the wall above the heater, doing little pirouettes as the ship rocked back and forth. Maureen stared at them and her thoughts traveled back to her ninth-grade drama class. The class in which she'd been cast, by the unanimous vote of her peers, to play the title role in *Medea*. Oh, how she now longed for some of that mythical sorceress's magical powder to sprinkle on Meghan's garments and then watch as the girl burst into flame! It was a deliciously wicked and satisfying thought, but one that she entertained only for a moment, knowing, as she did, that her ire against the girl was misplaced. Meghan was just a younger, fatter version of herself, just another victim of the real sorcerer, Artaud, and there had been times during the past week, as they both stood before him in the chief scientist's cabin, that Maureen had longed to turn to Meghan, woman to woman, and scream, "Don't be so stupid! Look at how he's screwed me over! Do you really think he's not going to do the same to you?" But then, Maureen herself had witnessed firsthand how he had screwed over his wife and that hadn't deterred her from hopping right into his bed, telling herself that with her he would be different, with her he would be content.

The reason for the simultaneous appearance of the two rivals in Artaud's cabin was in response to a summons for what he called "a strategy session." A more apt name might have been "a blackmail update" or "minion directive," since the meetings involved nothing more than the two of them—Meghan and Maureen—standing in front of Artaud's desk and listening to him dole out their under-handed tasking for the day.

In the first such session they were both instructed to be blind observers, to notice nothing during their marine mammal shifts and to try to distract the other observers so that they wouldn't see anything either. In the next session a few days later, they were given their sabotage orders: Meghan was to destroy the hard copies of all the observer forms, Maureen was to destroy the electronic. Whatever Jerry's tasking was, Maureen never knew, and the goal of it all remained a mystery to her. When she did inquire about the motive for their actions, Artaud flatly replied, "That's not something you need to know."

Later, back in her room, Maureen had tried to figure it out on her own, had rolled various ideas around in her head, but the more she thought about it, the more confused she became. It just didn't make sense. Sure, the marine mammal observing was annoying, tedious, slowed things down a bit, even left a few small gaps in the data set, but not to the point that it justified sabotaging the entire stupid operation. It was like using a machine gun to mug an old lady. Effective, but was all that firepower really necessary?

When the empirical data failed to answer her questions, Maureen used her voyeuristic privilege as the network administrator to secretly scrutinize the incoming and outgoing e-mail of her partners in crime, but even that was not very enlightening. Artaud knew what she was capable of and thus kept his correspondence in the realm of the mundane. He made no secret of his irritation with the marine mammal observing, but his complaints were public and betrayed no hint that he was trying to sabotage it. As for Jerry, he rarely wrote or received anything work related. Occasionally he would write to a manufacturer to get some information about a part, or a wiring diagram, but for the most part he sent only simpering, gently scolding e-mails to his child-bride-to-be, usually regarding the recklessness of her spending. And then there was Meghan, whose replies to her parents' eager missives became increasingly vague and remote until they were nothing more than one-line responses, usually something like, "Everything's fine, too busy to write."

Too busy indeed. If they even knew the half of it, they'd probably charter a boat and come get her themselves.

Day after day Maureen analyzed their e-mail, but never did it give her any clues. So, having no alternative, she reluctantly went along with Artaud's game, playing a part in his mysterious scheme. She became a blind observer, she sabotaged Davis's computer, which had, ultimately, been pointless since the idiot hadn't been backing up any of his data anyway. Meghan, on the other hand, had, by destroying the hard copies of the forms, actually done significant harm. Or at least so it seemed. She had taken the hard copies all right, but had not interpreted Artaud's command to destroy them to be synonymous with "shred" or "burn" and had, instead, simply deposited the stolen paperwork under her mattress, where it was plainly visible through the slats to the embittered occupant of the lower bunk. Maureen had, of course, noticed it there. And when she did, she promptly took the forms down to the E-Lab and scanned them all, thinking they might be of some value to her down the line. When she was done, she put the originals back under Meghan's mattress so that their second "disappearance" would not be noticed.

And that was where the story became even more puzzling because, excluding their clandestine trip down to the E-Lab, the forms had not moved, which made Davis's proclamation that he'd suddenly found them an obvious lie. A lie that, when publicly announced at breakfast one morning, had caused the scrambled egg–laden forks held by Artaud and Meghan to freeze in midair. Their eyes locked over the table and they subtly abandoned their meals and left the galley. And, sure enough, when Maureen finished her breakfast and returned to her cabin to brush her teeth, she noticed, without surprise, that the sheets and blankets on Meghan's bed had been violently molested and that the papers were gone from under the mattress, their ashy remnants probably just then emerging from the smokestacks and scattering themselves over the frigid ocean.

But the question remained: Why had Davis lied? It was a nagging inconsistency in the story, but probably nothing more than his pathetic attempt to save face.

She had been in the bathroom brushing her teeth as she mulled all this over. When she finished, she spat, rinsed her mouth, and ran her tongue over her smooth teeth, inhaling the fresh, clean, satisfying minty sensation. A feeling that was almost as satisfying as the knowledge that scans of the former mattress-bound documents were safely ensconced on her hard drive. She wasn't really sure what she was going to do with them—at least not yet—but she did know that they were worth something, and for that reason she intended to hang on to them.

She went back to her bunk, lay down, and closed her eyes, trying to sleep. She felt she should have been more upset about Artaud throwing her over for Meghan, but there was no accounting for taste. She was confident enough in her looks to know that if he wanted someone fat, then there was nothing she could do about it. She wasn't going to get some reverse form of anorexia to try to get him back. She smiled at the absurdity of the prospect, but then just as quickly the smile vanished as she remembered the tiny embryo that was possibly growing inside her and wondered how much it would balloon, distorting the abs and slender hips she fought so valiantly to maintain. She sat up on the edge of the bunk and felt hot tears roll down the sides of her face as she imagined herself as a guest on the stage of one of the seedier daytime talk shows, Artaud on one side of her, Worm on the other, the baby swaddled in a blanket on her lap. The host held a microphone in one hand and an envelope containing the results of the paternity test in the other. In the audience, still wearing her white hygienist smock, looking down and shaking her head, was her mother. That last thought sobered her, and as she wiped away the tears and snot she heard her mother's voice emerge from her own mouth: "Stop it, Maureen. Just stop it."

She thought of Worm and of how much she hoped this pseudo baby was his. She wanted it to be his, first and foremost because she wanted it not to be Artaud's. But there was more to it. . . . In spite of the unknown paternity, she was not even entertaining the idea of terminating the pregnancy. On the contrary, she now found herself moving gingerly around the vessel, holding the rail whenever she ascended or descended the stairs, thinking about what she was eating, and shying away from coffee and all other caffeinated beverages. She imagined the baby alive and with her and knew that she wanted it. And with those maternal thoughts in her mind she got up, abandoning sleep for a while, and went back down to the E-Lab, where she downloaded e-mail and then set to work reading through it all, determined to find something—anything—that would get her out from underneath Artaud's thumb. She didn't waste time browsing through the junk anymore—she didn't have time—but in this batch it appeared that there was nothing but junk: another e-mail from Artaud to the NSF, complete with a bullet-pointed list detailing the ways the observing was adversely impacting his science; an obscene mash note from Kristi to J_Dude; nothing at all from Jerry or Meghan. She then went to Worm's account, half-expecting to find him bragging to his friends about his repeated conquest of her. He didn't seem like the type to brag, but sometimes it helped, especially when she liked the person whose personal electronic space she was about to violate, if she had a rationalization, however slender, that she could give herself.

There was an e-mail from Worm, evidently in response to one from his mother, and she hesitated before opening it. In order to better grasp the subject, she started reading the earlier e-mail to which he had hit Reply.

Dear Bill,

Bill? That was his name? She'd sailed with him all these years, slept with him twice now, was possibly carrying his child, and had never known him as anything other than Worm. *Bill?* She looked off into space and whispered the name a few times in different tones. Bill, BILL! *Bill,* Billy. No, that wasn't good. *William.* No, not that either. She went back to reading:

Your father and I wanted to thank you again for your visit. I loved the sweater, of course, and the pipe you gave dad has become quite the conversation piece at the club. They were both lovely, thoughtful gifts but again, the gift of your time is still the best one you could have given us, especially at our age. I know we're not as exciting as your friends—off climbing mountains or diving for shipwrecks, but we do try to make it fun for you while you're here. At least we do the best we can.

Maureen paused and tried to picture this woman. A small frame, maybe with short gray hair cut in a pixie, half glasses on a chain around her neck, lots of chunky silver and turquoise jewelry. She read on:

I know it's selfish of me but I was so sorry to see you go this last time. It seems we just get started talking and then you have to rush off again. Of course, we do consider ourselves lucky (and thankful!!!) to have had you for New Years. It makes me think of that poor Mrs. Staggs (Bruce and Kelly's mother—he's on his second trip to drug rehab, btw (cocaine), and she married that African American man) sitting all alone out at Autumn Manor. Her children almost never call or send her e-mails. And do you think they visit her, or bring the grandchildren (three now, a girl and two boys. Cute kids. Such beautiful skin)? Of course I only hear her side of the story during our red hat lunches. I'm sure the children would have plenty to say in their defense. Anyway, when I talk to her I count my blessings that I have your father, and that we're both healthy enough to still get away for the winters to this heavenly place.

About your father: He looks healthy, I know, and he's never one to complain, but his knees bother him and I do so worry about his cholesterol. I don't want to worry you, just want to underscore how much more we treasure your visits with each passing year. That's all. You have your own independent life, and we're so happy you're happy, off alone like that. Shows real strength of character, the capacity to be alone. I should study you more closely so that if, heaven forbid, your father goes first, I'll know better how to carry on. . . .

Maureen leaned back and marveled at the fact that there were other mothers as clumsily inept at subtextually inducing guilt in their children as her own. His parents were old, that much was clear, it appeared he was their only child, come to them when they were well into middle age, and they cherished him, almost to the point of smothering. But there was something quaint about their epistolary attentions, so unlike the stilted, Doric correspondence she received from her own mother. She read the message again with feelings of tenderness and envy. She imagined her mother and Wor—er, Bill's, mother meeting over tea, or daiquiris, or whatever old ladies drank, and kvetching long and hard about their neglectful spawn. Then she shook her head at the sheer ridiculousness of the idea and went on reading.

> I hope you're not upset about my trying to arrange a
> meeting between you and Lori Brewer. I only want you to be
> happy, and she really is just the nicest girl. Pretty too! I think
> I said that already, but she really is. And so interested in
> meeting you again. I spoke to her on the telephone after you
> left—she called to wish us Merry Christmas (even though
> she's Jewish)—and I told her you'd expressed interest in
> meeting her when you visit later this spring. You are still
> planning to come, I hope . . . It means the world to your
> father. Me too!
> Be safe, my son.
> Much, much, love,
> Mother

Now that she had some context, Maureen scrolled back up the page and read Worm's response.

> Mom,
> Thanks for the message. And thanks for all the hospitality
> and gifts. You guys always go overboard with that stuff.
> There really isn't anything I need. The golf and the dinners
> out would have been enough. But thanks all the same for the
> check. I'm sure I'll find some way to spend it.

It's been a tough cruise so far. The scientist is, as dad would say, a horse's ass, and the work's been tough. I'll be glad when this one is over and under my belt. The scenery has been spectacular and I'll have to show you some of the pictures when I see you next, which will probably be sometime in the spring, maybe early summer. I will come, I promise. But I'm not making any promises about Lori Brewer. I really wish you would stop already with the matchmaking. I don't want to go out with Lori Brewer—or any of the others. At least not now. It's got nothing to do with her. I'd even be willing to give her half a chance, if it would make you happy, Mom, but if I did that I don't think it would be fair to Lori Brewer. I'm sure she's a great girl, she sounds great from all you say about her, but I've kind of got my eye on someone else already, and I'm not ready to give up on that yet. Guess it's that old Yankee persistence. Anyway, that's where things stand with me.

Give my love to dad,
Bill

She sat there for some time after reading that just staring off into space. She wasn't surprised by what he'd said—she knew he liked her, he'd told her as much himself after their last encounter in the ice tower—but something about seeing it in print, written to another person, gave it a permanence and weight, that she hadn't felt when she'd heard him say it to her face. And how did she feel? Touched? Angry? Frightened? She couldn't say. To her, he was like some article of clothing she'd bought on a whim. She had no idea where she'd wear it, didn't really have anything that went with it, but there was something about it that she'd liked enough to buy it. Such impulsive purchases either went on to become her favorites or, after many months of sliding down along the closet bar, were removed from the hanger once and for all and given to Goodwill.

It was nice to consider the possibility of Worm developing into one of her favorites, nice to imagine even the possibility of a life together with him, but no sooner did the idea enter her mind than it was stomped on by the white-soled hygienist's shoe of her mother.

And the stomp was followed by the voice, repeating the same thing it had always said: *Don't be naïve, Maureen. Men are all the same. This one probably just wants you for something, for what you can provide or produce, not for yourself. No man will want you for yourself. This one will be the same as all the others. Just look at the trap you stepped into this last time—with both eyes wide open, no less. The trap you're still trying to get out of. This one will be no different. No different.*

Chapter 39

Davis divided his time in half during the next week: part of it he spent recreating the paperwork, and the other part he spent ensuring that the observing was being done. In fact, he became hypervigilant about watching for whales, even going so far as to spitefully order shutdowns when he had seen nothing in the water *but* water, figuring that if they were going to fabricate trouble for him, then he would do the same to them. Screw their science.

Davis vented his frustrations to the only person he felt he could confide in: his brother, Don.

> **From:** Davis.Garner@HAH.pss.gov
> **Sent:** Wednesday, February 08, 2006 12:24 PM
> **To:** RadDadDon@gmail.com
> Subject:
> Hey brother,
> Imagine the worst times with your kids—the times they ignore what you tell them to do, have a sarcastic comeback to everything you say, or throw a public tantrum in line at the grocery store because you won't buy them candy. The days when your only rational response to their repeated cries of "Whyyyyy?" is "Because I'm the dad and I said so." Imagine

that, and then imagine the same behavior, but with adults instead of children, and you'll have some idea what this cruise has been like.

He then went on to relate the details of the missing paperwork and his certainty that he had not lost it, and closed with a few niceties to the family. Then he hit Send and closed his laptop. He pushed it to the side of the desk, opened the drawer, and pulled out the stack of blank forms and sign-in sheets he had printed up. From his bag, he removed every color of pen and pencil he had and set them between his laptop and the stack of paper so they wouldn't roll around. He picked up a blue pen, filled out one line of the form and sign-in sheet, then set the pen down, picked up a pencil and, writing with his left hand, filled in another line. Then he switched to a black pen, which he held in his right hand, filled out one line, switched hands, filled out another, etc. . . .

He made it through about three days of the nearly thirty he needed to recreate before ennui and the rhythmic rocking of the ship overwhelmed him and, like Dorothy in the field of poppies, he lay his head down on the desk, closed his eyes, and emitted an exhausted sigh. But he wasn't really exhausted, just overwhelmed at the enormity of the task before him. And since procrastination is never more decadent and sweet than when one has a lot to do, Davis surrendered himself to it. His left hand was palm-down on the desk and his left cheek was resting on it. His eyes were open, following the bolt on the string of the Reality Detection Device— back and then forth, back and forth. . . . He changed his focus to the pen in his right hand as he balanced it between his fingers. Then he pressed the tip to the paper and began doodling, nothing fancy at first, just a series of random curlicues. Soon those doodles morphed into mythical planets orbiting an imaginary star, then into fish, incongruously swimming in space, then more fish with conversation bubbles coming out of their mouths, starfish and seahorses, and soon the solar system had transformed into an underwater seascape, complete with sunken ships and elaborate reefs. He sat up and rubbed his eyes. He opened the desk drawer, shoved the onerous forms back inside, and pulled out the long-neglected spiral notebook containing the onerous sketches and plot musings for his book. He flipped to a blank page and continued drawing on the same theme, not really with any purpose, letting one vague scenario lead into the next like the panels of a comic strip. Then he flipped back to the pages containing the *Mick the Maggot* story and reread it. It was a basic "return of the prodigal son" story and, as such, it really was not that bad. It was, he assumed, just the maggoty characters that Estelle had objected to. He flipped forward again to the pages of undersea drawings and tried to apply the situation from the former story to these new drawings, with Mick now taking the form of a whale. There would still be exotic locales, ensnaring situations from which he would have to escape with the assistance of a cast of oddball supporting characters, maybe even a quirky sidekick who spoke in some exotic dialect. Then, at the end, there would be a sugary reunion with the family. Blah, blah, blah. He capped the pen, closed the notebook, and set his cheek back down on the desk and watched the RDD. Back and forth, back and forth, back . . . and . . .

"Dude, what gives?" Davis blinked his eyes open, inhaled, and sat up. "Were you asleep?" It was Worm.

"No," Davis said, wiping the drool from his chin with the back of his hand. Worm tapped at his watch.

"You were supposed to be up on the bridge forty minutes ago."

"My shift isn't until seven."

"It's quarter to eight."

Davis touched the space bar of his laptop, bringing it to life. He looked at the small clock displayed in the lower right-hand corner of his monitor: 7:42. How could that be? He had been asleep since just after lunch, had completely missed dinner. He gathered up the sheets of outlying sketches and put them all in a file folder.

"What were you working on?" Worm asked, trying to see over Davis's shoulder.

"Nothing. Paperwork. I'll be up in a minute."

"Oh, and hey, they're almost out of the new forms," Worm said, "so you better print up some more."

"Right. Thanks."

When Davis got to the bridge, after making stops at the bathroom to pee and at the mess hall to grab a handful of cookies (but completely forgetting to collect the forms he'd sent to the printer), Andrew was there, talking to one of the mates about college basketball. Both pairs of binoculars, their straps wound around them, were on the countertop next to the notebook. Annoyed, Davis signed himself in below Andrew's name, picked up a pair of binoculars, glanced through them for, oh, less than four seconds, then picked up the radio.

"Back deck, bridge. Copy."

A few seconds later came the scathing reply: "Bridge, back deck, over!"

"Whale sighted off the starboard bow. Repeat: Whale sighted within the safety zone. Shut off seismic. I repeat. Shut off seismic!"

Andrew and the mate turned and looked out to sea.

"Where?" the mate asked, squinting in the direction Davis had indicated.

"I don't see anything," Andrew said.

"It's right out . . . there," Davis said, pointing vaguely to his right. "Four, maybe five altogether. Hard to tell. Look like belugas, maybe a narwhal." The mate, aware that those species of whale were indigenous only to the northern hemisphere, opened his mouth to protest, but then realized what was going on and his mouth relaxed into a sly grin. It took effort for Davis not to smile back, but he maintained the mask of seriousness.

"But I don't see anything!" Andrew whined.

"Oh, they're there all right," Davis said. "They're probably diving now. You know, to get away from the seismic blast. Keep watching. They can hold their breaths a long time. Here," Davis said, thrusting the other pair of binoculars at Andrew. "They're a lot easier to see when you use the tools that have been provided for you."

Davis turned, left the bridge, and stomped back down the four flights of stairs to retrieve the forms. On his way back up he made another foray into the galley, selected an apple from the bin in the refrigerator, and then stood munching on it, staring out the port hole. He knew they'd be looking for him, knew they were probably screaming into their radios trying to reach him, demanding to know what he'd seen, where it was, how long before he'd give the "all clear" for them to re-start the guns. He was sure they wanted a lot of things from him just then, but, he reflected as he chomped on the mealy apple, people didn't always get what they wanted.

Between 8:00 and 10:00, when Davis and Andrew were relieved from their shift by Meghan and Kristi, Davis ordered two more shutdowns on the basis of phantom sightings. Jerry was off shift, so there weren't any tantrums from him, but Artaud radioed up after each sighting.

"What do you think you're doing?" he asked, his tone almost successful at concealing his annoyance.

"What am *I* doing?" Davis asked, his voice dripping with feigned innocence. "Why, my job, of course."

And each time there would be an exasperated sigh on the other end, followed by silence, then the sound of the radio clicking off.

That night, in spite of the long nap he'd had at his desk, Davis slept like a dead man, only waking when his roommate entered the cabin and slammed the metal door. Davis sat up, bumped his head on the ceiling, and again asked, in a bewildered voice: "What time is it?"

"It's time for you to be outta here," his roommate said, and then began reciting the familiar "your time is your time; my time is my time" bit, but by then Davis was up and had the water running in the shower. He dressed and made it to the galley ten minutes before the breakfast service ended, wolfed down some cold eggs and a stack of rubbery pancakes, and then dispensed some of the bitter ink that passed for coffee into a paper cup and went to the Environmental Room to check his e-mail. He sipped the coffee, waiting for it to cool down as the computer warmed up.

The messages were typical of those received by an insignificant employee: two messages forwarded from the office regarding some subtle change in corporate policy; an ad for Viagra without a prescription; a brief message from Jake asking him to call "when you've completed the thing we discussed yesterday"; and then another piece of spam that he hesitated before opening since the sender's address was invisible and the subject box contained nothing but the word "important." Hesitated because he had been warned, in one of the many office trainings, against opening mysterious e-mail like this, lest some worm or virus infect the network, but he did it anyway, figuring there were, among his colleagues, already plenty of viral worms, so one more couldn't possibly hurt. When the message opened, it was a single line of text, cryptic but not foreign to him:

You've got to climb to the top of Mount Everest to reach the Valley of the Dolls.

That was it. No offer to buy prescription drugs, no link to see underage girls performing with farm animals, no request for assistance in obtaining an African fortune, not even any message (sent with high importance) from the Denver office manager, notifying the office staff that refrigerator #3 was going to be cleaned out that day at noon, or that a green Chevy Malibu, license # 643-PIB, had its lights on. Just that single line of text. Davis recognized it, of course. It was a line from a book that he was, as a stereotypical gay man of a certain age, familiar with. But for Davis, as an author of considerable mediocrity, there was a special, more intimate connection. For in that book about the drug-addled sexploits of a fame-seeking trio of girls, he had always taken an odd form of solace, not in the subject matter (which was actually quite typical to the genre) but in the fact of the book itself and its having been roundly dismissed by readers and critics alike as trash. Solace, because although Davis's work, too, had been dismissed as trash, every now and then a piece of trash managed to work its way to the top of the pulpy heap, bewitch the imagination of the public, and sell thirty million copies, as *Valley of the Dolls* had done.

Figuring the message was probably some esoteric reminder from Estelle that his deadline was looming, he considered the message for, oh, about three seconds before deleting it along with all the rest. He then opened the drawer to take out the forms he had started recreating the day before, thinking he would do some work on them before he went on shift, but the folder containing the forms was gone. Again, there was a momentary surge of panic as he considered the possibility of his having misplaced it. In a frenzy he flipped through notebooks and folders on his desk, opened drawer after drawer, but then abruptly stopped himself and sat back down in the chair. He had not misplaced anything. He had stuck the folder in the drawer with the file folder containing his book. The latter was still there, the former was not. Again, the Shakespearean quotes cluttered his mind, although this time they were of a more sardonic bent. Instead of *"Treachery, oh, treachery!"* or *"Horrible, most horrible!"* the quotes that came to mind were more pedestrian. Things like, *"If this were played upon a stage now, I could condemn it as an improbable fiction."*

He narrowed his eyes and began lining up suspects in his head. Worm had been the one to get him out of the room, so Worm seemed like the prime suspect. But that was the faulty logic of *"Fleance killed, For Fleance fled."* No, it could not have been Worm, although . . . love for a bossy woman had (in that same tragedy, no less) driven a man to do far worse things. And there was little doubt that Worm was in love with just such a harpy.

Davis moved down the line to Maureen. She had nosed into his physical and electronic space so often that it would not have been at all surprising to discover she had been the one to do it this time. He suspected she'd had something to do with his computer crashing, so it was not inconceivable that she would violate his desk and steal the forms. But why? Again, love has made people do worse things. And she was in love with that He-Whore, as Worm so charitably referred to him, although "was" was the operative word there, since it was no secret to anyone on board that Artaud had abandoned her bony body for the ample bounce and cushion of young Meghan.

The next to appear in Davis's mind was Artaud himself. Davis was certain he was behind the theft, but he was just as certain that Artaud, like most men in positions of power, would not sully his hands by carrying out the deed himself. He would have given directions on what to do but would have left the actual dirty work and heavy lifting to others.

That left Jerry or the undergrads, any and all of whom had motive and means to do it. And that was just the problem: There were too many suspects and too few allies. *Fine,* Davis thought, rubbing his hands together and arching an eyebrow, *if that's how they want to play, that's how we'll play.*

Chapter 40

Since all of his work on the forms was being stolen from his desk as fast as he could churn it out, Davis shoved it back in the drawer and focused instead on his book. Although his plan had been to re-cycle the *Mick the Maggot* story in a nautical setting with marine mammal characters, he now, to use an old sailing term, changed tack. Instead of a plain old coming-of-age story, a story in which the main character's insatiable curiosity was to blame for leading him astray from his mother and siblings, this story would be more of an epic journey, a children's version of *The Odyssey* with a sub-text of environmentalism and revenge. Instead of a fly, his protago-nist would be a juvenile whale separated from his mother, not by his own curiosity, but by her violent death. A death (maybe he would even call it a murder) that would occur when she, and all the rest of her pod, were driven ashore in a tragic attempt to escape the earsplitting sound of blasting seismic guns.

The details of the story came into Davis's mind faster than he could type them into his laptop:

The main character, Bob, maybe he would be a false killer whale. . . . Yes, yes, that would be perfect—a dolphin in killer whale clothing—Bob would not die in the seismic event that drove his mother and the rest of his pod to beach themselves, but his young ears, still in their formative stages, would be destroyed and he would suffer significant hearing loss. Yes, that would work. There would be some kindly humans on shore to help him back into the water. They could help him, but not his mother or the others, who were too large and cumbersome to rescue. And once Bob is put back out to sea, where he mourns his loss and despairs his situation, he will settle to the sandy bottom of the ocean where barnacles attach themselves to him. Two of these will attach close to his ears, and when they speak he will actually hear them. They'll become his living hearing aids, offering commentary, criticism, and guidance, much like the little angels and devils that appear on characters' shoulders in old-timey cartoons to illustrate internal moral struggle. Yes, yes, that will work. Estelle would love that. She preferred stories that had little, if any, moral ambiguity.

Davis paused in his writing, pulled out his sketch pad, and attempted to draw some cute, semi-anthropomorphic barnacles. The first attempts looked more like squashed pies, the second looked like puckered anuses, but on the third try he managed to draw some that actually looked like what they were supposed to. He returned to the story:

With the help of the barnacles, Bob befriends a young killer whale, Sam, who thinks that Bob is, because of his similar markings, another killer whale. Sam introduces him to his mother and the rest of his pod, who feel pity for his orphan status and take him under their flipper, so to speak. And for a while, Bob is able to assimilate with this new pod. He learns their way of life, learns their language, their methods of hunting. At first the other whales just think he is smaller than they are because he lived on his own for so long and is undernourished, but soon the adults in the group realize he is not one of their species and they cast him out, à la the Ugly Duckling.

It is then that he befriends a . . .

Here, Davis paused and tapped his pen on his chin.

It is then that he befriends a . . . what? A tuna? No, that would never work. It would make people think of the old Starkist commercial. A dolphin? No, that might bring to mind the TV show *Flipper!* Granted, none of his young fans would remember or have ever been exposed to either of those lowbrow cultural icons, but their parents and teachers—the ones who would most likely be reading the story to them—would have, and, after the scathing reviews on his last book, Davis very much wanted to avoid giving potential critics any easy ammunition.

Okay then, some other sidekick. But what? An octopus? A squid? Maybe a seal or a walrus? He opened one of the drawers in front of him and pulled out the big book of marine mammals. Whales, porpoises, dolphins, seals, otters . . . Nothing seemed quite right. He set the book aside and pulled out another, this one on large, predatory fishes. Tuna, swordfish, Patagonian toothfish, shark . . . At the end of the shark section he found something called a whale shark. Technically it was a shark, but one with the docile manners of a whale, basically a big-boned, clumsy, filter-feeding oaf. A toothless, harmless shark. Yes, that would be perfect. Something that, like Bob, looked like one thing but was actually another. Anyway, the details could be worked out as he went along, but Davis felt he was really on to something and he went back and forth between notebook and laptop, developing the story:

With the assistance of his new friend, Wally the whale shark, and the continual advice and assistance of his hearing aid barnacles, Bob will hunt and grow and avoid the many perils of the sea—marine predators, Japanese whalers, drilling platforms, Navy sonar, pollution, and of course, earsplitting seismic.

Maybe, Davis thought, pausing and again tapping his pen on his chin, maybe Bob's deafness could give him a sort of sixth sense—an ability to feel the sound waves from seismic or sonar before they arrived, and thus give him the ability to warn other marine mammals and enable them to escape harm. That would make his disability into an asset, another wonderful lesson for the kiddies, and would make him a valuable asset to underwater friends and foes. Perfect! Davis returned to the synopsis:

Eventually, a pod of whales that Bob rescues from a vicious seismic attack will be another pod of whales that look just like him. He won't know it, of course, but will have it pointed out to him by Wally and the barnacles. This new group of whales will be so grateful they will embrace him and ask him to join their pod, even offering him the comeliest of their females to be his mate.

Hmmm, he'd have to give some more thought to that saccharine, slightly sexist, ending but he definitely had a start, and with gleeful fingers he tidied up his synopsis and then e-mailed it to Estelle with a simple *How about this?* in the subject line.

Once the message was sent, he noticed that the unread e-mail icon was blinking in his in-box. He saw the words *Check It Out* in the preview of the subject line, but again he hesitated before clicking on it, fearing it might contain some sort of malware that might infect his computer and ruin his synopsis, but curiosity won out over caution and he double-clicked on the icon. When he did, he saw the same message as before:

> You've got to climb to the top of Mt. Everest to reach the Valley of the Dolls.

He stared at it for a long time. There was nothing in the From line, so he had no idea who had sent it, but now he doubted it was Estelle. So, what the hell did it mean? He closed his laptop and went up two levels to the TV lounge. It was close to the time for a shift change, so the room was empty, the large flat-screen TV that dominated one wall was gray and blank. The DVDs were kept in plastic sleeves in several phone-book-sized notebooks. They were in no particular order, so Davis had to spend almost an hour thumbing through them looking for that elusive title. Out of the five hundred or so movies, there were only about ten that did not involve a car chase, martial arts, or a gun fight. Not surprisingly, *Valley of the Dolls* wasn't there. Not that it really mattered. He had seen the movie numerous times, knew the plot, characters, and most of the awful dialogue by heart, but none of it helped him understand the e-mail. He closed the notebooks, put them back on the shelf, and went down to the galley. Chicken Time. He was standing in line, waiting to see what crap was on the menu when another thought occurred to him. He stuck his silverware in his pocket, left the galley, and went back up the stairs to the 03 Conference Room.

Because it was Chicken Time, the conference room was empty. One whole wall, stretching the length of the room, was a floor-to-ceiling bookshelf, containing mostly well-worn airport paperbacks, all held in place on the shelf by wooden bars. Tilting his head to the side so he could better read the spines, Davis started at one end and walked backward, scanning the titles as he went. He made it through the first row but didn't see the book. He bent down to better see the second row of books, tilted his head the other way, and again walked backward scanning the titles. There were five rows, and midway along the fourth he caught sight of the Pepto-Bismol pink cover and removed the book from the shelf. It flipped open to a page with a bookmark. A bookmark that was actually a compact disc in a paper sleeve. Davis took out the disc but there was no label, nothing on it to indicate what it was. He went over to one of the public computers along the opposite wall, logged in, and popped the disc into the tower. It seemed to take forever to load, but once it did Davis clicked on it and an unnamed file folder icon appeared. He double-clicked on it and again he waited. When it finally opened there were about a hundred unnamed files, labeled with dates. He clicked on the first one, and when it opened it took him only a moment to realize that these were the forms that had been stolen.

Instinctively, he looked behind him to see if anyone was watching him. Seeing no one, he closed the file, removed the disc, and carefully placed it in an inside pocket of his fleece jacket. Up to that point he'd known someone was trying to hinder his efforts. Now it appeared that someone was trying to help him. . . . But who?

Chapter 41

For almost two days after finding the disc, Davis said nothing about it to anyone. The one he chose to confide in was not Jake, but Worm, who listened to his story, turned the book over, and examined the back cover before handing it and the disc back to Davis saying, "Maureen."

"What?"

"Maureen," he repeated. "She sent the e-mail, hid the CD in the book."

"Please," Davis scoffed, "how would you know that?"

"I saw her reading that book at her desk. I can kind of see her from behind, when I'm in the computer racks."

"You watch her that closely?" Davis asked, but then regretted his question when he saw Worm blush. "But why . . . would she do that? I mean, come on, the woman would sooner kick me than smile at me."

Worm nodded his agreement but restated his point: "It was her. No telling why, but I say we ask her and find out."

Since it was almost Chicken Time, they decided to delay her in the lab and confront her while the others were eating. When they got there, Maureen was alone, standing at one of the computer racks. They approached and stood behind her, each hesitant to speak. Maureen sensed their presence.

"What is it?" she snapped, not turning to face them.

"Someone," Worm began, but then paused to clear his throat. When he resumed speaking his words spilled out quickly. "Someone returned the observer forms to Davis—the ones that disappeared. They put 'em on a disc and put the disc in a book in the 03. Then that person sent him an e-mail telling him where it was."

She continued staring at the computer racks, but her murky reflection in one of the dark monitors showed them that they had her attention. She hesitated a few seconds before responding. When she did, she directed her speech to Davis, although she did not look at him.

"I thought you said you found the forms. Wasn't that, like, a week ago?"

"I did." Davis nodded. "I did say that, but it wasn't true. You knew that."

"Oh, I did?" she said, tossing off an unconvincing laugh.

"Yes."

"And how would I have known that?"

Davis shrugged.

"But that doesn't even matter," Maureen continued. "What matters is why you would lie about losing them."

Davis, afraid of incriminating Jake, did not immediately reply.

"Go on," Worm prodded, "tell her."

"I said I found them," Davis began, "well, because I was told to say that."

"By?" Maureen demanded.

Davis lowered his head. His reply was almost a whisper: "Jake."

"So, your boss told you to lie. . . ."

"He said he was getting a lot of pressure about the marine mammal policy and that he was going to have to write a report about it at the end of the cruise. If there was no data, there could be no report. And when I told him the forms were stolen, he didn't believe me. But they were stolen," Davis insisted, "and the new ones I've made up since then have been stolen, too, just yesterday. But like Worm said, someone gave the original batch back to me."

"Lucky for you," she said, sliding a tiny horizontal keyboard out from the rack and attacking it with her fingers. Davis had to restrain his desire to yank on her ponytail and snap her neck. Cervical dislocation. How tempting.

"I tried to tell him it wasn't you," Davis said, giving a nod at Worm. "Tried to tell him that you'd never do anything so kind and selfless, but he's got his own stupid ideas about you."

She finished typing, slid the keyboard back into the rack until it clicked into place, and turned to face them both, arms folded across her chest. "Well, I'm sorry to ruin your sleuthing, Hardy Boys, but it wasn't me." She stood for a moment looking from one to the other but then dropped her arms to her sides and walked out of the lab. When she was gone, they both stood staring at the door.

"Okay," Davis said, "I think I believe you."

"Yeah, I had my doubts for a second there, but not anymore."

Maureen knocked on the door to Artaud's room. Meghan opened it and Maureen managed a wan smile as she squeezed past. Once inside, she was disconcerted to see Jerry seated on the couch. Since there was nowhere else to sit, Maureen had to decide whether to sit next to him or to stand. She chose to stand, taking a place behind him. Looking down, she noticed how much his hair had grown during their time at sea. It curlicued out of his ears and was growing, ivy-like, up and over the collar of his shirt.

"Okay," Artaud said, walking over to the door and making sure it was locked. "Now that we're all here, let's get started. We still have several more days of mapping before we have to pull in the gear and head for New Zealand. Several more full days of data that we need to acquire. That means we can't have any more shutdowns."

This vague proclamation was greeted by silence. Maureen eventually broke it: "And just how are we supposed to stop them?"

Artaud looked up, his heavy brow hooding his eyes.

Maureen kept talking: "That big pest knows something's up. He's not going to let up on the observing now, even if he has to stay up there, awake, for four days straight."

Now Jerry turned around in his seat and narrowed his magnified eyes at Maureen. "What do you mean he knows something's up? How does he know? Have you been talking?"

"No," she countered, again crossing her arms on her chest. "Of course not, but he talks . . . to me."

"Maureeeen," Artaud said, his inflection slow and ascending. "Why would he talk to you? He doesn't even like you." This indisputable fact caused them all to turn to her in unison, and she noticed that even Meghan was nodding her stupid bovine head.

"Maybe so," Maureen said, examining her fingernails in an attempt to appear unconcerned. "Maybe so, but he still needs help with his computer, so he has to talk to me. In fact, just this morning, he told me about the second set of forms going missing. Now, was that really necessary?" she asked, trying to banish the nervousness from her voice and infuse it with more of its usual derisiveness. "If you ask me, it was just stupid. We're near the end of the cruise. How much damage could he do?"

"Plenty," Artaud sighed, rubbing his eyes. "Plenty. But I think you might be right about him being obstinate. The number of shutdowns we've had is ridiculous. He's just doing it to make trouble."

Jerry nodded. The room fell silent. The dull buzz of the engines moved from background noise to something more ominous and insistent.

"So," Artaud said, resuming his instructions from where he'd been interrupted, "the next four days are crucial. We'll have to do whatever we can to keep the guns firing." He leaned forward in his chair and addressed Maureen: "You can fix it so that his radio malfunctions, right? Maybe tinker with the binoculars, or call him down to the lab to take a phone call. If necessary we can plant a bottle in his room and tell the captain he's got liquor stashed in his room. That might slow things down. Meghan, why don't you put something, laxatives maybe, in his food. If you can think of anything el—"

"Are you serious?" Maureen asked, stepping forward. "You can't be serious. . . ." She looked at Artaud, at Jerry, and then at Meghan, who looked away, refusing to meet her gaze.

"Worm's almost a bigger problem," Jerry said, ignoring her. "I try to keep him at work on the back deck as much as I can, but he's a slippery one. I wish he'd just slip over the side so we wouldn't have to deal with him."

Maureen's ball cap felt tight on her head. "What do you mean by that?" she asked, again trying to mask her concern.

"I mean," Jerry said, "I wish we could get rid of him." Artaud nodded agreement.

Again, Maureen looked at all three, trying to register if they were serious or not. Meghan kept her eyes screwed to the floor, her fingers absently pulling on a loose piece of thread on her work pants. The girl was afraid, Maureen could tell, and she felt something close to sympathy for her.

"Now, c'mon," Maureen said, trying to sound confident. "Let's not . . . overreact. I can handle Worm." She was really sweating now and noticed that the stray wisps of hair on either side of her head were beginning to curl.

"And how you gonna do that?" Jerry sneered.

"Look, the guy's been after me for years," she said, realizing the truth of what she said only as it came sailing out of her mouth. It was one of those things that she had known, but somehow had never, until that moment, consciously considered. "I'll do what I have to do to keep Worm busy. Just quit talking about . . . other options."

"That'd be great, babe," Artaud said, "thanks for volunteering, but I think you're going to be too busy with other things to act as a distraction for Worm."

"Busy? With what?" she asked. Artaud came around to the front of the desk and sat on the corner of it, keeping one leg on the floor and swinging the other back and forth.

"I'm going to need you to edit all the new data and get an end-of-cruise data disc ready before we head back to Lyttelton, preferably before we cross 60 south."

"Why so soon?" Maureen asked. "I mean, what's the rush? We usually don't do that until we hit the dock." It had been stupid to question him, and she should have known better than to think she might get an answer. Artaud just sat there, leg swinging. Maureen didn't look at Meghan but she could sense the girl's fear. And she herself was frightened. Stealing silly, amateurish data and tweaking someone else's computer was one thing. Setting people up for a fall, figurative and literal, was another.

When she was finally dismissed, twenty minutes later, Maureen went to her room and locked the door. In the bathroom, she vomited up her breakfast and then sat down on the lid of the toilet, removed her ball cap, and put her head in her hands. At first, she tried to stop the tears but then leaned back and let herself cry, realizing as she did so that she was gently rubbing her belly. Once the crying had subsided, she yanked several feet of toilet paper from the roll, wiped her eyes, blew her nose, and took her ball cap from the door handle and positioned it back on her head. She went back into the room, picked up the phone, and tapped in Worm's room number. He answered, his voice groggy with sleep.

"You're the EMT, right?"

"Maureen?"

"Yes. I need to see you now."

"Now?"

"You've got the keys to the hospital?"

"Yeah."

"Can you meet me there in ten minutes?"

"You all right?"

"Yes. Fine. Sorry. No emergency. Ten minutes."

She hung up, stared at the phone for a few seconds, then picked it up again and punched in the number for the bridge. When the mate answered, she asked to speak to Davis. After what seemed an eternity, in which she imagined him waddling his way over to the phone, he finally answered.

"This is Davis."

"It's Maureen," she said, cupping her hand around the receiver and speaking in a whisper. "I can't explain, but I need you to listen closely to what I'm going to tell you and you need to do exactly what I say, okay? This is for your own protection."

"Okay."

"Don't eat anything Meghan gives you."

"Okay."

"I know it sounds crazy, but just don't. You should probably be careful about anything you eat. If it's in a wrapper or an unopened container, it's probably safe. Also, try not to leave your cabin empty. Make sure you're there or your roommate's there. And if you've got any liquor or drugs stashed away, now's the time to get rid of them."

"Okay, but—"

"I'm serious."

"Okay."

"Listen, I can't explain anything. I know you've got no reason to trust me, but you should."

"I do."

For some reason, his saying that so readily caused her throat to constrict and her eyes to sting again. Not sure if she was going to cry or throw up, she covered the receiver with her hand and swallowed hard a few times. When she regained control and could speak again, she said:

"Just, um, watch your back for the next few days, okay?"

"Yes. Will do. Thank you."

She was about to return the receiver to its wall mount when she heard "Hey, wait!" She brought the receiver back up to her ear.

"What?"

"Are you all right?"

Again the tightness and the stinging.

"Yes," she said, and hung up. The crying started again. She looked at her watch through the mist. Still five minutes. She paced back and forth in the tiny cabin, mentally rehearsing what, and how much, to tell Worm. She needed to warn him, but how could she do that without revealing everything? And how could she stop this crying? She went into the bathroom, ran the cold water until it came out of the tap at a temperature just above freezing. She filled her water bottle and then drank it all down as fast as she could. The brain-freeze headache that followed did the trick. The water was still running. She bent down and splashed her face with cupped handfuls of it until she felt a tingly numbness. She turned off the tap, stood up, and toweled off, tucking her hair back into place. She appraised her reflection—not great, but better than it had been a few minutes before—and then left her room.

When she got to the hospital, she stood at the door, rolled the tension out of her shoulders, and knocked. Worm let her in. The room, roughly the size of two cabins, seemed bigger because there were no bunk beds. Instead there were two stretchers, each made up with a military precision. Since there was no doctor on board, the company had trained select contractors to act as emergency medical technicians. Worm was the designated EMT for this trip.

The job rarely involved more than dispensing seasickness medication, or the occasional stitching and dressing of a cut, so she was not at all sure he'd be able to help her with her request. Worm waited for her to speak.

"Are there . . . any pregnancy tests in here?"

At first he thought she was joking. He laughed and was trying to think of a snappy response, but her pained expression showed that she was not joking. He turned, went over to one of the cabinets, and ran his finger down an index sheet that was taped to the door. He stopped near the bottom, ran his trembling finger across the page, and then tapped on the end. He fumbled with a ring of keys, eventually found the one that was needed, and opened an overhead cabinet. Inside, he rummaged around and pulled out a cardboard box about the width and length of a checkbook. He turned and handed it to her without question. She went into the bathroom and closed the door behind her.

When she emerged several minutes later, he had not moved.

"Well?" he asked. She lowered her eyes and nodded.

"Is it . . . ?"

She looked up, tears in her eyes, but did not respond.

"I mean . . . Am I . . . ?" he asked.

This, she knew, was where it could get ugly. She hoped it wouldn't, wished that she could lie, but knew that she couldn't. She let her chin fall onto her chest and again her lips trembled. The tears dropped onto her shirt. "I don't know. . . ."

They each retreated into their thoughts and were silent.

"Artaud?" he asked. She nodded, her nods degenerating into spastic sobs.

"Hey," Worm said, taking a step toward her. "Hey, don't do that." He raised his arms to embrace her, hesitated a moment, afraid she might protest, but then took another step forward and did it anyway. She remained rigid at first but then leaned into him and sobbed into his shoulder, muttering, "I'm sorry, I'm so sorry," over and over. He buried his nose in her neck, inhaling the heady scent, and gently kissed her. They remained like that for a long time until she was still. When he released her, she turned away and quickly plucked several tissues from the wall-mounted dispenser, not wanting him to see her tear- and snot-covered face.

"Are you going to . . . I mean . . . keep it?" he asked. She turned to look at him and was surprised to see tears in his eyes. She nodded, realizing that since her first inkling of the possibility of her being pregnant there had never been any question in her mind about whether she would keep it or not.

"Would you . . ." he began, but didn't finish.

"Would I what?" she asked. He tried to find the words, but eloquence was elusive. A minute passed before he spoke: "With me," he said. "Have it with me, I mean. Would you have it with me?" They stood about two feet apart and each scanned the other's face, trying to discern what was going on in the other's head. She started to speak but he stopped her, afraid of her answer.

"Don't," he said. "Don't tell me now. Just promise me you'll think about it."

"But you don't mind?" she began. "Doesn't it bother—"

He put his arms around her and whispered: "Just think about it."

She let him hold her, enjoying the warmth and security of his arms, but the feeling was short-lived as she remembered that she still had to tell him the rest of the story. She broke away from his embrace and retreated to one of the stretchers, perching herself on the edge and dropping her chin into her hands.

"There's more."

"Guys?"

"No," she scoffed, even managing a little laugh. "No more guys, you're the only two. More to the story. Complications."

He sat next to her and put an arm around her shoulder. "Tell me."

She unfolded her sodden wad of tissues, blew her nose, and sat up straight.

"I did something stupid," she began, then laughed at the unintended understatement. "Okay, so maybe there've been a lot of stupid things lately, but this one thing in particular was really stupid."

For the next fifteen minutes, they sat together and she told him the story about her theft of Madeleine's seismic tapes, about Artaud's subsequent blackmail. She had just started on the details of the treachery she'd engaged in on this trip when Worm jumped up, punched his palm with his fist, and exclaimed "That fucker!" He then walked over to a wall and punched it, which was foolish since it was steel and did nothing but break open the skin on his knuckles. She stood up, got him to sit back down, made him promise to relax, and then opened one of the first-aid kits and bandaged his hand, gently scolding him: "I already warned Davis to be careful. Now I need to warn you, too."

"*Warn* me!" he said, his anger rising again. "Warn me about what?"

"It's maybe nothing, please don't shout, I hope it's nothing, but they're set on getting this last bit of seismic done, no matter what, and, well, that Jerry, I don't know . . . he scares me. He said some things about wanting to get rid of you."

"What are they doing?" Worm asked, jumping up and walking to the other side of the room. "What's this all about?"

She shook her head. "I don't know. Artaud doesn't tell me anything. Even when we were . . . together, he didn't tell me much."

She filled Worm in on what she'd done and what she knew, but it didn't seem to enlighten him much. He just kept shaking his head and repeating: "What are they doing? We've got to find out what they're doing."

Maureen looked at her watch. It was two o'clock in the afternoon. She and Worm were due back on shift at six and she hadn't slept yet. She stood up behind him and put a hand on his shoulder. "Let's both go get some rest, hmm? We can meet again tonight."

"We should bring Davis in, too," he said. "Don't you think? He could probably help us out."

She walked to the other side of the room and stood facing the wall. He came up behind her and put a hand on her shoulder. "What is it?" he asked.

"The *tapes,*" she cried, turning, her hands in fists at her sides. Worm was confused.

"What about the tapes?"

"Davis doesn't know about that. Nobody knows about that but you, me and Artaud, and probably Jerry. If other people find out . . ."

"Okay," Worm said. "Okay, I get it. You're thinking you'll get in trouble." She nodded, looking down at the floor. He led her back to the bed and sat her down. "Look, I'm not going to let anything bad happen to you. Believe that, okay? But I'm not going to lie to you, either. There might be consequences for what you've done.

Then again, there might not be, I don't know, but you have to consider that possibility."

"I'll lose my job," she said gravely, "I might go to jail." Her words hung in the air.

"You might," he said, pulling her into an embrace. "You might. But we'll try to avoid it."

As they were about to leave the hospital, Worm grabbed her sleeve.

"On the upside," he said, looking down at her stomach, "just think of the stories the kid will have to tell!"

"What do you mean?"

"I mean, his parents met in Antarctica, he was conceived on Easter Island, he might be born in prison... He'll always have something to talk about."

"That's not funny!" she cried, but couldn't keep herself from smiling.

Chapter 42

Macaroni and cheese with little cut-up hot dogs in it. That was the main course at Chicken Time that evening. As a green vegetable there were some pale, prunish lima beans, frost damaged from their years in the freezer. In spite of the blandness of the culinary fare, Davis longed to load up his plate with the stuff, but the dire warning from Maureen echoed in his head, so he passed by the vats of warm food and took a juice box and a cup of instant noodles instead. As he stood filling the cup with hot water from the coffee machine, Worm came up next to him, set down his steaming plate of food, and proceeded to fill his water bottle from the dispenser. Davis nodded hello and looked longingly at the plate. Worm nodded back and, without looking away from the stream of water, said, "We need to talk. Come to the aft control room when you're done eating."

"I'm about to go on shift," Davis said.

"It won't take long," Worm said. "It's important."

The aft control room contained all the knobs and hydraulic controls used to operate the aft crane and the aft A-frame. It was also one of the few places on the vessel where smoking was allowed, so the air was stale, and the windows yellowed and grimy. The only approach to the room was via a metal catwalk from the 01 deck, so anyone approaching could be seen and heard a good ten seconds before they reached the door. As Davis approached, after having consumed his unsatisfying dinner, Maureen's face appeared in the tiny square window on the door. He was not surprised to see her there, but when he entered the room he was surprised by her appearance. She was still dressed in her same work uniform but her face was puffy and her overall appearance unkempt. The baseball cap was askew and there was a long strand of hair dangling loose in front of her left ear. She seemed not to notice it. In fact, she seemed almost not to notice Davis. She opened the door to let him in, closed it behind him, and resumed watching out the window.

"Do you want to fill him in," Worm asked her, "or should I?"

"You can tell him," she said, and while Davis listened, Worm related the details of Maureen's theft and the threats Artaud had made against both Davis and Worm. When he finished, Davis scratched his head. He was not surprised by any of it. Confused, yes. Surprised, no.

"Well," he shrugged, "I guess that explains why I can't eat. But I still don't get it. Is the seismic really that important?" Davis asked. "They're just mapping the seafloor, right?"

"Trust me," Maureen said, still facing the window. "There's more to it than that."

When she didn't elaborate, Davis ventured: "Anything you'd care to share?"

She spun around and shouted, "I don't know anything else! Artaud stopped telling me anything right after I gave him the tapes. I don't know what they're doing, but it's not just mapping."

"You're sure you don't know?" Worm prodded. "I mean, you don't have any idea what it is?"

"No!" Maureen shrieked. "I told you already, I don't know! But you have to believe me, there is something."

A door slammed and they heard footsteps on the metal catwalk. The attention of all three was directed, as if by the pull of a magnet, to the little window. The steps, slow and heavy, clattered along, pausing a short distance from the door. Davis held his breath. Again, the mechanical hum of the engine came from the background to the forefront as they all stood waiting. There was the sound of crinkling plastic, the roll and click of a cigarette lighter—once, twice—followed by one, two, three puffs of smoke wafting past the window.

To the casual observer, there would have been nothing wrong or suspicious about the three of them, Maureen, Davis and Worm, together in the aft control room. It was a little odd that none of them was smoking but, because of the views from the room's large, albeit grimy, windows, and the protection it provided from the wind and cold, nonsmokers did occasionally frequent the aft control room as it afforded a warm place to sightsee. The fear of the room's three occupants just then was that the person on the other side of the door might be someone other than a casual observer. They watched the clouds of exhaled smoke pass by the window and then, in what seemed like slow motion, they watched as the metal door latch, operated by some unseen hand, moved down. The lock disengaged and the door slowly opened, admitting a burst of cold air, but instead of the hairy, bespectacled visage of Jerry, they were relieved to see the smooth, catlike features of one of the Filipino deckhands.

"Oh!" he cried when he looked up and saw the three terrified sets of eyes. "Sorry." He was about to close the door behind him but hesitated; not wanting to go back out into the cold, he held up his cigarette and asked, "Can I come in and finish?" They all nodded their assent and the mate entered and closed the door behind him. Maureen turned toward the window.

By their silence, it was clear that he had interrupted something. He grew self-conscious and his puffs on his cigarette were frequent, quickly filling the room with smoke. He walked to the aft window and gazed out at the guns blasting bubbles in the water behind the boat.

"How many more days?" he asked.

"About six," Worm said. "Then we turn and head back to Christchurch."

"That will be nice," he said, extinguishing his cigarette in an already overstuffed ashtray.

"Yes," Worm agreed. "Nice. Sunny weather, cold beer."

As soon as the deckhand had gone, Maureen laid into Davis again: "You have to stop ordering shutdowns!"

"Huh? You heard him," Davis said. "There's still a week left."

"I'm serious."

"Yes, I can tell that. But I still don't understand why."

"Because!" she shouted, as if the answer were obvious.

Davis sighed and shrugged his shoulders. "So I'm just supposed to . . . what? Pretend I don't see anything?"

"Yes."

Worm leaned in. "She might have a point, dude."

"Yes, she might, but again, I don't have any idea what it is," Davis said. "What have I got to be afraid of? I can see why Maureen shouldn't help—not that she ever really has—but isn't it going to look even more suspicious if I suddenly just stop what I've been doing the whole cruise?"

"True," Worm said with a nod.

Maureen shook her head. "You don't understand. They aren't playing around. If you don't stop, they're going to stop you."

Davis experienced a sudden leap of excitement in his stomach as he considered the controversy his "little observing policy" was generating. Never before had he been involved in, let alone the creator and enforcer of, something so significant. He felt both proud and protective of it, and with a swell of self-righteous indignation, he crossed his arms on his chest and proclaimed, "I'm not stopping."

Maureen opened her mouth to protest but was too incensed by Davis's defiance to even speak.

"Listen," Worm interjected, attempting to stamp out the ember of their argument before it exploded into something larger, "fighting about this is stupid. You've both got good points, but they seem to miss the main point, which is finding out what they're doing."

"I agree completely," Davis said.

Maureen moved away from them and reoccupied her position by the window. For several minutes they were all quiet. Outside, the sun came out from behind a cloud and reflected off the sea, waves crashed against the towering chalk-white cliff of the ice shelf—a cliff that stretched on, unbroken, as far as the eye could see in either direction.

"There was a lot about this job that was tedious," Maureen sighed, her tone wistful. "But I just loved it. Most of the other network admins I know have jobs where they do nothing but stare at a monitor all day while their ass widens to fit the chair, but this job— my job—was different. A few times each year I got to leave the desk and the computer and the paperwork and the meetings—I got to leave all that behind and come down here," she said with a grand sweep of her arm at the cinematic view they were transiting past. "Here, where I was surrounded by smart people doing mean- ingful work. I wasn't doing the science myself, of course, but I got to feel I was a part of it, a part of something bigger, something im- portant, something more significant than enabling people to buy crap online, something better than making video games to rot the minds of pimply teens, better than developing systems to track sales data. I was helping smart people make genuine discoveries about the world, helping them take their theories and turn them into truth." She put both hands on the sill and leaned in close to the window, squinting at the reflected brightness. "And I got to do all that in a place like this."

There was a long silence after this soliloquy. Davis, too, stared out at the glittering scenery and realized how right she was. This was a special place; the jobs they were doing were extraordinary and important. He understood then just how much she had to lose.

Worm exhaled and spoke to Maureen: "How 'bout you stop using the past tense?"

She turned away from the window and looked at him.

"Granted," he said, "from where you're standing your situation doesn't look good, but it's not over yet. And c'mon, Artaud's the one who asked you to steal his wife's data, the one who's now using the fact that you did it to blackmail you into doing all sorts of other stuff. Put the two of you on opposite ends of a justice scale and you'd be catapulted into the air."

"Maybe," she said, turning back to the window.

"No, not maybe," Worm said, his impatience evident. "Defi- nitely. And don't you get it? This is all the more reason we need to go after him and find out what he's doing. Whatever it is," Worm continued, "it's not honest, and it's not ethical. So if you're looking for some sort of redemption for what you've done, why don't you knock off the self-pity and help us figure this out."

Maureen stood like a monument, staring out at the sea. She didn't answer, did not give any indication that she had even heard what he'd said.

Worm regretted his outburst, regretted that he had been so hard on her. He stared at her back and flexed his bandaged fist, the pain in his knuckles taking some of the attention away from the anxiety he felt in his heart.

The silence stretched on.

"I have no business being here," Davis said, seemingly apropos of nothing, which was fine because neither Worm nor Maureen seemed to be listening anyway. He went on: "I don't mean right at this moment, I mean in general—I have no business being down here, on this boat, in Antarctica. That probably doesn't come as a surprise to either of you since it's pretty obvious that I don't know anything about science, or boats, or computers. I'm here because I fucked up, tested positive for HIV and needed a job with benefits." Davis paused, giving his words a moment to sink in. Worm turned and adjusted his glasses, Maureen kept her gaze fixed on the landscape out the window.

"And while that reason may make sense," Davis went on, "it is not, I'll admit, the most principled. Oh, I do try to do the work as best I can, but for the most part I'm just a big fraud."

He stopped talking as abruptly as he started. Worm rubbed his eyes.

"Dude," he said, "that's some heavy stuff. And I appreciate your honesty, but, um . . ."

Davis finished his sentence: "What's the point?"

Worm nodded.

"The point is that Maureen's right, the people down here—the scientists, the technicians, the crew and mates—are all really smart. It's like a boat full of owls. But there's something different about Artaud, something that rings false."

Maureen scoffed and rolled her eyes. "No offense," she said, "but how could you, of all people, given what you yourself just said, know that?"

"I dated a TV weatherman," Davis said.

"What the hell does that have to do with anything?" she snapped.

"Yeah." Worm nodded. "Again, what's the point?"

"If you'll shut up for a minute, I'll tell you."

Maureen rolled her eyes and waved a hand in the air. Worm shook his head and folded his arms. Davis continued: "The point is, TV weathermen are not scientists. They pretend to be, but if someone were to toss them a hardball scientific question, they'd crumble. So my dating one of them gave me a good nose for pseudo scientists. And the two guys—Artaud and Mark the meteorologist—are more alike than different. Do you remember that science lecture Artaud gave on the last cruise?"

They nodded.

"Well, I remember sitting there and thinking, 'Wow, this is some slick presentation, but something doesn't sound right.' At the time, I brushed it off as my own stupidity."

"That was probably wise," Maureen said. Davis let the remark slide and went on:

"But the more I thought about it, the more I thought, 'Function is definitely behind form here, style is in front of substance.' And it was the same feeling I used to get whenever I watched my boyfriend do the weather report. There was a lot of professional polish, a lot of technical jargon, prophetic warnings of tornadoes, flash flooding, or snow above eight thousand feet (all combined with the appropriate hand gestures and concerned facial expressions), but the guy really didn't have a grasp of what he was talking about, and I knew that his only real interest was in the show's ratings and his own popularity."

"It would be nice if the situation were that simple," Maureen said, "but it's not. Yes, he does come off as a phony, can sound like a bad infomercial pitchman. And yes, the worst part is that I fell for it. But as much as it makes me sick to have to admit it, he's also a competent scientist." She sat on one of the steps and rested her chin on her palm. "I've seen him go over the raw data. He knows what he's looking at and he knows what everyone in the lab is doing."

"She's right," Worm added. "And his research does keep getting funded."

That, Davis thought to himself, meant nothing. Plenty of incompetent people got funding or got jobs they weren't qualified for. It was just as Zif Selig, the genius behind *Foot in the Door: How to Get the Rest of Your Body In, Too,* had taught him: wedge one foot in and then bullshit the rest of the way. And with any luck, your résumé or proposal would be reviewed by someone having a particularly bad day. By someone who was, say, nine and a half months pregnant with twins and desperate to fill an open position before she went on maternity leave.

"Then there's got to be another reason that he wanted Madeleine's data."

They mused over this for a while in silence, their thoughts all trailing off in different directions but never reaching a common conclusion. Davis and Worm discussed several possible scenarios, but Maureen was only half listening. Her attention kept getting pulled back to Davis's being HIV+. Not because she felt uncomfortable about it (she was too smart for that), or even because she felt sorry for him (she didn't really know him well enough). No, her mind kept going back to the HIV because she saw what drastic measures it had driven him to take and made her realize that her own self-centered existence, an existence in which she had been able to come and go, from one end of the earth to the other, for months at a time, would, because of what was growing inside her, most definitely change. She would have something else that demanded her attention and something—someone—who would, at least for a while, prevent her from traveling, prevent her from going to sea. But the strange thing was that she didn't feel any resentment about it. She had felt enormous resentment about having her life similarly upended by Artaud's treachery and her own stupid mistake with Madeleine's tapes, but somehow this little being growing within her, taking up her real estate and consuming her natural resources, only made her smile.

She surfaced from the depth of her thoughts and stood watching Worm and Davis, theorizing and plotting, and suddenly it all seemed so trivial to her and she began to laugh.

The two men stopped talking and looked at her. She laughed even harder, tears coming to the corners of her eyes. Davis raised an eyebrow.

"What's so funny? I don't get it."

"Nothing," she said, still giggling. "And everything."

"Okay," Worm said. "So are you with us, then?"

She nodded.

"Good," Davis said. "Then what's the plan?"

None of them had an answer to that question, and since the sand was rapidly descending out of the top of the hourglass, the solutions they came up with were not brilliant, and borrowed heavily from what they'd seen on television. Worm, the most diplomatic of the three, said, "Maybe we could negotiate with Meghan, try to reason with her and show her how she's being misled."

This seemed wise, since the one point on which they all agreed was that Meghan was, so to speak, the weakest link in the chain leading to Artaud and Jerry. Davis, still stinging from the girl's sneakiness in deleting the whale photographs from his camera and her part in stealing his paperwork, scoffed at the diplomatic approach and, thinking of a detective show, proposed that they "blackmail Meghan. Threaten to tell her mom and dad that she's really out here banging the teacher and stealing data."

Maureen, whose grudges against the girl were even more specific and pronounced, grew excited at the turn the plan was taking and suggested they take it a bit further and "waterboard Meghan. I totally know how to do it, and it really is physically harmless. The noise could be a problem so we'd have to find a pla—"

"Whoa!" Worm cried, waving his hands in the air. "Time out! No! We're not blackmailing or waterboarding anybody, okay? Meghan's a kid, for Christ's sake, so just stop that."

Chastened, the two resumed thinking.

"Listen," Worm said, looking down at the floor and pacing back and forth. "I helped string network cable on the 02 deck last year. Most of the wire runs go along a void in the ceiling and then drop down the walls into the rooms."

"I don't know where you're going with this," Maureen said.

"There's a void in the ceiling on the port side of the 02 deck. Not a big void, neither of you could fit in it, but I think I could. There's just enough space that I could crawl up into the ceiling, get over the MPC office and listen to what Artaud and Jerry are talking about when they make their nightly phone call. I don't think there's any access to the chief scientist's cabin, but I can definitely get in the ceiling above the MPC office."

Davis wondered why Worm would need to bother with all that

when all he really needed to do was crouch down in the hallway outside the MPC office and listen at the gap under the door, but since Worm seemed so enthusiastic and sure of his ceiling void plan, Davis said nothing. Besides, his mind was on something else entirely.

"You don't need to climb in the ceiling," he said, "or do any of this complicated eavesdropping."

He had the full attention of them both. His eyes were fixed on Maureen.

"Why are you looking at me like that?"

Davis clicked his tongue. "I think you know why. . . ."

"I think I don't have any fucking idea why," she countered.

"Oh, come on," Davis said. "The e-mail."

"What e-mail?"

"The e-mail that you're able to hack into and read."

Maureen's cheek twitched.

"I mean, you can do that, right?" Davis said.

"That's not . . . really ethical," she stammered.

"But you can do it. And ethical or not, it hasn't stopped you in the past."

"I don't know what you mean," she said, rising and wiping her hands on her pants.

"I mean," Davis said, "I know you've read mine."

She maintained her air of unconcern. "Your what?"

"My e-mail."

"Please!" she scoffed. "I have not!"

"Please. You have so."

She avoided looking at either of them; her face was bloodless.

"Oh, come on! The jokes, remember? Those stupid jokes you stole from me and passed off as your own in the Palmer Station bar? How does a penguin make pancakes . . . ? Come on, you know the punch line."

Worm looked from one to the other, confused.

"I'm not rubbing your nose in it," Davis went on. "Hell, I'd probably do the same thing if I were in your shoes—"

"Wait a minute . . ." Worm said, his brow pinched together. He turned to Maureen. "You read other people's e-mail?"

Maureen hunched her shoulders forward and glared at Davis.

"Whoa! Back up," Worm said again, the gravity of the situation sinking in. "Back up! Did you read *my* e-mail?"

"I only bring it up now," Davis said, ignoring Worm, "well, because it seems like it might be a useful tool—"

"You didn't read *mine,* did you?"

"—if you really want to know what Artaud and Jerry are doing."

"Wait," Worm said, his eyes darting around behind his glasses. "You read my *e-mail?!*"

Maureen groaned. She brought her palms to her temples and held them there, as if by doing so they might keep her head from exploding. Then she whipped them back down by her sides and yelled "Yes, all right? I'm a bad person. I steal, I lie, I sleep around, and yes, Bill, I read your e-mail."

"Bill?" Davis said. "Who's Bill?"

Maureen pointed at Worm. "He's Bill."

"You read my e-mail? I can't believe you read my—"

"Shall I tell you about him?" Maureen asked, turning to Davis. "Yes, yes, since you brought it up, let's drag it all out. First of all, his name's not Worm, it's William Oliver Radley III. If you draw lines down from the first and the third line of those three hash marks at the end of his name it looks like an M, so the nickname is really just an acronym. Clever, eh? Let's see . . ." she said, tapping her chin with her index finger and looking up at the ceiling, "what else did I learn about Bill? Well, like the majority of Deadheads, Phish followers, and white boys with dreadlocks, he comes from a wealthy East Coast family—went to prep school, parents live in a huge house in Westchester, and then, of course, there's the winter villa in Jamaica. Mom and Dad, well, they would probably have preferred someplace with fewer, you know, poor people—the Bahamas, say, or maybe a Yucatán resort—but Bill talked them into it, didn't you, Bill? And once they got there, well, the golf was magnificent! They found a gated community just minutes from Kingston. A place protected by high stucco walls with broken beer bottles embedded in the cement. A great place for snow birds to nest in the winter. And they are happy there, for the most part, but, like so many people in the autumn of their lives what they really crave is the company of their child, and what they crave even more than that is for their child to have a child, which is, I guess, where I come in," she said, patting her stomach. "Let's just hope they don't demand a paternity test."

"You're pregnant?"

"Although if they're willing to settle for Lori Brewer—a spinster, a librarian, and not exactly a member of the Episcopal Church—they'll probably be okay with a grandchild that looks nothing whatsoever like their son."

"That's enough!" Worm shouted.

"No," Maureen countered, "I don't think it is." She figured she had nothing to lose at this point, so she continued: "I've had a shitty week and I think I'll drag it out to the bloody end. I'm sick of keeping all these secrets! I know all about the torch you've been carrying for me, although I really didn't need to read your e-mail to know that. Do you think I couldn't sense you ogling me through the computer racks when you were back there puttering around? Did you think I didn't notice you watching me when I'm in the gym? Did you think I didn't know who stole my underwear from the dryer?"

"I never stole—"

Maureen cocked her head.

Worm blushed. "Well, I never wrote about it in an e-mail."

"And you!" Maureen hissed, turning her attention to Davis. "Yes, I stole your stupid jokes. So what! I also know about your missed deadlines, your stupid story ideas, and how you don't do much of anything but nap in the bathroom."

"I used to do that," Davis said, stepping forward to defend himself, "but I don't anymore."

"Whatever."

"I've worked my ass off on this cruise!" he protested. Then, eager to make it seem that he was taking the high road in the argument and conveniently forgetting that it was he who had pulled it into the gutter, he added: "But that's not important right now. What's important is that you can get into the accounts and, if that's the case, then how hard would it be for you to find out what Artaud and Jerry are up to?"

Maureen closed her eyes, shook her head in disbelief, and then looked at Davis again. "Can you really be that stupid? Don't you think I've already tried that?"

"You have?"

"Of course I have. Do you think I just sat on my ass and let the guy blackmail me without trying to find a way out of it?"

"And?" Worm asked.

"And I didn't find anything. Oh, I learned that Jerry has a mistress who is draining his bank account and that Artaud has a stable of stupid patsies just like me, but other than that, nothing."

Chapter 43

Later that afternoon, the three sat down and sketched out their plan: Once the evening Chicken Time rolled around and most everyone was preoccupied, Worm would, as previously described, crawl into the ceiling and make his way along the void until he reached the MPC office. There he would wait, batlike, until Jerry and Artaud entered the office to make their evening phone call. On the desk next to the phone was a delicately perforated and innocuous-looking DVD case, inside of which Worm had placed his iPhone, rigged so that its Voice Memo application could be remotely triggered at just the right moment by a transponder that he, Worm, held in his hand. In that way, the damning evidence could be recorded and played back in a dramatic courtroom scene, after which the villains would be led away in shackles and justly punished for their crimes, the nature of which would by then, presumably, be known.

For her part, Maureen would use her feminine wiles to obtain a master key from one of the Filipinos (if she could find one of them who didn't turn and walk the other direction whenever they saw her approach), and would then use that key to obtain entry to the chief scientist's cabin (terrain that was not unfamiliar to her). Once there, she would hack into Artaud's personal laptop, download to a thumb drive as much damning evidence as possible, and sneak out just as easily as she'd snuck in.

Davis? Well, Davis, as we know, was largely unskilled when it came to technical matters, so it was decided that he should, as he himself had earlier suggested, remain on the bridge and continue his marine mammal observations, although with much less zeal and vigor, unless, of course, he was radioed from Worm or Maureen to "see" something and order a shutdown, thus creating the necessary distraction to enable one or the other of them to complete their work.

Of course, things did not quite turn out as planned. Oh, Davis did maintain his observing vigil, seeing nothing unless ordered to do so by his new partners in crime, but the enforced blindness made him irritable and impatient since it added a layer of falsification to one of the few things about which he had, up to that point, been honest. And as it was, he was already irritable and impatient since he had, for the past three days, consumed nothing but instant noodles, cans of tuna, and boxes of sickly sweet fruit drink. To distract himself, he focused his attention on his book; refining the story line and polishing the sketches.

After he'd sent the initial synopsis for the whale story to Estelle, he'd almost forgotten about it. That lack of concern was, to him, a good sign. He had not had it when he'd hit the Send button on the message containing the synopsis for *Mick the Maggot*. He knew the response would not be good. With the tale of *Bob the Whale,* he had not worried a bit after he'd sent it, knowing somehow that it was good and would be acceptable to Estelle. Intuition that proved correct when, two days later, he received her response:

From: EstelleWillBookem@aol.com
Sent: Monday, February 13, 2006 6:22 PM
To: Davis.Garner@HAH.pss.gov
Subject: Okay, now we're getting somewh—
lly got potential here! I love, love LOVE the environmental angle! Of course, it won't fly with Republican parents but let's face it, they're more likely to plop their kids down in front of the TV than read to them, so they're not really our target market. No, this will be BIG with liberal educators,

tree hugger parents and best of all, reviewers! But there might even be some crossover because really, who doesn't like whales? And more importantly, who doesn't like a good story?

Carry on with what you're doing and have some sketches to send me when you get back. Don't blow it.

Best,
Estelle

After the noon Chicken Time, Davis and the captain were back on the bridge. The captain lit a cigarette, loosened his belt, and looked over Davis's shoulder at the sketch he was working on

"That there's definitely a whale," he said. "But you's more likely to see the real thing if you raised your head now and again and looked out the window."

Davis emerged momentarily from his artistic trance and raised the binoculars to his eyes. He made a quick, mechanical scan of the surrounding sea, then lowered the binoculars and returned to his sketch.

The captain went on: "You've lost some of your swagger for this little job."

"Well," Davis sighed, "it hasn't exactly made me any friends on this trip."

The captain nodded. "True," he said. "True. But are thems the kind of folks you want as friends?"

Davis considered this. No, most of thems were not. And he had relished having the power to shut down their operations, especially after he'd discovered they had been trying to shut down his, but now, he reminded himself, he was playing along with someone else's plan, and his own agenda had been relegated to the backseat. And he knew, in spite of the sting it caused his integrity, that his blind watching was the correct thing to do, especially since, in the past two days, everything Maureen had warned him about had, in fact, happened: Twice he'd returned to his room to find his duffel bag open and his toiletries tampered with. Another time, he had found a half-empty bourbon bottle stuffed clumsily under his mattress. In spite of his intense desire to consume its contents, he remembered Maureen's warnings about the laxatives, as well as the consequences of being caught with alcohol in his possession, let alone on his breath, and he poured the amber liquid down the drain, wrapped the empty bottle in toilet paper, and immediately disposed of it in the laundry room trash can.

Until they arrived back in port there were only two things that were important to him: the thumb drive containing the scanned observation forms from this cruise, and his sketchbook containing the drawings for his children's book. He kept them both with him always, sleeping with them under his pillow and even taking them into the bathroom with him. Whatever happened, they would not get those.

The radio on Davis's belt crackled. "Observer, this is E-Lab. Come in, please." It was Maureen. Davis brought the radio up to his ear, leaving the speaker volume up so that the captain could hear it.

"E-Lab, this is Observer. Copy."

"I've got some free time now, so I'm ready to start work on your laptop." This was the code they'd decided on to indicate that Maureen was ready to go into Artaud's room, and that Davis should order a shutdown.

"Roger that. Thanks."

"Roger nothing," Maureen snapped. "Mind telling me where you put it? Over."

"Sorry. It's in the Environmental Room. Over."

"Roger. Out."

Davis returned the radio to his belt, closed his sketchbook, yawned, and looked at his watch: 13:20. He raised the binoculars and looked to port. A plump seal was sunning itself on a drifting berg. Davis pivoted a quarter turn. The roar of the ship had frightened a group of penguins and they belly-paddled across another berg and plopped, one by one, into the water. He pivoted another quarter turn so that he was facing starboard. No bergs, only open ocean. He held his gaze there for about twenty seconds, then lowered the binoculars and picked up the radio.

"Back deck, back deck, come in, this is bridge, copy." A moment later Jerry's reply crackled back:

"Bridge, back deck, over."

"Whale sighted on the starboard bow. Repeat, whale sighted within the safety zone. Shut down all seismic operations, copy."

"God damn it!"

As soon as the order for the shutdown echoed through the lower decks, Maureen tiptoed out of the E-Lab and went up to the 03 deck. Armed with her knowledge of computers, an empty thumb drive, and the room key (for which her feminine charms had proved worthless, requiring her to pay real currency), she approached the chief scientist's cabin and knocked on the door. No answer. She knocked louder, waited, turned her key in the lock. The hinges gave an ominous moan as she pushed the door open and slid in. The room was dark. There was tinfoil covering the portholes to keep out the sun, so she stood for a moment as her eyes adjusted. Then she scanned the room; the unmade bed, a pile of clothes on the floor, an open suitcase ... the laptop! It looked like an open mouth on the desk. She had, of course, memorized Artaud's keystrokes when they were dating (or whatever it was they had been doing) and her hope was that since then his password, Λ#1$ignT1st, had not been changed. She sat in front of the desk, limbered up her fingers, and then allowed them to descend and perform their short, rapid tap dance. Once finished, they hovered above the keyboard while a tiny animated hourglass revolved on the screen, once, twice, thrice. . . . When the desktop icons cascaded into view she punched a fist into the air and mouthed a triumphant "Yesss!" Then she opened his My Documents file and her eyes ran down the list of subfiles. She knew she needed to hurry, but an inherent masochism caused her to click on a file labeled "pics4." When it opened, the contents appeared as a list, so she changed the view to thumbnail and was horrified to find not only pictures of her own flat, fried-egg breasts, but also an enormous rack that could only belong to Meghan. There were others, of course. Many others. The bastard! How had she been so stupid? Letting him photograph her tits because, as he had put it, they were "like two just-plucked apricots, still warm from the sun." Oh, brother. She scrolled down and found pictures of vaginas, erect penises, bare asses, both male and female, and other things she truly wished she had not seen. She was just about to delete the photos of herself but, figuring that might arouse suspicion, she closed the file and tried to focus, running searches for files containing the words "seismic," "tenure," "funding," dragging and dropping any-thing that seemed important onto the thumb drive. The trouble was, she didn't quite know what she was looking for, so the whole operation felt as rushed and random as a looting.

There were voices in the hall. Maureen raised her head and lis-tened. They were coming closer. She slammed the laptop and stood up so fast she knocked the chair down behind her. She barely had time to right it and take the two steps necessary to reach the bath-room when she heard the key in the lock. She froze. She was stand-ing between the sink and the toilet, trying to hold her breath. The door from the hallway creaked open and then slammed shut.

"Have a seat." It was Artaud. "I'll be out in a minute."

She heard him moving across the carpet toward the bathroom. The shower was behind her. The curtain was on metal rings stretched across a metal bar. She couldn't pull it back for fear of the noise so she bent down, grabbed the lower, slimy edge of it, and ducked under and behind. The light went on. She was crouched in the stall and only gradually opened her eyes. A shadow loomed over the curtain. It did not move. Did he sense she was there? Could he see her? Was he listening for some noise? Her pulse pounded in her chest and head. What *was* he doing? The trickle eventually came, followed by the steady stream of water hitting water. While it continued, she allowed herself to take a few shallow breaths. This was too much. She was dizzy, afraid of passing out. The stream slowed to a trickle, a few spurts, then stopped. There was the rustle of clothing, the upward pull of the zipper, and finally a flush. The light went out. She exhaled. Of course the bastard had left the seat up! She was surprised that something so trivial and petty came into her mind when the real worry was the thumb drive that she'd left sticking out of his laptop.

There was conversation in the main room and she strained to hear it. Both voices were male; the other person was probably Jerry.

"I thought you were going to do something about the shut-downs."

"I thought *we* were going to do something about the shutdowns. I've done what I can, but he's slipped out of every trap we've set."

"Maureen?"

"Probably."

"What do we do?" Silence.

"I don't know," Artaud said. "I'll talk to her after dinner. We've only got two days left to map this last quadrant. How much more time do we need?"

"Eight, maybe ten hours, more if we keep getting shut down."

"Okay. Worst comes to worst we can get her to fudge the data in the report. It's the least she can do, considering."

"The call still on for tonight?" There was no immediate response, so Maureen assumed Artaud had nodded.

"Don't let on that there's trouble."

"What? You think I'm stupid?"

"I'm just saying, we've got to reassure him, tell him it's all going fine. No hesitation, all right."

"Right."

"Let's go eat." The hinges whined, the door slammed, and the key turned in the lock. Maureen remained crouched in the shower another five minutes. When she was sure they were gone and not coming back, she pulled aside the curtain, walked back into the main room, plucked the thumb drive from the laptop, and went to the door. She stood and listened. Nothing. She turned the knob on the lock slowly to the right, letting the tumblers disengage one by one. Then she opened the door a crack, admitting a slit of fluorescent light from the hallway. Empty. She pulled the door open, stepped out, and walked as casually as she could to the stairs.

When he got word from Maureen that Artaud and Jerry planned to make their call right after Chicken Time, Worm went off shift, yawning and making numerous comments to his coworkers about how tired he was. Five minutes later, he and Davis were in the hallway on the 02 deck. They pushed in one of the ceiling panels and then Davis bent over and cupped his hands together. Worm stepped in and Davis hoisted him up. The height of the void was only about ten inches, and Worm was very light, so Davis's over-enthusiastic hoist sent Worm's head smashing into the metal deck above.

"Ow! Damn it!"

Davis lowered him again and he tumbled to the floor, rubbing his scalp.

"You okay?" Davis whispered. They were both looking around the hallway.

"Yeah," Worm said, squinting the pain away. "Fine. Just go a little slower."

They performed the operation again, and this time Worm's slender body snaked forward into the tiny space. When his feet were no longer visible, Davis put the panel back in place, consulted his watch, and walked away. He'd been instructed not to linger in the hallway but to return every ten minutes and discreetly tap on the ceiling with a small tube of metal conduit to see if Worm was finished and ready to come down.

In the dark, Worm took a few minutes to orient himself. He'd calculated that the MPC office was about fifteen yards from his entry point. The space was so narrow that in order to move along he had to extend his arms in front of him, as if he were diving or swimming. He wore a headlamp, but it was largely useless since he was unable to lift his head. It wasn't necessary anyway since the perforations in the ceiling, much like those in a Band-Aid, allowed just enough light to come up from below, and once his eyes adjusted to the dimness and the pattern, he could see what was below him, if not where he was headed. The distance he needed to cover was only about twenty feet, but progress was slow. Keeping his head down and his arms outstretched, he propelled himself along with his feet, his torso sliding along the two-inch-wide metal beam. The space was hot; he could feel his clothes becoming damp, and sweat from his forehead dripped into his eyes, but his movement was so restricted that the only way to get rid of it was to rotate his head from side to side and try to wipe his face on his shoulders. When he reached the edge of the MPC office, he stopped. Through the pinholes, he was able to make out the green vinyl flooring, the familiar desk, the filing cabinet, two chairs, and in one of the chairs, a person typing on the desktop computer. Worm stopped moving, the person stopped typing. It was a man, but he was wearing a hard hat, so Worm couldn't see who it was. The man was about to return to typing but then cocked his head, as if listening for something. He stood up and turned his gaze up to the exact corner of the ceiling Worm then occupied. It was Martin, the MPC. Worm tried to be quiet but his breath, due to the heat and the compression on his lungs, was coming and going in quick gasps.

"Who's up there?" Martin demanded. Worm said nothing. "Is someone up there? Who is that?"

Worm gave in. "It's me," he said. "Worm."

"What the . . . ?"

"I'm . . . just . . . checking some cables."

"By yourself?"

Worm gulped. He knew where this was headed. Anytime anyone climbed into the headspace area, they were required to fill out a confined space permit, detailing the work to be done. The permit was a technicality, limiting the vessel charterer from liability should something go wrong, but since Worm's foray into the ceiling had been surreptitious, he had not, of course, filled out the paperwork, had not even requested permission to enter the space and, most to his detriment, did not have someone assisting him, other than Davis, who was not qualified, and was probably not, at that moment, anywhere nearby.

"I've got the tech writer with me," Worm said. "Well, not with me, exactly. Down the hall." Martin turned and walked toward the door of the office. Worm thought he was going to look for Davis, but instead he closed and locked the door to the office and returned.

"Get your ass outta there!" he hissed, looking up at Worm. "I thought you went to bed!"

"I did. But then I remembered something I forgot to do. Up here."

"You know how much trouble you'll be in if the captain finds out? C'mon! Now!" Martin stepped up onto the desk and pushed up one of the panels. He grabbed Worm's outstretched arms and pulled him, filthy and sodden, down into the room. He had just opened his mouth to scold him when there was a knock at the door. The two looked at each other, eyes wide, and both knew they needed to be complicit.

"Just a sec," Martin called as he and Worm hurried to reposition the ceiling panel. When the door was unlocked and opened, it was not, as feared, a crew member or the captain, but Artaud and Jerry. They looked at Worm, his face and clothes covered in grime. Martin spoke:

"He was just cleaning up in here."

"Well he'll have to finish later," Jerry barked, looking at his watch. "We need to make a phone call." Martin nodded and escorted Worm out of the room. As he was being pulled along by Martin, headed for an inevitable tongue-lashing, Worm reached in his pocket to hit the trigger for his homemade transponder and was dismayed to pull out three separate pieces, the device having been crushed when Martin pulled him out of the ceiling.

"Hold on a second," he said, shaking free of Martin's grasp and using both of his hands to try and snap the thing together.

"No, c'mon," Martin insisted. "Now!"

As he was being scuttled away, Worm held the pieces together with his free hand and aimed it over his shoulder back at the office. He pushed the button repeatedly but knew that it was a futile gesture.

Davis, having no knowledge of Worm's exposure and capture, continued to return to the spot in the hallway, where he tapped tentatively on the ceiling. Nothing. It had been almost an hour by then and he was beginning to worry. He peered around the corner and saw that the door to the MPC office was closed. The hallway was empty, so he walked to the door, tucked his sketchbook and tapping device under his arm, and knelt down, just as he had done the last time, so that he could listen at the gap under the door, careful to keep his key in hand as a ruse should he be caught. He lowered his head to the floor. The door from the stairs swung open and Davis quickly went into his Lost Key role, patting down the floor with his free hand. He looked back to see who was coming. It was Maureen. He held a finger to his lips and made a sideways nod at the door. She stopped. Davis got up slowly, went down the hall to where she stood, and then pulled her back into the stairwell.

"Where's Worm?" she asked.

Davis pointed up. "I think he's still in there."

"Are they in the office?"

"Yes."

"On the phone?"

"Yeah. I could hear them fine but I'm not sure what they're talking about. Maybe you should go and listen."

"No way! If I get caugh—"

"You won't get caught. They can't see you, and you can hear everything. If anyone comes, keep a key in your hand, or better yet, take off one of your earrings and pretend you're on the floor looking for it."

Davis pushed her toward the hallway, but she resisted. Then, without a word, she reached up and began unscrewing one of her earrings.

"I'm not going to keep coming back to check for Worm," Davis said. "I'm sure he'll stay up there until they're done talking. I'll be in the aft control. Come get me when they're done."

Maureen gave a solemn nod and stepped into the hallway. Earring in hand, she stepped lightly down the hall and lowered herself, bringing her face very close to the floor. Artaud and Jerry were there and they had the caller on speaker. Davis had been right, she could hear *everything!*

Chapter 44

Davis had been in the aft control room for about fifteen minutes when he heard footsteps coming along the catwalk. When the door opened, he was surprised to see that it was Worm and not Maureen.

"What are you doing here? I thought you were in the ceiling."

Worm, still covered in grime, his shirt and pants ripped, headlamp still tangled in his sooty dreads, shook his head. "Yeah, that didn't work out so well. I got busted."

"No!" Davis cried. "How? Did they hear you?"

Worm then explained how it hadn't been "them," but Martin who had found him.

"But this is the worst part," Worm said, removing the pieces of the broken transponder from his pocket to show Davis. "I got nothing."

Davis had just begun to tell him about Maureen when the door at the other end of the catwalk slammed shut and they heard quick footsteps headed toward them. Before they could see who it was, Maureen pulled open the door, stepped in, and dogged it shut behind her. She leaned forward and put her hands on her knees, trying to catch her breath.

"I know," she huffed. "I know!"

"Know what?" Davis asked.

"I know what he's doing. I know. And you're not going to believe it."

They both waited for her to continue. She rose and looked back out the door to be sure she hadn't been followed, then she went round the room from window to window, making sure they weren't being watched. Behind them, the seismic umbilical stretched out into the water and the guns continued their methodical, explosive farts, leaving an irregular wake of bubbles, but there was no one around—the back deck was empty.

The knob on the electric heater in the aft control room had broken off and never been replaced, so it was always on and made the room oppressively hot but, in spite of that, Maureen was pale and trembling.

"It's okay," Worm said, "relax," and he reached out to touch her. She ignored the gesture and returned again to the door, peering out the tiny square window. She returned to the aft end of the room, looked out at the back deck, and then came back and faced them, steadying herself against the rocking of the boat by leaning on the control panel behind her.

"He's selling the seismic data," she announced. "To an oil company." She paused for dramatic effect, but her proclamation did not impress the small audience.

"Well," Worm said with a smile, "you said I wouldn't believe it, and you're right. I don't. And how did you get that idea in your head?"

Davis jumped in: "I was just starting to tell you before she got here. I was listening at the door but I couldn't understand all the technical stuff they were talking about, so I told Maureen to go and listen."

"And I heard it all!" she said. "And it all makes perfect sense! That's why he's having us pass over everyplace twice and why he's changing out the guns."

Worm nodded and closed his eyes. He was calculating, thinking back, doing the mental math.

"I don't get it," Davis said.

Worm smiled and opened his eyes. Maureen rolled hers.

"Artaud's a seismologist," Worm said. "He's studying what they call 'the basement'—the hard stuff, down deep. For that he needs low-frequency, big-boom guns. The higher-frequency guns are usually used when they're looking at the sediments. You can't even see the basement on the high-frequency data; the sound doesn't penetrate that far."

Davis gave a comprehending "aahhh!," but Worm knew he was bluffing, so he continued his explanation:

"If you're looking for oil, you'd probably use both frequencies, but mostly the higher ones since that's the only way to resolve any detail in the sediments."

"Because the sediments . . . that's where the oil is?"

Maureen looked at her palm and then smacked her forehead. "What do you think oil is, dumbass? It's decomposed dinosaurs, and plants, and other biological crap."

"Oh," Davis said. "Yeah."

"God!" Maureen cried, her annoyance taking away her shivers. She looked at Worm, waved a hand at Davis, and shrieked, "We don't have time for him!"

"What that means," Worm said, adopting a patient, professorial tone, "is that oil is only found in the sedimentary layers. When the biological matter gets trapped in the sediments, after a few million years it turns into oil. That's why he'd be looking in the sediments—if he were looking for oil."

"What do you mean 'if'?" Maureen cried. "That's exactly what he's doing! I just overheard him on the phone!"

"Relax," Worm said, again reaching out a reassuring hand, but Maureen spun around and swatted it away.

"Why do you think he's got Jerry? Why do you think we're going back and forth like this with the different guns? We did the same thing on the other side of the continent on the last cruise. Why do you think he had me steal Madeleine's data? They want seismic profiles of everything!"

"Look, I agree, something's going on," Worm said, "but oil? C'mon."

"What! Why not?"

"Why not?" Worm said, making no attempt to stifle his amusement. "Where do I start? First, it's in total violation of the Antarctic Treaty. No mineral exploitation—by anyone, anywhere—remember? He'd never get funded again for anything if he got caught selling that kind of information. And think of the political stink it would cause. Look, I know the guy's probably desperate for tenure, or money, or academic fame, but c'mon, do you really think he'd go that far?"

"Yes!"

Worm and Davis looked at each other.

"You know how flimsy that treaty is!" Maureen cried. "It lasts, what, twenty-five more years? And you know that most countries barely pay lip service to it now anyway. Look at Chile, look at Argentina, and Norway, and the U.K.! They've all staked their claims, divided the continent up like a pie."

"Yes, but those are claims that no one really recognizes," Worm added.

"Well, someone thought they were legitimate enough to make a map of them! It's hanging right over the desk in the MPC office. You've seen it a thousand times. And the Japanese whalers, the unregulated fishing vessels!" she continued. "Look at all the respect they show for the treaty. This whole place is just a big, unclaimed frontier that the countries of the world can't wait to get their hands on!"

"Yes, but—"

"You know as well as I do that everyone is here for a reason, and it's rarely the reason they give to the public. Everyone's playing a role down here: You've got Japanese whale hunting dressed up in bad drag as 'research,' geologists pretending to study climate change, you've got countries plopping down base after base, allegedly for the sake of science when you and I and anyone even mildly coherent about world politics knows that what they're really doing is establishing a presence, occupying territory, taking possession, which is all just a polite form of colonialism. And what better place to colonize! Untapped mineral resources, no pesky indigenous population to deal with, no government, no police!"

"You're upset," Worm said. "You're overreacting." As soon as the words were out of Worm's mouth, Davis knew enough to retreat to one of the corners. Maureen's back arched, her chin jutted up and out, bow-like, and as Davis watched he actually saw the blood rise up her neck and suffuse her cheeks. The explosions in the water behind her seemed a mere preview of what was to come.

But she surprised them both. She swallowed several times, let her fists unfold at her sides, and slowly lowered her head. Her voice, when it came, was modulated and mannish, like a recorded version played at a slower speed.

"I'm not overreacting—you're not listening. I know what I heard and I've just explained to you how and why it is conceivable that what I heard is correct. When you get your phone from the office and listen to the recording, you'll see that I'm right."

Worm squirmed. Davis saw him reach his hand in his pocket, but he did not remove the pieces of the broken transponder and explain to her what had happened. Instead, he shrugged and jumped back into the argument: "Okay, then let's go down your path and pretend for a minute that Artaud is selling his data. Do you really think there's an oil company out there that'd buy it?"

"Yes!"

The expression on Worm's face was patient, but condescending. "You're not thinking clearly. You're upset," he said, and again Davis leaned back to avoid the verbal and possibly physical reaction he felt certain was about to erupt. He looked over at her and saw that she was, indeed, shaking with rage, but before she could let loose, Worm held up a hand and continued:

"No, really," he said, "calm down and think for a minute. Think about how many times you've been down here, how many times we've almost gotten stuck in this ice. Do you really think it's possible to get oil from this seabed?"

She opened her mouth to protest but then stopped herself, realizing she had no real argument to make. When she did find her voice it was only to say, "What do you mean, 'do I think it's possible?'"

"I mean, look where we are," he said, turning and gesturing with both arms out the windows at the white-capped waves and the island-sized icebergs off in the distance. "Weather-wise, this has gotta be the snottiest, nastiest place on the planet. And those bergs, they're not just sitting there, they're floating around. And some of them are as big as small states. Imagine one plowing into a drilling platform, or ripping through a pipeline. Not to mention the fact that the water we're sailing on right now will be frozen a foot thick in less than a month. And the pressure from that ice would crush an oil tanker like a bag of potato chips. They can barely get the supply ship into McMurdo every year, you really think they could drill for oil out here?"

"I don't know if they can or not, but I do know someone thinks it's enough of a possibility to pay Artaud to look into it; to pay him for the data."

"How do you know that?" Davis asked. She ignored him and went on.

"Look at the price of gas! I read a report that said the price of oil would have to top a hundred dollars a barrel before they'd consider drilling in high latitudes. Well, guess what? It's over a hundred now, and come on, do any of us really think it's going to go back down?"

"Point taken, bu   "

"Twenty-five years ago no one thought it would be possible to drill deep-water wells, but look at what they're doing now! Look at the Russians!"

"The Russians?"

"Yes, the Russians. They just sent a submarine down in the Arctic and put a flag on the bottom of the ocean at the North Pole. You gotta ask yourself why? Is it because they're now flush with capitalist wealth and want to build a new Santa's workshop? No! It's because they want to claim the mineral rights! Maybe they don't have the technology to access and retrieve it now, but that technology will come, just like it did for the deep-water wells. And if the world keeps warming up—and you know it will—all these areas now covered with ice probably won't be."

She stopped speaking and stood in the middle of the room, her feet spread, her torso swaying. The wind was picking up, the waves were hitting the boat from the side. Davis could feel the dizziness returning, the tightness in his forehead. He reached in his coat pocket and felt the vial of Bonine.

"And they are doing it," Maureen said. "I heard them—Artaud and Jerry—they were talking to some guy with an accent, I couldn't tell where he was from, about handing over the report and the maps in exchange for money. Money that's going to be handed over to them in New Zealand. Again, you'll hear it all for yourself when you listen to the recording."

"Yeah, I kinda think that's not gonna happen," Worm said, removing the shattered transponder from his pocket and setting the pieces on the counter. He explained how it had broken and how the phone had probably not recoded anything. They dwelled on the reality of this disappointment for a while, no one saying anything, but then Maureen hopped up and started pacing.

"So all we've got is what I heard," she said, talking more to herself than either of them. "And if you guys don't believe me, it's doubtful that anyone else will either. We need more evidence. And I think," she said, pausing at one end of the room and drumming her fingers on the door, "that Jerry might be the key."

"Jerry?"

"What do we really know about Jerry?" she asked, shaking a finger. "We know nothing. He's supposed to be a seismic technician, but he seems smarter than that, and where did he come from?" She turned and walked aft, hands behind her back, head down.

"What are you driving at?" Worm asked. She didn't answer, still lost in her own thoughts, pacing. Her hands were in front of her now, her fingers moving, as if performing some complex calculations. She stopped abruptly and looked out the window.

"I didn't find anything on Artaud's computer..." She trailed off. "I'll look over what I've got again, of course, just to be sure, but I don't think there's anything there. Nothing that would connect him to anything other than his academic work. He's too smart to be that careless. But Jerry..." She emerged from her own thoughts and turned to Worm and Davis. "I need to get into his room, into his laptop."

"You are not doing that," Worm countered. "No way!"

"I have to," she said. "We have to. And we have to do it tonight. I'll have to pay the Filipinos for the key, but I think I've got enough cash."

"No way!"

She ignored Worm and approached Davis, who was still cowering in the corner. She bent down, her face very close to his.

"We'll do it just the same as we did before," she told him, her tone low and conspiratorial. "You announce a sighting and order a shutdown. I'll need some extra time since I'm not as familiar with Jerry's computer, but I think I can do it."

"You are not doing this," Worm said. "It's too dangerous. You're the one who said he was talking about offing people."

"If you're squeamish," she said, turning her head to Worm, her eyelids lowered "you don't have to be a part of it, but it's kind of your fault that we have to do it in the first place. I mean, if we had the recording . . ."

Chapter 45

Twenty-four hours after they left the aft control room, Davis was back on the bridge waiting for the clock to strike the seemingly insignificant hour of 11:40. That was ten minutes into Chicken Time and was the time that he and Maureen had agreed upon for Davis to make a "sighting" and order a shutdown. The wind and waves had calmed, so Davis was out on the deck behind the bridge enjoying the sun and the air. He glanced at his watch. Five more minutes. He walked to the port side and looked down at the water. It seemed the boat was barely moving. When the alarm on his watch beeped, he took his radio from his belt.

"Back deck, back deck, come in, please."

No response. He tried again.

"Back deck, this is bridge, whale in the safety zone. Cease fire!" He had taken to using the military term as an added annoyance to Jerry. "I repeat, cease fire."

Still no response. He thought his radio might be dead, so he went back inside. It was then he realized the boat had almost stopped.

"What's going on?" Davis demanded. "I ordered a shutdown."

"Save your breath," the captain said. "They ain't listening. They're pulling in the gear."

"What? Why? I thought we had two more days."

Pointing over to the chart table, the captain said, "Look at the satellite image that came in this morning." Davis walked over and stared down at an oversized black-and-white printout. It comprised several images stitched together to form one picture. Looking at it, Davis could make out a layer of gauzy clouds. Under that he saw the water, the edge of the continent, a few random icebergs. It was a beautiful picture but one that gave him no indication as to why they would be stopping early. He'd expected to see a dark storm cloud moving in, or maybe even the recognizable whirlpool of a hurricane, but nothing seemed out of the ordinary.

"What am I looking for?" Davis asked. The captain walked over, took a laser pointer from his breast pocket, and pointed out a thin, filmy layer between the water and the land.

"That there's ice," he said. "It's covering the last little area they wanted to map."

"Can't we break through it?"

"We could," the captain said, "but not with all the gear in the water. That ice would shred it."

"So what are they doing?" Davis asked.

"Giving up and wrapping up early. Looks like we'll have a few extra days in Christchurch."

With the binoculars still around his neck and the ubiquitous sketchbook clutched under his arm, Davis flew down the four flights of stairs to the E-Lab, hoping to catch Maureen before she went up to Jerry's cabin. When he got to the lab, her chair was empty. He ran down the hall to the galley. About half of the tables were occupied, but she was not there. He saw Martin and asked if he'd seen her or Worm.

"Worm's on the back deck bringing in the gear," Martin said. "Haven't seen Maureen."

Artaud was seated at the science table. He motioned Davis over.

"You know we're wrapping up," he said. Davis nodded.

"We got your last order for a shutdown, but I guess they were a little too busy out back to respond. What did you see?"

"See?"

"What kind of whale?"

Davis ignored the question and left the galley. He stood in the hall uncertain what to do. Jerry's cabin was one floor up, but Davis didn't know if he should go there or not. Instead, he ran to the aft control room where he could get a view of the back deck and see if Jerry was there. The marine techs were busy pulling in the snake-like umbilical, but they were all wearing hard hats, sunglasses, and identical jackets so it was hard to make out who was who. To get a better look, he went down to the lower deck, walked through the empty shop, and looked out at the back deck. From this vantage point, Davis could better discern who was who, but he did not see Jerry. He saw Worm, his mess of hair creeping out from under his hard hat, and Davis tried to get his attention, but there was too much noise and activity for Worm to notice. In a sweaty panic, Davis ran back upstairs to the 01 deck. On the whiteboard in the hall a spreadsheet with everyone's name and room number was taped up. Davis ran his finger along the sheet, found Jerry's room, #107, and walked down the hall, counting off the numbers on the doors as he went. As he approached, he slowed down and softened his step. 107. He brought his ear close to the door and listened. Nothing. He had not planned to knock, had not really planned anything, but he did knock and then instinctually straightened up and cleared his throat. No answer. No noise inside. He knocked again, harder this time. "Jerry?" he called. "You in there? It's Davis." Nothing. Something was not right. He tried the handle but the door was locked. Maybe Maureen had heard that the seismic was ending and had aborted her mission. He decided to return to the E-Lab and look for her again. On the way down, he collided with Artaud on the stairs.

"Hey," Artaud smiled, "slow down there."

"Sorry. I'm looking for Maureen, have you seen her?"

"I have not," he said, "but she's probably holed up somewhere working on the data report."

"Any idea where?" Davis asked, his tone impatient. Artaud shrugged and shook his head. He stood on the stairs and watched Davis descend. Once he was gone, the smile dropped from his face. He turned and went up two flights to the chief scientist's cabin. He knocked, waited a few seconds, during which he looked up and down the hallway, then unlocked the door and went in. The over-head light was on. Jerry, still dressed in his work clothes, was sitting on the couch, one leg crossed over the other, reading a magazine;

Meghan was on the floor, her back against the wall, head down on her arms. She looked up at Artaud, then over at Maureen, who was facedown on the floor, her hands and feet bound with zip ties, a sock tied around her head as a gag. Maureen, too, looked up at Artaud, her eyes wild and afraid.

"All right," Artaud began, his eyes on Maureen, his voice low, "how about you tell me what's going on."

Jerry, his focus still on the magazine, spoke:

"Caught her in my room, messing with my computer. She knows," he said, reaching into his pocket and retrieving Maureen's plastic thumb drive. He tossed it over to Artaud. "Go on, take a look."

Artaud went over to his laptop, logged in, and stuck the thumb drive in a USB port. When it was recognized, he clicked on it and ran through the files.

"She's got some of my old e-mails from Lopez and McGuffin," Jerry said, "financials an—"

Artaud cut him off. "Why did you have that information on your computer? I thought we agreed th—"

"There wasn't much, and I thought I had it buried. She rooted it out. She's got stuff of yours on there, too," Jerry said.

Artaud's eyes traveled down the list and as he read, his dark, heavy eyebrows merged and he fingered the scar on his jaw. It was all there, a history of their transactions with the company, e-mail correspondence detailing the areas Lopez and McGuffin wanted surveyed, the frequencies they wanted used, amounts they were willing to pay.

Jerry stood up and pulled on his coat. "I've been gone too long already. I've got to get down there and make sure they get everything dismantled and packed away. I'll be back in two hours. Then we've got to make decisions. She's not the only one we need to worry about, you know that, right?"

Artaud turned his head to Jerry, but his eyes were still on the screen. "I know."

"And whatever we do, it's got to be done soon. They're going to start wondering where she is."

"They already have. I told them she's working on the data report."

"That'll buy us a little time, but not much. The sooner we get the gear on board, the sooner we can turn for home. And the sooner we turn for home, the sooner we'll be back in rough seas and people will start disappearing and stop asking questions."

"What are you thinking . . . I mean about what we should do?" Artaud asked. He closed the laptop and gave Jerry his full attention.

"I have no frickin' idea," Jerry said, donning his hard hat and glasses. "But we've gotta start thinking of something."

There was silence after he left. Maureen wasn't struggling, Meghan was hunched over, her face hidden in her arms, and Artaud was staring at the door. He told Meghan to go down to the lab and help the other students dismantle the equipment and pack it up.

"What are you going to do?" she asked. Artaud stood up and went over to her, taking her in his arms and stroking her hair.

"Nothing bad, sweetie, I promise, don't you worry. I just need to talk to Maureen for a bit. You go downstairs."

When she had gone, he locked the door and got down on his hands and knees next to Maureen.

"I guess I'm going to have to compile the data report myself now."

She still had control of her neck, so she turned her head away from him. He grabbed it with both hands and turned it back to face him. She bit down on the gag and glared at him.

"Such a naughty girl you've turned out to be," he said. "What a lot of trouble you've caused. You could've had a cut of the action if you'd been a little bit smarter. All you had to do was ask. Yes, I had you trapped, I kept you doing what I wanted you to do, but the thing you never realized is that blackmail is a double-edged sword. You could just as easily have turned it back on me. I would've made a deal with you, paid you some hush money. But instead," he said, grabbing her by the hair and yanking her face up close to his, "instead, you tried to fuck me over! Didn't you?"

Again, she bit down on the sock and tried to pull her head back.

"And now I've gotta do something about you and your friends. Now instead of one problem to solve, I've got three." He let go of her head and let it drop to the floor.

Artaud got up and left the room, locking the door behind him. Maureen struggled with her wrists and ankles, trying to pull them apart, but the plastic dug into her skin. She tried to shake loose the stinking gag, to push it out with her tongue, but it was pulled too tight and knotted too well behind her head. She was immobilized. The thought of being thrown overboard like this, hands and feet bound, only able to breathe through her nose, sent an electric panic through her body and she thrashed and kicked. She tried to scream but all she could manage were low, guttural sounds from her throat that were not loud enough to be heard over the ship noise. Her breathing became fast and short. She started seeing amoeba-like constellations moving in front of her eyes like a kaleidoscope and knew she was hyperventilating. She closed her eyes and tried to make herself calm down, tried inhaling and exhaling at regular intervals, tried not to panic. She tried to picture the little being inside her, a tiny shrimp, nothing more than a mass of swarming cells suspended in a dark sea, connected to her by a slender thread, connected to her, depending on her. Somehow that calmed her, made her feel less alone, more determined to get out.

She had no idea how long she'd been there. Her hands were fastened behind her back and her shoulders ached from being arched for so long. Artaud returned at one point to change his clothes, but he paid no attention to her other than to note that she was still there. After that, no one returned for a long time. At one point Maureen felt waves hitting the beam, rocking the boat from side to side, and she knew the vessel was turning. A few minutes later and the rocking was gentler, fore and aft, indicating that they were sailing into the waves. The engine noise had increased; the captain had fired up the remaining two engines. They were headed back to New Zealand.

Sometime later, Artaud, Jerry, and Meghan returned to the room. They did not speak but were working together to prepare something. Maureen could only see Meghan, who was off to the right in Artaud's bedroom, emptying all of her belongings out of her black duffel bag. Jerry approached and stood over her.

"Almost done?" he asked. Meghan nodded, but did not look up at him. He picked up the duffel bag and brought it over next to Maureen. Instinctively, she tried to roll away from it, but Artaud was on her other side and stopped her roll with his feet. He walked around so that he was standing up by her head; Jerry went down by her feet and together, on a count of three, they lifted her up. She bucked and screamed, twisted and turned. They set her back down. Artaud got on his hands and knees, lowered his head until it was inches from her face, and looked her in the eyes.

"If you keep doing that, we won't bother to keep you alive; we'll just throw you overboard, understand?" She nodded through her tears. "Play along and this will be painless. We're just moving you."

The two men took their positions again and lifted her onto the bag, turning her onto her side and tucking her feet in. Then they bent the rest of her body and pulled the sides up. It was like being placed inside a giant mouth. The zipper started at her feet, and by the time it reached her shoulders she was screaming again, gasping for breath. Jerry stopped zipping and Artaud leaned in close.

"This is your last warning," he hissed. "Shut up!" She did as she was told. Artaud gave a nod to Jerry and his hairy paw pulled the zipper up and over her face, sealing her in darkness. She felt herself being picked up, tossed over someone's shoulder, and carried, on unsteady legs, out of the cabin. The sea had come up. With her sight gone, her other senses were more acute and she felt the syrupy nausea of seasickness in her head. Again she struggled to control her breathing, not wanting to throw up in the bag, and all the while terrified that she might feel cold air, indicating that they had taken her out on deck to throw her over. Would she drown first or be overcome by the cold? She hoped it would be the latter. But which deck could they take her to where they could not be seen? There were surveillance cameras on the starboard side and back deck. They were live feeds to the bridge and to monitors in the E-Lab, but they did not record. Someone might see if they threw her off from either of those points. Were there cameras on the port side? She couldn't remember. She heard a door open and felt slow, descending steps. Her mind was too distracted to count the number of steps, but she could feel whenever they reached a landing at one deck and began the descent to the next. They'd started on the 03, had gone down two flights, and were headed to the main deck. That was where the labs were. That was where they could slip her over the side without a splash. She panicked and started to squirm.

"Stop it!" It was Jerry. She held still.

They emerged unsteadily from the stairs into the hallway; she could hear that they were closer to the engines. She tried to picture where they were taking her but was disoriented. They set her down on her side and unzipped the bag an inch to give her some air. She was on the floor of one of the labs but she couldn't tell which one. There was something solid next to her face. She nudged her nose into the hole and managed to push the zipper down another inch. She rolled her head but could only see up the face of a nondescript cabinet. There was some sort of bolt on a string above her swinging back and forth.

"How do we get the others in here?" Jerry asked.

"We get her to make some calls. They'll come if they hear her."

"She'll talk?"

"What choice does she have?"

Worm and Davis stayed on in the galley after all the others had gone. Their mood was morose. They were sailing north into a storm. The wind was blowing forty knots, swells were increasing, and there were whitecaps and streaks of white foam on the surface of the waves. The ship was in a semiregular seesaw motion, up and then down, giving the feel of a carnival ride as the waves rolled along the keel. The barometer was falling, which had previously been Maureen's cue to make her rounds of the ship to ensure that everything was strapped down or locked away. As it was, her own desk in the E-Lab remained cluttered with notebooks and pens, her empty chair swiveled around and around.

"Do you think they've got her?" Davis asked.

Worm pushed the food around on his plate. "I don't know."

Neither had heard from Maureen since their last meeting in the aft control room, hours before.

"Should we tell the captain?"

"Let's wait a bit. Maybe she's on to something."

"But don't you think we would have heard by now?"

Worm twirled a lock of his hair around his finger and looked straight ahead.

An hour later, while Worm made rounds of the ship looking for Maureen, Davis was back in the aft control room, waiting. Although he'd ingested a double dose of his Coast Guard Cocktail in anticipation of the storm, he still felt like shit. Outside it had gone dark but from where he was sitting he could see the waves crashing over the back deck. This was the first time in almost a month and a half that Davis had not seen some light from the sun. Whether that was because they were headed north, because the austral days were getting shorter, or because of the severity of the storm, Davis did not know. It was a bad storm. The last meal in the galley had been sparsely attended. Most had already taken to their racks.

Davis held his sketchbook and a pen in his lap, but even if he had been able to sit upright without hanging on, he was too distracted to work on his book. The tightness in his head and the up-and-down motion of his stomach were bad, but they were nothing compared to his overall feeling of dread. The phone rang. Davis looked at it. He had never even noticed that there was a phone in the room, so its ringing seemed portentous. He jumped up and answered.

"Hello."

"Davis?" It was Maureen.

"Where are you? We've been looking for you. Are you all right?" There was hesitation, as if they had a delay in their signal and she was receiving his words a few seconds after he spoke them.

"Yes, I'm all right."

"Worm's looking for you. I'm in the aft control. You should come here. He's really worried."

"Worm's here," she said. "He found me."

"Where? Are you coming back here?"

"Why don't you come to us," she said. Her voice sounded almost girlish. "I'm in the Environmental Room."

"Why there?" Davis asked, picturing the cramped room under the stairs that had doubled as his office.

"Just come."

The line went dead. Davis held the receiver in his hand and stared at it. Something was not right. He couldn't think what it was at first, but then it hit him: Maureen's voice. There was no edge to it. He had almost not recognized that it was her. He hung up the phone and stood there, hanging on to the counter, his torso swaying with the waves. He put his sketchbook under his shirt so it wouldn't get wet and then made the perilous trek along the catwalk back to the main deck. From there it was one flight down to the Environmental Room. The hallways were deserted but brightly lit from the overhead fluorescent lights. As Davis passed the cabins he heard movies playing on some of the TVs, but for the most part it was quiet. Everyone was down for the night.

When he reached the Environmental Room, he stopped. Again, something was not right. The door was closed and there was paper taped over the small window. He stood a few feet away, listening. He pulled the handle down, pushed open the door, but before he could take a step inside someone grabbed his wrist, pulled him in, and the door shut behind him.

"Davis, run!" Maureen cried, but Meghan clasped her hand over her mouth. Jerry got Davis's arm behind his back and pushed him forward. Artaud grabbed his other wrist and pulled it back, and before he knew what was happening they had both his arms behind him and his wrists fastened together with a zip tie. Maureen and Meghan were directly in front of him, Meghan's hand still over Maureen's mouth. Worm was on the floor, bound and squirming, like a fish trapped in a net. Davis emitted a high-pitched yelp, but before it was fully out of his mouth, the sleeve of a shirt came over his head and was pulled tight between his lips. Jerry was in front of him, bending down to bind his ankles. Davis raised a foot and kicked, hitting Jerry in the jaw with his toe, but that first kick and the three that followed were not all that effective. The room was too small for him to draw back his legs and get any momentum, so all his kicks did was make Jerry so mad that he head-butted Davis in the crotch. The pain was intense, the reaction immediate: Davis bent forward and brought his knees together. Jerry worked fast, binding his ankles together with another zip tie. They sat him in a chair, fastening his hands to it with another zip tie.

There was not much talk once the three were subdued. The captives were all wide-eyed with terror, but none of the captors would look at them directly and acted almost as if they weren't there. Davis was led over to the floor next to Worm and was pushed down to a seated position.

"You sure there's enough gas in the tanks?" Artaud asked.

"Yes, checked the regulator. It's full. I don't think they've used any of it. There weren't any birds on this cruise."

Meghan, who had refastened Maureen's gag, looked drugged, her face showing as much animation as that of a stroke victim. She leaned against a wall and stared at the Reality Detection Device, her eyes following each swing of the small bolt.

Davis and Worm looked at each other, helpless.

So this was it, then, Davis thought to himself. It all made sense now. The small room, the gas bottles, the grouping them together. They weren't going to be thrown over the side, they were going to be gassed to death, just as Worm had planned to do to the injured birds. Maybe they were even using the policy Davis had revised. They would probably come back once they were dead and arrange their corpses so it looked like an accident, like they'd been working on something and had been overcome.

"Meghan, sweetheart," Artaud whispered. She looked up at him for a moment, then back to the RDD. He stepped over Worm and put his arm around her, leading her toward the door. He turned to Jerry, who was busy with the regulators on the two gas bottles, and said in a low voice, "I gave her a sedative. I'm going to take her upstairs, see if she'll lie down. I'll be back in a few." Jerry gave a cursory nod, a saccharine smile as Artaud led the dazed girl out. The ship pitched and rolled and the whole room seemed to pivot and turn like a house lifted off its foundation. And yet for all the motion, the only thing actually moving in the room was the RDD—the bolt swinging aft, hovering for a second or two, and then sliding fore again, never quite making it into the Danger Zone. The three captives looked from one to the other, wild-eyed and helpless. There was a knock at the door and then the handle turned and Artaud stepped back in.

"She all right?" Jerry asked.

"For now. She'll be out for a while."

"You should've kept her with these three. She'll talk."

"I know, but we needed her help. Get them started and we can bring her back down."

Jerry turned the knob on one tank and it emitted a low hiss.

"This is ragged," he said.

"What is?"

"This," Jerry said, gesturing at the bottles. Then giving a wave at the captives, "Them."

"Yeah, I know, but it'll work. And it's clean. They won't trace it to us."

"You sure? The body count's pretty high."

"I know, but this'll look like an accident. C'mon, let's go."

Both tanks were hissing now. The two men went out and switched off the light. The door clicked shut. The paper over the window shaded most of the light from the hallway. The door wasn't sea-tight, so there was a small crack of light visible at the bottom edge but, as Davis watched, something was wedged in that crack from the outside, blocking the light from getting in and the CO_2 from getting out. They were being sealed in.

In a few minutes, Davis felt the effects. There wasn't a smell but he felt like he was having an asthma attack or an allergic reaction. His chest was expanding more with each breath but seemed to be admitting less. His eyes began to water and he noticed an acidic taste in his mouth. He could hear Maureen and Worm struggling, could feel Worm kicking his feet. Davis kicked with his own but it did no good.

There were loud voices outside, then a banging on the door. The small strip of light returned, then the door was pulled open. Davis was losing consciousness and couldn't focus. The figures were backlit and fuzzy, but when the light was switched on he was relieved to see the enormous frame of the captain, and behind him, several members of the crew. They dragged Davis's chair out into the hallway, and just before he passed out he saw Meghan standing off to one side.

Chapter 46

Fifteen months later

As book signings go, it wasn't the worst. The room was three-quarters full, parents hovering in the back, the floor in front of Davis littered with kids sitting Indian-style, listening as he read, not from a book, but from a PowerPoint projected on a screen behind him. Sacrilege? Maybe, but his presentation was dual-pronged: The first part was a nonfictional presentation on traveling by boat in Antarctica, and the second (and, he hoped, more profitable prong) was a reading from his just-published book, *The Whale's Tale*.

The initial reaction to the book was tepid. There were, of course, the usual snotty reviews from the TUCBAs, which Davis read but then found that he was able to ignore, especially since they were soon eclipsed by hearty sales figures and positive reactions from both young and old attendees at his readings.

At this particular reading, there was abundant applause when he finished, and a line of eager children, newly purchased books in hand, quickly formed to the right of the table that had been provided for him. The line was progressing along, and Davis was doing a good job of taking the time to talk to each child and personalize each inscription, while still being mindful of the low threshold for waiting that most four- to ten-year-olds have. He'd been at it for

over an hour when he looked up and there was only one person remaining in line: a tall blond woman in a baseball cap pushing a
stroller.

"I called the office," Maureen said, "but they told me you
weren't working there anymore."

"No," Davis said.

She gave an understanding nod, rocked the stroller back and
forth, then remembered why she had come and pulled a heavy,
cream-colored envelope from her purse. "I was going to mail this
to you," Maureen said, "but I heard you were going to be here
today so I thought I'd bring it by in person. Bill's at sea, but you
probably knew that. Anyway, the wedding is set for when he gets
back. We wanted to have it in Jamaica but I'm not allowed to leave
the country, so we're having it here. I hope you can come."

Davis opened the envelope, glanced at the date, and said, "I'd
love to come, thank you." He rose, came around the table and gave
her an awkward hug. Then he crouched down to look at the baby.
A toad-like creature with bulbous eyes, pursed lips, and several
chins stared out at him from beneath the stroller's canopy.

"You want to hold him?" she asked, and then, not waiting for
an answer, lifted the thing, bald and wriggling, up and out of his
seat and handed him to Davis.

"He's not a looker," she said, giving his cheek an affectionate
pinch. "I know they say all babies are beautiful, but I think you'll
understand when I say I'm glad this one isn't."

"Yes," Davis laughed.

"And Worm says he doesn't want to know, can you believe that?
I think I'm okay not knowing, too. But come on, look at that nose!"

Davis ran his finger down the large beak, feeling the bump in
the middle. When he got to the tip, the baby erupted in giggles.

"What's his name?" Davis asked.

"Oh, it's the only thing Worm was adamant about—Ernest."

"That's perfect!"

"It suits him. And I guess it's better than William Oliver Radley
the Fourth, which is what the grandparents wanted."

Davis finished up with the signing, and he and Maureen left the
store and headed to a nearby park. They walked along the clay path
and talked about what had happened since their return, about

Maureen being dismissed from Polar Support Services, about she and Meghan bargaining with the prosecutor and being given probation in exchange for their testimony against Artaud. As they walked along, she spoke with dread about Artaud's upcoming trial and all the publicity that was sure to erupt.

"I wish it could all just be in the past," she said. "I've got a lot to look forward to and don't really want to dwell on my past mistakes."

"What are you going to do?" Davis asked.

"You mean for work?"

"Yes."

"Just this," she said, tapping on the stroller. "Be a mom for a while. Then I'll see."

"But you loved that job. You must be upset about being forced out."

"I'm really not," she said. "I did love it, and I do miss it, but to be honest, I always felt like I was putting my life on hold when I went down south. I feel much more, oh, I don't know . . ."

They walked along, Maureen holding the baby and Davis pushing the stroller, until they arrived at his car. The top was down and he dropped his leftover books on the backseat. He said his good-byes to Maureen and the baby and then got in the driver's side and started the motor. He had just put on his sunglasses and was about to put the car into gear when Maureen rushed over and tapped him on the shoulder. He lifted his glasses and looked up at her.

"I don't think you're going anywhere," she said, pointing down at his front wheel. Davis leaned out of the car, looked down, and cursed. The front tire had been booted.

"Can I give you a lift somewhere?" Maureen offered, turning and putting the baby back in the stroller.

Davis thought for a moment, then pulled out his cell phone.

"Let me call my boyfriend. I can probably borrow his car. His office isn't far from here."

As he waited for his call to connect, he looked at Maureen and put his finger to his lips.

"Hi, it's me . . . Oh, it went well. Big crowd, lots of sales. . . . Yes . . . Listen, I'm having some car trouble. Any chance I can borrow yours this afternoon? No, no, nothing like that, just won't start.... Okay, yes, it's booted.... No, I think I've got the money, just need to get downtown and pay the fines.... Thanks. I'll be right over."

He hung up. Maureen and the baby were both grinning at him. Davis rolled his eyes. He got out of the car, retrieved his books from the backseat, and together they walked back across the park to her car.

"Sounds like he's got you figured out," Maureen said.

Davis nodded. "Yeah, I suppose. It's kind of nice, actually. He knows that for all practical purposes I'm a total mess, but he still likes me. Can't do much better than that, can you?"

"Where'd you meet him?"

"Oh, my brother introduced us. They work together. Rob's a great guy, and included with his many manly attributes, his job has domestic partner benefits, so I've got my meds covered for a while."

"So, I never asked you," Maureen said. "Why did you leave PSS?"

Davis sighed and related the story about his return to the office; about how he had initially been heralded by his coworkers, all eager to hear about his near-death experience—a dramatic, almost heroic story that, for a while, gave him something akin to credibility within the cubicle. But the fame and respect didn't last long, and after a few weeks, they were all at it again, lobbing their conversational grenades and arguing over minutiae.

"And then," Davis said, "just as it got to the point where I was about to become homicidal, or suicidal, or both, I got a call from my agent saying that she'd managed to sell one of my earlier stories."

The story was, of course, *Mick the Maggot,* which Estelle had rechristened with the less offensive but still euphonious *Where the Fly Flew.* The advance from that sale, together with the little bit of money he'd managed to save from his time at sea, enabled him to quit PSS and start looking for more suitable work.

"That's great!" Maureen said. "But if it doesn't work out I'm sure they'll take you back. I mean, after all that happened. And you have to admit, the job does generate some good stories."

"True," Davis laughed. "True, but I never really had any business being there. You knew that from the start."

She was about to protest, but he stopped her.

"Don't," he said. "You were mean, but you were right: I didn't belong there. It was like being on stage every day, and I wasn't a very good actor."

"Can you make enough to live on with just the writing?" she asked.

"Please," Davis scoffed, pointing at the booted wheel. "I can't even make enough to pay my parking tickets, but I'm hopeful, I guess. Besides," he said, giving the stack of books under his arm a thump, "it's the only thing that's ever made me feel . . . authentic."

They walked along protected from the July sun by a green awning of trees. The baby started to cry, so Maureen lifted him out of the stroller and held him high above her head, tickling his underarms with her fingers, swinging him pendulously from side to side.

Authentic, she thought as the baby giggled down at her, *yes.*